HOPE AWAKENED

USA TODAY BESTSELLING AUTHOR

CHARLENE HARTNADY

HOPE AWAKENED
Cover art by Melody Simmons
Edited by Brigette Billings

Proofread by Lynn Glockle
Produced in South Africa
charlene.hartnady@gmail.com

Hope Awakened is a work of fiction and characters, events and dialogue found within are of the author's imagination and are not to be construed as real. Any resemblance to actual events or persons, either living or deceased, is purely coincidental.

First Paperback Edition 2021

PROLOGUE

"Tell me!" Ekon boomed. "Spit it out already." His patience was waning.

"You're not going to like it, Sire." Kwan stepped closer into the circle of flickering candlelight.

Of course he wasn't going to like it. He hated anything to do with his blasted brother, usurper of the throne. *His* throne. "Out with it," he urged, needing to know. He could guess. Ekon hoped he was wrong. From the grave look in Kwan's eyes, he knew it was bad.

Ekon inclined his head, urging him to continue. "My spies tell me that the three of them are to be mated… and soon."

"When?" his voice boomed.

"In three days."

"So soon?" Ekon snarled.

"I'm afraid so." Kwan nodded.

"It's an abomination," he barked. "Did you have a look in the book of lores? Two males and one female… it can't be legal!"

Kwan looked reluctant to answer. "I found nothing," he finally said, head bowed.

Ekon closed his hand into a fist and smashed it into the wood of the table. It splintered, cracking right through the center and falling to the ground in a pile of tinder. Then he pulled in a deep breath. "I'll just have to go to Plan B, then."

"What is Plan B, my lord?" Kwan looked skeptical.

"Simple. I will take their first-born chicks. Take Leukos' heir. Whoever has the heir is king, right?" He would do whatever it took to see Leukos dethroned and in a cage where he belonged, with that traitorous bastard, Magnar, beside him. The two of them could rot.

Kwan looked flustered. "I'm not sure the rules were meant to be interpreted in that way."

"Nonsense!" Ekon spat. "I'm not sure why I never thought of it earlier. It could have saved a ton of heartache."

"As always, you are wise beyond compare." Kwan bowed low.

He could see that the male was still skeptical. "Don't look so worried, Kwan. What could go wrong?"

CHAPTER 1

SEVEN MONTHS LATER...

"I'll see you in a week, Mr. and Mrs. Simons," Hope said, smiling at her patient, who put a hand on her heavily rounded belly. Hope felt an instant pang as she watched the woman's hand move in a lazy circle. Hope should have been pregnant by now, or at least trying hard to make it happen. That was her plan… their plan. Her life was all mapped out. *How had things taken such a wrong turn?*

"Thanks so much for everything. We can't wait to meet our daughter." Mr. Simons took his wife's hand and looked at her with such love. Hurt bubbled to the surface, making Hope clutch her chest with one hand to try to quell the emotion. Her heart tightened, and she had to look away from the happy couple. At that moment, Hope realized that her ex had never looked at her like that. It was an upsetting thought. What was even more alarming was that she didn't think that anyone had ever looked at her like that.

I need to stop this pity party right now! she thought to herself.

What was there for her to say? Just like anyone in her situation, she had her good days and her bad days. She couldn't help but get irritated with herself on the bad ones. At the same time, Hope realized that she had to cut herself some slack, otherwise, she'd go mad. After all, it had only been five months since she caught her husband cheating on her with her—

"Your eleven o'clock is here," her receptionist, Sandy, said. "Mrs.—"

"Hi, sis."

Hope felt her blood run cold. Even though it was the middle of summer and the AC wasn't working optimally, she still felt a chill work its way down her spine. Gooseflesh broke out on her arms. With a lump in her throat, she glanced at her sister and then around the waiting room. There were several more patients already there. As much as she wanted to tell Lizzie to get lost, she couldn't make a scene. Instead, Hope took the file from her receptionist without acknowledging her sister.

"Follow me," she said as she walked into her office. She closed the door behind them and pulled in a deep breath.

"How are you keeping?" Lizzie asked. She had a sweet-looking smile on her lying, scheming face. There was nothing sweet about Lizzie.

"What do you want?" Hope folded her arms, realizing for the first time what Sandy had just said.

Mrs.

Her receptionist had definitely said 'Mrs.' before Lizzie cut her off.

"I, um... I..." Her sister took her bottom lip between her teeth and shoved some hair behind her ear.

Oh, my god!

Holy fucking shit!

Hope felt her blood go from cold to boiling hot in an instant. Her eyes were glued to the ring and wedding band on her sister's finger. It was Emmet's grandmother's ring. The same one he'd given her all those years ago. Her eyes prickled, but she blinked back the tears. She'd be damned if she let her sister see her cry. *Not happening!* This was unreal.

"You and Emmet got married?" Hope said, her voice more even than it should have been, given the situation. "Our divorce was finalized a couple of weeks ago and you've already tied the knot? I mean, the ink was barely even dry." There was an incredulous tone to her voice, but that couldn't be helped.

"Um... yes. I'm so sorry. We... we got married." Lizzie's eyes fluttered closed, and she bowed her head.

"I don't want your apologies, Elizabeth. Why are you here?"

"It's Lizzie." Her eyes flashed to Hope's for a second before going to the shiny tiles at her feet. "Please call me Lizzie," she whispered.

Hard ignore! Hope knew that it hurt her sister whenever she called her by her full first name, but she didn't give a shit. It had hurt her far more when she found her sister in bed with her husband of over five years.

Emmet and Hope had fallen in love in high school, gotten engaged in her second year of residency, moved in together and were married a year and a half later. Everything was storybook. They were supposed to establish their careers first before starting a family. Emmet the lawyer and Hope the Ob-Gyn. The perfect couple. The perfect house. They were supposed to start trying for a baby once they had their careers up and running. Once they had the white picket fence. They would have been trying long before, if Emmet hadn't made all of those excuses about why they needed to wait just a little longer. It wasn't until Hope walked in on the reason for all of those excuses. Namely, Lizzie and Emmet were having an affair. It wasn't just sex, and it wasn't just the one time.

Her sister looked her in the eyes. "I tried to call you, but you wouldn't answer. You haven't read any of my messages. I tried to tell you about the wedding, Hope."

"Can you blame me for ignoring you?" Hope frowned. "For not wanting to speak to you?"

"Please, Hope. I'm begging you to try to forgive us. We know it was wrong," Lizzie pleaded. Her big brown eyes were filling with tears. Unfortunately for her sister, Hope had seen this all before and heard it all before. She was left cold by the display.

"You slept with my husband for eight months. The two of you went behind my back all of that time. You lied and cheated. The two most important people in my life…" Hope shook her head, feeling her throat clog and her eyes sting. She could still see them together in bed. Emmet making slow, passionate love to her sister. Betrayed by her two best friends. They were together in *her* bedroom… in *her* bed… *their* marriage bed. Some things were unforgivable.

"I know." Lizzie held up her hands in defeat. "We did a terrible thing. A horrible… terrible thing. It was an accident… It just—"

"An accident?" Hope tried to keep her voice down. "Spare me the bull." She pushed out a breath. "I've heard this all before. I don't feel like having the same conversation all over again. I'm going to assume you came here to tell me about your marriage. Congratulations. The two of you deserve each other." Hope couldn't believe this was happening. She never thought that the relationship would last. Relationships born from lies and deceit hardly ever worked out. Yet, here they were… married. *No!* It was too much. "Now if you'll excuse me I—"

"That's not why I'm here." Lizzie shook her head.

"You apologized; you can go." Hope looked pointedly at the door.

"That's not it either." Her sister got a look in her eyes. Lizzie licked her lips and clasped her hands in front of her. She was nervous. What the hell could she possibly have to tell Hope that was worse than her and Emmet getting married?

There was nothing. There was—

Oh god!

That wasn't true; there *was* one thing.

At least, only one she could think of.

No!

Surely not!

That would be cruel. It would be more than she could take.

It felt like a pile of lead landed in her stomach. Her mouth went dry. "It was a shotgun wedding?" Hope whispered. She felt her heart break as she looked into Lizzie's eyes. She hadn't thought that things could get any worse. She was so wrong. Her sister had taken her life… her dream… everything. It felt like she was drowning.

Her sister pulled in a deep breath. "It wasn't a shotgun wedding." Lizzie shook her head. "I am pregnant, though. I'm three months along." She touched her belly in much the same way Mrs. Simons had, pulling her bottom lip between her teeth.

Hope wanted to punch her sister in the face. She wanted it so badly it scared her. Just like when she caught them in the act. If it weren't for her sister being pregnant, Hope would do just that. As it was, she forced her hands to unclench. She worked hard at controlling herself, taking even breaths. "You told me. You can go now." She gestured towards the door behind her sister. At least Hope would have fifteen minutes to pull herself together before her next appointment.

"I was hoping you would be my Ob-Gyn. Not just that, I want you to be the baby's godmother. I want you back in my life, Hope. I miss you. Emmet misses you, too. As a friend, of course," she quickly added.

Hope swallowed thickly, feeling ill. She tasted bile in the back of her throat. "I can't!"

"Please," Lizzie begged. "Do it for Mom and Dad. They're in the middle of this. They miss you so much."

"They took your side."

"There are no sides, Hope. They want me to be happy… us to be happy. All three of us."

Hope had nothing to say to that. She didn't care what any of them wanted. She felt both sick to her stomach… and numb.

"They want you to be happy too," Lizzie said.

"Funny way of showing it." She couldn't hold back.

"Please, Hope. Can we at least try to be a family again? Will you help me with this baby? I need you."

"I can't, even if I wanted to," she said, a little too harshly. "I'm leaving at the end of the month. I've accepted a position elsewhere."

"What?" Lizzie gasped, "Where? You've worked so hard to build your practice." Her sister looked around them.

"I can't say where I'm going," Hope said. "I've signed a nondisclosure agreement."

"A nondisclosure?" Her sister's eyes widened. "That doesn't sound right. Why would you have to sign a nondisclosure? You're making me nervous."

"I'm not at liberty to say." Even if she were, she wouldn't tell Lizzie. "I have a locum standing in for me here in case things don't work out. I'm fine. Moving on with my life," Hope lied. The fact of the matter was that she only made up her mind to take the position right then. She hadn't been able to decide whether to uproot her whole world. Only now, she realized that she had nothing left here. No real reason to stay. Not anymore. Besides, it was a six-month contract. She'd come back when her heart was on the road to recovery. When she could deal with everything going on here. Hopefully, she'd reach a point where she didn't want to punch her sister in the face anymore. Hope had a long way to go!

Grabbing the handle of the door, she opened it, standing to the side. "I wish you all the best, Mrs. Robertson." It hurt her to say the words, but she forced them out. She was thankful that she'd reverted back to her maiden name. "I hope you and Emmet have a long, happy life together. Good luck with the baby."

"You make it sound like we won't see each other again."

"If only that were true," she muttered.

Lizzie's face turned pink. "Don't say that, Hope. I really am sorry. Emmet too. Please be careful." Lizzie put a hand out to touch Hope, but she moved out of reach. Her sister held her gaze for a few moments before she finally turned and walked away.

"I have a phone call I need to make," Hope said to Sandy. "Give me five minutes, please."

"No problem, Doctor," Sandy said, looking up from her computer.

Hope closed the door with a soft click and leaned back against the cool surface of the wood. It was difficult to hold back all the emotions inside her. Her eyes stung. Her throat had a lump in it the size of a small building… that's how it felt. All of her muscles were clenched tight. She took a couple of deep breaths. This was not the day for tears. This was the day for action. The wallowing needed to stop. All of the self-pity, too.

Hope realized that if she stayed, she'd keep holding on to all the anger. All the hurt… the frustration… all the crippling pain and regret. Hope realized that it was time to act… it was time for a change. Although she didn't have the full details for this assignment yet, it sounded interesting.

CHAPTER 2

Worry churned in Reece's gut. Why had the king summoned him?

Many things had changed in the last couple of moon cycles. Reece was no longer Leukos' second-in-command. Not since the king and Magnar had both mated the same human female. Magnar had stepped up to take the second's position, which made sense since the male was no longer a Fallen… no longer the enemy. He was now Reece's direct superior and a part of the royal family. Reece didn't have a problem with Magnar. In fact, he liked the male… even respected him.

Reece slowed, hovering over the landing before touching down. His clawed talons scraped on the surface. He shifted into his human form before announcing himself at the royal chamber door.

He needed to stop being so damned negative. Perhaps the king had summoned him with good news. Maybe he was going to get the promotion he had been working so hard toward. It was between himself and Shard. Reece felt his whole body tense up. His beast clawed to be freed. It wanted the male's blood. He hated that bastard with every fiber of his being. There was no way he would ever report to the likes of him. Shard was a hothead and a traitor. Unfortunately, he had proven himself to be a decent leader. The males respected him. That was because they didn't know Shard like he did. The male was not to be trusted.

He and Shard were evenly matched when pitted against each other. They were pretty evenly matched every which way you looked at it. That was why it had taken Leukos so long to choose between them.

Worry churned in Reece's gut. If Shard was promoted over him, he might have to leave his home and his people. It wasn't what he wanted. If Shard got the leadership position, he would have to… would be forced to go. Hate burned within him, strong and true. Years may have passed, but nothing had changed for Reece.

Nothing!

Was the king giving him the position, or was he going to let Reece down gently in person? After essentially being demoted, he deserved to be given the title. He, of all people, knew that life wasn't always fair, though. It could go either way. By feather, he wished he knew the answer. Shard, ever the thorn in his side. He gave his head a shake. He needed to be focused for this meeting.

"Come in," Leukos shouted from inside.

With a soft sigh, Reece pulled the billowing curtain aside and entered the nest. It was large and airy. Gold, wood, and stone were the primary materials used in the making of the structure. A whole lot of gold. It glinted from all sides of the nest. From the door handles to the candelabra. Even a large tub to the one side of the bedroom was made from solid gold. "Sire." He inclined his head.

"Enough with the formalities," Leukos said.

Reece nodded once in acknowledgment. He noted that Magnar and the queen were also in attendance. Magnar wore a double-breasted suit, just like the king. "Your highness." He gave a quick bow through the waist in the direction of the queen, noting how much more prominent her belly was beneath the dress she was wearing. The clutch was coming along nicely. That was good news. The birth of an heir was going to be a joyous day, indeed.

"Call me Claire," the human smiled. "I can't get used to all the fanfare." She flapped her hand at him, not really looking his way.

This was the last thing he expected. Why was the queen there? Magnar was understandable, but the queen… not so much.

"Please take a seat." Leukos gestured to a nearby chair.

Magnar threw a pair of pants at him. "The queen still finds nudity… off-putting."

"Not off-putting." Claire shook her head, her ponytail bobbing in time with the movement. "I'm just not… used to it. Not yet. You don't have to dress on account of me. I don't mind at all," she said. Reece noted that she still didn't quite look at him. Her cheeks looked a touch pink.

He took the pants and pulled them on, doing up the zipper and clasp. Humans called them jeans. They were uncomfortable. Not as bad as shoes, but a close second.

His prick and balls felt squashed. He wanted to adjust himself, but refrained.

"Thank you for coming." Claire finally locked eyes with him as she sat on one of the nearby sofas. Leukos and Magnar sat on either side of her. Magnar put his arm along the back of the chair. The king put a hand on her lower thigh.

It was a strange set-up. One Reece couldn't quite understand. It was normal for their species to share females. They had been compelled to do it more and more as Feral females died off. Four or five males to one female was completely normal. At least it was normal up until mating. Then the female would pick her favorite and they would mate. He couldn't think of a single three-way mating within their species. Especially with a human female. He thought they were timid about such things. Claire couldn't even handle nudity, but she was fine with being pleased by two males at the same time. He turned his attention to the king and the meeting at hand.

"You're probably wondering why I called you here today," Leukos commented.

Reece nodded. "I am, indeed." He felt his body tighten and a frown form on his forehead.

"You need not worry any further," Magnar said. "We asked you here to offer you a very important role."

"An *all* important role." The king sat forward, his expression grave.

His heart beat faster. This was it. They were about to offer him the position of the head guard. Shard could go to hell.

"It was a tough decision choosing between the best our warriors have to offer," Leukos went on. "I chose you, in the end."

He couldn't help but smile. "I am honored, Sire."

"There isn't a greater role than head royal guard." Magnar leaned back more into the chair, his hand brushing the back of the queen's neck.

"It would be a…" Reece began. He suddenly realized what Magnar had said. "Head royal guard? Forgive me, Magnar… Sire… What is a head *royal* guard? I'm going to assume it's different to the head guard position?"

"It is a new position," Leukos said. "A more important one. My spies tell me that Ekon plans on stealing our chicks as soon as they are hatched." There was a hard growl to Leukos' voice. His eyes narrowed. "They have it on good authority that he intends to go through with this crazy plan of his. The wheels are already in motion."

"The Fallen king is unstable, to say the least." Magnar leaned forward, clasping his hands in his lap. He sighed. "This is a major task we have set for you. One that must be seen as the most important role that there is."

"Exactly," his king said. "Do not underestimate this position. The future of our people is at stake. The heir to the throne is inside my mate's belly." Leukos placed his hand on Claire's rounded stomach.

"*Our* young." Magnar's voice had an edge, too. Reece found himself wondering who the father was. Did they even know? Would it be questioned?

"It will be alright," Claire said, putting her hand over Leukos' one. He could see the fear in her eyes. "I know Ekon isn't… I guess he has mental problems, but he would never take babies that aren't his." She shook her head. "No! That's pure madness." She was trying to convince herself. But, from the way her chest was rising and falling quickly, he could see that she wasn't succeeding.

"No, my sweets." Magnar put his arm around Claire. "This is merely a precaution. One of us will be at your side at all times. Then there's Reece. Not only is this male a fantastic warrior—a stronger male does not exist," he looked Reece's way, "but he is the best at risk management. At looking for weaknesses… finding problems before they become an issue. Reece will keep you safe." Magnar touched her belly, too. "Between the three of us, you have nothing to fear."

Despite the shocking news, he still felt his chest warm at the compliments. He was both proud to be given this role and frustrated because he might be missing out on the head guard position.

"Okay." Claire smiled. She looked somewhat placated.

"Do you need time to think things through?" Leukos asked. "I would urge you to take the role. You would need to pick out three strong males to stand at your side. Individuals you trust to keep the queen safe. Males who would fight to the death. Those who can stand in your shoes when you are resting. Ekon's spies are everywhere. You will need to choose wisely. Claire is due to lay within the next moon cycle. There are plans in place to take down Ekon, but they could take several months… moon cycles," he quickly corrected. It was clear that he had been keeping the company of a human. "Your place would be here at her side. You and your team. This is especially important if we are both called away." Leukos and Magnar shared a look. They were both frowning darkly.

"There will need to be two shifts," Reece said. "Myself with another male, and then another team of two males. I would want Locke leading the second team."

"No problem," Leukos answered quickly. Too quickly, perhaps.

"Who will take the head guard position in my absence?"

Magnar and Leukos shared a look. Reece didn't like what he saw. Apprehension, definite tension.

Leukos' jaw was tense. "Shard will take up the position temporarily as head guard."

Blast and damn!

Reece had to work hard to hold back the emotion. He knew it! If he took this role, he would lose out to that bastard, Shard. If he didn't take it, he would be snubbing the king and queen… Magnar too. He finally sighed softly and nodded once. There was no other option for him but to take it. Mainly because it was the right thing to do. Ekon was dangerous. Left unchecked, the male could destroy the Feral species. Destroy his people, and just when they had found a way forward with human females. They could take mates and successfully breed. It was something he had given a lot of thought to. Once he was promoted to head guard, he planned on taking a female of his own. Everything had been carefully mapped out in his head. It was time for him to move on. It was time. It wasn't supposed to happen this way, though. *What now?*

"All we ask is that you keep the queen and our chicks safe for the next three moon cycles." Leukos stopped there, his jaw tightened, his eyes were blazing. The need to protect his female, to take down any enemies, had to be riding him hard. Reece could see it all over his king.

"Do this for us and you will be given the head guard position," Magnar added when Leukos looked too shaken to continue. Reece had never seen his king like this.

"Of course, I will," he said. "You should give the head guard position to whoever is best suited." It burned him to say it, but he forced himself. "I will watch over the queen and the chicks when they come because it is my duty. I am greatly honored to be chosen for this role. I will give you my life… willingly, your highness," Reece told the queen.

"Thank you, Reece." Her eyes glinted with unshed tears.

"We have already decided," Leukos said, "that you will be given the head guard position. Three moon cycles, and it's yours, Reece. All we ask is that you keep what is most precious to us—to our people—safe from that madman. Removing him will need to be done with tact and care. We have a plan, we just need time to execute it. Once he is neutralized, we will be able to breathe easy." He sighed. "That's the problem with Ekon, he always uses a scapegoat. It's never him directly to blame. We'll get him soon enough. We can't have the Feral fighting amongst themselves or joining the Fallen. This needs to happen one step at a time."

"Understood. In the meantime, you can rely on me," Reece said, looking each of them in the eyes. Three months and he would be head guard. Three months and he would be able to move onto the next phase of his life.

Until then, his life belonged to the queen and the unborn chicks.

"One last thing," Leukos said.

"Yes, Sire?" He caught the look in the other male's eye and quickly said, "Yes, Leukos."

His friend smiled. "We have hired a human healer. She specializes in pregnancy and birth."

"A human?" Reece said, frowning. Claire was mated to Feral males, about to lay eggs. "With all due respect, we have healers. The chicks will not be human. We know this already."

"I'm human," Claire stated the obvious. "I love Delise. She knows what she is doing. She's been nothing but kind to me. However, I think I would feel more comfortable with an Ob-Gyn as well. There has only ever been one human who has done the whole egg-laying thing." Her eyes widened. "We're covering all our bases." She looked at each of her mates in turn.

"That makes sense," Reece said. "Excuse my insolence," he said to Leukos and Magnar. "Forget I said anything." He gave a head bow to the queen.

"Doctor Bristol is arriving tomorrow," Leukos said. "Please meet her and show her the accommodation. You will need to make her feel welcome and ensure her safety, particularly when she is with Claire. We foresee that she might end up being a target as well."

"Of course." Reece nodded. A human was an added complication, but if the queen needed a doctor, then he would step up. "No problem. No harm will come to either female."

"Good! One other thing," Magnar added. "With the threat of Ekon looming, I don't like the idea of the human being alone in the accommodations at night. Depending on the shifts you and your team work, I would prefer it if one of you slept in the room next door to the doctor."

No!

It was the first thing that came to mind. He drew in a breath, gathering his thoughts. The last thing he wanted was to fledgling-sit a human.

"I could put a general guard on duty, but I would prefer it if we kept it to a small group who oversees the human. There are very few who I trust implicitly. Since the four of you will oversee her already, when she is with Claire, it makes logical sense to have you, or another male, do it," Magnar said. "Our first choice would be you. The second choice would be a male you can trust to take the duty seriously. Locke perhaps?"

"No problem," he pushed out.

"It's more of a formality than anything else," Leukos said.

"Of course, Sire." He inclined his head, praying for the next three months to go quickly. A human! Reece didn't like it. A human female complicated things.

CHAPTER 3

The helicopter slowly descended. Hope couldn't take her eyes off the creatures flying all around them. Half eagle and half lion. Griffin shifters—or Feral, as they liked to call themselves—were huge in their animal form. Their hindquarters were furry and muscular. They had long tails, with dark fur on the tip. Their top half was that of a majestic eagle, complete with wide, feathered wings and sharp beaks.

The helicopter touched down on the grass with a bump. Tall towers littered the open field. They looked to be two or three stories high and were bigger than they had looked from up in the air.

One man stood waiting about a hundred yards away. He was huge, with wide shoulders and thick biceps. The guy was wearing a pair of jeans and nothing else. Hope didn't think he even wore shoes. She strained her eyes to see. *Nope, no shoes.* Strange. Then again, she had been briefed that nudity was normal and should be expected.

A movement to her right drew her attention. Hope watched in shock as one of the creatures, who had just landed, reduced in size, seeming to collapse in on itself. Limbs shortened. Feathers sucked back into skin. Within seconds, a man stood in the place of the beast that had descended.

A naked man.

This was normal. She'd been briefed on the species and what to expect. Just the basics. Mainly the differences between their two species. Shifting. Naked guys. Seeing it in the flesh was a whole different matter to a briefing, however.

She turned back to the man wearing jeans. He had moved much closer. The rotors of the helicopter had stopped turning, and the noise had died down. "Thanks so much for getting me here safely, Peter," she said to the pilot, who was flicking switches. She removed her headset, hanging it back on the designated hook.

"Sure thing, Dr. Bristol," the pilot said, turning back towards her and giving her the thumbs up. "Good luck. You're going to need it."

Really? Why did he think that? Instead of asking, she grabbed her bags.

"Let me help you," a gruff-sounding voice said from outside the chopper.

Hope looked out of the open door… and there he was. His eyes were a startling golden color. The Ferals' strange eye color had formed part of her briefing, but she still hadn't been prepared for this. They were mesmerizing… along with the rest of him. For a few seconds, all she could do was stare. He had broad shoulders and gleaming dark hair that was probably a little too long to be considered fashionable by human standards. It suited him. As did the five o'clock shadow he had going on.

Wait a minute!

Was she checking him out? No! Maybe... So what if she was? If there were hot guys to look at, she was looking, dammit. Especially if they were naked a lot of the time. It was the main reason she had taken this assignment. No, it wasn't. Hope had run away from her problems. She was quite happy to admit that. Thing was, Hope could look all she wanted, but she wouldn't touch. She planned on giving the whole 'rebound relationship' thing a skip. Instead, she was going to focus on herself. Finding herself and learning about herself as a single woman. That meant no men. No shifters, either. She didn't need someone to tell her what to do and what not to do and then to lie and cheat behind her back. No thanks! In fact, she might never want to be with a man again.

"Are you okay?" The gorgeous guy gave her a questioning look.

Shit!

"Um... yes! Um... I'm... um... fine." She managed to lock eyes with him again. She stared into his golden orbs. They were beautiful.

"Do you want me to turn around so that you can get a better look?" His eyes were narrowed on her.

"Turn around?" she repeated, sounding like an idiot.

"I take it you've never seen one of my kind before." He was completely deadpan.

She couldn't gauge whether he was teasing her or calling her out on all the gawking. "Sorry... no... that's fine, no turning around necessary, and no, I've never seen a Feral before. Is that how I say it?"

"Yes." He lifted his brows. "Your bag?" He looked pointedly at the baggage at her feet.

"It's heavy," she warned.

"I'm a Feral. Were you not told that we have superior strength to you humans? We are superior in many ways."

"Lucky you," she grumbled. "Here it is." She shoved her bag at him. It would be her bad luck to meet a grouchy asshole as her first Feral person.

The big guy was as strong as he looked because he caught her big-ass bag, putting it on the floor next to him like it weighed nothing. "That one too?" he said, glancing at the much smaller medical bag at her feet.

She gave the other bag to him as well. Hope watched as he put that down as well. Then he lifted both his arms up. "Your turn." He looked bored. "Come on, Doctor. I swear I won't drop you."

It was quite far down since she was so short. She wasn't that tall. Her hesitation was justified, even though he looked like he could carry five of her without a problem.

"Put your hands on my shoulders," he instructed. "I won't bite."

"I know you won't bite."

"I won't drop you either." He deadpanned. "Grab ahold of me, you will be fine." He sighed, like this was the hardest job he had been given. Like she was the biggest bother.

Hope put her hands on his shoulders. *His very wide, naked shoulders.* "Okay," Hope stammered, doing as he said. His skin was warm and smooth.

He reached up and took her hips in his large hands.

She had to work hard not to yelp when he took her out of the helicopter, setting her on her feet.

Hope just stood there like an idiot, her hands still on his broad shoulders. Her eyes on his face. *Wow!* She'd never met anyone quite like him before.

"You can let me go now, Doctor. Unless you really do want me to turn around so that you can get a better look. It might be better to get it out of the way so that we can move on." He definitely seemed irritated this time. There was no humor evident.

"Oh! I'm sorry. I guess it's all going to take some getting used to, that's all." Hope took back her arms, letting them hang at her sides. "It's just… I've never met a Feral. Although, we haven't actually officially met, have we? My name is Hope… I'm Doctor Hope Bristol. You can call me Hope, though."

"My name is Reece. I will call you Dr. Bristol. I am here because the king requested that I welcome you. I have just been appointed as the head of the royal guard. My duty is to protect the queen and the soon-to-be hatched young."

"Hatched?" She shook her head. "I'm still trying to wrap my head around all of this. I was briefed yesterday. Everything was quite vague about this assignment up until then. I'm happy to be here and it's nice to meet you."

He frowned heavily. "Wrap your head around? Why would you want to wrap your head around—? What do you need to wrap your head—?"

"It's a human saying. I need to get used to being here. I can't wait to find out more about your kind," Hope said brightly, hoping to get a smile out of the serious Feral.

"I do not know much about humans." He frowned. "I am going to shift now, so that I can transport you to your accommodation. Are you afraid of heights?"

"No." She shook her head.

"Good."

It all happened so quickly. There was no time to do anything. No time to look away or prepare. Her mouth fell open when Reece unsnapped the top button of his jeans and pulled them down. Her eyes were immediately drawn to his... to his penis, which was long and thick and slanted slightly to the left. He was a big man in all respects. His thighs were thick and powerful. His abs... were very much there, all eight of them. His penis looked... No, it couldn't be! It looked like he had a semi. Reece took a few steps toward her and it swayed. There was nothing in the briefing about this. Perhaps it was perfectly normal for a Feral. There was no saying.

"Have you seen your fill?" Reece's rough-as-nails voice broke into her mushy, hazy brain.

Her cheeks instantly heated. "I'm... I'm sorry." She was still looking at his cock. What was wrong with her? "Yes!" she practically yelled. "I... wasn't expecting you to get naked quite so soon or quite so quickly." She looked into his eyes, which were steely.

"I thought you said you were briefed."

She swallowed thickly. "I was. They even gave me a booklet."

"You should study the booklet, Dr. Bristol." Again, she had no idea what he was thinking. Was he angry? He looked angry. She was messing this up. Five minutes on Feral soil and she was ruining things.

"You need to get used to naked people... naked males. If it's something you can't handle, then this assignment won't work. I can advise my king to find another human healer."

She swallowed again. "I can handle it. I've seen you naked now." She shrugged. "No big deal. Doctors see naked people all the time" *Not like you!* Not like him! Not like this. Her heart was hammering in her chest. Her hands felt clammy. She'd get used to it soon enough. It wasn't a big deal. The fact that up until today, she had only ever seen one man naked. At least, living and breathing. Cadavers didn't count. Holy mackerel, her mind was all over the place. "All good," she added when he didn't say anything. She even shrugged.

His eyes narrowed as he scrutinized her. "Are you sure, Dr. Bristol?"

"Absolutely."

"Fine." He took a few steps away from her and she had to fight to maintain eye contact. All she wanted to do was to gawk at him some more, which was strange since she wasn't normally like this. Good-looking guys had never made her uncomfortable or made her want to stare. Then again, he was spectacular, and he wasn't human. Not even close. That was the biggest point of interest; how animal-like he was, even in his human form. She was allowed to react the first time meeting a Feral up close. After this, she'd maintain decorum. It wouldn't be long before seeing sexy naked guys would be an everyday occurrence.

Her mouth fell open all over again when he started to shift. When the most gorgeous golden feathers sprouted from his skin. When claws and scales took the place of arms, and fur began to sprout from powerful legs. Wings emerged from his back. They were wide and impressive, just like the rest of him. A griffin shifter, up close and in the flesh. *Wow!* He made a screeching noise as soon as he was fully changed. It was loud and terrifying. Goosebumps rose on her arms. She watched, transfixed, as he gripped her bags and his jeans in one taloned claw.

The second claw came at her. "Um… I don't know about—" Before she could say anything more, he had her in his grip and was taking to the sky. She screamed in both exhilaration and fear. Probably both in equal measures. The fear soon dissipated as they sped across the sky. His huge wings barely seemed to flap. It felt amazing as the wind rushed past her, whipping her hair about her face. This was hands-down, one of the most remarkable things to ever have happened to her. A laugh was ripped from her. She couldn't help it. It was like all the pent-up anger and frustration eased a smidgen for the first time in months. She felt something lighten inside her. Hope felt that she'd made the right decision to come here. If nothing else, she'd have lots to look at. She stared up at the great griffin as he flapped his wings.

CHAPTER 4

Reece wasn't entirely sure that this female had all of her faculties. She gripped his claws tightly and screamed as he ascended. Not so long after, she laughed. A little later, she laughed a second time.

Laughing.

Why was she laughing like that?

What was so funny?

Quite frankly, he wasn't sure that she was the right person for the job. All she had done so far was stare at him. How would others of his species react when she stared at them like that? It was rude. You would swear that she had never seen a naked male before. From a regular human he might expect as much, but not a healer. What was the big deal about a naked male?

Then again, he had reacted to her. It was a shock to him that he had. Something he hadn't expected, since the human was so tiny. So unferal-like. Perhaps it was her feminine scent that had set him off. Reece had started to feel his prick stir under her scrutiny. His balls had pulled tight and his prick started to prepare to mount.

Even though he wasn't convinced about Dr. Bristol, he needed to keep that particular fact in mind. His harder, thicker cock would explain her staring. Then again, it was his understanding that human females were timid. The doctor hadn't shrunk away. She was brazen in her scrutiny of him. Perhaps she was on Feral territory to do more than just be a healer to the queen. Perhaps she wanted to choose a Feral mate of her own. The idea didn't sit well with him. He was going to keep a close eye on her and report back to his king if there was anything untoward. The queen was relying on this healer to help her through the laying.

He was worried about Claire. The queen needed someone who would give her their undivided attention. It was a good thing that Delise would also be in attendance.

Reece spotted the human accommodation in the distance and descended slowly. He landed on the lawn in front of the squat-looking nest. It was at ground level and didn't look appealing to him at all. Reece carefully put the female down. She staggered a step or two, grinning from ear to ear.

"That was exhilarating. Thank you," she told him as he put her bags and his jeans down next to her.

He noted that she averted her eyes when he began shifting back into his human form. Her gaze was firmly on the nest in front of her. The human gasped loudly. "That's some house. Am I the only one who will be living there?"

"Either a colleague or I will stay with you. Do not fear," he put up a hand, "we will stay out of your way. It is a precautionary measure to ensure your safety during these troubled times."

A frown formed on her forehead. "I was informed during the briefing yesterday about a dangerous Feral wanting to become king. He was dethroned years ago. He thinks that if he steals the royal babies, that he will be king again?" She shook her head. "Is that right? I have to say that I'm a little concerned."

"Yes, you are correct." He watched as her eyes clouded. "You are in no danger, Dr. Bristol," he tried to reassure her. "The Fallen king Ekon wants to kidnap the chicks as soon as they are born. His reasoning is that whoever has the heir is the rightful king."

"Forgive me, but it all seems a little... strange that he would do this. I don't know enough about your culture." Her frown deepened. "I guess I'm trying to figure out just how much danger I might be in. I think it's terrible that the queen has to worry about this during what should be a magical, exciting time of her life." He saw what looked like fear flare in her eyes, hence all the questions. It made sense that she would be apprehensive.

"It has nothing to do with our culture. Ekon isn't of sound mind. His reasoning is flawed, but it won't stop him from trying to carry out the task. He desperately wants the throne back. We can't let that happen." Reece picked up her bags. "Like I said, you have nothing to fear. Ekon has no interest in a human healer."

"Why not just arrest him?" Her eyes were wide.

"Ekon has his followers. He's known as the Fallen King. Taking him down, even attempting it, could start a war. Certain protocols need to be followed. Do not worry about Ekon. You only need to worry about the queen and the chicks."

"Noted." She nodded. "Thank you for the explanation. I was given very little information yesterday. I was wondering." She lifted her eyes in thought. "It was bugging me."

"There are security measures in place. You have nothing to worry about."

"Only," she chewed her bottom lip, "I will need to see the queen regularly. I'm sure I'll need to spend a whole lot of time with her in the coming period. That would put me in the line of fire."

Reece couldn't believe what he was hearing. He dropped the bags and stopped walking. "You have the facts. I'm sorry that some of the information was omitted. You are not the target, Dr. Bristol. There is some risk, though. Again, I will reiterate, if this assignment is not going to work for you, then I urge you to leave now. The queen is going to lay her eggs in less than a moon cycle. If you are not the right person for this job, speak up now so that we can replace you. It would need to happen sooner rather than later. Should I call the helicopter pilot? Perhaps he hasn't left yet. If he has, he can come back to collect you."

Her eyes narrowed on him as he spoke. She sucked in a deep breath. "No, you don't have to call him back. And stop saying that I'm not the right person." Her eyes narrowed even further as they locked with his. "It's starting to seriously irritate me. Just because I'm someone who likes all the facts, does not mean that I need replacing. The more I know, the better. I could help you keep the queen safe."

He choked out the start of a laugh. "No, human! You are small and weak. You could not help. You would get in the way. There is nothing you could do to—"

"Stop there!" Her soft voice had turned gruff. "I have eyes and ears. If I know what I'm looking for, and understand the situation, I could perhaps alert you or one of your guys to something unusual. I could be a big asset. I refuse to go into this blindly. I might not like everything I encounter, but that does not mean that I'll run home with my tail between my legs. I might be small, but I'm fierce."

He cocked his head, looking down. Humans didn't have tails. What was she talking about? As to being fierce… please!

"There won't be much to hear or see since they will not send a large army. It will be a few trained males who would use stealth to try to take the chicks."

"Exactly. I can help you. I can be an extra set of eyes and ears. I can scream loudly if I see anything. I have a decent set of lungs."

He had noticed. Her squeal at take-off had been piercing. "Fine. Just stay out of the way so that you don't get hurt. Having a human injured or killed on my watch would be a major blemish on my record."

"Heaven forbid your record is affected." She rolled her eyes.

"I take my job seriously, Dr. Bristol."

"As do I. Forget I even offered to help." She huffed. "This Ekon person may not even make a move." She shrugged.

"Oh, he will make a move. Or at least, one of his men will make a move. I will stop them." He opened the door, standing back so that she could go inside.

"Oh, my gosh!" The human covered her mouth with both hands and walked in a small circle. Her eyes were very wide. "This place is gorgeous! That view."

"The view would have been better from up high."

"I saw that you guys live in towers." Tiny frown lines appeared between her eyes.

"Nests," he corrected her. "We build our nests on tall rocky structures. We have to shift to enter and leave. We fly wherever we want to go; we don't have vehicles. We are a base species who spend a lot of time in our animal form."

"Interesting. And this house?" She looked around them.

"We built this house as a human accommodation. You really need to read that booklet." He felt annoyed. This was taking too long, and the human was asking too many questions. He had a feeling she was going to ask more, so he might as well explain everything. "Our people lost most of our females almost twelve years ago. They—"

"I heard about that. Clutch sickness, I believe the illness is called." She looked solemn, her eyes darkening with concern.

He nodded. "We were a species of males for many years. The Feral have since discovered that we are compatible with humans. The nests are not deemed suitable and therefore, we are making adjustments. The royal nest now has an elevator. Humans get around in four-wheelers. We are busy installing electricity. Many of our nests are equipped for humans. They have electricity and running water. We even have cellphones and computers."

"That's great. I'm glad to hear it since I would like to be able to stay in touch with the outside world. This really is a lovely space." She continued to peer about.

"This is the first house our species built especially for humans. Females seeking nonhuman mates come and stay here from time to time. There have been quite a few matings as a result, including the king. We are building more units for mated couples. It is a work in progress. We are learning as we go along. For example, although this is a four-bedroom house, there is only one bathroom. That small oversight still needs to be rectified."

"That's fine." She shrugged, "I don't mind sharing."

Reece didn't like the idea at all, but kept his thoughts to himself. He was trying to be cordial to the human. His king wouldn't want it any other way.

"The swimming pool is beautiful," she gushed, opening the back door and stepping onto the deck.

Reece didn't say anything. It was getting late. He had things he needed to do. Namely, his team would be assembling soon for their first meeting. He had greatly underestimated how long it would take him to welcome the healer. In his opinion, aside from one or two small hiccups, it had gone very well. He had done his duty sufficiently.

Dr. Bristol put her hand into the water. "It's perfect. I can't wait to take a dip." The female must have caught the look on his face because she went on, "What? Don't you like swimming?"

"I'm half bird and half cat. The thought leaves me cold. A quick, hot shower is one thing. Choosing to immerse myself in water for any length of time..." He shook his head. "If you'll follow me, I'd like you to choose a room so that I can help you with your bags."

"Oh! Of course. I'm sorry." She paused mid-stride. "Are you always this serious, Reece?"

What kind of question is that? "I am on duty. As I mentioned before, I take my job very seriously. I hope you will do the same."

Her eyes widened for a moment. "Of course I will. I already told you that." She walked ahead of him. "Which bedroom would be best?" she asked as they arrived in the hallway.

"They are all very similar. This one is closest to the bathroom, so perhaps—"

"I was asking from a security standpoint. I mean, I know it's strictly precautionary, but perhaps there is a bedroom that would be better from a strategic standpoint?"

The female had a point. He'd give her that. Perhaps he had underestimated her to some degree. "Take the second bedroom," he said. "That would put myself or one of the others between you and the threat. Just precautionary, of course."

"Okay, then." They bypassed the bathroom and the first bedroom. She walked into the next room. "This is lovely," she said, stopping dead.

He had to stop abruptly, almost bashing into her. He put down the bags and walked backward—not before he caught another whiff of her scent. He couldn't say what she smelled of exactly. All he knew was that it was good… amazing even. She smelled soft and feminine. He wanted to step forward… step in closer and get another whiff. Reece refrained. In a couple of months, he could get his fill of female scents. *Not now!* Not with this particular human. Dr. Bristol was strictly off-limits to both him and the rest of the royal guard. He would be sure to convey that to his team. "I will leave you to settle in," he stated, his voice a rough rasp. Reece didn't wait for her response. He turned and left.

CHAPTER 5

The breeze ruffled his hair. The sun was warm on his back. On days such as this, he preferred to hold meetings outside. It kept a male's mind clear.

"Is everyone clear on their duties?" Reece asked.

"Yes." Andy was frowning heavily. "I can't believe that Ekon would stoop this low."

"I can't either." Locke ground his molars together. "You can count on us, Reece. We will work tirelessly to keep the queen and her young safe."

"We'll pulverize anyone who tries to touch those chicks." Zaire's eyes were blazing.

"I'm glad to hear it." Reece looked at them each in turn. "It is of the utmost importance that any and all information surrounding this assignment stay between the four of us. There are spies everywhere… even high up in our ranks."

"Who?" Andy asked. "I mean, I know that there are spies but who is high up?"

"I can't say for sure." Reece's mind went straight to Shard. Anger and hate churned in him. "Suspect everyone and trust no one. I'm talking about the movements of the Royals. The timeframes for the laying. Whether the chicks have hatched or not. All of this information is strictly confidential. I chose the three of you because I trust you and only you." Andy was still quite immature. Locke had potential but also had some growing up to do. All of these males were strong warriors and above all he trusted them with his life. More importantly, he trusted them with the life of the queen and the chicks.

"Understood." Zaire nodded.

"Any questions?"

They all shook their heads.

"Good! That brings me to the last item on the agenda," Reece said, eyes on the three males before him. "Dr. Bristol."

"That's the human healer who will be helping the queen lay her eggs?" Locke asked. His eyes suddenly glinted with mischief, which irritated Reece immensely.

"Yes," Reece said, nodding once. "She arrived not too long ago and is settling in at the human accommodations."

"She's here already?" Andy asked, eyes wide. "I heard that she's still quite young and unmated. Is that true? Is she beautiful? I'll bet she is."

Reece's feathers rubbed, but he worked hard at pushing the emotions to the side. These were unmated males in their prime. Males with needs, who rarely got to mingle with females. It was unnatural. He needed to try to have some understanding of their urges. It was tough, since this was very serious.

"Yes! Is she gorgeous?" Zaire's eyes were bright.

"No!" Reece growled. "I mean… I don't know if she's beautiful." He shrugged.

"What do you mean you don't know?" Locke said, grinning. "You met with her, didn't you?"

"Yes, I met with her, but I didn't take note of what she looked like," Reece said, drawing in a deep breath.

"You take note of everything." Zaire frowned. "I'm sure you would have—"

"Yes, okay… yes!" Reece blurted. "The human is beautiful. She has dark, shiny hair and big blue eyes. She's very small, even by human standards, but that is her only flaw. It doesn't matter, though; not at all, because she is off-limits to all of us."

"No!" Zaire shook his head, looking horrified. "It was the one thing about this assignment that I was excited about."

"Well, get unexcited fast," Reece snapped. "What this assignment needs is focus and dedication. What have we just been talking about for the last half an hour?" Frustration welled.

"Oh, I can be focused and dedicated, alright." Zaire grinned. "What could it hurt if—"

"The queen's life is at stake. Her life and the lives of the chicks. The life of the heir to the throne… of our people. You have a job to do. A job that will be a lot more effective if your pricks stay dry. Do you hear me?" He looked hard at them. "There will be plenty of opportunity for human females in a couple of months, when this assignment is over."

"Months?" Locke looked horrified.

"This particular female is off-limits. What you do in your spare time and when you are on leave is up to you." Reece sounded exasperated. "Do not try anything with Dr. Bristol… that's all I'm saying. There will be serious repercussions when you are caught, and I *will* find out. Also, you will address her as Dr. Bristol, not by her first name. Are we clear?"

All three males nodded.

"Good. We officially start tomorrow. You can all take the rest of the day off. I want you clear-headed and resolute. A more important assignment has never existed. Our careers hang in the balance. Moreover, lives hang in the balance. We need to protect the king, the queen, and the chicks with our lives." He was repeating himself, but it was obvious that it was necessary. He had expected a reaction to the human, but this was too much. Reece was also worried about what they would do when they saw her in person. The human was greatly attractive. It was going to make his life that much more difficult.

"Understood," Locke said. The other two nodded. There was no more stupid banter or silly grins.

Good!

"You are dismissed," Reece said, folding his arms.

He watched Zaire and Andy shift and fly away. Locke was still at his side. He turned to the male, who was grinning like an idiot. "What?" He didn't like the look the male was giving him.

Locke chuckled. "You've made the female off bounds because you want her for yourself. Admit it."

"No!" Reece shook his head. "You are wrong. That female is not my type at all." In truth, it had been so long since he had tried to win a female. His focus had been on his career for so long that Reece wasn't sure he even had a 'type' anymore. He had zero clue when it came to females, especially humans.

"If you say so." Locke looked at him like he didn't buy it for a second.

"It doesn't matter, though. She is part of my… our assignment. That makes her even more off-limits to me since I am in charge."

"That's a big pity, Reece. I think you could do with—"

"Don't even say it." Reece shook his head. "I was going to take the night shift, and have you watch over her during her rest cycle, but I'm beginning to think that it might be a mistake. Can I trust you with this female, Locke?"

"Of course you can trust me. The question is whether you can trust yourself." The male laughed, irritating him no end, even though he knew that this banter was unfounded since Locke had never seen the female.

"I trust myself just fine."

"I won't touch her." Locke put up both hands. "You gave an order, and I'll obey. Also, I think you like her more than you're letting on. You admitted to finding her attractive."

"I said she was beautiful. I also said that she wasn't my type."

"Beautiful and attractive are the same thing. I think you are protesting so much because you want this human." He winked at Reece, ruffling his feathers.

"I don't want her. Stop being a prick! I'll work nights. You can fledgling-sit the human." His voice had a hard edge.

"Are you sure? You'll miss out on—"

"I'm more than sure. It's the last I want to hear about it. Another word from you and I'm going to give you overtime."

Locke held up his hands. "Okay, boss. If you change your mind and need to swap, let me know."

Reece scowled. "I won't change my mind on any of it." Why did he feel so angry if this was the right decision? The last thing he wanted was to live with the human or to have to fledgling-sit her. This was the better solution. He was sure that the attack on the queen would come during the dark of night. He needed to protect the Royals. He needed to ignore the human. Locke would do a great job. "That's settled, then."

"I'll go and pack a bag," Locke said. "Do you want to introduce me to the female, or should I just go over there and take care of it myself?"

"Dr. Bristol… that's her name, you should use it."

"Of course." Locke smiled. "Would you like to be there when I meet Dr. Bristol, or should I pack and head over myself? I'm good with human women. I have plenty of experience."

Hearing him say that grated him. "I'll introduce you to the doctor." He pushed out a breath. "Are you sure I can trust you with her… with something so important?"

Locke rolled his eyes. "For the last time, yes! Even if she throws herself at me naked—which she won't do, I'm just making a point here—but even if she did throw herself at me naked, I swear I'll turn her down."

Reece snorted. "You wish she'd throw herself at you naked."

Locke laughed. "I can't help it that human women love me."

Reece choked out a laugh and shook his head. "What I wouldn't give to have your confidence."

"I'll meet you there shortly?" Locke raised his brows.

Reece nodded. He took a few steps away from Locke and shifted, making for the human accommodations.

CHAPTER 6

Hope dipped her toes into the cool crystal water. It was perfect. The weather was lovely and hot. She'd sat in the sun for half an hour soaking up the rays, and now it was time for a refreshing swim. She made sure that her towel was nearby, then she peeled off her sarong and dove into the water.

It took her breath away for a couple of seconds before her body became accustomed to the temperature. She swam a number of lengths before going to the edge and admiring the view. There were mountains in the background as far as the eye could see.

Sure, there were dangers and definite cultural differences, but this felt right somehow. She'd wanted a change in her life. Something new… an adventure. This was an adventure alright. Hope chuckled to herself as she dipped under the water for a few seconds before coming back up. A smile was still firmly plastered to her lips.

"Do you always laugh so much, and for no reason?"

Hope squealed as she turned towards the voice. She clasped a hand to her chest when she saw Reece standing there. "Oh… hi. You shouldn't sneak up on a person." She wiped the water off her face.

He was in the same pair of jeans as before. His eyes dipped down to her chest. She looked down as well. *Oops!* The water was a little cold. Her nipples had taken center stage through the thin fabric of her bikini. She'd ended up going with a bright green number with black trim. It worked well with her dark hair and light complexion. In hindsight, perhaps a darker color would have been more practical. If she'd known she'd have to share a house, she might have chosen differently. The good news was that the Ferals were used to nudity. She didn't need to be modest.

Reece frowned, looking anything but interested. Not that she thought he would be. That was the thing, though. She was average-looking, even though she had striking blue eyes and dark hair. She was a little on the short side, maybe even slightly dumpy, but she had good boobs… no, *great* boobs. They were her best asset, aside from her hair. You would never say so, judging from his disapproving look. "I'm not sure that's appropriate work attire." His golden eyes locked with hers.

"I'm not on the clock right now. I start tomorrow morning. The trip here was long and noisy. I thought I would have a snack and something to drink, followed by a quick swim before unpacking." She gestured to an empty plate and glass on the table. "I was sure I had the afternoon to myself. I thought I was alone." Why was she having to explain all of this?

He held her gaze for a few long seconds before nodding once. "That is a suitable explanation." He still didn't look happy.

Hope couldn't believe how serious he was. She wondered to herself if he ever had fun. If he ever let his hair down and relaxed—smiled even—once in a while. She somehow doubted it. He pulled in a lungful of air. His chest expanded, making her look down. What a chest it was. Broad and muscular. No hair except for a light smattering on his garden path... that was it. Reece cleared his throat.

Shit!

She needed to stop checking him out already.

"My colleague, Locke, will be here soon. It might be better if you put more clothing on. Just a suggestion."

"Oh? Who is Locke and why is he coming here?" She waded over to the steps and got out of the water, grabbing her towel.

"He is on the second shift responsible for overseeing the royal safety, and your safety too." His voice was gravelly.

Hope continued to dry her body and moved on to her hair.

"Locke will share this house with you. It will be up to him to keep you safe at night."

"Oh..." Hope looked up at Reece, who was staring at the view ahead. "I thought you were going to be the one to do that."

"Locke has more experience with humans. He has a better understanding of your kind." He looked back at her. "I think you will be more comfortable with him." His eyes dipped down, and he frowned before looking back up at her face. "You will need to put some clothes on." His voice was gruff. He sounded angry. "He will be here shortly."

"I thought that Ferals were comfortable with nudity. You warned me earlier about having to accept that."

"You are *not* a Feral." He definitely sounded angry.

"Why does that make any difference?" She shrugged.

"It just does." Reece pressed the tips of two of his fingers to the corners of his eyes for a second or two before releasing. He sighed. "Feral males are highly attracted to human females."

"You are?" she gasped. It was hard to believe, since they were larger than life. Like movie stars and linebackers rolled into one. Humans were... dull in comparison.

"Not me!" he all but snarled. "I find you all too small and too weak. I'm not sure how human females withstand mounting. You do *not* appeal to me."

Mounting? She could guess exactly what that was. Funny how hearing him say that gave her a strange feeling in her lower belly. Hope wasn't sure why, since he was referring to hardcore sex. Sex hectic enough to break a human. Hope had always been into slow and tender... into making sweet love. Maybe she'd been wrong on that count all these years. Her husband had gone looking for it elsewhere. Then again, affairs weren't always about sex. Thinking about that made her feel worse. She pushed thoughts of her failed marriage aside.

"It's sad somehow that you don't like humans... in that way." She frowned. "Doesn't that mean you won't ever mate or have kids? I mean that's fine if you enjoy being on your own." She couldn't help but think how all of that gorgeousness was going to waste. Then again, he was a big grouch. Although, if he took sex half as seriously as he did everything else, he'd be amazing in bed. Okay… her thoughts had taken a turn back into murky territory.

"That is none of your business, Dr. Bristol." He folded his arms.

Oops! He was right. "My apologies. I was just wondering… that's all."

There was a flapping sound. She saw a griffin shifter descend behind the house. It had to be Locke.

Reece's throat worked; his eyes were aimed in that direction. "Get dressed," he snapped, looking at her.

He was obviously used to giving orders. The only thing she had nearby was the sarong. Although Hope felt like arguing on principle, she complied, tying it around her hips. Since they had to work together for the foreseeable future, she would play nice. Just this once. If he thought he could boss her around about everything, particularly in her own time, he was mistaken.

Instead of looking placated, as she expected, Reece gave her a dirty look. "You need to conceal your mammary glands, Doctor. They are large, and that covering is hardly sufficient. You will need to cover up in front of my males at all times. No skimpy outfits. No parading around half-naked." He shook his head, looking disappointed in her.

Firstly, mammary glands?

And secondly, what was his problem?

And thirdly, *asshole!* He was starting to irritate the hell out of her.

This was her home for the foreseeable future, and she was off duty. Not only that, Hope was with a species who spent half their life in their animal form and almost all of the rest of the time naked or practically naked. *What the hell!* "I will wear what I want in the comfort of my home." She pointed at the house. "It's not my fault I need a guard. Not my fault that this crazy king is fixated on stealing the babies. My breasts are covered sufficiently." She pointed at her boobs. Thankfully, her nipples were back under control. The bikini was sexy, but the right size for her. "I won't walk around naked… only because that's not how I roll, but guess what, if I change my mind, I'll do what I want whenever I am off duty. I don't report to you. Whatever this ego trip is that you have going on, I suggest you stop right now, or there's going to be serious friction between us."

Friction.

Her belly tightened.

Stop!

What the hell?

He pulled in a deep breath, his eyes still blazing. "Walk around like that in front of Feral males and you will attract unwanted attention, I can promise you that," he said in an even voice. "We are a base species, Dr. Bristol. You have been warned. I didn't mean to offend you in any way." His jaw was tight. "I made it clear to my team that they may not mount… have sexual relations with you. If you choose to stay on at a later stage, once the threat has been terminated, then you may take as many males to your furs… um… to your bed as you wish. You can take all the time you want choosing a mate, if that is what you wish to do. But I would ask you to refrain, for the time being, from testing compatibility with any males… most especially those from my team. We all need to be focused on the task at hand. The queen and her unborn chicks are the main focus. Not you, Doctor!"

"Your team? You told your whole team that I'm off-limits? Did you think that just because I'm single, I might want to have sex with everyone?" What was wrong with this guy? She'd done nothing to warrant this attitude. Did he actually think that she wanted to sleep with his entire team and then some? Test compatibility? What did that even mean? She didn't want to know. No, thank you! "And also, I know I'm not the main focus. I'm good with that."

"My point is that you are young… in your prime and unmated…" He nodded a few times. "So yes, I do think that. And it would normally be perfectly acceptable to have relations with whomever you wanted." He shrugged.

She made a squeaking noise because she didn't know what to say. Quite frankly, she had been rendered speechless.

"I'm going to tell you what I told them… refrain. Please don't! Don't tempt my males with your sizeable mammary glands and soft skin. Don't give them mounting signals, because they will have a hard time turning you down."

"A hard time turning me down?" she snorted. Hope still couldn't believe what she was hearing. "Not you, though?" She wasn't sure why she said that. It wasn't like she wanted anything to do with this asshole.

"No!" He shook his head. "Not me." He actually looked afraid at the prospect. Afraid that he would break her? Huh! What he didn't understand was that she was made from tougher stuff. Not that she was interested in him, though. Forget that. "I can't ban you, Dr. Bristol, but I can come down on them hard. I'm talking fifty lashes with a silver-tipped whip and a week in the cage."

"Silver-tipped whip?" Hope half-whispered, but only because she couldn't believe what she was hearing. *How barbaric!*

"You're scaring the human, Reece." An ultra-tall guy walked onto the wooden deck. His footfalls were soundless since he wasn't wearing any shoes. Like Reece, he only had pants on. A pair of gray sweats, to be exact. It was clear from the considerable outline that he was 'commando' underneath the sweats. Hope felt her cheeks heat; she kept her eyes on the guy's face. "You must be Dr. Bristol," he said, smiling broadly. "I'm Locke." He held out his hand.

She took his hand and shook it. "Call me Hope." They let go of each other's hands.

"Hope?" He shook his head. "I can't call you that, not if I want to avoid that silver-tipped whip." He winked at her. "Thanks, though, *Dr. Bristol.* I appreciate the sentiment."

"Locke will stay here with you," Reece said. "He will stay out of your way and keep you safe."

"By staying focused on the job at hand," she said.

"Exactly," Reece said.

Locke rolled his eyes. "I can see that you got the full speech too."

"This is serious," Reece grumbled.

"Of course." Locke nodded. "You were right." He smiled. "Dr. Bristol is very beautiful."

Reece had said that about her? Really?

Reece's jaw tightened, so maybe it was true. Maybe he had said it. "You are taking my words out of context," he muttered. Now that made sense.

"Stop while you are ahead, my friend." Locke touched Reece on the back. "I am sure you are very busy. I am here now, Dr. Bristol is safe."

"I should show you the sleeping arrangements," Reece said, looking from Locke to Hope and back again.

"You're in the room right next to the bathroom, and I'm one up from that," Hope said to Locke.

"I think we're good," Locke said to Reece, who visibly bristled.

His jaw tightened up further, and his eyes narrowed. "You're sure?" It came out in a bit of a growl, reminding her that they weren't human. Humans didn't sound like that.

Reece turned his golden eyes onto her. He was sizing her up, as if trying to decide if he could trust her. *Holy freaking shit!* Reece didn't want to leave because he was sure that she would jump Locke the second he did. This guy was too much!

"Yes, I'm sure. I'm going to unpack and hang out in my room. I will stay out of your way, Dr. Bristol."

"I'm going to shower quickly," she held up a hand, "if that's okay with you? Apparently, we're sharing a bathroom."

"Absolutely fine. I'll shower later, before bed."

Hope pushed out a breath. "I'll go and shower, then. I still need to unpack. I see that there's a ton of easy meals in the refrigerator. I'll probably grab one of those and hit the sack early."

"Why would you hit a sack?" Reece was frowning heavily. "Is that how you humans work out?"

Hope rubbed her lips together to stop herself from laughing. She knew she would piss Reece off if she so much as smiled.

"It means to go to bed," Locke said. "Sack, furs, bed; they're all the same thing." Locke shrugged.

Reece did not look happy at all. His mouth was pressed into a tight white line. She could see that he was clenching his teeth. "Fine." He nodded. "I will leave you to it. I look forward to your debriefing at shift changeover tomorrow," he told Locke.

Locke nodded once.

"I'll see you both later," Hope said, then headed to her room. It was clear that Reece wasn't going to be the first person to leave. That he had something to say to Locke. He probably wanted to threaten the poor guy. To tell him that even though he lived with a temptress, that he needed to ignore all of her—what had he called them? Mounting signals? It was absurd. Completely ridiculous.

Hope unpacked a few things, then grabbed a pair of sweats and a t-shirt out of her bag, together with her toiletry bag, and went back into the hallway.

Locke was there. He was about to go into his bedroom. He smiled when he saw her. "You good?" he asked.

She nodded. "For the record, I promise I won't throw myself at you. I'm not here to meet men… to sleep with as many guys as I can." Her face felt flushed. She hadn't realized how upset she was until right then. "You're safe with me." She tried to laugh, wanting to ease the tension building inside her. It came out sounding even more tense.

Locke gave a soft laugh. "I must apologize on behalf of Reece. I know he comes across as… as a—"

"An asshole?" she pushed out.

He nodded and smiled. "Yes, somewhat of an ass, but he's a good guy. He hasn't had it easy. He has no experience with humans… none whatsoever. His job *is* his life. Even though he comes across as an asshole, I promise you he isn't one. You'll have to take it from me until you get to know him."

"So, he just acts like one? He seems to think that I'm some sort of seductress hellbent on sleeping with everyone on his team and then some."

"I don't think he knows what to think. Reece is so far out of his depth with you—a female—a human female at that…" He paused for a moment. She could see that he was gathering his thoughts. "He has no idea what to think or how to manage the situation. He's flying blind, and Reece doesn't cope well unless everything is ordered and neatly in a box."

"He should educate himself and not take his own insecurities out on me. How is it that you have experience with human women when he doesn't?"

"Many of our males, myself included, have spent time on human soil, interacting with and learning about humans. I have been several times. In fact, I met someone on my last trip, we have been texting back and forth for a while."

"That's great," Hope said. "So, I'm assuming that Reece hasn't interacted with humans? Crossed over into our lands, even once?"

"No." Locke shook his head. "He's always too busy. Like I said, work has become Reece's life. All work and no play has made that particular male dull indeed." He laughed.

She joined in. "You're telling me."

"He will lighten up when he gets to know you." Locke looked at her strangely. He had something resembling a smirk on his face.

"What is it?" she asked, cocking her head.

"Don't take this the wrong way, but I think he's attracted to you."

"Reece, attracted to me?" She pointed at herself, frowning. "I think you have that wrong. He doesn't even like me. He said that humans are weak and unattractive."

"He likes you just fine, Doctor."

"You can call me Hope."

"I can't." Locke grinned. "Orders. He's seriously attracted to you and doesn't know what to do with that attraction."

"Nothing! That's what he can do with it, unless he wants a punch to the throat."

Locke choked out a laugh. "I like you, Doc. I like you very much. It's such a pity you're meeting Reece under these circumstances. I think you could have—"

"Don't even go there." She held up a hand.

"That's the thing. Reece won't do anything about it. He might drive everyone around him mad, but he won't lay so much as a finger on you or show the least bit of interest. He's too professional for that."

"That suits me just fine. I'm not here for love… or even sex, for that matter. I came for a change of scenery. I just got out of a long-term relationship. I don't want anything to do with men."

"Good thing Reece isn't a man... he's a keythong." Locke winked at her. "The highest-ranking non-royal. He is a catch."

"You are a fabulous wingman, but I'm not interested. Not even a little bit."

Locke frowned. "That's perfect, since the situation doesn't warrant it right now. Things will settle down... you'll see. Reece will calm down. You won't see him much, since he is working at night and asleep during the day. Maybe five minutes here or there."

"I'm happy to hear it." She wasn't sure why, but that wasn't entirely true. She felt a little disappointed hearing Locke say it. "Suits me just fine," she mumbled anyway.

"Give him a chance, Doc. First impressions are not always correct."

She nodded once. "Thanks for clearing a few things up for me."

"Anytime. Call if you need anything. I will leave my door slightly ajar."

She nodded once. Hope wasn't buying it. Not for a second. Reece wasn't attracted to her. Surely she would have seen something in his eyes or on his face... something? She did agree that he was a driven workaholic who took things far too seriously. Also, he didn't have a clue as far as humans were concerned. Their species were very different. Some of the reasons for the clash between them had stemmed from that. It got her thinking.

"One last thing," she asked Locke before he could leave. "Why would he think that I would want to have sex with every guy around? Were Feral women quite promiscuous? It's not a bad thing if they were." She didn't want it to seem like she was putting their species down. She just wanted to understand them better. Particularly men like Reece, who weren't very familiar with humans.

Locke kept his eyes on hers. "That's a very good question. There were far more males to females and so females would spend time with several keythongs before finally deciding on a mate. You could definitely say that our females were highly promiscuous."

"So, a Feral woman would date different guys, one after the other?"

Locke shook his head. "No, a female would test compatibility with several males at the same time."

"Compatibility?" she murmured. There was that word again.

"Compatibility in bed, Doc. So, whether a person was a good fuck or not. I don't mean to be crude, but that's how our species tests whether they are a good match. It is an important aspect of a relationship. In fact, unlike humans, it's one of the first steps taken before starting a relationship. If a female is attracted to a male, then compatibility would be tested. A female would fuck various males before spending time with any or all of them."

"Bed hop?" Her mouth fell open.

"Yes." Locke nodded. "It was perfectly normal for a female Feral to have four or five males at the same time. Sometimes even more than one male in her furs at once."

"Okay, well, that makes sense as to why he would be so worried. Humans don't do things like that. Well, not as a rule. Not me!" She widened her eyes. "Not that I'm judging. I know that the royal couple comprises two men and a woman and that's perfectly fine. It wouldn't be for me, though… that's all." She shrugged.

"Relax. I know what you mean, Doc. And Reece will realize it soon, as well."

She nodded once. "Okay, then. I understand Reece a little more. I'm glad we had this chat. I will make an effort to get along with him and to cut him some slack." She just had to hang in there until he realized as much. No problem! She'd faced worse challenges in recent months.

CHAPTER 7

THE NEXT DAY…

Her hands felt clammy. Her mouth felt dry, even though she had just taken a sip of her water. She stuffed the bottle back in her purse.

"Follow me, Dr. Bristol." Locke smiled at her. "Don't look so nervous."

"Do I look nervous?" She smoothed the front of her suit.

"You look petrified. They won't bite… I can promise you that much."

"They're royalty. A real king and queen. It's Claire and Leukos. Not that I will call the king by his first name, mind you. Then there's Magnar… is that right?"

"Yes, Magnar is also mated to Claire."

"Does Magnar have a title? Is he a king too?"

Locke pushed the button to the elevator, and the doors opened. "After you," he said, gesturing inside.

Hope didn't move. She kept her eyes on Locke's.

"Magnar is not a king and therefore he does not have a title." Locke gestured inside again.

Hope walked in. "So I can call him Magnar, then?"

"That is correct. They are very down-to-earth… you'll see. There's nothing to be concerned about."

Hope pushed out a heavy breath she had been holding and looked down at herself for the tenth time.

"You look great. Professional, and yet… very pretty. I'm not sure Reece will approve." He chuckled.

She rolled her eyes and laughed, too. Right up until the elevator dinged, and the doors opened, then all humor evaporated.

The first thing she saw were two almost naked people. They were clearly Feral from their builds and yellow eyes. One of them was a woman, which was interesting. She was the first Feral woman Hope had seen.

"Hello, human," the woman said; her wrinkled face was open and friendly. "Welcome." She was wearing a skirt and nothing else. Her breasts were large and sagging. Her skin was brown and leathery.

"Hi there. I'm Dr. Hope Bristol."

"I am Delise. I am the head healer." She put out her hand.

Hope did the same. She smiled when Delise grabbed her wrist. Hope took the other woman by the wrist as well. It was obviously customary among the Feral. Come to think of it, that booklet she received before coming here was far too thin. Not nearly enough information. They shook.

There was a guy standing next to her. He had what looked like a furry cloth over his privates, and that was it. Hope looked over at him, and he inclined his head without further introduction.

"This is King Leukos." Delise drew her attention, gesturing to a man dressed in a three-piece suit. He was tall and very attractive.

"Please, you must call me Leukos, Doctor."

"Then I insist that you call me Hope." They shook hands, only this time, the king took her hand when they shook, instead of her wrist.

"I am Magnar," another really good-looking guy said. He had longish hair, with a hint of stubble on his face. He wore jeans and a button-down shirt. "This is our mate, Claire," he added.

"Hi there." A beautiful woman smiled at her. She had big, bright blue eyes and gorgeous, long blonde hair. They were a similar height and even though Claire was very much pregnant, Hope suspected that they had a similar build as well. "I'm so glad you're here. I'm glad to have an Ob-Gyn on board, even though I know that Delise has a wealth of knowledge."

"I'm happy to be here, too. I can't wait to learn everything there is to know about the Feral species and to help you deliver these… um… eggs." She smiled. It felt weird talking about eggs instead of babies. "I will need to tap into your expertise, Delise."

"I, too, have much to learn from you, Doctor," Delise said. "Although there are many similarities between our species, there are also many things that are very different."

Hope nodded, thinking about Reece for some reason. "That is very true."

"This is Evander. He is our first male healer. We are trying to make progress as a species. Up until recently, there were no female warriors and no male healers. Things are changing. Evander has learned everything there is to know about egg-laying. Now he needs to learn in practice."

Evander inclined his head. "I am greatly looking forward to learning from both of you."

"How exciting… the first male healer," Hope said. "I think that with our combined knowledge, we should do just fine." She glanced at Claire when she said that.

"I hope so." The queen went pale and clutched her rounded belly. "There has only been one Feral-human egg-laying."

"And it was a success," Delise said. "No clutch sickness. The chicks are all thriving."

"That's fantastic news." Hope nodded.

"The clinic is almost ready," Leukos said. "We left you office space, Doctor. You must order the furniture and items you need."

"It's a personal space," Magnar chimed in. "We are hoping that you decide to stay longer than your six-month contract."

"That's very sweet. I worked hard to get my business going at home. I can't stay away for too long." She made a face.

"Perhaps we can convince you." Leukos put an arm around Claire. "There will be many more pregnant females in the future. Our males have started taking mates. We are encouraging it. There is no future without children. If you stay on, you would have your hands full in no time. Mark my words."

"We'll have to see." There was no way she could stay on beyond the six months. There was too much she'd end up losing. Hope left it at that.

"Shall we take a seat?" Claire said.

"We thought it would be best if we had a discussion about the two species. Everything surrounding being with clutch and the laying," Delise said. "We can meet at the clinic tomorrow. You can examine Claire then."

"Sounds like a plan." Hope nodded.

Claire hung back while they all made their way to the living room area. "It's so nice to see another human face," she whispered. "I hope we can be friends."

"That would be great." Hope followed Claire, watching as she positioned herself between the two men. Both of them were her husbands. It sure was different. Different was interesting, though. She had wanted an adventure, after all. Claire seemed so nice. She couldn't believe that somewhere lurking in the shadows was an evil madman intent on stealing her babies as soon as they were born… hatched.

CHAPTER 8

By scale and by feather.

Blast and damn!

Was the female trying to kill him? Was she? First those tiny coverings yesterday, and now this.

For feather's sake! Now he was thinking back about the female yesterday in the swimming pool. Dripping wet. Green was most certainly her color. The doctor might be a tiny thing, but she was lush in all the right places. Not just her chest… her ass was plump, too. Reece knew it would jiggle when—

"Reece! Hey… Reece!" Locke waved a hand in front of his face.

Damn! Reece realized that Locke had been trying to get his attention. The male had a smirk across his whole face.

"What?" Reece snapped. "Stop that!" he growled when Locke slowly let his hand drift in front of Reece's face again.

"Red is a good color on the lovely doctor, don't you think?"

"What are you talking about, Locke?" he growled, his hands fisting at his sides.

"I noticed you staring, and I don't blame you." He shrugged, still smirking.

"I'm monitoring the goings-on… that's all." Dr. Bristol was walking Claire out of what would be a fully functional hospital one day. Right now, it was a handful of rooms. He scanned the horizon for a moment or two. He needed to keep his attention on the job at hand. The doctor was a distraction. He glanced her way.

As Locke pointed out, Dr. Bristol wore a bright red suit. The skirt came to mid-thigh, showing off rather lovely legs. Her footwear wasn't very practical. "Are her… foot coverings…"

"Shoes," Locke commented.

"Can her shoes be used as weapons?" They were black with a long spike sticking out under the heel.

Locke broke out in laughter. "You really need to spend some time with humans."

"Once this assignment is over," he grumbled. "Answer the question."

"They're called high heels. Human females love them. They're supposed to make their legs look longer… better. Human males think they are sexy on a female."

He frowned. "What happens in the case of an emergency? The doctor won't be able to run away. I would understand if the… shoe…" It was a strange word to wrap his tongue around. "If the shoe doubled as a weapon." It made no sense to him that people would choose to wear such things. They looked uncomfortable.

Her legs looked great, but he suspected they would, even if she was barefoot.

"I suppose they could double as a weapon, but shoes aren't meant to be used in that way. Like I said, human females think it makes their legs look better."

"Dr. Bristol doesn't need them."

"Her legs are great already."

Reece turned to look at the male, intent on giving him a piece of his mind. Locke laughed. "I'm teasing you."

"You're not! You fully believe what you just said."

"I said it to tease you, but yes, her legs are just fine without the heels."

Reece looked back at the talking females. Even though Dr. Bristol wore a suit jacket, it was tight-fitting and accentuated her… abundant curves. The top button strained. "Perhaps it would be good to implement a dress code. No heels or skirts. No tight clothing in general."

"Stop thinking with your prick. If you want to piss the doctor off in a bad way, start dictating to her how she should dress. It would be a bad move."

What the hell?

Locke had it all wrong. "This has absolutely nothing to do with my prick." He spoke under his breath. "Dr. Bristol could break her neck if she tried to run. Climbing would be impossible with such a tight skirt. The outfit isn't practical for these conditions."

"She's comfortable. It's obviously her normal work attire. The skirt isn't too short and high heels are normal for human women. Leave her be. It's not like she's the main target. Even if she could run—let's say she was in sneakers—she still couldn't outrun or outmatch a Feral. Heels, no heels… it doesn't really matter."

Reece sighed. "I suppose you are right. I never thought of it like that."

"Try to take it easy on the doctor. You are quite… intense at times. It can be intimidating to a human."

"Did she say something to you about me?" Reece felt his heart start to race. He wouldn't be surprised if she had. Truth be told, he had been a little… a little overbearing the previous day. His response to her lack of clothing was… Well, it was exaggerated. His physical reaction to her had shocked him. His prick had hardened. Even his balls had tightened uncomfortably. His throat had turned dry. Every instinct told him to mount her. To take her until she screamed his name. Until she creamed all over his prick. It was shocking that he should have such a reaction, especially considering she was off-limits.

"No, she didn't say anything." Locke shook his head, bringing him back to reality… and not a moment too soon. Just thinking about his discomfort was making him hard all over again. *Blast it all to hell!* "She didn't have to say anything about your behavior. Her face spoke volumes when you mentioned silver-tipped whips and cages. Humans are timid. You would do well to remember that."

"She needed to understand the ramifications."

"You were berating her before she, or anyone else, had done anything wrong. It doesn't matter the species, no one likes being knocked down for something they haven't done yet."

"Sometimes it's better to preempt than to deal with the fallout," Reece said, eyes firmly on Locke for a few moments before he scanned the perimeter once again.

"I guess it depends on the situation. Go a little easier on the doctor, please."

"We'll see about that." He shoved his hands into his pockets. That was the one good thing about these human covers; they gave you something to do with your hands sometimes. "How did it go today?" he asked soon after.

The queen laughed at something Dr. Bristol said. "As you can see," Locke grinned, "the two of them are getting along very well. Everything is going smoothly with the clutch. The queen is in good health and good spirits. Delise and Evander just left. All is well."

"Good news," Reece said.

"Indeed." Locke nodded.

"It was so lovely to meet you," Claire said, grabbing Dr. Bristol's hand. "You should come to dinner sometime to get to know us. I know my mates seemed really stiff and formal, but they're actually huge amounts of fun. They're such great guys. You're not weirded out by… the three of us, are you?"

"Not at all." The doctor squeezed the queen's hand. "I think it's great. So progressive. The dynamic must be interesting and fun."

Great!

Progressive!

Interesting and fun!

Hmm… Her statements were thought-provoking. As it stood, he felt justified having had some hard conversations with Dr. Bristol. The human didn't seem anywhere nearly as timid as Locke was making her out to be. Firstly, she'd stared at his cock long and hard when they'd first met. Her unabashed staring had been brazen and unexpected. Then she was perfectly comfortable parading around half naked. He had heard that humans could be shy about such things, but not Dr. Bristol. Now she was telling the queen how she found their three-way mating to be great and progressive.

He might not have much experience with humans, but Dr. Bristol wasn't a typical human, not by a long shot. Reece had no idea what to make of her. No idea how to proceed when it came to her. Good thing Locke was in charge. He would keep getting updates. He would keep monitoring the situation, but otherwise he was going to take a step back where the doctor was concerned. As much as he hated it, he was attracted to her.

CHAPTER 9

THREE DAYS LATER...

Hope was both nervous and excited. She gave herself a final once-over in the mirror, wondering for the tenth time if she shouldn't rather put her hair up in a ponytail. No! She was leaving it down. It looked good, loose around her shoulders. Her dress was a little shorter than she would have it for work. It had a high neckline which actually accentuated her breasts. The sleeves were long, since the evenings could be chilly. She touched the fabric of her dress, which she'd bought in hopes of an evening such as this. It was a deep royal blue.

Royal.

Fitting since she was having dinner with the royal family. With Claire and her two husbands. She really liked the other woman. Claire was sweet and bubbly and warm. Even though the queen was her patient, she could tell that they were going to be firm friends.

There was a solid knock on her bedroom door.

"I'm coming," she yelled, quickly reapplying lip-gloss over her stay-fast lipstick. She looked good. She felt pretty and feminine; better than she had in a long time. Too good perhaps?

Screw that asshole! Reece was making her second-guess herself. His comments from the other day had stuck in her head. She had been standoffish with the two other Ferals who oversaw the safety of the royal family. Zaire and Andy didn't deserve it. She wasn't rude to them, but she wasn't her normal, jovial, chatty self, either. It wasn't right. Reece had gotten inside her head, and she hated that fact. So much so that she was evicting him right now.

Hope grabbed her jacket off the bed and slung it over her arm. She touched her hand to her purse, which was already on her shoulder. Then she headed out.

Locke was waiting in the hallway. "Are you sure I can't take you to the royal chamber myself?" He looked nervous.

"Let me guess, Reece is here."

Locke winced. "Yes. I can tell him you're running late or something. I can see he's in a mood. He might end up being rude to you. You look amazing, by the way." He gave her the once-over.

"Thank you! Thank you for the kind offer, but your shift ended an hour ago. It's been a long day. Reece can suck eggs."

Locke's eyes widened. "I haven't heard that saying before."

She smiled. "I think it's an older saying. Something my grandmother used to say every now and then. It means that he can get over himself."

"I figured as much." Locke grinned. "I agree with you. If Reece is... a stuck in the... in the muddy water... Did I say that right?"

"Almost. A stick-in-the-mud. You can leave the water part out." She giggled.

"If Reece is a stick-in-the-mud, please ignore him," he tried again, still grinning.

"I will." She widened her eyes. "I'd better get out there before he thinks that we're having sex or something." She rolled her eyes.

Locke laughed, "He wouldn't think... Actually, you're probably right." He chuckled. "I have to say, my girlfriend is jealous. She doesn't like that I'm living with another woman."

They started walking towards the front door.

"Girlfriend?" She looked at him pointedly. "Since when is your text buddy your girlfriend? I'm assuming it's the same lady you told me about the other day."

"Yes." Locke's eyes glinted. "Her name is Tracey. She's a ba... barista," he pronounced the word carefully, "at a coffee shop. I spent a couple of days with her when I was last on human soil. We've been texting back and forth for two months. I called her yesterday, and we had a long chat." He grinned broadly, looking thrilled. "I asked her not to see anyone else because I was serious about her, and she agreed. I'm pretty sure that would make her my girlfriend, since we're serious about each other?"

"It would absolutely make her your girlfriend; how exciting. When are you going to see her again? Long-distance relationships can be tricky."

He looked downtrodden. "I don't know. I had hoped to get back there around now. I'm due some time off, but then this assignment came along. I put in for leave anyway, but I don't think that Reece will let me go."

"That's not fair." They walked outside. Reece was standing a little way away from them. Her stomach gave a lurch. She tried not to look at him, looking at Locke instead.

"It's understandable, since this is an important assignment," he said, rubbing his chin. "Sometimes we have to wait for the things we really want."

Hope nodded. "And sometimes waiting is the worst possible thing you can do." She'd had a niggling feeling that something was up in her marriage. That something was up with Emmet. It was a niggle she'd ignored. Letting Emmet insist that they wait before trying for a baby was a mistake too. Perhaps a child would have been the glue to keep them together. Now she was in her thirties and newly single. She'd more than likely never have a baby. "Anyway, I'm sure she'll wait for you. She's one lucky girl." She touched his arm as they walked towards Reece.

Oh, boy! From the frown and hard eyes, she'd say that Reece was angry. Of course he was. She took a deep breath. She had told Locke that she would try to be nice. That she would make an effort. "Hello." She waved. "Sorry to keep you waiting."

"Good evening, Dr. Bristol. It's not me who you are keeping waiting." He shook his head. "The Royals are expecting you at seven-thirty sharp. That means that we have five minutes to get there if we want to be on time. You're not squeamish, are you?"

She shook her head. "No…" She sounded skeptical.

"Do you get motion sickness?"

She shook her head again. "No. Why are you asking?"

"That's good to know. We're going to have to move fast once we're in the air. You might want to put that on." He gestured to her jacket. "I'm not sure that such a short dress was the right clothing choice." He scrutinized her legs with the same disapproving look as before. Locke was so wrong when he said that Reece was attracted to her. This wasn't attraction… not even close. "I see you have those stabbing shoes on again."

"Stabbing shoes?" She giggled. She couldn't help it. "I like that."

His mouth twitched. She wasn't sure whether he found it funny or was annoyed. "I have to fly you there at speed, Doctor."

"Put on the jacket," Locke said. "Make sure your purse strap is around your shoulder and torso. You can hold your heels." He winked at her.

She smiled back, even though she knew it would probably piss Reece off. Let the asshole think what he wanted. When she turned back to him, he was naked. The linen pants he had been wearing were nowhere to be seen. He was holding a bag that looked to be made of animal fur. She assumed the pants were in there. "Can you hold this for me? You may put your shoes and purse inside." His golden eyes locked with hers.

"Um… sure… of course. I wish you'd warn me before stripping like that." *Holy freaking moly.* Her face felt hot in an instant.

"I thought you'd be used to it by now." Those frown lines were back.

That was the thing; she should be used to it. Dammit, she *was* used to it. When it came to Locke it was… it was different. She just looked away. It wasn't a big deal if she saw a hint of something. Heck, it didn't matter if she saw all of it. Hope felt nothing. She'd seen Zaire and Andy shift once or twice… also, nothing. They were gorgeous… all of them and yet… nothing. Right now, her heart was pounding right out of her chest and her hands felt sweaty. "I am. It's just… A heads up would be good." She widened her eyes, trying to look normal. Her cheeks felt like they were a bright shade of red.

"Heads up." Locke laughed. "Heads up would not be good at all." He laughed harder.

Heads up as in… as in… She also started laughing. "You're terrible." She pointed at Locke.

"Heads up? I don't get it," Reece said. "My head is up." He touched his head. The one on his shoulders.

That made Locke laugh harder, which made Hope laugh harder. Reece got this murderous look. *Shit!* This was bad. It was a terrible way to start the evening. Especially since she was supposed to be making an effort to get him to like her. Not like her, as in *like* her. Accept. Yes, *accept* was a better word. She needed to get him to accept her. It was never going to happen if she was laughing at him like this.

"I'm sorry." She put her hand up. "Locke's being an idiot."

Reece gave Locke a scathing look and for a moment she felt guilty for dropping him in the shit. Not! He should know better where Reece was concerned.

"Humans call the top of a prick a head," Locke said.

"A heads up, is giving someone notice or informing them before you do something." she added.

"The doc told you to give her a heads up. I said that wouldn't be appropriate." Locke chuckled.

"You're such a juvenile," Reece said, his voice a deep rasp which had goosebumps rising on her arms.

"You said that your head was up." Locke choked out a laugh.

"This *isn't* appropriate," Reece said, completely deadpan. How did he do that? "I think we should go, Dr. Bristol."

"I hope you have a lovely evening, Doc," Locke said, his eyes still glinting with mischief.

"Dr. Bristol," Reece admonished Locke, his eyes were narrowed on him.

"Dr. Bristol." Locke winked at her as soon as Reece looked away. Why was he so hard on himself? Because make no mistake, although he was hard on those around him, he was even harder on himself.

Hope knew that she should look away, but she couldn't. She watched as Reece took a few steps back. She watched as his muscles moved beneath his skin. Mesmerized as his body changed, quickly morphing into that of a griffin. He was formidable. She could see why he was the highest-ranking shifter here. Aside from his discipline, he was huge. So strong. Just like before, his tail thrashed from side to side and he gave a terrifying screech that had all her hair standing on end. She swallowed thickly, unable to take her eyes off of him.

"Um, Doc...?"

Reece screeched again, this time rearing up on powerful back legs.

"I mean," Locke gave a shake of his head, "Dr. Bristol… the bag." He pointed at her feet. To the fur bag lying there. "Reece is impatient to leave but I'm sure you understood that, even if you don't speak griffin."

Reece made a rumbly noise from deep in his chest.

"Oh, shoot." She slipped out of her heels, which she placed into the bag, together with her purse. Then she put on her jacket and secured the bag around her body.

"See you later," Locke said.

"Thank you," she said, turning and waving.

"Have fun!" he yelled, as Reece picked her up. "Don't stay out too late," he added.

She heard the start of a laugh, but Reece shot up into the air. All she got was a rush of wind in her ears. Her stomach gave a lurch. She had to close her eyes because they stung from the rush of air. Her hair whipped around her face. She clung to his scaly claws. Usually, she enjoyed her flights. This was something different. She made a mental note never to be late if Reece was taking her. Thing was, this was a social engagement. A few minutes here or there didn't matter, did it? Anyway, she was going to be ready early from here on out. Thankfully, the flight didn't last very long. Within two minutes they were swooping down to the ground. Her stomach lurched again, and she gave a yell. This time there was no excitement involved. No wonder he had asked her if she was squeamish.

She breathed the biggest sigh of relief when he slowed and carefully touched down. He put her down slowly, until her feet touched the earth, which was cool between her toes. With a rumble, he let her go, but she kept her hold on his talons. She was breathing hard, trying to catch her breath and her faculties. When she finally let him go, Hope staggered a step or two in order to keep her footing. Reece shifted. He turned towards her, his golden eyes blazing in the moonlight.

They narrowed on her, almost making her want to take a step back. "Are you okay, Doctor?"

"Yes." Her voice was stronger than she thought it would be.

"Good. I'll take the bag."

She nodded once and pulled the strap over her shoulder, keeping her eyes on his.

"Thank you," he said as he opened the bag, taking out his pants.

She watched as he pulled on the linen pants. Then he took out a thin-knit sweater. He pulled that over his head, running a hand through his hair. "You might want to pull your dress down, Dr. Bristol." He rummaged in the bag and handed her something.

She looked at her hands. Her heels. Then what he had said registered. She looked down and true as nuts, her dress had ridden up... all the way up. Her jacket was gaping open and the hem of her dress was sitting around her hips. She groaned, giving the hem a yank. She was wearing black lace panties. Quite see-through lace panties. "My brain is a little fuzzy from that flight," she stammered, giving her head a shake. "Maybe this wasn't the best outfit," she mumbled to herself, probably sounding a little like a madwoman.

Hope staggered a few steps when she lifted her foot to put the heels on. "I'm off balance and a little light-headed," she said, holding onto her knees and bending over at the waist. Who could blame her after that? The flight had been something she was sure trainee astronauts went through at NASA. Possibly worse.

"Apologies," Reece said. He had the good grace to look sheepish. "Perhaps I pushed a little too hard trying to make up time. We're already seven minutes late," he said as he removed a watch from the fur bag, strapping it to his wrist. "Here," he held out an arm, "lean on me."

She took a step towards him and clasped his forearm. Holy shit but it seemed to be made of steel. The other thing she noticed was how good he smelled. It was tough, but she refrained from sniffing in his direction. Only just! That would look weird. She quickly pulled on her heels, letting him go as soon as she was done. Then she took a deep breath, praying she didn't break her neck on the things. Hope had already made a fool of herself that night. At least he was being nice… well, nice for Reece.

"Ready." She smoothed her dress.

He was looking at her strangely… no, make that, he was looking at her hair. She ran a hand through, and holy moly, what a rat's nest.

"Oh, no!" she moaned. "I didn't bring a hairbrush." She tried to smooth her wild tresses. "I should have worn it up." Then again, she hadn't been expecting that mad flight.

"It looks nice down," Reece said, not looking at her. Then he cleared his throat like he regretted the compliment. "Turn around." His voice was gruff.

She did so tentatively. Was he still being nice, or was this where it ended?

"I'm going to use my fingers to comb your hair. Is that okay?"

"Yes... sure." As it turned out, he *was* being nice... super nice.

Using his fingertips, Reece carefully combed her hair, starting at the tips and working his way up to her scalp. She was mortified when she groaned as his fingertips raked against her scalp.

"Shit... um... sorry. It's been a while since... Well, since I got a massage." What she was going to say is that it had been a while since she had been touched in any kind of an intimate way. When she really thought about it, she and Emmet hadn't had sex in the last few months that they were together. He hadn't so much as held her hand. Even their kisses had turned into quick pecks on the cheek. It had been ages since anyone had touched her like this. The thought unnerved her. The fact that she enjoyed it unnerved her even more.

"Are you feeling okay, Dr. Bristol?" Reece asked as he pulled away. "Your hair is fine now. I'm sorry if that was uncomfortable for you. I know that it was inappropriate. I was trying to help you."

"Thanks, and yes, I'm fine. It wasn't inappropriate. It was sweet, and I'm grateful. I was just thinking about something. It's not important. Thanks for your help and for getting me here safely."

Reece sighed, looking at his watch again. "It turns out that my plan backfired. Flying so fast has resulted in us being later than we would have been had we traveled at a normal speed. I will keep that in mind for the future."

His seriousness was pretty cute at times.

No!

Wait!

She needed to stop this. A rebound thing was a bad idea. A rebound thing with Reece was a terrible idea. Not to mention that he wouldn't be interested, anyway. There was that particular fact to consider as well, and it happened to be a biggie.

"Shall we go to dinner?" he asked.

She frowned. *We*. What did he mean by 'we'?

Reece frowned. "You didn't know I was invited?"

"No. That's great, though." She smiled. "We can get to know each other better."

His head whipped her way. "There wouldn't be much purpose in that, since we can't be friends, Dr. Bristol."

Stick-in-the-mud was an apt description of this man. An apt description indeed. As he walked just ahead of her, scanning the area for threat—at least, she assumed that was what he was doing—she couldn't help but take him in… again. It was crazy, but the guy was just as gorgeous fully clothed as he was naked. The way the pants clung to his meaty ass. The way they rode low on his hips. How the knit of the sweater accentuated his shoulders. She groaned internally. She was attracted to an anal-retentive… she wanted to call him an asshole because he had acted like one a couple of times. Yet, she knew that lurking somewhere inside all of that brooding seriousness was a nice guy. Deep, deep down inside.

CHAPTER 10

They walked in silence. Reece still wasn't sure how he had kept his prick from becoming fully erect. By tar and feathers, this female was testing him at every turn. Firstly, wearing that sexy garment and then showing him her snatch. It shouldn't matter. He was used to nudity. It was something that normally didn't bother him. Dr. Bristol was not a Feral. She was a human. A lush, delectable human. That part of the equation *did* bother him a whole lot. His jaw tightened just thinking about it. Other parts of him threatened to tighten, too.

Griffin shifters had the best vision out of all the shifters, only not at night. But the moon was full, and his eyes were much better than a human's were. It took all of his willpower and then some, not to stare at the junction of her thighs. The covering she wore was filmy. He'd caught a glimpse of her thick snatch fur.

Fuck!

It was a human cuss word that many of the males used after picking it up on human soil. It seemed fitting to use it right now. *Fuck! Fuck!*

Then she'd groaned like that when he'd touched her. Was she trying to kill him? The sound had gone straight to his cock. His balls had tightened. Reece found himself thinking about his own stern warning to the others on his team. His own words were ringing in his ears about how this female was out of bounds. There was so much at stake. Too much!

"Good evening, Dr. Bristol," Zaire said as they arrived at the royal chambers. The male smiled so widely that Reece thought his face might crack in half.

"Hi, Zaire." Dr. Bristol smiled back.

"You look… you look absolutely…" The male's eyes raked over her body in a way that irritated the feathers right off of Reece. In a way that had him grinding his teeth, but only because he had eyes too. "You look fantastic. Like a million bucks… no a billion bucks." Zaire winked at her. "A million wouldn't be enough."

Dr. Bristol giggled. "Thank you. That's sweet."

"I mean it, you—"

"That's enough!" Reece practically roared the words. "Your job is to keep your eyes and ears open for anything out of place. I will do the same from inside the chamber." He pointed at the top of the tower. "Do not hesitate to sound the alarm. Rather a false alarm than a missing queen because you didn't want to come across as a fool."

"Yes, Reece." Zaire bowed his head for a moment in deference.

Good!

"Bye, Zaire. I will organize a takeout for you." The female waved.

"That would be wonderful, Dr. Bristol." More of that stupid smiling.

Reece pushed the button a second time for the elevator. The doors opened a few seconds later. Reece held back, waiting for the doctor to go in first.

"What is a takeout?" he asked as soon as the doors closed behind them. The elevator started to move.

He could see her bite back a smile. It aggravated him that he didn't know enough about humans. "It means that I will put some dinner into a container and bring it to him. It's exactly how it sounds… a takeout."

He frowned. "Zaire can go and get food during his break. There is no need to give him any. We all have more than enough."

"I know that he has food, but bringing him some would be the nice thing to do. Zaire is guarding the royal house," she shrugged, "we are going to enjoy a lovely meal. It would be wrong not to take him something later."

Reece grunted. He disagreed, but he didn't say anything. Thus far, he had done a good job of alienating her. Thing was that he didn't want Zaire getting the wrong idea. Reece was going to inform the male that the doctor was very considerate. That it did not mean that she was giving him mounting signals. Humans were strange creatures. Interesting and strange.

He also needed to be sure not to pick up the wrong signals himself. Like the way she stared at his prick when he was naked. He had been told that human males were not so well endowed. She was probably startled every time he disrobed. That had to be it. She wasn't interested in him. Not after he was so hard on her that first day. Even if she was attracted to him, it wasn't like he would ever act on it. He couldn't!

The elevator dinged, and the doors opened.

"Hi!" The queen waved at them. What was it with humans and waving? Dr. Bristol also liked to wave. "How are you, Hope?" The females hugged each other tightly.

"Good, and you?" the doctor asked as they released each other.

They began talking about a whole lot of nothing. Things like clothing and hair. He wasn't sure why.

Reece turned his attention to his king. "Sire." He bowed to Leukos. "Magnar." He inclined his head to the male.

"Glad you could make it, Reece." Leukos smiled broadly. "Please call me by my name. We are here as friends."

"I am technically on duty," he reminded his king.

Leukos snorted. "Ekon wants our chicks, which means that Claire is relatively safe." His eyes darkened. "At least up until they are hatched. At that point all bets are off."

"With all due respect, I would rather not take any chances," Reece said.

"I have several very trustworthy spies amongst the Fallen," Magnar pointed out. "Ekon wants our chicks." His voice turned deep and menacing. "Leukos is right… we can relax somewhat for now."

"I will keep my wits about me if it's all the same to both of you."

Leukos laughed. "Of course, my friend." He patted Reece on the back. "That is one of the many reasons why you were chosen for this assignment."

The two females were looking at them expectantly. All three of them turned in their direction. Reece noticed that they were quite different. Claire had golden hair, and Dr. Bristol's hair was a very dark brown. Like chocolate. A human delicacy a few of the males had brought back. He had enjoyed the taste of chocolate very much. Dr. Bristol was smiling, her eyes glinting in the candlelight. The chamber had electricity, but Claire had chosen to keep things traditional for the evening by lighting the many candles in the chamber.

"It's lovely to see you again, Doctor," Leukos said; he put his hand out, intent on shaking hers.

Dr. Bristol flapped her own hand at him. She hugged the king instead. *Blast and damn! Hugged. The king.* His eyes widened. "It's Hope, please. I'm not working right now."

"Of course. You are absolutely right." The king smiled and touched a hand to Dr. Bristol's back.

Reece pushed out a pent-up breath.

"I agree. We're having a meal together," Magnar said, giving the doctor a bear hug. "Welcome to our home. We are glad that you have become such good friends with our mate and in such a short time."

"I'm happy too," Dr. Bristol said. "I was a little worried that I might end up alone, staring at four walls every day. Not that I mind being on my own. It's just that it's nice to have a friend."

"I hardly think you would ever have a problem with meeting people," Magnar said. "You are a nice person and, if I might add, you're attractive." He looked at Claire. "I'm just stating a fact, sweets." He winked at his mate. "You should never be lonely, staring at four walls."

"I decided to take this position in order to—"

"Hold that thought," Claire said. "Can we pick up this conversation once drinks are poured?"

Blast! Reece had been leaning forward, wanting to hear what Dr. Bristol had to say. She'd clearly stated that she didn't like to be alone. Did she take this position with the intention of finding a mate? It sounded that way. He felt his feathers rustle and his fur stand on end. If that was why she was here, she could wait until this particular assignment was fulfilled. After that, once she was reassigned, she could look at testing compatibility or dating. Humans apparently dated each other. They ate meals together and talked about all sorts of nonsense.

Reece was sure to keep listening for Zaire sounding the alarm. At the same time, Zaire might miss something. He needed to keep watch as well.

"Reece!" Leukos said. It was obvious that it was not the first time that he had called to him.

"Apologies, my lord." He inclined his head. "I was listening for anything out of the ordinary."

"Think nothing of it. I opened a lovely Bordeaux. Can I offer you a glass?" Leukos' eyebrows were raised. He lifted the bottle in his hand.

"No… thank you, Sire…"

"My name, please," Leukos said.

"No thank you, Leukos," Reece said. "I'm technically on duty."

"It's not like you can get drunk." Magnar laughed, "Or even tipsy, for that matter."

Reece was not familiar with the word, although he could guess. He didn't like wine. Chocolate was great but wine and that other morning beverage… the dark one… They were a big no to him. Both pungent and acquired tastes. As far as he was concerned, wine tasted disgusting. There were other human delicacies that were much better… to him, at least. "Perhaps a soda?" he asked. "The dark one with bubbles."

Leukos laughed. "I have Coca-Cola."

He noted that Dr. Bristol already had a glass of red wine in her hand. Claire looked like she was drinking juice.

Magnar poured the soda and handed him a big glass full of the beverage. "Thank you," Reece said. He took a sip. Now this was more like it.

"At least I don't have to *not drink* alone." Claire held up her glass to him.

He did the same back. Again, it was a human thing. He couldn't remember what it was called. He smiled at the queen. Magnar poured two glasses of red. One for himself and one for Leukos.

They made small talk for a while. The weather. How Dr. Bristol was settling in. How the clutch was coming along. Several other topics. He tried to add to the conversation wherever he could, but for the most part, he listened to what the others had to say. Moreover, he kept guard, which was technically why he was there in the first place.

They finally sat down to dinner.

The queen bit down on her bottom lip for a few moments. "Most of what we have on offer is traditional Feral cuisine," she said to Dr. Bristol.

"Oh… that sounds interesting."

"I hope you enjoy eating meat, Doc?" Magnar added.

"I like meat." Dr. Bristol nodded.

"I'm talking mountain goat stew and elk steaks." Magnar lifted his brows.

Dr. Bristol swallowed hard. "I would be happy to try them."

Leukos laughed. "There's also salmon, root vegetables and salad." He wrinkled his nose. "We don't eat much rabbit food, but Claire enjoys it." He beamed at his mate, who beamed back.

"Vegetables and salads weren't high on the list of meals when I first arrived." Claire laughed.

"We've started a wonderful garden," Magnar said.

"I was very thankful for that once I became with clutch. I was a little sick for a while there." She touched her belly. "I couldn't eat too much meat. It made me ill. Vegetables and fruit were a must."

"We still have to bring fruit in," Leukos remarked. "The trees we've planted will take a couple of years before they yield a harvest."

Fruit was another human food Reece had taken to. "I enjoy oranges very much," Reece remarked, watching as some servers exited the elevators with platters. Things had certainly changed since they started taking humans as mates.

"You should try strawberries. In fact, any berries," Magnar remarked. "Strawberries are my favorite. So sweet and tasty."

"I have never heard of such a thing," Reece remarked.

"We stocked Hope's fridge. Perhaps she will share some of them with you," Magnar said.

"I would be more than happy to share." She smiled at Reece.

He nodded back. There was no way he was sharing anything with Dr. Bristol. It wouldn't be appropriate. Not at all.

Leukos held out a platter to Dr. Bristol. "This is the goat stew."

"It's quite delicious." the queen remarked. "It's slow-cooked for hours until the meat is falling off the bones."

"I'll try some." The doctor took the ladle and dished up a tiny portion.

"What about some elk steak?" Magnar held out the platter this time.

"Um..." Dr. Bristol looked worried.

"It's probably undercooked by human standards." Claire wrinkled her nose.

"We can send it back and ask for something more well done," Leukos commented.

"No." Dr. Bristol shook her head. "Don't worry about it. I'll have the stew and some of that salmon... as well as the sides. That salad looks amazing."

Reece dished up for himself, sure to let Dr. Bristol and the Royals dish up first. The elk steaks were cooked to perfection. He was sure that the humans would like it if they tried it. Then again, humans didn't have an animal side like the Ferals did. He couldn't imagine being that weak.

They ate in silence for a few minutes.

"The stew is good," Dr. Bristol said. "But the salmon is to die for."

Reece heard a rustling noise outside. He put down his knife and fork, wishing he could just pick up the meat. It took forever with all the cutting. *What was the point?* He had teeth. Humans had teeth too, and yet they insisted on eating with these things.

There it was again… another rustling noise followed the sound of a twig snapping.

"Excuse me." He put his napkin on the table next to his plate.

"What is it?" Leukos asked.

"Nothing, my lord. I want to do a quick check."

"Now?" Magnar's eyes lifted. "Can't it wait?"

"I won't be long. I won't be able to enjoy my meal otherwise." Reece headed for the terrace. He listened. Then quietly stepped outside. He noted that Zaire was walking the perimeter. Chances were good that it was he who had made the noises. He held his breath and listened some more. There was a soft rustling as he walked over a grassy patch.

Satisfied that all was well, at least for now, Reece went back inside and sat down.

"All good?" Claire asked. She clutched her eating utensils tightly, to the point where her knuckles were white.

"Yes, my queen. I did not mean to startle you. Just doing my job," he said.

"You have nothing to worry about, sweets." Magnar put his arm around his mate and gave her a reassuring hug.

Claire sighed. "Good! I don't ever want to see that madman again."

"You met him already?" Dr. Bristol said; her fork was midway to her mouth. "When?"

"I sure did," Claire said. "He had Magnar kidnap me. His intention was to take me as a mate. He essentially wanted to marry me against my will and get me pregnant as soon as possible, so that Leukos couldn't have me."

"Oh, my gosh… that's awful! You kidnapped her, Magnar?" Hope's eyes were wide.

"It's a long story. I was on Ekon's side. There were some cracks visible, but I didn't realize until that moment how unstable the male had become. Up until then, I had thought that Claire would meet Ekon and that she would fall in love with him."

"It obviously didn't happen that way."

"Not at all." Claire shook her head. "It was apparent quite quickly that he had several screws loose."

"His true side was revealed." Magnar stated, clearly thinking back to the memory. "I felt terrible for what I had done to Claire and helped her escaped, becoming a fugitive in the process."

"Magnar took me back to Leukos, even though he knew he would be in big trouble." Claire added, putting some salad into her mouth.

"He didn't exactly bring you back," Leukos interjected. "We captured him. Rescued you, my love."

"I didn't need rescuing. Magnar was bringing me back, my darling. You know that."

"Leave him, sweets. Leukos is still pissed with me for everything that happened." Magnar grinned at Leukos.

The king rolled his eyes and chuckled. "I'll never let you live it down."

"I don't want to ever see Ekon again. He can't have my babies." Claire was ghostly pale.

"You have the best male on the job." Leukos gave Reece a hard stare before looking back into his mate's eyes. "You are in good hands… as are the chicks." His voice softened.

Reece read the warning loud and clear. His tail was on the line here. The nervous tension quickly dissipated as Magnar began to tell funny stories about when he and Leukos were young. Reece tried hard to relax. He couldn't!

CHAPTER 11

THE NEXT DAY...

Hope stirred the sauce as it bubbled, in a pot, on the stove. She replaced the lid and leaned against the counter. The sun was just setting over a magnificent horizon. This was certainly a view she could get used to looking at every day.

"Hey," she said as she caught sight of Locke. His shoulders were slumped. There wasn't the usual spring to his step.

He gave her a feeble half-smile, which wasn't like him at all.

"What's wrong?" She frowned.

"Nothing. I'm fine." His smile widened, but it seemed to her like he was trying to look like he was fine when he was far from it.

"I'm making spaghetti bolognese if you're hungry," Hope tried. "I'm sick of those ready-made meals. There'll be garlic bread as well." She lifted her brows.

"Nah, I'm good, thanks." He shook his head. His eyes were clouded. "I'll grab something later." He opened the fridge, choosing a soda. "I came for one of these." He held up the can. His whole demeanor screamed that he was dejected. He reminded her of a sad puppy.

Locke loved to eat. On a normal day, he would wolf down three of those ready-made meals in one sitting. She had made egg and bacon the other day and although Locke didn't touch the eggs—for obvious reasons, Ferals didn't eat eggs—the big shifter practically inhaled everything else. She had to make another pack of bacon just for him. He never said no when it came to food. Never! This was bad.

Hope turned the heat down on the sauce. "Tell me what's going on." She fixed him with a stare. "I don't mean to pry, but you look like you need to talk."

"It's nothing." He shook his head.

Bullshit! "Out with it, buster. I can see that something is up."

"My leave was declined. I'd really hoped to get a couple of days off. I was told that I have to wait until at least two months after the royal chicks are born." He sighed. "I haven't seen Tracey in ages. I don't want to add a couple of months onto that. I had hoped that I could catch a break before the chicks come. There are plenty of males who could do this job just as well as I can, but…" He shrugged. "I guess I understand where Reece is coming from. There is a lot of pressure on him to keep the queen and the chicks safe. There are spies among us. He can't just pick anyone but…" He sighed.

"All of those reasons are valid, but you deserve time off. You said that you are due some leave."

"Overdue." He widened his eyes and cracked open the soda, taking a sip.

"It's not fair."

Locke shrugged. "It's understandable. Thing is, I asked for one measly weekend… hardly a long time. I'm not upset with Reece, just the situation."

Locke was such a nice guy. "I'm so sorry," she said.

"I'm worried that Tracey might meet someone else. Her ex has also been sniffing around. He was the one who ended it, and now suddenly he wants her back. I wouldn't blame her if she moved on, one way or another. Long-distance relationships are tricky, as you said."

"If she moves on so easily, maybe she isn't the right girl for you," Hope offered, folding her arms. Sometimes the truth hurt.

"I've known her all of a couple of months. Spent days with her in the flesh. I can't expect her to wait forever for someone she hardly knows. It's just that we really hit it off. It wasn't just the sex… it was everything. I enjoyed spending time with her in every way. A weekend would sustain our new relationship until I can spend some real time with her. We've been talking on the phone every evening for hours." He got this wistful smile.

"I know, I've heard you laughing." She couldn't help but smile as well.

He widened his eyes. "I'm sorry. I hope I didn't keep you up."

"Not at all. I swear I wasn't listening in."

"Oh, I know," Locke sniggered. "Humans have terrible hearing."

"Hey!"

They both laughed. Locke turned serious. "I'm going to call Tracey now with the bad news." He shook his head. "I wish I could see her, that's all. I feel depressed. A couple of months seems like a very long time."

It *was* a very long time. Hope had to agree with Locke. Long-distance was tough when both parties saw each other fairly regularly. It was impossible when the length of time grew too long. Phone calls and texts were great, but face-to-face contact was paramount.

"How was dinner last night?" he asked, taking another sip of his drink.

"Great. I don't think that elk steaks are for me." Hope made a face. "But everything else was delicious."

"And Reece? Did he give you any more trouble?"

"No." She shook her head. "For the most part, it was almost as if he wasn't there. If he did speak, it was to point out that he was on duty. He checked the perimeter several times. His behavior freaked Claire out once or twice."

Locke shook his head and then choked out a laugh. "Sounds like Reece. I'd be worried if he was talking, jovial, and happy."

"Did something happen to make him like this?"

"We all have our pasts. A skeleton or two in the closet." Locke's answer was cryptic. She saw it as a confirmation of sorts. Something had happened. It had to be bad.

"Did his mate die from clutch sickness?" she blurted, feeling bad the instant the words left her mouth. "You don't have to answer that. I'm prying. I should ask Reece directly." He would never tell her anything. He was like a closed book. All she'd learned about him during the course of last night was that he liked Coca-Cola and oranges. Oh, and rare elk steak. That was it.

Locke shook his head. "I know you're not trying to pry. You're trying to understand him better. Knowing things about a person's past will often help do that. He didn't lose a mate. Although…" He looked like he was thinking it through. "What happened to him was probably worse. At least to a male like Reece."

Worse?

What could be worse than losing the person you loved?

Hope couldn't ask, even though she was desperate to know. She'd pried too much already.

"I need to call Trace," Locke said, his eyes instantly clouding.

"Good luck."

"Thanks," he mumbled, already turning to leave.

"Let me know if you change your mind about dinner."

He gave a half-hearted nod.

THE NEXT DAY…

Claire got onto the examining table and propped the pillow behind her head.

"Comfortable, sweets?" Magnar winked at her.

"Yes… very."

He leaned down and kissed her gently on the lips. "Good to hear it."

"Great stuff," Hope said, partly to remind them that she was still in the room. "I take it that Leukos can't make it?"

Claire shook her head. "He had an important meeting with the dragon kings."

"Dragons?" She felt her eyes widen in surprise. In fact, she was quite sure that they looked like saucers. It couldn't be helped because… dragons. *Holy shit!* She supposed, when all was said and done, that it wasn't so far-fetched, considering that she was working for griffin shifters. That there were wolf and bear shifters, too. Even vampires. The vampires advertised openly about wanting to mate with human women. Dragon shifters, though. *Dang it! Dragons!*

Magnar laughed. "You should see your face." He nodded. "Yes, dragons. It's not common knowledge that they exist. Your nondisclosure agreement is in place to protect all of us." He looked at her sternly for a moment.

"Of course. What happens on Feral soil, stays on Feral soil," she blustered, berating herself for overreacting.

"Exactly." He seemed to relax. "Anyway, Leukos is in a meeting… he couldn't cancel."

"No problem. There will be quite a few more of these before Claire… um… lays the eggs. Shall we get started?" She looked down at Claire.

"I'm ready when you are."

"I'm going to perform an abdominal palpation, same as last time," Hope said.

"Of course. Go right ahead." Claire smiled.

"You know the drill." They had done this once before. "It would be great if you could pull your shirt up to just under your breasts."

Locke cleared his throat. "I will wait outside. Shout if you need anything." With that, he left the room, the door clicking behind him.

"What?" Claire said. "No jokes, no smiles, what's up with Locke?"

"Yes," Magnar remarked. "He isn't himself today."

"Locke has a girlfriend," Hope blurted. She chewed her bottom lip. Maybe she shouldn't have said anything. Then again, it wasn't a secret.

"That would explain it." Magnar grinned.

"Hey." Claire smacked him on the side of the arm.

Hope giggled. "That's not why he's upset. He really likes this girl. They've been chatting for a while now. He had hoped to get a weekend off to go and see her, but his leave was declined."

Magnar frowned. "I wonder why." He rubbed his chin.

"Something about this assignment being too important." She shrugged. "He'll take his leave in a couple of months. He's missing his girlfriend… that's all." Hope wanted them to understand the situation. She didn't want them getting the wrong idea about Locke.

"This assignment is all-important, but so is the mental health of this team of royal guards. I think that now is the right time for leave—before the chicks hatch."

"That was his thinking. Reece feels differently and Locke respects that. He might be a little down for a few days. It's important that you understand why that is." Hope breathed in deeply. "Anyway, I've overstepped. I probably shouldn't have said anything. He has assured me that he is fine. Shall we get back to the examination?"

"Yes, let's," Claire said. "Like you said, I'm sure he'll be himself in a day or two. Poor guy." She pulled her top up.

"Push your pants down a little as well, please."

"Sure." Claire smiled brightly. She lifted her hips, allowing the garment to be pulled down a few inches. Magnar was nice enough to help out.

"Great." Hope rubbed her hands together to ensure that they were warm to the touch. "Here goes," she said before gently placing them on the other woman's belly. It didn't take long for her to feel the three lumps. "They're definitely bigger already, and it's only been a week since I arrived."

Claire breathed out. "So, everything is looking good? Delise said that she is happy with my progress. She says that she thinks the eggs will come sooner rather than later. She gives me two weeks."

Hope made a noise of affirmation, continuing to palpate Claire's stomach softly. So far, she and Delise were working well together. Evander was very keen, which she liked. He asked loads of great questions, some of which were helpful to her as well. "Everything is looking and feeling great. How are you?"

"I'm starting to get a little tired here and there. My lower back hurts if I overdo it, but other than that, I'm fine."

"All is perfectly normal," Hope said. "I want to weigh you. Same as last time. I also want to take blood and run a couple of routine checks." She put up her hand. "It's nothing to be concerned about."

"You have Vicky's file," Claire said, frowning. "Do you plan on comparing us?"

"I will use Vicky's tests and general pregnancy and birth as an indicator of what is considered normal, but it won't be the be-all and end-all. If some of your results vary, then we will take it from there. Everyone is different, and every pregnancy is different. In other words, we're not going to panic if results are different."

Claire sighed. "Good to know."

"Do you guys have any questions?"

"Sex," Magnar blurted. He grinned, and Claire laughed. Hope could hear that the other woman was embarrassed.

"What about sex?" she asked, urging them on.

"Is it still okay? We're technically still in the honeymoon phase of our relationship. We still have plenty of sex. There are two of us, and one of Claire, so… it's… it's a lot… that's all. Is it okay to be having regular sex with two men, or should we slow down?"

"As long as you feel fine," Hope said to Claire. "As long as you don't feel pain or cramping or anything else out of the ordinary, there's no reason why you can't have plenty of sex. In fact, the body produces hormones when a woman orgasms, that have been nicknamed the 'happy hormones' because they make you feel relaxed."

"In other words, you're prescribing sex?" Magnar asked, eyes bright.

"As long as it feels good, then go for it."

"Don't worry about that, Doc," Magnar grinned. "We do everything in our power and then some to make sure it feels better than just plain good." He winked at Claire.

Claire giggled. "Magnar," she admonished, "I'm sure Hope doesn't want to hear about our sex life."

"No," she shook her head, "that's absolutely fine. You guys need to be able to tell me anything or ask me anything. What happens in this room, stays in this room. Doctor-patient confidentiality. A healthy sex life is important."

"In that case, can we leave now and get going?" Magnar asked, still grinning.

"Stop it, babe! Behave yourself." Claire's cheeks were blood-red.

Hope chuckled. "Let's get the rest of the information I need, and you can be on your way." She looked pointedly at Magnar, who grinned.

"Now you're talking," Magnar said as he helped Claire up.

It made Hope wonder if she'd ever had such a healthy sexual relationship with Emmet. Maybe in their very early days. The honeymoon period, as Magnar put it. Still, she wasn't so sure anymore. Had their marriage seemed perfect because she had made it out to be that way in her head?

CHAPTER 12

LATER THAT DAY...

Willing her hand to steady, Hope took a deep breath and continued applying the paint to her nails. Part of her felt she was being silly. She was in the middle of nowhere. It wasn't like anyone was going to look at her toes. But then again, *she* had to look at her own toes and she happened to like them painted. Not silly at all. Therefore, here she was, carefully applying coral-colored varnish to her toenails.

Just when she had one foot done and the big toe on her second foot half-finished, she thought she heard shouting from down the hall.

She listened, cocking her head. The house was massive. It was hard to tell.

No, wait... there it was again. More shouting. *What in the world?* She had just put the brush back in the container and was twisting it closed when a hard knock sounded on her door. Two seconds later, Reece strode through the door. His eyes were blazing. He wore a pair of linen pants. White this time. The fabric looked good against his bronze skin. His muscles looked out there. Like he'd been pumping iron.

"Come in… I guess," she deadpanned. "You do know that it's customary to wait until a person invites you in? What if I had been changing?" Changing would have been better than this. As it stood, she was wearing an oversized hoodie that was about a million years old and looked it. Her hair was in a messy bun on the top of her head.

His murderous expression became even more murderous. She hadn't thought it possible. His eyes seemed darker. Like thick honey. "Do you make a habit of interfering, Dr. Bristol?"

"What?" she frowned. "Where is this even coming from?"

"I was pulled aside by the king and interrogated on the way I run my team. Do you know why he would have done that?" He narrowed his eyes for a second.

Why the questions? What was going on here? Hope spotted Locke hovering around in the hallway outside her bedroom. He seemed to be pacing. She couldn't catch a glimpse of his face. "Why would I know something like that?" she finally said, her voice timid. It felt like a trick question. Like he was trying to trap her into saying something she might regret.

"Leukos wanted to know why I refused to give Locke leave. He didn't think that it was fair. Something about the queen being upset. Then it turns out that they heard all about it from you."

"Hang on just a minute—" She put up a hand.

"I won't hang on for any length of time, Doctor. This is my team and my assignment. I don't appreciate you interfering."

"I wasn't interfering. Locke was depressed because he was denied leave. Claire wanted to know why he didn't seem himself. She was the one who picked up on it. She was the one who asked me about it."

"So now you're blaming the queen for your flappy mouth. Why am I not surprised?"

She sucked in a breath. "I do not have a flappy mouth, and I'm not blaming Claire." She shook her head.

"Seems like it to me."

"I'm explaining what happened… that's all! But since you're shouting at me for my wrongdoings, let me just point out that I think it's wrong that you wouldn't let Locke go for one lousy weekend."

"He *is* going. Well done! Your meddling worked. Locke is going and you're stuck with me, instead." With that, he stormed out.

The front door slammed as Reece left the house moments later. Locke came into her bedroom. He looked sheepish. "I didn't mean to get you into trouble. I'm so sorry about that, Dr. Bristol."

"Come on!" she growled. "You should really call me Hope. We live together. We've become friends. It's stupid how formal you have to be all the time."

"I can't call you Hope. It would be going against orders."

She made a noise of frustration and rolled her eyes, flopping back on the bed. Reece was damned infuriating. She sat back up after a few seconds.

"I'm so sorry," Locke said again, running a hand through his hair.

"Listen to me," she said, "you have nothing to be sorry about. You should never have been denied the leave in the first place. I don't feel bad about telling Magnar and Claire. They picked up on your somber mood and I told them what was going on. I also explained that Reece was only looking out for the royal family and that you were ultimately okay with it. If Reece had given me half a chance to explain, he would have known that."

"I shouldn't have put you in that position in the first place." Locke looked upset. "I shouldn't have moped around at work. It wasn't professional." She could hear Reece in that statement.

"Stop," she said. "Stop right there. This isn't on you." She smiled. "So, when do you leave?"

His eyes lit up. "Tomorrow after my shift. I get two whole nights on human soil. I can't wait to tell Tracey." He didn't move. His eyes stayed on hers. Locke looked tense.

"What are you waiting for then?" She lifted her brows.

Instead of heading off, phone in hand, Locke lingered. "Maybe I shouldn't go." He shook his head.

"Of course you should go."

"Reece is angry. You—"

"He'll get over it. I'll apologize to him. He blames me, not you. I don't mind at all." She shrugged.

"He's not too thrilled with me, either. It might be hell sharing a house with him for a whole weekend."

"I'll be fine. How bad could it be?" She rolled her eyes.

Locke still looked hesitant. "Reece can be—"

"I know how Reece can be, and I'll cope. Call your girlfriend and tell her the good news. I'm a grownup. I promise you I can handle that stick-in-the-mud."

Locke pushed out a breath. He finally grinned, his eyes lighting up. "Thank you, Doctor. I won't forget this. I really hope you're right about being able to handle Reece."

"Of course I'm right." She laughed.

CHAPTER 13

Act normal.

Be cool.

You've done nothing wrong.

Reece wasn't even there yet, and she was feeling stressed out. Her stomach churned. Hope had decided that she wasn't going to hide away. *Reece could go to hell! There!* She sucked in a deep breath, feeling marginally better.

Locke appeared from down the hall. He had a light travel bag slung over his shoulder. There couldn't be much more than a toothbrush and t-shirt in that thing. "Packing light?" she asked.

Locke nodded. "I'm sure we'll spend plenty of time getting reacquainted." He bobbed his brows.

She laughed. "That may be so, but every woman loves to go out for a nice dinner as well as lots of… you know."

He frowned. "Sex, Doc. You can say the 'S' word, you know."

"I'm an Ob-Gyn. I'm quite familiar with sex and how the reproductive organs work. Sex… sex… sex!" She grinned. "See, I—"

"I'm not sure that's an appropriate conversation to have, Dr. Bristol," Reece said from the door. She hadn't heard him come in.

Great! Just freaking great. Something else for Reece to take out of context.

"I'll go and…" Locke pointed at the hallway that led to the bedrooms. "I forgot to pack… something." He sauntered off.

"You needed to hear the whole conversation," she tried, regretting her words instantly.

"I doubt it." He had a leather bag over his shoulder. It was significantly fuller than Locke's had been. "Just to be clear, you might talk about inappropriate subjects and walk around in inappropriate wear while Locke is living in this house, but that's not going to happen while I'm here."

Holy shit, he was too much. Too damned much! "That's not fair."

"Lots of things aren't fair, Dr. Bristol. The fact that I have to fledgling… babysit you for the weekend isn't fair either, and yet here I am."

"I'll stay out of your way," she said.

"Sounds like a plan." He started walking away. "I'll take the room across the hallway from you." With that, he was gone.

Asshole!

Talk about a bad mood. *Screw him!* If he wanted to be in a bad mood and to have a shitty weekend, that was on him. Hope wasn't letting him get to her. She'd planned to make him pizza as a peace offering, but he didn't deserve any.

She'd make pizza for herself. Forget Reece! Hope had half a mind to put her little pink pajamas on and walk around like that. No bra! The asshole would immediately assume that she walked around that way in front of Locke. He'd think less of her. Not possible! That jerk couldn't think less of her if he tried.

Things couldn't possibly get worse. A whole weekend with that sexy asshole was too much to comprehend. What was wrong with her? She didn't like him, and yet she was still attracted to him. The whole thing was just plain crazy. Surely it wasn't normal for there to be such a big disconnect between a person's brain and their body? Her phone dinged. Come to think of it, the device had dinged a couple of times in the last five minutes. Her stomach churned. Three missed calls from Emmet. There were two messages from her sister saying that the baby was fine, asking her to call them. At least her sister used the word 'please.' Emmet left one message.

Call me! Now!

Another jerk who thought he could order her around. Emmet could go straight to hell. Pizza! She needed one badly. Claire got back to grating the mozzarella. She wanted extra cheese with bacon. Lots of bacon. Then, there was ice cream for dessert. Double chocolate. All would be well after that.

CHAPTER 14

Reece watched as Dr. Bristol bent over to check inside the oven. Her ass was up in the air. The doctor even bounced it around a couple of times while she looked at whatever she was cooking. The female was making it impossible for him not to look. As it was, her butt looked amazing wrapped up inside those blue jeans.

"Are you just going to let that ring?" he asked. The sound of her phone was annoying, to say the least.

"Yes." She nodded her head.

"You're not going to answer it?"

"No!" She shook her head, her eyes firmly inside the oven. Her ass was still in the air.

"Turn it off then," he growled.

"Try asking nicely." She stood tall, facing him. Eyes narrowed, she folded her arms, plumping up her breasts. Not that he was looking. Reece hated that he noticed them in the first place. This female was trouble. Going behind his back, making his name mud in the eyes of his king. It irritated the feathers off of him.

"I was told that I am too harsh on my males." He ground his teeth together, but only out of irritation for saying anything in the first place. His plan was to leave it alone. To ignore her for the weekend. Of course, an hour in, and his plan was already upended.

Blast!

"It's not just them you're hard on," she grumbled.

"This isn't about you."

"I didn't say that it was." She exhaled through her nose, like she was trying to pull herself together. Why would she need to do that? If anyone needed to find calm, it was him. "Maybe you should listen to Leukos and Magnar. Perhaps you *are* too harsh."

This female had no idea. None! "There is no such thing as too harsh when it comes to Ekon and the Fallen. Make no mistake, they're circling like vultures. The queen is in danger. The royal offspring even more so."

"There *is* such a thing as too harsh. Locke needed these two measly days." She showed him two fingers. "He'll be better for it."

"And during those two days, the queen is at elevated risk. Two days is a big enough crack, Dr. Bristol. Here I am with you, instead of with her, where I am needed."

"Someone else can take Locke's place. You could have sent one of the others to babysit me."

"Most of our males are too weak to watch over you."

"Weak? I've seen Andy and Zaire, and there's nothing weak about them. Okay…" She looked him up and down. He liked how her eyes seemed to change. They became more hooded. He shouldn't like that. "You're definitely stronger but… that doesn't mean one of them couldn't be here, instead."

"I'm not talking about that kind of weak. Not in the physical sense."

She frowned. "What do you—?" Her mouth fell open. "Back to that? You still think I want to have sex with everyone here," she growled. The sound shot straight to his cock. "You think they would be too weak to turn me down? For the last time, I'm not here for sex."

"Feral males can be persuasive."

"I don't care! Stop it! You're pissing me off. And since I can't kick you out, I need you to stop with your bullshit. I'm sorry I interfered. I'm glad Locke got his leave. Can we drop it?"

"Locke underestimates his abilities. He is one of the best we have. He still needs to mature some more, but that male has huge potential. He is irreplaceable. You wouldn't know any of that about him. The kings don't realize what they have in him yet either. I've had to replace him with someone else. A male I don't fully trust." Why had he divulged that? It was more information than she needed. "If you think for a second that Ekon won't hear of Locke leaving, you're mistaken. There are only so many I trust. One of the few has now left… thanks to you." He felt his jaw clench. "Just as we have spies, so does the Fallen King. His eyes are everywhere. I am struggling to let this go. This is why."

"I refuse to give in to panic and fear."

"You have nothing to worry about. It's the queen who does. Again, Dr. Bristol, this isn't about you."

"Stop saying that! I know! And for the record, I know that Locke is irreplaceable. Just saying." She narrowed her eyes.

"You don't know anything," he growled. Anger rose up in him. Was Dr. Bristol attracted to the male? That had to be it. It had to. She was jealous that he was gone. All the males sought human attention whenever they were on their soil.

"I'll have you know that—" Her phone started ringing… again!

He looked at the device on the table. "This is becoming a nuisance. You are a nuisance." His voice came out harsher than he intended.

Dr. Bristol looked at her phone; she made this noise, sounding annoyed. That made two of them. She swiped at her phone. "What?" She paused, listening. "I'm busy. My life doesn't revolve around you anymore. It hasn't for a long time, so forgive me for not dropping everything as soon as you called." He'd never heard her sound so cold and angry.

Dr. Bristol listened to whoever was on the other side, a little longer this time.

"What?" She frowned. "You can't be serious. How is that possible? How can this be fixed?" Her eyes flashed from left to right as she listened.

Reece forced himself to go to the refrigerator. He found a Coca-Cola in the door. His attention was still on Dr. Bristol and her conversation, even though he was trying hard not to care.

The person on the other end was talking. Reece couldn't quite make out the words.

Dr. Bristol did something unexpected. She started laughing. It wasn't a normal kind of laughter. It sounded slightly off. Like she didn't really mean it. The person on the other end talked louder, which made her laugh harder.

"Wait just a minute," she said between gasps of air. "Does that mean you're not married to Elizabeth? Or does it mean that you're married to both of us?"

Married.

What?

It was his understanding that the doctor was single. Not that it was important. In fact, it would be better if she was mated. He wasn't sure why she hadn't divulged that fact. She had plenty of opportunities to do so. It irked him that she hadn't said anything.

The male on the line said something loudly. It didn't take long for his voice to normalize again. Dr. Bristol rolled her eyes and sighed. Then she pinched the bridge of her nose for a second.

"Let me get this straight. I only just arrived here, and no, I can't tell you where I am, only that it took me a long time to get here. I just started my new job a week ago, and yet you want me to drop everything in order to sign the papers again. All because of a technicality."

There was a pause while the other person spoke.

"No... I can't." She shook her head.

There was shouting again on the other end.

"I can't tell you where I am. I signed a nondisclosure agreement. That means that sending the papers to me won't work. I suggest—"

The male interrupted, still shouting.

"I understand that she must be upset…" A pause. "I get it, I do, but there's nothing I can do right now. I'll let you know as soon as I— " Another pause. "I'm not trying to be difficult, Emmet. I'm not trying to get back at you. I can't leave right now." A longer pause while he talked. "Tell Lizzie that meditation works for stress."

Dr. Bristol held the phone away from her ear. Reece could make out snippets of the shouting. There were cuss words interlaced in the dialogue. When the noise died down some, she put it back to her ear. "I'm hanging up now. I'm sorry this happened. Believe it or not, I don't want to be married to you either." She not only put the phone down, but turned the device off.

"You're mated?" The words came out before he could stop them.

"Apparently so." Her face crumpled, and she burst into tears. They streamed down her cheeks.

Dr. Bristol put a hand over her face. Her shoulders shook, and she made sobbing noises.

It was the last thing he expected to happen. The very last! He didn't know what to do. If several Fallen males arrived at that moment, he would know exactly how to handle the situation. He'd know whether to fight or to run. He'd hold his own in battle if staying was the right option. From time to time, a male needed to take a beating to protect those around him. He would know if that was the right choice. These were decisions that came naturally to him. A crying female… No! He had no idea what to do with this.

"Do you want some water, Dr. Bristol?" She was losing fluids. Maybe they needed replenishing.

She ignored him and cried harder. Her sobs sounded like pure agony.

Blast and damn! He walked closer to the miserable female. "What can I do, Doctor?" he asked.

"It's a disaster. An absolute disaster." She shook her head, sniffing loudly. "I thought it was over. That... that..." The sobbing started up again.

"Um... Dr. Bristol... perhaps..." He touched the side of her arm for half a second, not knowing what to say to her. Then he tried squeezing her upper arm softly. "I'm sorry... this happened to you," he finally said, feeling like an idiot.

Dr. Bristol sniffed a few times; she was blinking her eyes rapidly. Did it mean that she was about to cry some more? Maybe harder than before? Perhaps she was trying to stop. He prayed the latter was true. "Whatever it is, there has to be a solution."

"No solution." She shook her head. "Well, there is and there isn't." She wiped a hand over her face, rubbing her eyes.

"That doesn't make sense, Dr. Bristol."

"Call me Hope. It's not that hard and I insist, after you just witnessed me making a fool of myself."

"You haven't made a fool of yourself. People cry... sometimes. It's a normal thing to do if... if warranted, Hope." It felt strange to call her that.

Dr. Bristol gave him a watery smile. "See, that wasn't so hard. If I had known it would just take a good cry to get you to relax a little, I would have done so days ago." She sniffed again.

"I'm glad you didn't. I wish you would stop now," he added when he saw another tear roll down her cheek.

"I'm trying." She wiped her face. "I really am." More of those blasted tears followed.

"It can't be that bad."

"It's worse. My life is such a mess," she moaned. At least she didn't cry harder. The tears were slowing.

"Maybe talking about it will help. I probably won't be qualified to offer you any advice but… sometimes…" *Blast!* He was messing this up. "Sometimes, getting something off your chest is help enough." He glanced at her chest, feeling instantly bad for noticing how plump it was in that t-shirt. Dr. Bristol… Hope was mated. She had a mate! At least it sounded like she had one.

She nodded. "You're right. We won't be friends after this, though." She put her hand up, looking stern.

"Of course not."

Dr. Bristol laughed. She wiped her eyes again. "I'm only kidding." She turned serious. "Are you sure you want to hear all about it?"

He nodded. "Very sure… if it will help you." He also really wanted to know. Was she mated, or wasn't she?

"Okay, then. But first…" She turned towards the oven, sticking her ass in the air again as she looked inside. "It's done," she declared, standing.

Hope fetched a plate. She opened the oven, carefully sliding some food onto the large plate. "I wasn't going to offer you any, but I suppose I have no choice now." She made this cute snorting noise.

"You eat," he said. "I plan on grilling a steak once you are done in here."

She cut the… food, into slices.

"What is that?" he asked, looking at the strange meal.

"Pizza."

He frowned.

"You don't know what pizza is?" She sounded shocked.

"I guess not." He shook his head.

"I made this one from scratch. It's cheesy, tomatoey goodness. I put a couple of pepperoni slices on top. Pepperoni is meat," she added. He was grateful because he had no idea. If he wanted to find a mate one day, he'd have to get better at this. Perhaps he could learn from Dr. Bristol.

"You eat, Doctor." It didn't look all that good. It was flat and mostly light yellow. Something yellow would certainly taste strange.

"Hope… call me Hope."

"You eat, Hope… please." He gestured to her plate.

"Okay, then." She sat down across from him at the small kitchen table.

"Would you like some wine? It's supposed to help humans relax," he offered.

"No… thanks." She shook her head. "When I'm in a bad or sad mood, wine makes me feel worse."

"I can imagine. It doesn't taste good at all."

She laughed, even though he hadn't meant it as a joke.

"What about a soda?" He held up the can.

"That would be great… thanks." He handed her the drink, going to the refrigerator to get himself another one.

Then Reece sat across from her. He kept his eyes on her as he opened his can of soda. "Whenever you are ready, Doctor." He didn't want to rush her.

She smiled at him. "I can't believe I was getting ready to kill you not so long ago and here you are being all nice to me."

He frowned. "There is no way you could kill me, Doctor… um… Hope. I am too strong."

She laughed. "I wasn't being literal but thanks for pointing that out, just in case I get the urge again." She turned serious. "I was mad at you. You keep accusing me of trying to seduce your staff, when that's the absolute last thing on my mind."

"If you are already mated, then I get that. I wish I had known; we could've avoided some of our conflict."

Dr. Bristol inhaled deeply. "That's just it, I'm not… at least I thought I wasn't mated… married. I guess they are the same thing." She shrugged. "But it turns out that I am."

"Hmm…" He rubbed his chin. "I do not think that being mated and married are the same. Shifters mate for life. There is no divorce. We are tethered to one another in a way that is unbreakable. I wouldn't say that they are the same thing at all."

Her eyes seemed to cloud, and for a short while he thought she might start crying again. "They're not the same, then."

"I'm sorry I interrupted. Please continue. You will need to start at the beginning, please."

"I thought Emmet and I would be together forever. I really did. I was so clueless and stupid."

"What happened? Did you no longer want him?" Reece tried hard not to get angry. He could feel his feathers rub. He wasn't sure why he felt anger. Was it aimed at Dr. Bristol or her mate?

"I wanted him, but as it turned out, he didn't want me. He wanted someone else."

"What?" Reece growled. "No," he shook his head, "that can't be possible." He wasn't buying it. Who wouldn't want this female?

"Trust me when I tell you that it is." She took a bite of her flat food. Then she made a noise of enjoyment. Her eyes rolled back. "That's so good. You need to try a slice."

He started to decline, but she took a piece and handed it to him, giving him a napkin.

She chewed for a few seconds and then swallowed. "I worked long hours. So did Emmet."

"Emmet is your mate."

"My ex-mate. We're not together anymore."

He nodded, still struggling to comprehend that concept.

"My hours at work were pretty standard. I would start at roughly the same time and get home at the same time every day. If anything, I would have to work late… or rush off because of an emergency. It's the nature of what I do."

He nodded to show her that he was listening. Then he took a bite of the food. It was in his hand, and he wasn't really thinking. It was crispy and yet soft. It was salty and… He also made a noise of enjoyment, looking down at the flat yellow slice.

"Good, isn't it?"

He nodded. "Very. It is quite a shock. I didn't expect that. You are a good cook, Dr. Bristol."

"Thank you."

"Go on." He took another bite.

"Well," she swallowed thickly, "I had an emergency one afternoon, so I called Emmet to tell him I'd be home really late. I had a woman in labor, and it was taking a while for her to dilate. There was a good chance that she wouldn't end up dilating and that I would have to operate. I told him not to wait up, that I would be gone half the night." She took a sip of her drink. "The baby started showing signs of fetal stress soon after I ended the call."

"I'm not sure what that means."

"The baby was in trouble. We put machines on the mother to monitor her and the unborn child. Those machines were telling us that there was something wrong with the baby. We rushed her into the operating theater and opened her up."

"That's amazing. Go on."

"It turned out that the umbilical cord had wrapped itself around the baby's neck twice." She must have seen his confusion. "With human women, the baby gets its air and food from a pipe called the umbilical cord. This can sometimes wrap around the child's neck, which causes the pipe to pull away and become ineffective… to put it in layman's terms. The baby can suffocate inside the mother as a result."

"That would be terrible." He frowned.

"Anyway… we rushed her in for surgery and got the baby out before that could happen. It all took place soon after my call to Emmet. He wasn't expecting me back until hours later. I arrived home expecting to find him cooking or watching the television. I called out but there was no response." She licked her lips, putting her half-eaten food down.

"Where was he?" Reece asked when he could see her hesitation.

"He… well… he was in the bedroom." Her eyes were clouded with pain. "He wasn't alone."

"Who was with him?" Reece asked.

"My younger sister, Lizzie."

"What were they doing in your bedroom?" It couldn't be. Surely not.

"They were fucking." Her chest was rising and falling rapidly. "Actually, that's not true. They were making passionate love. They were so lost in each other that they didn't even notice me standing there. They didn't hear me gasp. They didn't… they…"

"I'm so sorry," Reece said. He put the food down. "That is… It's… I'm… I'm shocked."

"I was shocked too. I found out that it had been going on for a long time. For eight months. They were in love. They'd been meaning to tell me. They hadn't wanted me to find out like that. It felt like my world ended. My parents were upset. They wouldn't speak to my sister… or Emmet. He moved into her place. I was broken." A tear ran down her cheek. She wiped it away.

"That's not right." Reece shook his head. This poor female. "I can't imagine… I just… I would have killed the male. Taken his head from his shoulders."

Dr. Bristol giggled. "Oh, I thought about it."

"With your sister." He felt his eyes widen. "What did she have to say for herself?"

"Lizzie told me that she loved him."

"What about you? Her own flesh and blood? Did she not love you, too?"

"You raise a good point. One I raised myself… several times. My parents supported me for a while at first, and then…" She got this haunted look he didn't like.

"What happened with your parents?"

She took a sip of her drink. "They started to say things like, 'your sister didn't mean it' and 'Emmet isn't such a bad guy.'"

"He deserves death for what he did to you. At the very least, he deserved a hundred lashes and a long time in the cage. I would even go so far as to say that he deserved to have his prick removed. Maybe not with silver… that would be harsher than death. Still…"

"Um… okay… if you say so. Oh!" Her eyes widened. "I forgot that silver is your kryptonite."

"Krypto… what?" He frowned.

"You guys are allergic to silver."

"That is correct." He nodded. "So your parents took their side in the end?"

"They say that there are no sides. They've realized that Emmet and Lizzie are together now, and that they need to make the most of it. They had to forgive Emmet. They had no choice."

"There is always a choice," he said.

"I haven't spoken to my parents in about two months." He could see her eyes welling with tears.

"You're alone."

"It feels that way sometimes." She licked her lips.

"From what I can tell, you are still mated to this male." He struggled to keep the growl from his voice.

"I thought our divorce was finalized. That means that we ended the mating," Dr. Bristol explained.

"I got that." Reece nodded.

"Only it isn't. The paperwork had a mistake on it. My social security number was written down wrong. They swapped two numbers around. They only picked it up today, apparently. That means that we're still married, which is a disaster."

"I understand that now," Reece said. "I also understand why you wouldn't want to be with this Emmet bastard."

"Well, the thing is, Emmet married Lizzie a couple of weeks ago. At least, he thought he married her. Polygamy isn't legal in our state. That means that they're not married." She shook her head. "Lizzie is pregnant with Emmet's baby." Her eyes filled with tears again, and she blinked hard. He realized that she was trying not to cry.

"You still love your mate very much." Reece reached over and touched her arm. "I am so sorry. I'm sorry I ever thought you were trying to seduce one of the males. I know now that it couldn't possibly be true. I can see that you are devastated. If it's any consolation, I understand some of what you must be feeling."

"Why? Did you have something happen to you?"

"Nothing nearly as terrible. I'm so sorry, Dr. Bristol."

"Call me Hope… please."

"I'm sorry… Hope." He nodded once.

"All I want is for that chapter to close. I want our marriage to be over. I don't want to be married to Emmet anymore. I came here to start a new life. To find myself again. Now I hear that I'm still married to that asshole." She pointed at her phone, which was lying on the table. "As far as I'm concerned, Emmet and Lizzie can have each other. They deserve one another. I really don't want to have to go through it all again."

"A piece of paper doesn't mean anything." He shook his head. "It is what is inside a person's heart that counts. It sounds like the two of you haven't been mated for a long while now." For a moment, Reece was worried that hearing him say that would upset her.

He breathed out a sigh of relief when she nodded, contemplating his words. "You're right."

"Yes, I am."

"Emmet and Lizzie are a couple. They have been for a while now. I can't leave right now to go to sign those papers. That's something they will need to come to terms with."

"Yes, you will need to wait until the chicks have hatched and are thriving."

"I still don't get that." She picked up her food. "Babies are going to hatch from the eggs within hours of them being laid."

He nodded in agreement.

"But you still call them chicks."

"They will look like small human babies, but that doesn't mean that they will grow up to be human. They will learn to shift… to be Feral. They are therefore chicks."

"I find it interesting that, even though you mate humans, the offspring are just as much Feral as if they were born from a Feral couple?"

"That's right. Our seed is strong."

Dr. Bristol giggled. "I'd say. That's some seriously strong DNA."

"DNA?" He frowned.

"DNA are the building blocks of the body." She took a big bite of her food. Once she finished, she cocked her head. "So now you understand why I'm not here to find love… or sex… or any of that stuff."

"Why did you come, then? Did you run away from your problems?"

"No." She shook her head. "I felt like I was in a rut. Like I needed a different view." She pointed at the window. It was dark outside. He didn't think she was being literal. At least, not completely literal. "I felt like Emmet and Lizzie were moving on, and like I was stuck. I had this job offer fall in my lap and it felt like the right thing to do. I was Emmet's girlfriend. Then I was Emmet's fiancée. For a lot of years, I was Emmet's wife. Otherwise I'm a doctor. None of those things are who I am. I don't think I know who I am anymore. That's why I'm here."

"I'm glad you trusted me with your story. I think you made the right decision coming here. I'm sorry I treated you so harshly without even knowing you. I saw a beautiful female and… I… I guess I didn't know how to behave or what to think. It's no excuse. Please forgive me, Doct— Hope… please forgive me."

He watched as a smile slowly took residence on her face. Her eyes were red-rimmed and shimmery, but she still managed to look beautiful. What a fool that male had been to throw a female like this away.

"Of course… there's nothing to forgive. I think we got our wires crossed."

"Wires?" He frowned. "What does this have to do with wires? Wait just a moment… it's a human saying, isn't it?"

"See!" She laughed. "You're already getting better at this. It means we got mixed up. That there were mixed signals and miscommunication between us… that's all."

"That's easily rectified. We need to communicate better in the future."

"I like that plan. If in doubt… we talk it out."

"Sounds good to me."

"More pizza?" She held out her plate to him.

Reece didn't even realize that he had finished his slice. "Thank you." He took some more.

CHAPTER 15

THE NEXT DAY...

"A little more to the right," Hope instructed Zaire. "That's it." He put the cabinet down. "I still can't believe you can move that thing around by yourself." These shifters were even stronger than they looked, and they packed some serious muscle.

"It doesn't weigh anything." He picked up the sonogram machine like it weighed nothing.

"Um... maybe you shouldn't—" Hope made a squealing noise in the back of her throat when he held it up with one hand above his head.

"That cost a ton of money!" she yelled. "Don't do that." She shook her head. "Quit messing around and put it down," she added when he started twirling it around with his fingers.

Holy shit!

Zaire laughed, putting the machine back down. "Sorry to scare you, Dr. Bristol. I wouldn't have dropped it and it's not like you can use it, anyway."

"That's true." It was the one thing that was annoying with nonhuman pregnancies. She couldn't use an ultrasound to see how the pregnancy was coming along. It didn't work. The machine was gathering dust. It was purchased when they still hoped it might be possible. Now there was a new machine just sitting here, unused. She might recommend that it be donated to one of the many care facilities in need.

"What else do you need me to do?" Zaire lifted his brows. He hadn't so much as broken a sweat while they put her new furniture into her office.

"I will take it from here," a gruff voice sounded from the doorway. She didn't have to look up to know that it was Reece.

A feeling of awareness crept over her as she lifted her gaze. "Hi, Reece." She tried to play it cool, even though she felt anything but.

"Dr. Bristol." He inclined his head for a second, looking angry. She was going to ignore it. It was easy to get mixed signals from him. Reece was just being himself. That was all.

"Sure, Reece." Zaire smiled. "Would you like me to patrol the area?" He used his thumb to point outside.

"No, you can go to the royal tower. Keep a close eye on the queen. It won't be long before the change of shift. I will be there to hand over. Magnar and our king are with Claire, but that does not mean that you may let down your guard. You know what we discussed earlier." Hope briefly wondered what it could have been. She was sure it had to do with spies and Ekon and risk. She felt a shiver travel down her spine.

"I do, Reece. You can count on me."

"Hurry, then," he said.

"Goodbye, Doctor. I might see you tomorrow." He winked at her.

Reece growled.

"Sorry… I… um—" Zaire started to say.

"Go!" Reece roared. "Now!"

Zaire ran from the building. When Reece turned to her, his eyes were blazing. "I am sorry. I will have another talk with my team." He shook his head, looking disappointed. Anger simmered just beneath the surface. His muscles looked tense. Especially the ones on his neck and shoulders.

"Why would you need to talk to them, and why do you look so angry?" She held up her hands. "Since we agreed last night to communicate better with one another, I thought I would ask you. I don't understand this behavior. We were getting the clinic ready. Zaire was helping. You shouldn't be angry over that."

His whole stance softened. His shoulders relaxed. His eyes, too. "Zaire was showing off for you. He was giving you mounting signals. It made me angry."

"Mounting signals?" she repeated, frowning. "You thought he was flirting just then?" She held back a smile. Because Reece had it wrong.

"Definitely." Reece nodded. "It's how we… let a female know that we are interested in her. We show off our strength and skill as a warrior. Our ability to keep her safe. It is a turn-on for a Feral woman."

"So, him holding up the ultrasound machine," she pointed at the piece of equipment in question, "with one hand, was his way of flirting with me?"

"Yes."

"I think it was just a case of him fooling around."

"He was *not* fooling around. He was serious. He was trying to prove himself to you. It's not right. Not after everything you've been through. You're trying to find yourself, and yet you're surrounded by males who would like nothing better than to… than to… take advantage of you. That's not right." Reece was frowning. He was completely serious. So darned cute.

Hope wanted to tell him to relax. None of them were being rude to her. They were all really nice. They all gave her compliments all the time. In a way, it was flattering. Even pleasant. If anyone tried to take it further, she'd be quick to put them in their place. She didn't say any of this to Reece, because she didn't think that he would take it well. "If you feel like it's necessary," she finally said, "then you should talk to them. For the record, I'm not a Feral woman so it's lost on me." She shrugged.

"I do think it's necessary. I'll take care of it."

"Okay, then."

He looked around. "It's starting to come together nicely. This actually looks more like an office. Definitely not so sterile as before."

"I know. The whole clinic has a long way to go, but it's starting to take shape. I have my first appointment booked for Monday. One of the human women living here now with her new mate."

"That's great!" Reece's eyes lit up. He almost looked like he was going to crack a smile, but stopped himself at the last second. "Is she with clutch?"

"I don't know. It'll be her first time coming to see me. I wouldn't be able to tell you even if I knew. It's called doctor-patient confidentiality. I took an oath when I became a doctor."

"I hope it is a female with clutch," Reece said. "We need young for our species to stay strong and to thrive. Humans have given us hope. For the first time in years, we have hope."

"Hope." She smiled. "It's funny how my name is Hope and I'm here to take care of the future generations of your species, starting with the next royal offspring."

"It's great." His mouth twitched and his eyes glinted. "You have a lovely name. I'm glad you came."

"Me, too." It was weird. It *still* felt like they were tap dancing around each other. She wasn't sure why. It felt like they had broken ground yesterday. That maybe they could be friends. Yet, here they were, and it felt awkward between them. Possibly even more so than before.

"Are you ready to go, or do you need me to move anything else?" He looked around the room.

"Nope." She shook her head. "I think that's enough work for a Saturday. I'm taking what's left of the day off."

"Sounds like a good idea."

They walked outside. Reece took his pants off, and her cheeks instantly heated. Make that, her whole body ignited. She had to force herself to look away. To look anywhere but at him. If she looked, she wouldn't be able to stop staring.

And there it was. The reason it was still so awkward. The reason they couldn't be friends. It didn't matter that she was still married. It didn't matter that she was here to find herself. To leave her past behind. It did not matter that she didn't want a rebound relationship. Or even sex, for that matter. She was attracted to Reece. Hugely attracted to him. Up until recently he had come across as a colossal jerk. Her new problem was that it wasn't the case anymore. Beneath all his layers—the broody, anal-retentive layers—there was a really nice guy. A nice guy who was incredibly sexy. The fact that he didn't know it made him even more attractive to her.

It was one hell of a problem to have. One hell of a problem indeed. The only consolation was that he wasn't interested in her. He wasn't attracted to humans. It was a good thing. A fantastic thing. It meant that she wouldn't be tempted to act on her desires. She'd make a fool of herself if she did.

CHAPTER 16

Hope couldn't sleep. She tossed and turned, and tossed and turned some more. She finally picked up her phone and had another look at the messages. She'd had a back-and-forth exchange with Lizzie after getting home earlier. She couldn't put their conversation out of her mind. Hope scrolled through her phone.

> ***Lizzie:*** *Please come back. Surely you can get a day or two off. I need you to sign the paperwork. Please!*
>
> ***Hope:*** *I can't. I'm sorry. I'm on call 24/7. It's going to be a good couple of weeks before I can get away. I promise I'll be there as soon as I can.*

Hope was shocked at how much she meant it. At how little animosity she felt towards her sister. Towards *them.* She wanted the papers signed. She wanted to move on, once and for all. Needed it.

Lizzie: *Why are you doing this? I know you hate me. I know you don't want us to be together. Thing is, Emmet loves me. You guys are done!*

Hope: *This has nothing to do with Emmet. I want nothing more than to be divorced already. You're pregnant with his baby. He's with you now. The divorce not going through wasn't my fault.*

Lizzie: *I know how much you want to be a mother. You hate me since finding out about the baby. You love watching me suffer. It isn't good for the baby.*

Hope: *Emmet is with you, NOT me. He left me... remember? I can't leave here right now. I have certain responsibilities. Please try to calm down. You're right, stress isn't good for the baby.*

Lizzie: *You almost sound like you care.*

Hope: *I do care. You're my sister. Emmet loves you. A piece of paper doesn't matter. It didn't matter when he was with me, and it shouldn't matter now. He loves YOU.*

Her sister hadn't responded. Hope was worried. Emmet hadn't messaged her again, either. It was radio silence from him. Why? Why was Lizzie acting like this? Like she was desperate and afraid. What was going on with them? Although she shouldn't give a shit, she was worried about Lizzie. Her sister was pregnant, after all. It could affect the baby.

Hope had spent many months wishing for them to break up. She'd been waiting for it to happen. Expecting it to. A relationship based on lies wasn't much of a relationship. Except they'd stayed together. They'd gotten married—or tried to—and Lizzie had fallen pregnant. Now it seemed that there might be problems in paradise. Problems that had nothing to do with her. Yet she was the one being blamed.

What the hell?

More importantly, she was worried about her sister. Hope found herself hoping that Emmet and Lizzie were going to work things out.

Maybe she was finally starting to move on. Somehow it was happening, and quicker than she ever imagined. It still hurt. It was still something she would never fully get over or move on from, but she didn't want Lizzie to be hurt. Hope didn't want her sister to go through even half of what she had gone through. Maybe that made her crazy or an idiot. It didn't matter; it was true.

Hope sighed as she took note of the time. It was half-past two in the morning, and there she was, wide awake. She needed the toilet and perhaps a drink of water. Then again, chamomile tea would be better. At this rate, she wasn't going to get back to sleep anytime soon.

Hope slipped out of bed and padded into the hallway. She looked at Reece's door. He also left it slightly ajar. She wondered if he slept on top of the covers, with his head buried under a pillow, or— She gave an eye-roll. This needed to stop. Good thing Locke would be back the next day, and things could get back to normal.

She quickly went to the toilet. Hope didn't flush it; she didn't want to wake Reece. Perhaps she'd call Lizzie in the morning and have a long talk with her sister. It would be better than messaging back and forth.

She turned the corner into the kitchen and turned the light on. Hope gave a yell when she saw someone standing there. It took a second or two for her eyes to adjust.

It was Reece.

Of course it was.

Who else would it be?

He was standing with his back to her, looking outside. He had a glass of water in his hand. His ass was… it was… Could an ass be beautiful? Could a back be considered gorgeous? His shoulders were wide. He was all hard lines and roped muscle covered in bronzed skin. He was… turning around. *Shit! Holy freaking shit balls!* 'Balls' was right!

He turned slowly… very slowly. First looking over his shoulder and then turning all the way to face her. "I take it you couldn't ?" His voice was thick with disuse.

Don't look down.

Don't!

His hair was mussed. How could one person be this sexy?

"Ummm… ah…" *Speak! Spit it out, dammit!* "Yes… I mean, no, I couldn't… um… sleep. Sorry, you startled me. I thought you were in bed."

He gave her a half-smile. Now? In the middle of the freaking night, naked, and he chose to smile at her for the first time. It caused her stomach to flip-flop. It made her feet feel like lead. That was some smile. It lasted all of half a second and made it all the more attractive. "I was in bed. I couldn't sleep either. My mind works overtime as soon as I lie down."

"Maybe you just needed something to relax you." It sounded like she was flirting. Like she was alluding to sex. Was she? Maybe. No!

"I normally fly… hard, for a while. It works." He shrugged his big shoulders. "I can't tonight, though."

"You're babysitting me."

"That's okay, I don't mind. I was sick of lying there staring at the ceiling."

"So, you thought you would stare out at nothing, instead." She looked past him out the window, taking a few steps towards him. It was still beautiful, even though she couldn't see the view. The sky was slightly less black than the land. It was vast and dark and there was something to that. The stars twinkled overhead. There was a sliver of a moon. "It's magnificent," she whispered, almost to herself. She looked at Reece.

Crap!

Crappity crap!

It couldn't be. *No! Shit!* It was. Reece was staring at her chest. As in *staring.* There was a hunger in his gaze which moved downward to her legs before coming back up... slowly. It made her swallow hard. It made her nipples tighten. She folded her arms.

Reece lifted his eyes. He cleared his throat, looking down, but not before she saw it. Desire! He wanted her. He was just as attracted to her as she was to him. He might not like it, but he was. Reece turned back to the window, his movement abrupt. He put a hand on the pane, his fingers tight on his glass of water.

Shit!

This wasn't good at all. She needed to defuse this and fast. "Um..." She turned toward the kettle, putting it on. "Do you want some t-tea? I'm making some for myself. Chamomile. It always helps me sleep when I'm feeling wound up." She glanced down, biting her lip. She was in her little pink pajamas. The tight little tank top with hearts all over it, and the even smaller shorts. Her boobs were all over the place. She groaned inwardly. If she had known he was there, she would've put her robe on. Changed. Not come out looking like this.

The worst part of it all was that she did feel wound up. It had been a very long time since she'd had sex. Maybe that was it.

Wound up.

Yes, she was.

Was the length of time without sex strictly to blame? Um… no… It was the man across the room from her.

"I'm okay… thanks," he muttered, still facing the window.

"No, really, you should have some. Staring at the ceiling isn't fun. Just lying there is… it's awful," she stammered, sounding completely out of sorts… which she was. There it was, that awkwardness between them. It was glaring.

"I should probably get dressed." His voice was a deep rasp.

She glanced back, noting that he was still standing there. Hope didn't say anything. She should probably tell him that she'd seen him naked a ton of times, and that it didn't matter. But it did… matter. It mattered a whole hang of a lot. She made a noise of agreement as she hunted down a mug. She placed a teabag inside the mug.

"I'm going to stand here a little longer first. If it doesn't bother you."

"Not at all." She glanced his way. From this angle, she caught his reflection in the glass.

Oh god!

Ohhhhh!

This was worse than she thought. Way worse. Reece had an erection. It was impossible to miss on account of him being a big guy... a really big guy. Her heart went nuts in her chest. "Maybe I should find a robe or a sweater or something." Her eyes were wide.

"Are you cold?"

"No... but... I... um. Are you sure you don't want some tea? Tea would help." With his erection? It would not help with his erection. Why was she insisting on tea?

Oh hell! Reece had an erection. He was attracted to her. What now? This was a bit of a mess. All she felt was... good. It actually made her feel *good* that someone like Reece was having a moment because of her. Someone so serious, so together, was a little ruffled—because it was clear that he was ruffled—and all because of her. She had done this to him. Hope wasn't sure if she still could be sexy and desired and wanted. It turned out that she could. That she was. It was a rush.

Hope stifled a smile. She pulled in a deep breath, glancing his way. His ass was pulled tight. His glutes were working overtime. If she was a guy, she might just have an erection of her own right then too. This was manic. It made her laugh. It was a silly, slightly hysterical laugh she couldn't hold back. The situation was crazy. If anyone had told her, even a couple of weeks ago, that she'd be in a kitchen with a naked guy—a gorgeous, fully erect, naked guy—she'd have told them that they were certifiable. Yet, here she was.

"What's so funny?" Reece asked, glancing over his shoulder at her. He looked angry. He was frowning darkly. Hope knew that it wasn't anger.

"Um... nothing..." She giggled some more. "I'm sorry. I shouldn't be laughing. I think I'm going to put some more clothes on. Can I get you pants… a pillow? Something?" She made a face.

Reece grimaced. He put a hand over his groin area. "My sincerest apologies, Dr. Bristol. I…" He winced.

"Hope. It's Hope, please. I think we're way beyond formalities."

"I guess we are." Reece turned.

Holy fucking shit! His hand couldn't cover what he was packing. Not even close. Not even a little bit.

"You really shouldn't look at me like that, Doctor."

"I… I'm sorry," she mumbled. "I… um…" She whipped herself around and poured the water into her cup, hoping that the thing had actually boiled. She wasn't sure.

"I'm the one who should be apologizing. It's so wrong. After all you've been through, and here I am… I… I'm an asshole. I'm despicable. You are safe with me, I swear. I'm going to get dressed now." He took a step forward.

"It's fine." She turned and leaned against the counter. "You're not an asshole. We can't always help what happens to our bodies."

"I'm a grown male." He narrowed his eyes. "This is unacceptable."

"You're too tough on yourself. My body reacted to you as well. It's just not as obvious."

His gaze dropped to her breasts. Her nipples were still tight. Her breathing suddenly felt shallow. Like she wasn't getting enough air.

Reece looked away. "This is bad, Doctor… Hope. It's… it's not right. You should— I'm going to go now."

"We're attracted to each other. The way I see it, we can do one of two things," she licked her lips. "We can go with it or ignore it."

"Go with it?" He narrowed his eyes. "By 'go with it' you mean that we should... That..." His jaw tightened and his throat worked. "That's not going to happen. You didn't come here for sex, remember? You came here to find yourself. That means being alone."

"Things change." Where the hell was this coming from? Maybe it was the blood pounding through her veins. Perhaps it was the tightening in her lower belly. She'd never wanted anyone more. Not ever! Why not go for it? She had nothing to lose. It's not like it would go anywhere. She wasn't staying long-term. Hope was setting up the clinic. She was going to see the royal chicks born. In a few months... she would need to get back to her life. To her practice. Her locum couldn't stay on forever. Six months had been a push.

It probably wasn't the best idea, but it could be fun. Something quick and seriously hot. She'd always balked at the idea of rebound sex. Of hook-ups in general, but that was before she found her husband of five years in bed with her sister. It was before her life had gone to hell. Maybe it was time to live a little, to let loose some. Reece could do with some fun. They both could.

There was one thing Hope knew for sure, it would be like dynamite between the two of them. Truly explosive. "I'm not looking for a relationship. That part hasn't changed. Maybe I was wrong about being alone to find myself. Maybe I was wrong about forgoing sex. We're attracted to one another, so why can't we—?"

"No," he pushed out, his voice gruff. "Absolutely not! I gave an order to my males. An order to my team."

"You're the boss. It doesn't count for you."

"It counts double for me. As much as I…" He shook his head. "Not happening, Dr. Bristol." He marched out of the room.

Hope wondered if she should feel bad. If she should feel guilty for coming onto Reece. For trying to seduce him. For being everything he was afraid she would be. She didn't feel bad. For the first time in years, she felt alive. They were two consenting adults who were attracted to each other… big time. Why not act on it? Get it out of the way. Get each other out of their systems. Once or twice should do it. She just needed to find a way to convince him of that.

CHAPTER 17

What the hell was wrong with him?

The female had offered. Hope had all but put herself on a golden platter for him, and he'd turned her down. Perhaps if he mounted her once… just once. No! Not once. It had been an age since he had taken a female to his furs. He would need to mount her twice. The first time would be fast and over too quickly. The second time would be all for her.

Wait!

He needed to stop. He was thinking like he was going to go through with this craziness, and he wasn't. He couldn't. Reece needed to maintain focus. He wouldn't be able to do that if he mounted Hope… Dr. Bristol. If he tasted her snatch. If he felt her tighten around him. If he heard her cries of pleasure.

Blast!

By feather, but he was hard again. He was sick of being hard. Sick of taking cold showers. All he needed to do was make it through the day. One lousy day, and Locke would be back. They could go back to seeing very little of one another. There would be no opportunities after that.

His stomach growled loudly. It was mid-morning, and he hadn't eaten yet. He'd heard Dr. Bristol get up earlier. He'd listened to her shower. Not long after that, he heard her in the kitchen, dishes rattling.

Aside from showering twice, Reece hadn't left his room. He was a coward. Reece would think nothing of heading into battle, talons at the ready. Hell, he'd head up the charge. Yet, here he sat, in his room, hiding from a tiny female.

His stomach grumbled again. He put a hand to his abs. Blast it all to hell! He was done hiding and done being a yellowbelly.

Reece pulled on a pair of jeans. He hated how tight they were, but at least they would hold him together if need be. He couldn't understand it. It was like he was a damned juvenile again, with no control over his own body. The previous night was one of the most embarrassing ordeals of his life. He was mad at himself for what happened.

The way the doctor looked in her sleepwear would be burned into his mind for a long time. The plump swell of her breasts. The tight buds of her nipples. Her lush thighs. The full globes of her ass through the tight cotton. His balls tightened, causing him to groan.

Perhaps he needed to go on one of those weekends away. Perhaps once the chicks came, he could do it. Humans were delectable. He hadn't expected to be this attracted to one.

Reece took a couple of deep breaths before walking to the living room and kitchen area. Dr. Bristol was outside on one of the loungers next to the pool.

Blast! She wore those tiny covers again. He'd get something to eat and head back to his room. If that made him a yellow-bellied coward, then so be it.

Dr. Bristol spotted him. She sat up and waved like a mad person. He'd rather get feather rot than talk to her, especially in such a state of undress. What if she tried to seduce him again? How was he supposed to turn her down? A male only had so much willpower. They had a job to do. He had given his orders, and he needed to obey them himself. Also, she'd been through an ordeal yesterday. She'd had bad news, he'd be taking advantage if he mounted her.

Reece opened the refrigerator and grabbed two of those easy meals. He placed them inside the heating box and pressed a couple of buttons. They made beeping noises, but nothing happened. The box didn't start up. *What was wrong?* He tried again, pushing different buttons… still nothing.

Reece was getting ready to put the meals back and to go with bread instead when he heard soft footfalls behind him. He squeezed his eyes shut. No! Why couldn't she leave him alone?

"Everything okay?"

His heart rate picked up immediately. What a fool he was to be acting this way. "Um… yes… all good." He prayed to all the gods and pushed the buttons again.

Nothing.

Blast! It couldn't be that difficult to operate this thing. "There must be something wrong with the heating box," he muttered, steeling himself to turn around. To face her.

He was not a coward. He could face one measly human. Reece turned, practically holding his breath.

Dr. Bristol was smiling brightly. Thank all that was both furry and feathered, she was wearing a dress over her small coverings. She still looked amazing. The dress showcased her deep cleavage. It was flowery and pretty. "Morning, sleepyhead. I take it you decided to sleep in after your bout of insomnia."

"I haven't slept at all."

Her face darkened with concern. "Oh! I'm sorry to hear that. I just assumed since you… stayed in your room so late, that…" She chewed on her plump lower lip.

He shrugged. "It is what it is. I hope you managed better than I did." They were talking such nonsense. Next, it would be a discussion on the weather patterns. Things had gone from stilted to downright… uncomfortable between them. In a few hours Locke would be back, and they could go back to how things were.

"You don't have to heat those meals. I made a ton of pancakes and bacon. I used mashed bananas instead of eggs, so you can eat them. If you were hiding out to avoid me… I'm sorry I made you uncomfortable. The food is a peace offering." She gestured to the table, where plates were stacked high, full of delicious-looking things.

"More flat food." He frowned. "Are you partial to thin foodstuffs?"

Hope laughed, her eyes twinkling in the sunlight. "No… it's coincidental. They're pancakes. They're really delicious, I promise. I would suggest plenty of maple syrup drizzled over the top. I eat mine with bacon and syrup, but you need to see how you like them." She gestured to a jug filled with golden liquid. "These are the strawberries everyone was talking about the other night." She touched a bowl with red fruits inside.

"The flat food from last night was very good, so I will take your word for it. Thank you for the kind offering."

She handed him a plate. "Pizza is definitely one of my favorites." She pulled in a breath. "Again, I'm sorry. I shouldn't have come on so strong and in the light of day it was probably better that we didn't… you know…" She widened her eyes, licking her lips.

Reece wondered if all humans were this open and forthcoming. He liked it. He liked it very much. There was so much more to this female than he ever realized. "I'm glad you feel that way. I thought that you might be upset or that you…" He didn't finish his sentence.

"You thought I might try to change your mind?" She narrowed her eyes for a few moments, scrutinizing him.

"I thought you might try."

She shook her head. "No. I wouldn't do that. I guess you could say that I had a moment of weakness last night. For the record, I haven't changed my mind. I think it's better that we didn't, but if I could turn back the clock, I would proposition you all over again." She giggled, her face turning pink.

That didn't make sense. This female was confused. Her emotions were all over the place.

"Don't worry. I won't try to force myself on you, or try to get you to change your mind. Just know that if you do, I'm not going anywhere. It might be good for both of us if…" She closed her eyes and gave her head a shake. "There I go again. I'll leave it at that. Enjoy the food. I'll be out on the deck reading." She pointed to the door.

"Thank you. Your honesty is refreshing. I had heard that humans didn't like talking about sex… or their emotions."

"I guess some people are shy about it, but most of us are open. We're in the twenty-first century. Women can express their opinions on the subject."

"Absolutely." He nodded. "It's the Feral female who is in the driver's seat. They would be the ones to decide everything when it comes to mounting and choosing a mate."

"It should be equal. Both parties should have a say. Honesty is everything. It's something I've had to learn the hard way. I saw signs that there were problems in my marriage, and I didn't face up to them. I didn't talk to Emmet about the problems we were having. He lied and cheated. I can't help but think that if I had spoken up, that maybe…"

"That you might still be together?" he offered, when she stopped talking.

"Maybe." She shrugged, looking deep in thought. "Or perhaps we could have called it quits before he slept with Lizzie behind my back. So now, I've decided to be more forthcoming about the way I feel and the things I want."

Namely, sex with him.

Fuck! He was so damned tempted. This female was technically still mated. Dr. Bristol was off-limits for so many reasons. "Have they calmed down about your di-vor-ce not going through?" Another one of those human words he had to wrap his tongue around.

"No." She shook her head, her eyes clouding. "Lizzie won't speak to me. I even tried calling her earlier, and she ignored me. I see that she's read my messages, but she won't answer me. She thinks I won't go back home on purpose. She thinks I still want Emmet. That I'm trying to hurt her on purpose. I would never do that." She licked her lips. "Surely if I wanted Emmet so badly, I would be there contesting the divorce, not hundreds of miles away? It doesn't make any sense. She isn't being rational." He noted that her eyes glinted with unshed tears.

"Your sister needs time to process everything. She will come around. It might also be that she is over-emotional because of the child she carries."

Her eyes brightened, and Hope smiled. It floored him how beautiful she was. Blast and damn, but he was feeling things he shouldn't.

"You're right. I will keep trying. Hopefully she'll realize that I mean it. That I want a divorce just as much as they do. I'm going to go now. I'm sure you want your space on your off day."

He was enjoying speaking with her, but he nodded anyway. Putting some distance between them was a good thing. Reece watched her walk outside. He watched as she pulled her dress over her head, laying back down on the lounger. He swallowed, forcing himself to look away. Reece piled up his plate with everything. He tasted the syrup, making a noise of enjoyment. The pancake was good, too. Reece decided to take the food back to his bedroom.

Hope still wanted him. No, that wasn't true. She didn't really know what she wanted. That was the thing about coming out of a bad relationship. It left a person raw for a good long time. He would know. What happened to him all those years ago still left a bitter taste in his mouth. Walking away was the right thing for him to do. It was! He pushed his bedroom door closed behind him, hearing it click. He put the food down and then opened the door slightly. Reece didn't think that the human was in any danger, but he couldn't be too careful. He needed to stay vigilant.

CHAPTER 18

LATER THAT DAY...

Hope heard Reece clear his throat.

Her wide-brimmed hat blocked her view from down there on the lounger, so she was forced to crane her head to see him.

He looked so good in jeans. They were the light, faded kind. They hugged his narrow hips and muscular thighs. He had that whole 'V' thing going on. She quickly lifted her eyes to his, thankful she could hide her stares behind dark glasses.

"I'm going to fly for an hour or so." He gestured with his chin upwards. "There's only so long a Feral can sit between four walls. I need to shift. I need to spread my wings, to feel the wind between my feathers." He closed his eyes for a few seconds, the sun on his handsome face.

"Sounds good." She could see that he was excited about it. "I'm a little jealous."

He gave her a hint of a smile, making her mouth feel dry in an instant. "You wouldn't enjoy it much, Dr. Bristol. It's going to be hard and fast."

"Maybe I like hard and fast." She was wrong on every level. Hope had to bite back a smile when she saw how uncomfortable he became. Reece took a step back and then pushed his hands into his jean pockets. Then he took them out and folded his arms.

He was so darned cute. Hope had a soft spot for him. She wished for the tenth time that he had agreed to her proposal. Sex with no strings attached. No, make that sex with Reece, with no strings attached. "You don't… like it fast, Dr. Bristol." He got this shy look. "It made you feel unwell last time, and that was nothing compared to the speed I plan on going today." He chose to ignore her innuendo.

"Hope," she corrected.

"Zaire is outside. He won't intrude, but he's here if you need him. He'll keep you safe until I get back." He ignored her request to call her by her first name. Hope decided to drop it.

"Okey dokey. Have fun."

"I will." He turned and left.

Hope watched him walk away. She lay back down on the lounger, enjoying the afternoon sun. After a minute, she picked up her book and started reading. At some point, she must have dozed off, because she was startled awake when someone cleared his throat.

Reece.

Back so soon.

She frowned. Then again, the sun was lower on the horizon. She squinted, looking up. It wasn't Reece. His eyes leaned more to yellow than golden. His hair was white-blond, cut short against his scalp. He gave her a grin. "Hi… I thought I would come and introduce myself." He held out his hand. "I'm Shard."

Hope slowly rose to a sitting position. Her book fell to the floor. "Oh… oops." She picked it up, placing it on the lounger next to her. Then she took his hand, noting the firm grip. "I'm Dr. Hope Bristol." She stifled a yawn. Yep, she'd been sleeping alright. Making up for her bad night.

"It's lovely to meet you, Dr. Bristol. May I?" He gestured to the lounger next to hers.

"Of course." She felt around the back of her chair for her dress.

"Don't get dressed on my account," the guy—Shard—said. "We're shifters, nudity is completely normal, which means you're actually overdressed." He laughed.

She smiled, pulling her dress over her head despite what he had just said. Perhaps she was taking Reece's warnings to heart. She wasn't sure. Maybe it was the way this shifter was looking at her. Not that he outwardly checked her out or anything. It wasn't that.

"So, you're here to help the queen lay her eggs, Hope? You don't mind if I call you Hope, do you?"

She shrugged. "I don't mind. I prefer it when I'm not working, otherwise it's Dr. Bristol."

"Fair enough." He smiled. It was charming. Shard was a good-looking guy. He brimmed with confidence. "I'm the head guard, in case you were wondering. I thought I would drop by to… introduce myself and to check if there was anything you needed. Are all your security needs being met?"

"Nice to meet you, Shard," she said. "I'm all good. I don't need anything. My security needs are most definitely being met. Thank you for checking." She was eager to get back to her book, but didn't want to come across as rude.

"I'm glad to hear it. How are things with the queen?"

"I'm not at liberty to say. Claire is my patient. It's confidential information." She didn't think he was prying intentionally, but she couldn't discuss Claire's medical records with anyone without consent.

His eyes widened. "Of course. My apologies. Where are you from? I've been to various human cities over the last year or so. I've worked hard to learn about your species."

"Oh… planning on taking a human mate at some point?" It seemed like most of the guys wanted that.

"Definitely." He nodded. "I was mated. I lost my female to clutch sickness." His eyes clouded for a moment.

Hope felt sorry for him. She couldn't imagine all they must have gone through. "That's terrible. I'm so sorry."

"Yes, it was terrible. An awful, dark time in our lives. Many years have since passed and I feel that I am ready to… move on. Not that I would ever forget my love. Nerusha was everything to me. She was my world." He looked down.

"I can imagine," Hope replied. She wasn't sure what to say.

"Anyway, that was a long time ago." He looked into the distance; his eyes were still clouded. "On a happier note, what do you think of our beautiful landscape?" He smiled.

"Magnificent." It was Hope's turn to take in the exceptional view. She didn't think she'd ever tire of looking out over the vast lands.

"Will you be staying once the royal chicks are hatched?"

"Maybe for a couple of months. I'm helping set up the clinic. I'll probably be involved in finding my replacement, but I don't think I'll stay... no."

"That's a great pity, Dr. Bristol. I think that we could use someone with your expertise. Also, you are a very beautiful woman, if you don't mind me saying."

"Um... thanks," Hope said to be polite. Shard seemed pleasant enough, but... she wasn't interested at all. She hoped he wasn't going to come onto her or anything.

"Perhaps we could have dinner together one of these nights? I would love to get to know—"

There were heavy footfalls on the wooden deck. "What are you doing here, Shard?" Reece's eyes were practically on fire. They seemed to glow. His hands were curled into tight fists at his sides. His jaw was tight. He wore the same blue jeans, but the top button was undone, like he'd dressed in haste.

"Reece, good to see you." Shard smiled broadly. "I came over to introduce myself to Hope."

"That's Dr. Bristol," Reece growled. He took a step forward, and for a second or two, she was sure he was going to hit Shard. "Have some respect."

"My apologies." Shard got this smirk as he turned to her. "You said you were okay with me calling you by your first name?"

Now he was putting her on the spot. "I... um... don't mind."

"Well, I mind." Reece cocked his head. "Dr. Bristol is too polite to set you straight."

"Dr. Bristol," Shard winked at her like it was a big joke between the two of them. Like Reece was the joke—which she didn't like at all, "is an intelligent woman. The doctor would tell me if I stepped out of line."

"Why are you even here?" Reece took another step toward them, eyes on Shard. They were still narrowed and still blazing.

Shard stood. "I told you why I came."

"To introduce yourself. Funny you would wait until I was elsewhere to do so."

"You shouldn't leave your post," Shard smirked. "Or let your guard down. It's not on me that you did."

"I didn't let my guard down. Zaire is here in my place," he growled. "Don't change the subject. You waited until I was gone to pounce. That's a pussy move if I ever saw one. I see some things don't change."

Shard narrowed his eyes, his face twisting with rage before he caught himself and schooled his expression.

Hope stood up. She could see the animosity building between the two men. Shard's jaw was tight, even though he was still smirking.

"I'm fine. Everything's fine," she tried to defuse the situation. "There's nothing going on. Shard was—"

"Everything is not fine, Hope. This bastard waited for me to leave so that he could make a move on you. He snuck around because he knows it's wrong."

"Why is it okay for you to call Dr. Bristol Hope?"

"Dr. Bristol is my charge." Reece narrowed his eyes. "We are sharing a house." The two men looked like they were squaring off to fight. "I don't have to answer to you!"

"Charge?" He nodded. Shard took a step closer. "I can ask the doctor out if I want. She doesn't report to you. Unless," he lifted his brows, "unless the two of— "

"Unless nothing! You can stop right there." Reece's voice was barely audible, which was somehow all the more menacing.

"Okay, so then it's perfectly fine if— "

Reece took another step towards Shard and growled low in his throat.

"Um..." Hope stepped in between the two men. She looked from Shard to Reece and back again. "Wait! Stop this, please. I'm not interested in dating anyone at this stage. Thanks for the offer, but I have to decline," she told Shard.

"Don't decline on account of him." All traces of humor had long since left Shard's face. "We could have a whole lot of fun together, Doc." He didn't take his eyes off of Reece, whose muscles roped and bulged. Reece looked like he was going to hit Shard at any second.

Hope was sure Reece was going to shift. His eyes glowed brightly. He was magnificent and terrifying all at once. Reece made a screeching noise that had goosebumps rising on her whole body. "I'm giving you ten seconds to walk away," he told Shard.

"You can't order me around. I don't report to you. The way I see it, you're probably a rung below me at this point." He smirked. His eyes were hard and cold.

"You wish! I report to the king, not to you. Never to you!"

"Let's wait and see what— "

"Please stop!" Hope turned to face Shard, still keeping herself between the two men. "Please, just go."

"Getting tiny human females to fight your battles nowadays? Pathetic!"

Reece put his hands on her hips and physically moved her to the side. The two shifters bashed chests as soon as she was out of the way. Reece put his face in Shard's face. "You're a lying, cheating bastard!"

"I didn't lie or cheat. It was above board. It's about time you came to realize that, Reece. Just because things didn't work out for you doesn't mean—"

"Stop this! Stop! I mean it."

Shard took a deep breath and stepped back. Hope watched as he forced himself to relax. He even gave her a tight smile. "If we fight, the human might get hurt. I will do the responsible thing and back down. I will leave now, since I said what I came to say." He locked eyes with her. "If you change your mind about that date—"

"She won't change her mind!" Reece snarled.

"I can speak for myself," Hope interjected.

Shard grinned, looking pleased with himself.

Reece pulled in a deep breath. Every muscle tensed. His face was a mask of pure rage. His eyes... *Holy crap.*

"I think it would be better if you left," she told Shard.

"Nice meeting you, Doc!" He winked at her. "I hope to hear from you soon."

Reece growled, and Shard laughed as he turned to leave.

They watched until he disappeared out the front door. "That is why you shouldn't dress like that," he growled at her. "That asshole is exactly why I insist we call you Dr. Bristol. Maybe now you will understand why I act the way that I do." He took in a deep breath, his eyes still blazing. "If I hadn't arrived when I did..." He shook his head looking disappointed... in her? *Surely not!*

"What then? What exactly do you think would have happened?"

"I know that you are looking for sex. For a good time. I didn't give it to you. Perhaps you would have accepted Shard's proposition of a date. You do know that he doesn't actually want to date you. He wants to mount you."

"What? I can't believe you just said all of that." She made a noise of utter frustration. *Where did he get off?* "I wasn't born yesterday. I know exactly what he wanted."

"Why didn't you turn him down when he asked you?"

"I didn't get a chance to turn... No, make that—I *did* turn him down and more than once." *What was wrong with him?*

"Only because I arrived when I did. Perhaps you would have accepted otherwise. You turned him down to defuse the situation, not because you didn't want a date." He snorted as he said 'date.'

"I would *not* have accepted." He was making her so damned angry. "And so what if I had? What's it to you?" *Screw him!*

"That male is trouble." Reece pointed in the direction that Shard had taken.

"He seemed fairly sweet to me," Hope said it to anger Reece. He was really pissing her off with his accusations. It was getting tiring. Just when she thought they had moved on from that. She wasn't sure what she even saw in Reece. Why couldn't she be attracted to someone else?

"Don't let me stand in your way, then," Reece snarled. "Should I call him back?"

"You're not in my way. That's just it. I'm not interested in Shard! For the record, I can take care of myself, you know."

"Can you?" He folded his arms, looking at her like he thought she was full of hot air.

"You're the one who's the asshole, Reece. Just because I made my feelings of attraction known to you—*you*—does not mean that I want to sleep with the whole damned lot of you. I'm attracted to *you*. I wanted sex with *you*. Now I wish I hadn't said anything because you still keep doing this." She gestured wildly with her hands. "What's wrong with you?"

"There's nothing wrong with me. I'm a male in my prime."

"I wasn't talking physically wrong. Look, please forget I ever told you how I feel… forget it. That's all I ask. I've changed my mind completely. I wouldn't touch you if you were the last man on Earth."

"I'm not a man, I'm a Feral."

"Same thing." She shrugged.

"It's not the same, Doctor, not even close. If you want sex so badly…" He closed the space between them, putting his chest against hers in much the same way as he had with Shard. His eyes were blazing just as brightly. "I will be the male to give it to you."

CHAPTER 19

"I wouldn't touch you if you were the last man on Earth," she spat the words at him. Her whole stance was rigid.

This was going from bad to worse. Why was the female angry with him? He didn't get it. He had saved her from a bad situation. Didn't she see that? "I'm not a man, I'm a Feral." His voice was a deep rumble. That was half the problem; she assumed, somehow, that Feral males were the same as men. Ferals were base creatures at heart.

"Same thing."

"It's not the same, Doctor, not even close." Rage simmered just below the surface. He couldn't believe the nerve of that male. Reece would not stand by and watch Shard trample over everything all over again. That bastard wanted to take advantage of Hope, plain and simple. The doctor was too kind… far too sweet. Hope couldn't see what an asshole he was. She was going through a tough time. She didn't know what she wanted herself. Letting Shard mount her would be a mistake. One he could not allow to happen.

Reece would look after her and ensure her happiness above all else. That her needs were met and in every way. Technically, the king had asked this of him, *not* Shard or any of the others. That prick could go straight to hell! He was not getting this female. "If you want sex so badly," he closed the space between them, "I will be the male to give it to you." It was a simple solution. Why hadn't he thought of it earlier? They could've spent the night together. He could've accepted her advances.

If he was the one to mount her, he could control when and where it happened. He wouldn't let his guard down. Not for a minute. She wasn't interested in a relationship, so he could keep emotions out of the equation.

Reece expected her to reach up and put her lips on his, or perhaps give a coy smile. Instead, he was met with a scowl. Her blue eyes turned stormy.

"Don't do me any favors!" She rolled her eyes and turned around, picking up her things. "I cannot believe you would even suggest such a thing."

Confusion hit. What was wrong now? She had offered him sex last night. All of a sudden, she didn't like the idea. "Fine! Go to Shard… or any of the others. It—"

She turned around so suddenly he took a step back. Reece had not known that humans could move quite that quickly. Then she threw something at him. It hit him square in the middle of his chest. "What was that for? Why are you so angry? You wanted sex. I'm offering to give it to you. I might not have any recent experience, but I have not forgotten how to please a female, if that is your fear."

She groaned and scrubbed a hand over her face, looking at the floor for a few moments before locking eyes with him. "That isn't my fear. I'm sure you're quite capable."

That was a relief.

"Why are you doing this?" she asked. "Although I can guess," she muttered to herself, folding her arms.

Had she not heard him? "You want sex, Dr. Bristol. You mentioned that you were attracted to me. That is why I am doing it. I will give you what you need."

Hope sighed. "You're a lost cause." She picked up the object at his feet. He noted that it was a book. Then she started towards the house. Her jaw was set. Her whole stance radiated anger.

"Wait," Reece called after her. "I don't understand. I thought you wanted to have sex with me."

"I thought so too but it turns out I was wrong." She didn't turn back as she spoke, so he followed her into the living room.

"I still don't understand. Are you so enamored with Shard? Is that it? After seeing him, you don't want me anymore? Do you want him instead?" His voice became deep. His whole stance tightened.

She growled as she turned around. Her eyes were blazing. "For the last time, I am not a Feral. I'm not wired to have sex with a whole lot of guys. I liked you yesterday and today it's Shard. Tomorrow it might be someone different. Then it'll be back to you… No! That's not me." She touched her chest. "I'm attracted to *you.* At least I *was* attracted to you when I thought you were a nice guy. When I thought you wanted me too. I thought we could have something that could be mutually beneficial. A working relationship during office hours and plenty of sex at night for as long as we're both into it. It turns out that I was wrong."

"I *am* a nice male."

"Nice?" She snorted. "You're so far from nice it's crazy. You're a control freak."

"I *am* nice," he growled. "I'm honest. I have honor." He beat a fist against his chest. "I also try to do what's right. I have *your* best interests at heart. I am attracted to you, Hope. I'm greatly attracted to you, but I don't want to take advantage of you while you are in a vulnerable state." He felt everything in him bristle and tighten. "I certainly don't want a male like Shard taking advantage. He was once my best friend. Trust me when I tell you that he doesn't have your best interests at heart. He only thinks about himself. He has plenty of experience with human females. He wouldn't misunderstand you as much as I do but—"

"Stop there. I'm not interested in Shard or anyone else. I'm attracted to *you,* Reece. Only you. I don't want a relationship, but I also don't want to sleep with other guys. I don't know if that makes sense, but that's where I am at this point in my life. As to being vulnerable… thanks for caring, but I'm a grown-ass woman who can make my own decisions. I know what I want and what I don't want. I realize that this would be rebound sex. So what? Loads of people have sex to get over bad marriages. There's a saying," she scrunched up her nose in thought, looking sexy as anything, "you have to get under someone to get over someone… or something like that. It was just a thought I had. Probably not a very good one. My thinking was that it could be beneficial to both of us. You could learn about human women and I could—"

"Please stop there…" Her cheeks were a bright rosy pink. Her skin was slightly browned from lying in the sun. That flowery dress looked amazing on her. This would complicate things, but he was doing it. It had been a very long time since he'd wanted something this badly… or someone this badly. It was mutual. It was perfect. "I want you under me, Hope. I want you under me so badly, I—"

Hope dropped her book and jumped into his arms. His mouth closed over hers, his hands gripped her ass. *Fuck!* It was one hell of an ass. He groaned into her mouth, his tongue toying with hers.

Hope pushed herself against him. All of her softness mashed against him. She whimpered, and his hard cock pressed up against her belly.

He gripped her ass a little tighter. Then he dipped his head down and nipped at her throat. "I want you… so badly. I can't think straight…"

"Yes… we need to hurry," she murmured.

Blast and damn! "Locke will be home soon. I'm a fool for waiting this long." They were walking toward the bedroom. Reece still had his hands on her ass. She was walking backward. He was maneuvering her to where he wanted her… namely, his bed. "You're so beautiful," he whispered, pushing her up against the wall in the hallway, pressing himself against her. His mouth found the pulse at the base of her throat. He breathed in her scent while he kissed her neck.

Hope hooked a leg around his thigh. Her breathing was rapid. He could feel the thrum of her pulse against his mouth.

Reece cupped a hand over her snatch. He rubbed in the vicinity of her nub. Hope's eyes flew open and she moaned.

Good, she liked that. He figured that human females would be much the same as Feral females, but he wasn't entirely sure. He tried again, rubbing with one finger.

Her mouth fell open and she made a little noise of frustration, even though it was laced with pleasure. Reece reached under her dress, stroking her through the thin snatch-covering. She moaned and arched into him.

He yanked the fabric aside, looking into her eyes. Reece ran a finger over her seam. "Wet," he whispered.

"Yes…" Her eyes fluttered closed, and her head fell back as he rubbed his fingertip over her swollen nub, using her own juices as lubrication. "Oh… that feels good… Oh…"

Reece pushed a finger into her, and she groaned low, her mouth opened in an 'O.'

"So tight." He swallowed thickly. She was going to feel amazing on the end of his prick. "I'm not sure… um… what you need. It has been a long time since I was last with a female, and I… I have no experience with humans."

"This is a good start." Her voice was strained. Her hips rocked against his hand. "An amazing start."

He didn't want to assume. "Do you like sex on all fours… on your knees? Would you prefer that?"

"I don't have a preference… oh… oh…" He was thrusting a little deeper, moving his hand faster. "I don't mind either… ooohhh… way." Her breathing was ragged.

"What about my mouth on you?" His balls pulled tight just thinking about tasting her.

"That would be—" She sucked in a sharp breath as he put his thumb onto her nub, still fingering her. "Oh, god… Oh!" she moaned loudly. "I would love… love… oh… your mouth… your fingers are amazing too. Your mouth… ohhhh…" She was rocking harder against his hand. Her mouth was open a little, and her eyes were hazy. Her voice was laced with pleasure. Husky and yet high-pitched.

"I'm sure I will need to be very careful. You're so soft and tender."

"No!" She gripped his arms. "I want hard sex. Don't be soft and tender." Her eyes looked a touch panicked. Why would she panic at the thought of tender sex? He thought it would be the other way around. Reece definitely didn't understand humans… not at all.

He stopped moving. "You are a delicate human. It would not—"

She was panting a little. Two lines had appeared between her eyes as she frowned. "Listen, Reece, don't hold back. Take me like you would any other woman. I won't break… I swear. I don't want soft and tender. We're having fun. I promise, I'll let you know if I'm not happy with something."

"Noted." He rubbed on her nub a few more times. He was going to get her to cream on his hand. Then he'd take her into his room and make her scream his name a couple of times, wrapped around his cock. They had at least an hour before—

"Honey… I'm home!" a male voice shouted from the front door. *For the love of fur!*

Hope sucked in a breath. Her eyes went wide as saucers.

Reece looked up, cocking his head towards the front entrance. "Blast!" he whispered. Locke was home.

"He's early," Hope mouthed.

"I'll take care of it," Reece whispered.

"Where are you guys?" Locke shouted.

Hope frowned. "How?" she mouthed.

Reece opened the door into his bedroom. "Wait for me. We're finishing this!"

"Some other time." She shook her head.

Reece pulled her dress down. "No… now." He wanted to brush a kiss on her full, pink lips, but… it didn't feel right doing so. Too intimate, perhaps.

Thankfully, she didn't argue for once. Hope went in to his bedroom.

Reece walked out into the living room, just as Locke was getting ready to head down the hallway. He stuck his hands in his pockets, hoping that Locke didn't smell the musky scent of Hope's snatch. "Hi." *Blast!* He sounded too… nice. "What are you doing back already?" he growled. Now he sounded like he was interrogating the male. He and Locke were friends, which could be tough considering he was the male's superior.

Locke grinned, folding his arms. "Why? Did I interrupt something? Where is Dr. Bristol?" He looked around the room. "Is that her book lying on the floor?" He frowned, looking confused.

"In her bedroom. I think she is sleeping. Neither of us slept well last night."

"Oh." His grin widened. "Why would that be?" He narrowed his eyes, looking cocky.

"Not for any of the reasons that are going through your mind right now. I'm not sure on her part. I didn't get a chance to fly yesterday. I felt wound up."

"I'm sure you did," Locke said.

"Don't do that." Reece frowned. "I went for a flight today, leaving Zaire to watch over Dr. Bristol, and that bastard Shard came around." He ground his teeth just thinking about it. It still angered him, even though he and Hope had cleared the air. Excitement coursed through him at the thought of the little human. He needed to get rid of Locke, and fast.

"Oh, did he?" Locke lost all his good humor in an instant. "Why was he here?"

"He wanted to introduce himself to Hope," Reece snorted.

"Hope?" Locke lifted his brows. "You're calling Dr. Bristol Hope these days?" He lifted his brows.

"Um… we're on good terms now. At least, we *were* on good terms." It was the first thing that came to mind.

"Oh, I see." Locke scratched his chin. "What happened to ruin things?"

"Shard happened. I may have said some things to her after the bastard left. Things I regret."

Locke winced. "What things?"

"It doesn't matter. Only that she told me she can think for herself. That she doesn't need me to look out for her, or to speak for her. She told me that she doesn't think I'm very nice."

Locke chuckled. "Oh, shit! That's not good." He shook his head.

"I want to apologize to her. I need to fix this. I was out of line. You know how angry Shard makes me. That asshole waited for me to leave. He has no scruples. Hope threw her book when she stormed off," he muttered, looking at the object in question.

"Okay. We could talk until she decides to come out of her room." Locke smiled. "I'm sure you're interested to find out how my weekend went with Tracey. I can offer you a beer. We can—"

"No! Thanks," he quickly added, to soften the delivery. "I would rather wait on my own. Speak to her without an audience. Can you give me an hour or two?" Locke was technically still off duty. It would be wrong to order him to leave and might come across as suspicious if he did. Also, Reece felt bad about lying to the male. Locke might have become a friend in recent months, but he was ultimately Reece's subordinate. He was part of the royal guard. Locke could never know that this had happened between Reece and Hope. Never!

"You want me to leave after I just got back?" Locke frowned. "We flew fast all the way home. Jock and Flint were initiating races. I'm exhausted." He fake-yawned. Bastard was enjoying this.

"You? Tired? Get lost!" He gave Locke a hard look. "Go hang out with Zaire or Andy, or one of the others. I'll call you as soon as the doctor and I have talked. If you haven't heard from me in two hours, it will mean that Dr. Bristol is still holed up in her room." He shrugged.

"Should I go and check on her?"

"No... leave her. Give her some time to cool off. Shard didn't leave that long ago. If she doesn't come out, I will try again tomorrow. I don't want to force things." He shook his head, sighing. "I have to try to make it right. I acted like a," he frowned, "like a shudder. Is that the right word?"

Locke looked at him like he was crazy. "Um… no… that doesn't sound right."

"A shake?"

Locke shook his head.

"A jolt? These human words. They make no sense." He shook his head, trying hard to remember what it was.

"Oh!" Locke grinned. "A jerk. You acted like a jerk."

"That's it! And yes, I acted like a big jerk. I need to make it right so that we can continue working together."

"I most certainly won't stand in your way. I have my phone. Let me know when you're done. Or I'll be back in two hours. I'm hungry. I worked up an appetite on my weekend away." He rubbed his belly.

Reece smiled. "Did you have a good time?"

"I had the best time. Human females are delectable." The male licked his lips. "You are missing out." He gave Reece a look. "Anyway, let me get out of your feathers. I hope she forgives you."

"Me too."

"I'm sure she will." Locke smiled at him broadly. "Dr. Bristol is a very sweet female." He started towards the door, looking back over his shoulder.

Reece nodded. "I hope I didn't take it too far this time."

"Do whatever it takes to make it right." Locke laughed. Then he was gone, the door banging shut.

Reece frowned. That sounded like an innuendo. Did Locke suspect something? Probably. Suspecting and knowing were two different things.

"Is he gone?" Hope asked from behind him. Reece vibrated with need as he turned. To him, her dress seemed shorter, exposing more of her soft thighs. Her breasts looked plumper, straining against the fabric. Everything about her was beautiful, from her bright blue eyes to her tiny feet.

"He's gone but not for long." Reece advanced. There was no way he could stop this from happening. It was too late for that. It would be like trying to stop a volcano from erupting. A storm from raging. Not possible. He didn't want to. He prayed that Hope hadn't changed her mind.

CHAPTER 20

"What did you tell him?" she asked as she walked into the room.

Reece looked her way. "I said you were mad at me about the Shard incident." He took a few steps towards her, stopping just short of touching her. "That I messed up by overreacting. That I needed to fix it. That I needed to make it up to you."

"That sounds about right." She sucked on her lower lip.

"Locke advised that I do whatever it takes."

"That seems like good advice." Her voice was soft. Her breathing elevated. "Are you sure he bought—?" She gasped when he spun her around so that her belly was pressed against a large set of drawers.

He pressed himself against her ass. His erection was thick and hard. Her ass was soft and so beautiful. Hope moaned as he put his hands on her hips. "Is this okay?"

She had said she wanted rough sex. That she didn't want him to be tender.

"More than okay. This is perfect." Her scent was more prominent... more feminine. It had to be arousal. He breathed in deep through his nose, savoring it... savoring her.

"Do you want me inside you?" His voice was a low rasp, filled with so much need it scared him.

Her breathing had turned ragged, her hands were splayed on the wood. Her fingers white from clutching the edge.

"Is that what you want, Hope?" he said, when she didn't respond.

"Yes." A moan. "I want you, Reece. If I'm honest with myself, I wanted you from the first moment I saw you."

That's all he needed to hear. The urgency that rushed through him was almost more than he could take. He put a small space between them. "I won't hurt you," he growled as he yanked up her dress. He ripped off her covering, dropping the ruined garment on the floor. "Open your legs." He could feel his beast taking over. He could feel his nailbeds tingling. His feathers rubbing under his skin. He was sure his eyes would be burning brightly.

Thankfully, Hope did as he said and pushed out her ass. His breath was coming in short rasps. Reece clasped her mound. "Still wet," he whispered, hearing the awe in his own voice.

Hope sucked in air between clenched teeth. She rocked against his hand, urging him on. He pushed a finger into her welcoming flesh. Just one. He needed to bring her to completion. He wasn't going to last. Not after being celibate for so long. Not with a female like her. She arched against him and groaned. *So receptive.* His prick throbbed. His jeans felt excruciatingly tight. He wanted to rip them from his body, but for now it was better that he was held in check or he'd be too tempted to take her.

Reece pumped his finger in and out a few times before adding a second one. She groaned again, louder this time. He used his thumb and rubbed against her nub in time with each careful push. Her pussy flooded, becoming slicker. Her groans became more pronounced. Hope rocked her hips, thrusting against his hand. He loved how brazen she was. More than he had expected from a human. "Oh, god! Oh… oh!" He thrust faster, harder. "I'm going to… I'm nearly… Oh!" Her voice was high-pitched. "You should stop. We should… I want…" Very strained. "I'm going to come if you don't stop!" She groaned, low and deep.

"I want you to find completion," he ground out, leaning down so that he could say the words directly into the shell of her ear. He kept working her nub with his thumb while thrusting his fingers in and out of her welcoming flesh.

"Oh… Oh!!" Her pussy fluttered around his fingers. Reece inserted a third, keeping his ministrations soft and easy. Her snatch tightened around his hand. She arched back against him. She went from groaning and panting to completely silent for a moment. Then she all-out moaned. Long and deep. Her pussy spasmed around his fingers. He almost creamed in his pants thinking about what she was going to feel like around his cock. Hope jerked against him, taking what she needed. Once she was done, he gripped both her hips, steadying her.

"Would it be alright if—" he started to say.

"Yes!" Her voice was thick with need. "I'm on the pill, so you don't need a condom… unless…" she was panting hard, "you think it's necessary."

"I assume that this pill will stop a clutch?" he double-checked.

"Yes. It's ninety-nine percent…" she was still panting, "effective." Her snatch was a perfect deep pink. It glistened with her juices. Hope was ready for him.

Reece ripped the front of his pants open in his haste to get the zipper down. "The next time will be better," he ground out as he bent his knees. On a low growl, he crouched over Hope and entered her tight snatch in one thrust. It almost took his breath away. He growled as his hips hit her ass, as his balls slapped against her. Hope cried out, grabbing at the wood of the furniture. She mewled. Reece forced himself to count to ten… slowly. She needed to stretch to accommodate him. Also, he was so near to release already, and he hadn't started moving yet. "You feel so good," he rasped, his chest expanding as he heaved in a breath. He forced his hands to relax their hold on her hips. He didn't want to bruise her delicate skin.

Not delicate.

Not weak.

Hope was strong and ready.

She whimpered as she pushed back against him with her ass. "I need—"

"I know what you need," he whispered. His feathers rubbed. He was sure he looked part animal. His jaw might even be slightly elongated. Perhaps feathers had sprouted on his chest. His back hurt as his wings threatened to unfurl. That's why he had turned her around. It had been so long. Too long. He was so desperate for Hope. He already knew that he would need to do this again… and again. Once or twice would not be enough. He pushed those thoughts aside, pulling her dress up, bunching it in one of his hands at her hip.

"Take me, then." Her voice was pleading. She sounded just as desperate for him as he was for her.

Good!

Her snatch fit him like a velvet glove. Wet and so tight that being inside her almost hurt. He groaned as he pulled out, and then plunged back in.

Fuuuuck!

Reece bent his knees a little more to get a better angle as he pushed back into her, trying to ease his hold on her hips. Her head was thrown back. He pushed in again and again. Hard and deep. Hope moaned and groaned and mewled and panted. Her hands tightened on the wood. His sac slapped against her flesh. *So hot, so tight, so amazing.* Reece stopped moving. He was balls-deep and panting hard; his mouth felt dry. He held her from behind, his body caging hers. He forced himself to ease his grip on her hips. His nails had elongated into the start of what would be talons.

His balls were pulled so tight. His prick throbbed. Everything in him was wound tight. "I'm going to come," he ground out. *Blast and damn! Blaaast!* He had to hold on. This was about her. Not him. He could wait. He had to try to think about other things. Certainly not about how she felt around him… or how her eyes danced when she smiled. How adorable she looked when she was angry. Her full breasts. *Fuuuck!* He was grunting with every breath he took. Fighting, fighting, fighting the urge to let go.

Hope laughed. It sounded strained. "I want you to find completion," she used his words as she pushed her lush ass up against him. "Do what you need to do." She sounded husky. "I already came. Your turn."

"It's too soon." He couldn't seem to catch his breath. "I need you to come again. If I move so much as a muscle—"

"Don't worry about me, just… come…" She clenched her inner muscles, squeezing his dick tightly. He groaned, feeling sweat break out on his brow.

Reece jerked into her with a hard grunt. It had been too long. He'd been fantasizing about Hope since the first day he met her.

Reece squeezed his eyes shut as he felt her grip around him tighten. He thrust two… three… four times. And then he was coming and coming and coming. Seed flowed out of him in hard spurts. He roared as pleasure rushed through him. His movements became jerky. He put his head on her back as he slowed… groaning. Even after he stopped moving, he kept his head there, just feeling her. In awe of how amazing she felt. Soft and tight. So wet. His prick stayed hard.

Once he felt somewhat in control, he pulled out and turned her around. Her eyes shone with lust. For him. She smiled sweetly. "Now that wasn't so hard, was it?"

"We should have done that all of last night." He smiled at her. "You were right, I am an asshole."

Holy moly, but he was beautiful when he smiled. His face still had a pinched look. He was still breathing hard.

Hope looked down, noting that he was still hard. His cock was long and thick. It had a slight curve, even though he was hard. Like they hadn't even had sex. She felt wetness drip down her thighs, telling her that they had. That he had come. She felt a buzzing in her veins. She was turned on and desperate for more. Normally once was enough for her, regardless of how she got there. Right now, all she could think of was more.

Hope forgot her line of thought as Reece pulled off his pants. Peeling them down his thighs and stepping out of them, one leg at a time. His cock bobbed with every movement.

Reece moved between her legs; his gaze was firmly… there. On her girl parts. His eyelids were hooded. His eyes were a deep golden color. "Hook your thighs around my waist." His voice was deep.

They were doing this!

Again.

Heat pooled in the base of her stomach as he instructed her. As his eyes took her in.

Hope did as he said. Reece ran a finger down her slit, and she groaned. "You have a beautiful snatch," he murmured. "Lean back on your elbows or hold on tight." His jaw tightened. "I'm going to mount you until you come hard. I will hold out this time."

"Oh… um… okay." Her vagina gave a hard zing of need. Her clit actually felt like it was throbbing. "Sounds really good," she added. He was forward. Then again, she shouldn't have expected anything else from Reece. Hope leaned back, resting on her elbows.

"I need to see you." He lifted her dress.

She nodded, lifting her arms one at a time as he pulled it off. Reece looked down at her chest. His cock jutted out between them.

"This, too." He touched her bikini top. "It has to go."

She reached behind her neck and undid the tie; her breasts sprang free. Hope felt slightly unsure for a few seconds. Her boobs were big and not quite as perky since she'd hit her thirties.

His nostrils flared as he took her in. Reece looked at her like she belonged on the cover of a magazine. Like she was a pinup girl or something. "Fucking beautiful." She could see that he meant it. "Your eyes too," he added, looking into them. "Even your toes."

She giggled. "You're sweet."

"No, I'm not," Reece replied, cupping one of her breasts in his big, warm hand. "So damned sexy," he groaned as he squeezed her boob, rubbing his thumb over her nipple. He bit down on his lower lip and frowned, looking angry. Then he gripped her thigh, pulled it higher on his body, and lined his member up at her opening with his other hand. "I can't wait to take you again. I want to face you this time. I want to watch you find completion. My eyes might glow, and I… I might make loud noises. I'm part animal, and it might become apparent when I—"

"Hey." She leaned forward and cupped his cheek. "I would like nothing better than to watch you let loose. To watch you let go. I happen to like your animal side. I like you. Don't overthink this. Let's just do it already. You won't be too rough. I won't get scared if you let go… I swear."

Reece nodded. He was frowning hard. His eyes were glowing a little. "I look forward to hearing you scream."

"Scream?" She narrowed her eyes on him. "I moan and groan. I'm not much of a screamer."

His eyes got this twinkle, and he nodded. "If you say so, Doc." He said it like he didn't believe her.

Hope pulled away, leaning back on her elbows.

Maintaining eye contact, he slowly pushed into her. She was still really wet. His frown deepened with every inch. He made a soft grunting noise as he slid all the way home. Hope bit down on her lip. He was really big. She hadn't been sure that she would be able to take him. It may not have been possible if he'd been any bigger. Reece didn't move; sweat glistened on his brow. His muscles were out in all their glory. His abs... good lord, but they were fine. Reece sucked on his thumb and then used it in a slow glide over her clit. She moaned.

Holy freaking moly! He did it again, and she sucked in a breath, her eyes widening. Reece was balls-deep inside her, stretching her to capacity and not moving an inch. It was just his wet thumb that slid lazy circles around her clit, which felt really swollen. She pulled in a lungful of air and let it out slowly. "That feels good. You feel good," she pushed out.

Reece gave her the smallest of smiles and leaned down, latching his hot mouth over one of her nipples. Her back bowed. Between his mouth and his thumb... *Oh god! Oh!* She tried to move, wanted more, but his body held her in place. More accurately, his cock held her firmly in place. Her girl parts throbbed. All of them collectively.

She moaned. It was a harsh sound that reverberated around the room. Reece nipped at her nipple and a zing of need spread like wildfire, coursing through her whole body. His thumb barely brushed her puckered flesh. Soft little slippery circles that had her crying out with desperation. There sure were a ton of nerve endings in the clitoris. She could feel each and every one of them at work. He moved to her other breast and sucked on her there, too. His mouth was so warm. Reece was firm, but not too rough.

"Oh… Oh my… Oh!" Her voice was thick. Her breath coming in thick gulps. Another nip had her groaning so deeply it hurt her throat. She didn't care.

Then he was straightening up. His knees had to be bent, otherwise he would be not able to reach her. He gripped her thighs, lifting her legs so that they hooked over his shoulders. "Lie back and hold on."

She did as he said, barely fitting on the chest of drawers. There was a lamp on the end. She wanted to tell him to be careful. They should probably stop to move the thing, but— His finger glided over her and her clit throbbed. Her nipples were so tight they almost hurt. Reece leaned over her, looking her in the eyes. Her knees weren't that far away from her face. She hadn't known she was quite this flexible. His eyes bore into hers; it was intense. She'd never been more turned on in her life. She'd never been so desperate to come. When he started moving, the drawers creaked. In and out. Slow but hard. Deep. Controlled. Exactly what she would expect from Reece. Precision and concentration. Her mouth fell open, and it felt like her eyes actually rolled back in her skull.

Reece breathed in deeply through his nose. *Please let Locke stay away. Please!* She couldn't bear it if they were interrupted. Not when that coiling sensation had already begun deep within her belly. Not when she could feel that this might just be the best darned orgasm of her life. She grabbed hold of his thick biceps.

He kept going. Still slow and hard. Harder than she'd ever been taken before. Should have known she would prefer it like this to soft and gentle. She was moaning with every thrust. Reece made a grunting noise here and there. It turned her on even more to know that he was enjoying this just as much as she was. His gaze drifted to her boobs, which were jerking with every hard shove inside her.

His jaw tightened, and he swallowed. "So soft," he growled, barely sounding human. Somehow, even that was a turn-on. He tilted his head back and closed his eyes like he was barely holding on. He made a groaning noise. His muscles bulged. His features seemed more prominent, too. He was so stunning it almost took her breath away.

The coiling sensation became almost too much. The drawers were creaking louder. The chest of drawers slid a little across the floor with a scrape. The lamp teetered on the edge but seemed to hold on. She didn't care if the lamp broke. She didn't care if the chest of drawers broke as well. If the whole damned house fell down. Slow and deep had turned to hard and fast. His balls slapped against her with every thrust. Hope was making these shrieking noises. There was a wet suction sound from where their bodies joined. Even that excited her. She dug her fingers into his arms. Her boobs jiggled so hard, but it didn't matter to her. The table scraped again and creaked so loudly she was sure it would break any second. She didn't care about that either. Nothing mattered in that moment.

"Reece," she sobbed his name as the coiling reached its peak. Her hips jerked, and her head fell back. A rush of ecstasy raced through her, starting in her belly. It seemed to radiate out. It took her breath away. Everything stilled. Then her pussy spasmed hard. She gave a hard yell as everything let go.

Instead of slowing, Reece took that as a signal to redouble his efforts. His finger found her clit. She pointed her toes and gripped his arms even tighter. Too much, but so good! Hope screamed. It was ripped from her before she knew what was happening.

Reece roared. He jerked into her. Slapping, sucking, panting and moaning. The sounds they both made were laced with intense pleasure. Reece slowed, his hips rolled against her as he wrung out every last drop of pleasure from her. His frown was back, his mouth pursed. The movements slowed until he stilled altogether, staying joined with her. Reece was breathing hard. His face was serene.

He unhooked her thighs, putting them around his waist. "You are even more beautiful when you come."

"You're pretty damned gorgeous when you're roaring like a lion."

"You weren't watching me when you were screaming," he deadpanned. "Your eyes were tightly shut."

"I'll have to try harder to catch it next time." She bobbed her brows.

"Next time?" He raised his brows. "You want more?"

"Not right now but soon?" She lifted her brows... praying he agreed. She'd been right, it was dynamite between them.

"Yes, more would be possible." He frowned.

"Good." She nodded like a crazy person. "I'm not sure how we're going to make that happen without anyone finding out. Should we tell Locke?"

"No!" he pushed out. "No one can know. This needs to stay between us. I will come up with a plan that will allow us some time together."

"Okay. I would like that."

"I'll shower and pack. It would be great if you could stay in your room for a while after I leave." He winced. "You should shower as well. We Ferals have a decent sense of smell, even though it's bad for a shifter. It's way better than humans. I don't want Locke scenting... us... this." He touched her inner thigh. "I will tell Locke that you never came out of your room. You will need to act like you are upset with me tomorrow."

"I'll give you the cold shoulder."

He frowned. "Cold shoulder? I—"

She giggled. "It means that I will act cold towards you. I won't even look your way unless I really have to."

"Yes, do that. I will find a way to get more time with you to apologize."

"To make it up to me, because, although you did a good job... it wasn't nearly good enough."

His face morphed into one of horror. "I'm so sorry, Hope. I will do better next time. I swear to you!"

"Wait a second," she put a hand on his chest, "I was teasing you. You did an amazing job."

"I am out of practice but—"

"You're great! Do that again next time, and I'll be happy as Larry."

"Who is this Larry?" His voice got all gruff and raspy.

"I didn't realize how many human sayings I use. I will try to omit them going forward."

"No." He shook his head. "I want to learn."

"Happy as Larry just means very happy."

He cocked his head. "That doesn't make any sense, but I will try to remember it. Let me get you a warm towel to clean up."

"That would be great."

She watched his ass cheeks alternate up and down as he jogged down the hall. For a moment she was tempted to pinch herself. Hope turned to the front door. Thankfully, the window to the side of the door was frosted. If someone had come to the door, they would've heard them going at it like rabbits.

She felt her cheeks heat and she smiled broadly. That was the best sex she had ever had, and he was worried he hadn't been good enough. She chuckled softly to herself. Reece was going to be an amazing rebound sex buddy.

That's when she saw it. "Oh, shit!" Hope muttered.

"What is it?" Reece asked as he closed the distance between them. He handed her a towel.

Hope took it. "Look." She pointed at the broken lamp on the floor next to the chest of drawers. Apparently, her orgasm had been so good she hadn't even heard it crash to the ground.

"It's fine." Reece shrugged. "I will order another one."

"It's not fine." Hope cleaned herself with the towel while she spoke. "Locke is going to suspect that something is up. He's not an idiot."

"I will tell him that you threw the lamp at me and stormed back to your room."

"He won't buy that. He knows that I would never do something like that."

"Really now?" Reece rubbed his chest. "What about the book you threw at me?"

She choked out a laugh. "I guess you're right. You made me really mad."

"I know, and I'm sorry."

"We're having casual sex, but I'm not going to sleep with anyone else. You need to know that."

"Good to know." He hugged her for a few seconds. It felt good to be in his strong arms. She was glad she decided to take a chance to come all the way out here. Really glad!

CHAPTER 21

"There you are," Locke said, grinning. He was on the deck, tongs in hand as he watched meat cooking on the barbeque.

"And?" Hope lifted her brows. "How was your weekend away?"

"Great! Trace and I spent every minute together. I almost told her several times about being a shifter." He turned a steak; it sizzled on the barbeque.

"That smells delicious, by the way." She licked her lips. "Are you allowed to divulge such information?"

He made a face. "We have to get a female to sign a nondisclosure agreement first. I had the agreement with me in my bag, but… I don't know, it felt a little wrong, somehow. I couldn't bring myself to use the thing. I have to tell her, but I also have to keep my people safe." His eyes got a faraway look for a moment. "If I'm honest, I'm worried she won't want me anymore."

"If she has real feelings for you, she'll still want you."

"You're sweet to say that, but not everyone is as open-minded as you are. I think I know her well enough to know that she is an open-minded person, but this is big news. It's huge. You never know."

Hope nodded. "That's true." She thought she knew her sister. Her own flesh and blood—and look what happened. Lizzie still wasn't talking to her. She decided to give it a couple of days before trying again.

"Also, if I make her sign the agreement, it will look like I don't trust her. I do trust her. I just don't know if she can handle such a revelation."

"You don't have a choice in the matter, though. There are rules in place for a reason."

He looked up for a moment. "There's always a choice, so that's not completely accurate. If I really care about her, I'll trust her enough *not* to have to make her sign an official document before talking to her."

"If you're wrong, she could end up exposing the Feral species."

"She'd make herself look like a crackpot if she started spouting about griffin shifters."

"If enough people come forward with similar stories over a period of time, it will start to hold water."

"Do you think that could happen?" Locke took the last piece of meat off the barbeque, placing it on a tray. "I cooked for you, too. I figured you hadn't eaten if you were hiding from Reece. What is that all about?" He frowned.

"We haven't finished talking about *you* yet. I don't want to even talk about Reece." Hope had to work to stifle the biggest smile. She could feel it building inside her just thinking about him. She had this not entirely unpleasant soreness between her legs.

"There isn't much more to say. I like her a lot." Locke shrugged. "She wants to visit *me* next time. Which is a bit of a problem."

"Oh, boy!" She made a face. "That is a problem."

"I'll figure it out. I'm sure I'm worried about nothing. Tell me about your weekend. No, first tell me about the smashed lamp. You tried to throw it at Reece?" Locke laughed. He walked toward the door leading inside, glancing back at the last second. "Are you coming? I even made a salad."

"That's awesome. Thank you!" They walked into the kitchen and she grabbed some plates, hoping he would forget about Reece.

"Out with it. Tell me what happened already. Reece didn't say much."

"He's just infuriating, that's all." She shook her head. "Speaking for me when I'm perfectly capable. Then assuming that I want to sleep with everyone." She rolled her eyes.

"He's jealous. You know that, right?"

She frowned. "I don't know anything of the sort."

"What made you throw a lamp at him? It must have been really bad."

"I don't remember. It's all a jumble. He was rude, and I was mad. I don't think I've ever been that angry with anyone."

"Funny that." Locke rubbed his chin. "Reece also can't remember exactly why you threw the lamp." He scrutinized her for a second. "I buy it from him because he doesn't fully understand you… a human female."

"We fought. That Shard guy really set him off." She shook her head.

"Not his favorite person. That asshole should know better than to snoop around." Locke looked her over. "There's something different about you that I can't quite put my finger on."

"I'm tanned. That deck is amazing." She pointed in the general direction.

"I don't think that's it, but..." He looked at her for a little longer. "I suppose it could be. You look far too relaxed and happy for someone who just had a huge fight."

"Reece can go to hell," she pushed out. Hope didn't like sneaking around like this. "I'm not going to let him ruin my Sunday evening... that's all. I'll let him stew for a few days and then we can make up."

"Make up, huh?" Locke grinned.

She threw him a dirty look. "Not like that. What is it with you?"

"Nothing. I guess I think the two of you would make a good couple... that's all. The chemistry between you is off the charts. It could go from throwing stuff at each other to burning up the sheets in an instant."

"Stop it already!" She waved a hand. "You really think there's chemistry?" *Shit!* Was their attraction that obvious?

"Crazy chemistry. That's how I know it's jealousy making Reece a little nuts. You need to forgive him, and... just go for it."

"I'm not going for it." *Too late!* "He made that whole rule about—"

"Rules are made to be broken. It's about time that Reece lived a little. It's been so long since—"

"Since?" she asked when he didn't continue.

Locke shook his head. "Not my story to tell. Forget I said anything."

"Fair enough."

"Now let's eat before our food gets cold." He sniggered.

"What?"

"You and Reece…" He sniggered some more.

"There is no 'me and Reece,' you fool."

"Not yet, but soon." He winked at her. "Something is bound to give at some point."

She narrowed her eyes at him. "You don't know what you're talking about."

"I know exactly what I'm talking about. It's just a matter of time, mark my words. He's jealous because he wants you for himself."

"Stop right there! Let's change the subject because right now, he's on my shitlist."

"Remember what I said about going from throwing things to burning up the sheets. They're one rung apart on the ladder." He laughed.

She shook her head, looking at him like he was a crazy person, which he wasn't. Locke wasn't stupid. They weren't going to be able to mess around for too long. It looked like their rebound thing was going to be short-lived. Probably better that way. Hope couldn't help but feel disappointed. There was some relief there, too. These things had a way of turning into more, and more was the last thing she wanted.

"We can stream a movie tonight if you want?" Locke asked.

"Sounds good."

CHAPTER 22

THE NEXT NIGHT...

Hope pulled the heavy curtains aside. *Crap!* She looked out of the bedroom window. All was dark. All was quiet. Too quiet. A person could hear a pin drop.

This isn't a good idea! she quickly texted.

Three dots appeared immediately.

I agree with you.

Hope pushed out a breath, the window fogging for a few seconds. Not meeting up was the right thing to do. She knew that. Reece knew it, too, and yet, all she felt was disappointment.

Hope fired off another text. *We'll try again tomorrow.*

Another sigh fogged up the window all over again. She had warned Reece yesterday that Locke was onto them. That he hadn't caught on yet, but that it was just a matter of time. They'd texted back and forth since. That quick glimpse she'd gotten of him at shift change had her heart racing. Hope had to try not to look at him. True to their plan, she'd given him the cold shoulder. She looked back down at her phone, frowning when she still didn't see a response.

It was better this way. Much better. She let the curtain drop and was just pulling the covers back to get into bed when the softest tap sounded on the window. So soft she was sure she hadn't heard it. Her phone buzzed in her hand.

Knock knock!

What? He was here! Reece was here. She looked down at her pink pajamas. The ones that had gotten him so riled up the other night. They were simple, but sexy. A tight tank and little cotton shorts. They were a light pink with heart motifs.

Hope quickly pulled the curtains aside, trying not to make any noise. Her eyes widened when she saw him. A smile worked its way across her face. Being careful, she opened the window. Reece was naked. His cock was already semi-erect. He squeezed in through the window, immediately putting his arms around her.

"I thought you agreed that this was a bad idea," she whispered.

"It's worse than bad." He hardly made a sound, talking into the shell of her ear. "It's terrible."

"We're going to get caught."

"Not if you're very quiet."

"I'll be quiet." Her heart raced against her ribs. Thrumming hard in her chest. "The question is, will you be quiet?"

"I'm trained for stealth. Get on the bed and take this off." He touched her pajama shorts. "Tearing them off might be too noisy."

"My bed squeaks a little." She made a face. "I wouldn't suggest we use it."

He smiled. "You would choose the room with the squeaky bed." She liked this playful side of him. It was a side she hadn't seen before.

Reece looked around her room. She had the lights on the dimmest setting. Her dressing table was on the one side and the chest of drawers on the other. The chest of drawers was against the wall separating her from Locke.

Locke.

She prayed he was fast asleep. All had been silent for hours. It was the middle of the night. Still, she prayed they wouldn't wake him. On the other hand, it would be better if he knew. They could trust him to keep a secret. Reece was adamant, though. She was even a little shocked he was actually there. This was risky, and Reece was completely risk-averse.

"Come." He took her hand and led her to dressing table.

Reece gripped her hips and lifted her easily, her butt landing on the surface. Her bedside lamp was on, so they could see what they were doing. She noted that he was now fully erect. His thick cock bobbed a little as he walked. He looked serious. There were frown lines on his forehead. When he locked eyes with her, he smiled for half a second and her stomach did flip-flops. She'd never been this excited in her life.

Reece put a hand on either side of her. He leaned in and kissed her neck until he reached her ear. She felt his breath tingle for a second before he took her lobe into his mouth and nipped. Hope moaned softly.

"I've been thinking about you all day," he whispered. "Thinking about what I want to do to you."

"Oh…" She was already out of breath and he hadn't done anything yet.

"I need to taste you," he whispered. "Have to."

"Yes," she whispered back. Her eyes felt wide as he gripped her shorts in his hands. She lifted her ass so that he could slide them down her legs.

"So pretty," Reece said as he dropped to his knees in front of her. Then he picked up her foot, hooking her leg over one of his shoulders. His eyes were glued to her sex. She felt his breath against her slit. It both tickled and ignited an even greater need inside her. If that was even possible. He sniffed at her… there. And then made an almost inaudible groaning noise. Not human. The only thing she could think was that a human guy would never do that. If he did, he would be creepy as hell. When Reece sniffed at her, it ignited a fire inside her. A damned furnace. Then he licked her. His tongue was big and hot, and… She groaned, trying hard to be quiet. One of her hands was flat on the dresser and the other clutched at his hair.

"Shhhhh." He said it against her flesh, making her whole body break out in goosebumps.

Then his tongue zoned in on her clit and laved over it a good couple of times. *Good lord!* She was rocking her hips, but couldn't stop. The hand on his head gripped tighter at his hair. He sucked her. Opened his mouth and sucked. Not too hard, not too soft. She opened her eyes really wide, working hard not to make any noise. *Damn.*

He was good at this. Not rusty at all. Hope enjoyed oral sex, but Emmet hadn't felt the same. She was lucky if he went down on her once a year on her birthday. In hindsight, he was a jerk, and she felt sorry for Lizzie.

Then he pushed a finger inside her, and her mouth fell open. All thoughts of anything other than what was happening that moment evaporated as need churned inside her. She cried out softly when he crooked that finger, pushing it in and out.

Reece made a noise of enjoyment, his lips against her clit.

By now she was panting, working hard not to make moaning noises each time his finger slid back into her. There was a coiling sensation in the pit of her stomach. It was growing by the second. Her skin felt tight. Her—

Reece stopped. She tried to hold him there, between her legs, but it didn't work. He rose up, his hands pulling at her top as he licked his lips. Make that, licked her taste off of his lips. There was something really sexy about that. She lifted her arms, and he pulled her tank off. It felt like his hands were shaking. Was he that desperate for her? "I'm going to mount you now, Hope." His face had this pinched look.

The knowledge that he wanted her so badly made her feel really good… even though this was just sex and nothing more.

He cupped her breasts and squeezed lightly, running his thumbs over her nipples. Hope moaned again.

Reece cursed softly. "I wish we had more time."

"Me too." Her words were strained.

"Next time I want to taste you properly." He squeezed her boobs softly. Those thumbs working magic on her nipples. "Stick my tongue inside you while you come."

What could she say to that? It sounded too good to be true. A little dirty, too. It shocked her how much she liked dirty talk, especially from a strait-laced guy like Reece. Then he was sliding a finger over her clit, and she couldn't think. She groaned softly.

"Put your legs over my shoulders." He palmed his cock. Starting at the base and ending at the tip. It was one of the most erotic things she had ever seen. "Legs… shoulders." He lifted his brows.

She gave her head a shake to clear it. "I'm not sure…" she started to object, stopping as he lifted them and slid them over his shoulders. Yet again, she couldn't believe how flexible she could be. His finger kept up its strumming on her clit. *Holy shit!* Hope put her hands behind her and leaned back on them. Thankfully, the dressing table was big and sturdy. Her eyes felt like they might have gone back in their sockets as well as he kept up the slip and slide over that bundle of nerves. It felt so incredibly good. Between his tongue and now his finger, she was already close.

"We have to be quiet," he whispered as he lined himself up with her opening. Then he was pushing into her, one finger still on her clit. Had he been this big yesterday, or was she still a little tender? Thankfully, she was very wet. Within a few careful thrusts, he was balls-deep. Reece grunted softly as his hips hit her ass.

"Fuuuck!" Reece rumbled as he thrust in and out of her. His skin looked taut. He was frowning in concentration. He looked seriously pissed off. He looked magnificent. She couldn't take her eyes off him.

She was whimpering softly with every thrust. How could she not? It was that good right from the start. Her orgasm was right there already. That feeling starting to take residence deep inside her.

"Shhhh," he soothed as he bent down, closing his mouth over hers, eating up the noises she was making.

Then his thumb was between them, pressing on her clit, not moving but still so darned good it all but took her breath away. Reece took her hard and fast. She could hear the slapping of his balls, the wet suction noises her body was making. Even their ragged breathing while they kissed seemed noisy. Locke might hear. She should be afraid at the thought. Tense even. She wasn't. The thought of Locke finding out amplified everything she was feeling tenfold. When his thumb suddenly moved—*rub, rub*—she was a goner. Reece swallowed up her cries. He groaned softly, jerking into her. His other hand held her in place. Perhaps it was her imagination, but she was sure she could feel the hot spurts inside her. He jerked and grunted. She moaned, her eyes wide, her hands trying to find purchase on the wood.

Finally, he slowed down. Easing in and out until he stopped moving completely, letting her legs slide off of his shoulders but staying inside her. Reece pulled her close.

"Do you... do..." She licked her lips. Her mouth was dry. Her body was buzzing. "Do you think he heard?" she almost mouthed.

"I hope not." He pulled back, looking into her eyes. "I don't think so. We were quiet."

She frowned. "Are you sure?"

He nodded. "Yes." He grunted softly as he pulled out. "I wish I could take you to your squeaky bed and make some noise."

"Me too." She also wanted to talk to Reece. Get to know him better, since they were sleeping together. Again, maybe this was better than an in-depth conversation. She was curious about his past, though. There was far more to Reece than what met the eye.

He fetched her the towel that had been hanging over a chair, handing it to her. "You'll need to wash that with soap in the morning. Don't put it in the laundry with my seed all over it." She had to half-read his lips.

"Okay." She nodded.

Reece took the towel, placing it in a heap on the floor, then he picked her up and carried her to bed. He put her down gently. "I need to go. I left Zaire on his own."

She nodded.

"I'll see you soon?" He looked a little shy, which she found cute.

"Let's hope we can get it right." She shrugged.

"We'll get it right." He nipped at her earlobe. Hope bit down on her bottom lip to stop herself from making any noise.

Reece stood up. He switched all the lights off before climbing out the window.

Hope pulled the covers over herself. She had this stupid smile on her face. That was the best sex she had ever had. Hands down. Reece was a really good lover. *Nope!* He wasn't her lover. What they were doing was fucking, and it was amazing. She couldn't wait for them to do it again. This was perfect. It was bliss. Pure bliss.

Her phone vibrated. Her smile grew wider. It was probably Reece sending her a— She stopped right there as she read the text. It wasn't from Reece. It was from Lizzie.

Did you see any signs when Emmet was cheating on you?

Her heart sank.

CHAPTER 23

THE NEXT DAY...

Reece knocked on the door. He knocked again, and Locke answered. The male grinned. "Heeey, here to chew the fat?"

"I can't stay for dinner."

"Chew the fat means, are you here to talk? I'm sure you want to know all about my weekend away. Perhaps I can convince you to have a beer with me."

"I don't like alcohol."

"It's an acquired taste. That means you have to actually drink it to start liking it." He lifted his brows, moving to the side so that Reece could enter.

"I don't see the point. I don't like alcohol, so why force myself to drink it until I do like it? It makes no sense whatsoever and therefore, I won't do it." Reece shook his head as he walked inside. "Actually, I don't have much time. I can't have dinner or drinks. I'm still technically on duty. The queen is with her mates, and Zaire is watching the perimeter. I'm—"

"You're here to see Dr. Bristol?" Locke grinned all over again. Why was he grinning so damned much?

Reece needed to keep it together and to act naturally. "Yes. I want to talk to her… to apologize."

"I must say, that's big of you. You're normally not the type to back down first." He narrowed his eyes. "That was clearly some fight you guys had on Sunday. Neither of you will tell me much about it."

"There's not much to tell. I was a jolt… a jerk. I was a jerk. I said some things I regret and," he pushed out a breath, "I can admit when I'm in the wrong. I just don't happen to be in the wrong very often."

Locke laughed. "You were wrong this time?" Locke asked.

"Very wrong." He paused for effect. "Where is Dr. Bristol?" He looked around the room. He knew full well that she was in her bedroom. This was all planned. They really didn't have long. He didn't like leaving the Royals, even though he knew that the queen was safe for the moment.

"She's in her bedroom. I'll go and fetch her," Locke said. "I'm sure she'll—"

"No, wait," Reece called after Locke, who was already on his way, his hand on the wall that led down the hallway.

Locke stopped and turned. He was frowning.

"I will go to Dr. Bristol. I'll knock first and let her know it's me. Hopefully, she'll hear me out."

Locke's frown deepened. "You want to apologize in her bedroom?"

"Yes, I wouldn't mind some privacy. Unless you want to leave for ten or fifteen minutes? That'll work too."

"No." Locke shook his head. "I'm about to cook dinner. Dr. Bristol cooked last night. It's my turn."

"You go and start dinner. Wish me luck." Reece stayed completely neutral. "If you hear shouting, feel sorry for me." He widened his eyes.

"I'm not sure that you going into Dr. Bristol's bedroom is appropriate. I mean, if we take into account all the things you've said about being respectful."

Reece frowned. "What do you mean? I can still be respectful inside Dr. Bristol's bedroom."

"I mean, you're a male and she's a female. I don't know if it's appropriate. The two of you could—" he shrugged.

"Could what?" Reece folded his arms. "We're not going to do anything." He shook his head hard. "I will attempt to make things right, that's all."

Locke narrowed his eyes. Reece wondered if this was a mistake. He'd never been this desperate for a female before. To leave his post! He was taking risks. *It was wrong!*

At the same time, it was a calculated risk. Both Magnar and the king were with Claire. Zaire was there, too. This was the best possible time. He had said that he would choose when to mount Hope. When the risk was at its lowest. The time was right now. Leukos was leaving straight after dinner to go and spend a few days at a conference with the kings from the other species. They more than likely wouldn't get a chance until he got back. It was now, or… wait until Friday. Friday seemed too far away. Locke was fishing for clues, but the male didn't know what was going on. Reece was sure of it. He needed to keep his cool and stand his ground. "You know me, Locke. Nothing will happen in that bedroom. Now stop with this line of conversation. It is unnecessary."

Finally, Locke relaxed his stance; he rolled his eyes. "I was only teasing you." He laughed. "Like *you* would do anything against one of the rules." He rolled his eyes. "In fact, I wish you'd live a little, once in a while."

"I will live a little when I get my promotion. Right now, I will talk things through with Dr. Bristol. I'll apologize and all will be well. The queen picked up on animosity between us. Or should I say, from Dr. Bristol directed at me. I need to fix this. I can't have any blemishes on my record. Shard might end up taking the head guard position, and that can't be allowed to happen." It wasn't an outright lie. Reece was straddling a fine line. One that could end in disaster. And yet, he couldn't stop this. He had to see Hope. He had to touch her.

"Agreed!" Locke nodded. "You'd better go. Let me know if you need anything. Perhaps I could be your wingman."

Reece frowned. He was sure it was another one of those human sayings. He just nodded. "I will let you know. You concentrate on dinner. I'll concentrate on Dr. Bristol." His cock started to harden just thinking about the delectable human female. "I need to stop being so hard on her." That was just it; Hope loved it hard. He'd never had a softer, tighter, more receptive female in his life. Reece had always been a good warrior. He'd risen in the ranks quickly, and from a young age. He hadn't had a shortage of interested females. He just happened to pick the wrong one.

"I honestly… Don't bite my head off when I tell you this, but I think you're jealous of Dr. Bristol when it comes to other males. I think you should be honest with her. Explain that to her."

"I won't tell her that," Reece snorted.

"Even if it's true? I'm telling you what I see. It explains your actions when it comes to her. You're attracted to her. It's normal. You're a male and she's a beautiful female. Don't be so hard on yourself."

"It's certainly something to think about." Reece pulled in a breath. "It won't be something I tell the female… ever."

"I already told her my thoughts."

"Why would you do that?" he practically snarled, but only because it's what he would've done in this situation.

Locke shrugged. "She needed to know. She doesn't believe me. For the record, I think she's attracted to you, too."

"Even if it were true, there's absolutely nothing we could do about it. Not right now." If he had more willpower, he would stay away, but he couldn't. "Not until the threat of Ekon has been neutralized."

"You do know that you can have a relationship with someone and do your job all at the same time. Millions of people all over the world do it quite successfully every day."

"Dr. Bristol is my charge. Until that is no longer the case, we cannot be together in any way, shape, or form. I am in a leadership role; what I do and don't do sets a precedent for others and for the future. Now, if you will excuse me, I need to apologize. I won't be long."

"I guess you're right."

"I know I am." The crazy thing was that he believed every word of what he had just said, and yet his balls were pulling tight in anticipation of what was to come. What the hell was he going to do? This couldn't go on.

"I'll see you in a few." Locke jogged over to the kitchen.

Reece didn't wait. There was no time. He made his way to her bedroom and knocked on the door. "Um… Dr. Bristol, it's me, Reece. Can I come in?" He felt like an idiot, but they needed to take every precaution. Mounting during a shift. There was a part of him that wanted to leave right now, to stop this insanity. The other—bigger—part wanted to see Hope. Needed to see her.

"Reece?" Hope sounded truly shocked. "What are you doing here?"

"I want to talk. I need five minutes of your time… please."

"Okay, fine!" she pushed out, opening the door. "You have five minutes and not a—" She closed the door.

Reece pulled her into his arms. "I missed you. Make that… I missed this." He cupped her ass and kissed her hard for a few seconds before pulling away. He noticed that she seemed tense. Not herself. Her eyes held a sadness. "Are you okay?"

"I'm fine. All good. What about you?"

He shrugged. "Nothing to report. Boring… it's just the way I like it. No signs of Ekon, but the laying will be upon us soon." He noted that her eyes were definitely a little clouded. She didn't seem like her jovial self. He slid his hands onto her back. "What's going on? You look upset."

"It's nothing. We don't have time." She reached up to kiss him.

"It's *not* nothing," he said before her lips could touch his. "Speak to me. I can see you're upset."

"If we don't do this right now, there won't be time." She started undoing his pants. "You said that the king only gets back on Friday."

He put his hand over hers. "You *are* upset. I don't like seeing you this way. Is there anything I can do to help?"

Hope pulled away. She went and sat on the edge of the bed. It squeaked, which made her smile. "I told you it's noisy."

"I ordered you a new one. It should arrive tomorrow."

Her eyes widened. "You did? That's so sweet. Then again, I suppose you did it so that we can fool around in bed without getting busted." Her smile died, which he hated.

Reece nodded once, even though it wasn't true. He didn't want her trying to sleep in a squeaky bed. At the end of the day, her comfort was most important, but he didn't want to give her the wrong impression; he didn't tell her any of that.

"My sister, Lizzie, is worried that Emmet is cheating on her."

He frowned. "That's terrible! What a bastard. That male doesn't deserve to have anyone in his life."

"She's not sure." Hope shrugged. "She asked me if there are any signs she should look out for." Hope sighed. "I mean, can you believe that? The two of them cheated while Emmet and I were married, and now she wants to know what the warning signs were. At the same time, I'm worried about her and the baby. She found out that they're having a boy." Her eyes filled with tears, but she blinked them away. "I hope she's wrong, but a leopard doesn't usually change its spots…" She widened her eyes. "As in, once a cheater, usually always a cheater. It would make me feel better if he was cheating on her, because then the affair wouldn't be my fault. Something I did or didn't do. That line of thinking makes me feel incredibly guilty because, despite everything she did, I still love her."

"It was nothing you did." He kneeled on the ground in front of her, putting his hand on her thigh.

"For a while there I thought it might be. I'm not super adventurous in bed."

He frowned. "Aren't you?" Reece found that hard to believe.

"No… I'm not. I second-guessed myself a lot after I found out about the affair. About whether I'm pretty enough, sexy enough. Whether I should have agreed to sex when I turned Emmet down. We were together for years. I *did* get a headache sometimes. I wasn't adventurous at all with Emmet." She shook her head.

"You said it, Hope. You weren't adventurous with *him.*" He cocked his head. "Maybe the two of you weren't that compatible. That's not on *you.* You're so damned sexy." His voice dropped a few dozen octaves. "You're incredibly receptive. I wish we had more time, and that we didn't have to sneak around. I reckon you'd be plenty adventurous. You're amazing."

She gave him a fake dirty look. "You're just saying that because it's been so long." She giggled.

"Listen to me, Dr. Bristol. I may not have had sex for a long time before you, but I can safely say that you're amazing. Better than amazing, and I'm not just saying that." He wanted to tell her that she was the best. Hands-down, the best mount he had ever had, but he couldn't bring himself to do it. He wasn't sure how she would take it. "I have been with a few females in my time. I also happen to have a good memory… you're plenty sexy enough," he growled the last part, feeling heat coil in his belly. He felt his skin tighten. Just thinking of this female made him hot and needy.

"You're so sweet." She licked her lips. "I'm going to tell Lizzie to do what I should have done. She needs to get a private investigator. She needs to get his cellphone records. That way she'll know exactly who he's been in contact with. I'm staying out of it otherwise." Hope pulled her plump lip between her teeth. "We're not talking about Lizzie anymore, and we're definitely not talking about that asshole Emmet. We've wasted enough time on them."

"That's the right attitude to have." Reece stood up. "I'd better go, Hope. Don't take all of this on yourself. You're…" *Wonderful, amazing, kind, gorgeous… a whole lot more.* He couldn't say it. It wasn't like that between them. "You're so much more than you know. If that asshole didn't realize what he had, that's not on you. If he's doing more of the same to your sister, that's not on you either. I think you're incredibly compassionate to still be so worried about Lizzie. That's something special." She was something special, but thinking like that was dangerous.

Hope dropped to her knees in front of him. "I think we might still have a minute or two." She pulled down his zipper and then pulled on his jeans, which slipped down his thighs. His prick filled within one second flat. Heat flooded him. His balls pulled tight watching her lick her lips. Her full, glistening lips.

"Um… What… what are…" She took his cock in her hand. *Feather and tar!*

"I'm going to give you a blow job. Suck you off. Give you head. Suck on your dick. I'm not sure what the Feral term is."

His heart started racing. His mouth went completely dry in an instant. "Suck me? You want to take me into your mouth?"

"You look shocked." She narrowed her eyes. "You have had a blow job before, haven't you?"

He shook his head; excitement coursed through his veins. They were totally out of time. They really shouldn't do this. "No." He shook his head.

She frowned. "Really? Never?"

"Feral females only suck their mates…" He swallowed thickly, feeling his Adam's apple bounce.

"You're in for a treat, big boy."

Big boy?

What was that?

Hope pulled her dress over her head. She had pretty, filmy coverings on. They were pink. He could see her nipples and the fur on her snatch. Her cleavage was deep. Her breasts spilled over the tops of the coverings. Beautiful… simply spectacular. He couldn't take his eyes off her… off her mouth. She licked her lips again. Her eyes looked greedy, they were focused on his prick.

Hope cupped his heavy balls. He felt his eyes roll back in his skull and he made a soft groaning noise. It couldn't be helped. He was already feeling his balls pull tight.

"You really don't have to," he said, his breathing harder than it had been seconds before.

Instead of answering, she shuffled closer, her hand around his thick girth. "I can't wait to deep throat you." He watched as her cheeks heated. She clearly wasn't used to talking in this way. Reece liked it. He liked it a whole lot. He liked *her* a whole lot! Not just because she was doing this. Because of her… she was spectacular.

He made a noise of approval. It was all he could muster as her soft hand stroked his length.

Thankfully, Hope didn't make him wait. Any thoughts of Ekon, Shard, ramifications of what they were doing fled his brain as she took his tip into her mouth and swirled her tongue over his head. *Blast!* He groaned and threaded a hand through her hair. Then Hope took him deeper, using her other hand to work his shaft. Up and down. So warm and wet. It felt different from a snatch. It felt… He rocked his hips forward, his eyes wide; it felt fucking amazing. He watched as her mouth stretched around him. It was the most erotic thing he had ever seen.

Reece made a grunting noise, having to work to keep quiet. "Not going to last." He gritted his teeth to keep from moaning. "You are so sexy. Your mouth… your… Arghhh—" He twisted his fingers into her hair, working at keeping still. She was small, and he was so big. He didn't want to cause her discomfort by forcing himself into her mouth.

Hope kept it slow and easy, even though she should be rushing him to the finish. They didn't have time. He found that he didn't care; the world could go to hell. He wanted this to last. Looking on in amazement, he watched her pump her hand in time with her mouth and tongue.

A minute later and he was panting, making small circular motions with his hips. It couldn't be helped. True to her word, she sucked him as deep as he would go, taking the head of his cock to the back of her throat. At the same time, she fisted him quicker, using more pressure.

"By feather… By… oh… by—!" He gave a harsh growl.

She released him. "Shhh. You need to be quiet." Her hand kept working his shaft.

Hope took him back into her warm mouth. Hard and deep.

Reece muttered a soft curse. His fingers splayed on her scalp, they tangled a little deeper in her hair, and yet he remained careful not to hurt her or force her. He felt his balls pulling ever tighter. He could swear they were just about in his throat. He felt that coiling sensation deep within him.

"I'm going to come," he muttered as she increased the pace.

His hand gripped her tighter, almost against his will, and so he let go. "Hope," he choked out. "Hope!"

He knew he was being too loud. Hope worked him harder… deeper. Her hand pumping. Her breasts bounced a little despite being in the coverings. Her mouth… her hand… her tongue on his rim… her—

He clasped a hand over his mouth. His eyes rolled back as his seed erupted. He groaned into his hand as pleasure coursed through him.

She kept milking him. Drawing out his pleasure. He ran his hand through her hair as she released him. Reece was still hard. He still wanted her. Wanted to please her as much as she had pleased him. "Thank you," he whispered.

"Any time." She smiled up at him, looking at him through long lashes.

"You're incredible. I want you so badly, I—"

"Today was about you."

He shook his head. "It shouldn't be like that. You need…"

"I got exactly what I needed, don't you worry."

"I wish we had more time." His jaw clenched as he gritted his teeth for a moment. "I wish things were different."

"In a way… this is better." She licked her lips as she rose to her feet, making him want to cream all over again.

Instead, Reece pulled up his pants. He adjusted himself, pulling up his fly. "I'm holding you to it, Hope. Next time, it's all about you. I'm going to make you come so hard you'll forget your own name."

"Sounds good to me." She stepped forward, putting her hand on his chest. He leaned back. "As much as I want to, we can't kiss. Ferals don't have a great sense of smell, but Locke might smell my seed. You should brush your teeth and use mouthwash. We can't be too careful."

"Can we tell Locke that we're good now?" She let go of him.

"Yes, I still have a lot of work to do to fix things but… I'd say we're doing much better."

She giggled. "Okay then."

"I'll see you in a couple of days?" He lifted his brows.

"Yes… for sure."

Reece left, leaving her door slightly ajar.

"All good?" Locke shouted from the kitchen; it smelled like he was frying something delicious.

"All good." Reece put up a thumb.

"Took long enough." Locke lifted his brows.

Reece shrugged. "I need to get back." He pointed at the door, not waiting for Locke's reply. He removed his pants and shifted. They could do this. It would work for a while. The world wouldn't end just because he was mounting the doctor.

CHAPTER 24

Hope brushed her teeth twice and gargled a couple of times, too. Until the insides of her mouth tingled. Then she washed her face with soap. She even sprayed some deodorant under her arms for good measure. *That should do it.* She briefly considered showering, but that might set off alarm bells. Hope felt certain that Locke would never know what had gone down.

Hope smiled, thinking about what had just happened. It was the first time she'd actually enjoyed giving head. Only because Reece had been so into it. He'd loved it. He had this way of making her feel like the sexiest woman on the planet. It wasn't what he said; it was his actions, which counted so much more. This rebound sex thing was off the charts.

"What are you smiling about?" Locke asked as she walked into the kitchen.

Oops! She hadn't even realized that she was smiling.

"Um… nothing! No, that's not true…" she quickly backtracked. She could tell from the look on his face that he wasn't going to buy the whole 'nothing' thing. "I'm glad that Reece and I made up. It felt…'off' between us, and now we're all sorted. It's not nice when you work with someone and there's animosity." She shrugged. "That's all."

"Good to hear. Here…" He held up a spoonful of something. A stew of sorts. "Try this."

Shit! She'd planned to keep her distance from Locke, just in case. "I'm sure it's delicious." She waved a hand. "It smells fantastic. I'm just going to—"

"No, really. I think it's missing something. Try it." He held the spoon in her direction.

What could she say to that? Nothing, that's what. She needed to taste the food and act like everything was perfectly fine… which it was. She walked over to him and tried to take the bite.

Locke shook his head. "It's hot… you might need to blow on it first." Was there a tone to his voice? A glint in his eyes when he said 'blow'?

Nah! It was her very guilty conscience working overtime, that was all! She nodded once and blew softly on the food. Then she wrapped her mouth over the spoon and made a noise of enjoyment. "That's delicious. It doesn't need anything."

Locke folded his arms, still looking at her strangely. "Since when do you brush your teeth at this time of the day? I smell the minty freshness of…" He sniffed again. "Is that mouthwash? Were your teeth feeling dirty?" He cocked his head, still scrutinizing her.

"They felt a bit... furry. You know... I'm sure you've had it before." She ran her tongue over her teeth.

Stay calm.

Stay cool.

She didn't mind all that much if Locke knew about them, but Reece was very much against anyone knowing. She had to respect that. "You know," she carried on, "when your mouth doesn't taste great." Hope shrugged.

"I've never had anyone jizz in my mouth before. I'm sure it leaves an aftertaste," Locke deadpanned.

Holy shit!

Shit!

He knew!

Her mouth fell open. She tried to close it and failed. Tried to speak, and failed some more. He was probably fishing. She needed to get him off the scent. "Um... what...? You..." She pointed at the hallway entrance. "You think that—?"

"I know exactly what you were doing. Do you see juvi-plumage when I shift? No, you don't! I'm a male in my prime. I know what fucking sounds like."

Sounds like...

What?

No!

He couldn't have heard them. She and Reece hadn't even had sex just then. Locke was still fishing; she was sure of it.

Hope choked out a laugh. "You think...?" She shook her head. "No way!" *Shit! Shit! Shit! What to do? Deny! Deny! Deny!* "You're wrong." She wasn't making such a convincing argument here. She wasn't great at lying, full stop. "So off-base." She tried to throw out a careless laugh, but it came out sounding shrill.

"Something you should know about me—I'm a light sleeper. Something the two of you should know about yourselves—even when you think you're being quiet," he shook his head, "you're not quiet enough. All that grunting and whimpering and groaning." He laughed. "Even with my pillow over my head..." He laughed harder. Her face felt hot in an instant.

"You knew! You heard us?"

He gave her a mock dirty look. "Of course. I have good hearing for a Feral as well as being a light sleeper. You probably would have gotten away with it if I had been Andy. You would definitely have gotten away with it if I had been Zaire. He sleeps like the dead."

"I'm mortified." She covered her mouth with both her hands.

Locke chuckled. "I think it's freaking awesome. I'm so happy for the two of you."

She leveled him with a stare. "It's just sex."

"Just sex is perfect. It's exactly what the two of you need." He chuckled some more. "You'll have to tell me how you got Reece to ignore all the rules in his book. How you got him to embrace life, just a little. I've been trying for an age and nothing has worked."

"I have breasts, that's how." It was the first thing that came to her head.

He choked out a laugh. "You're right. You're absolutely right."

Hope scrubbed a hand over her face and sighed. She made a face.

"What is it?" Locke frowned.

"Reece and I agreed that we would have to stop if anyone suspected… if you ever found out. I was enjoying myself." She narrowed her eyes at him. "You've ruined everything. Why couldn't you just sleep like everyone else at that time of night?"

"Don't stop. Reece doesn't have to know that I know. No one does. This is the best thing that's happened to Reece in a long-ass time. You said that you were getting over a bad breakup. It's perfect for both of you. You can't stop. I'm assuming that the lamp breaking had something to do with—"

"Yes!" She nodded. "We fought because of Shard coming here, and then… we might have done the dirty, breaking the lamp in the process." She giggled.

Locke grinned. "Go Reece! I'm going to ask him if he wants to swap shifts."

She shook her head. "Don't! He'll know something's up. You have to promise me that he won't find out that you know. Please."

"Sure… okay." He nodded. "As I said before, I think it's great that the two of you are together."

"We're not together. It's just sex," she reiterated. "Really good sex, but that's all. It's the other reason I don't want you swapping shifts. I think I like how things are."

"Sneaking around. Grabbing quick fuck sessions."

She nodded. "I wouldn't have put it quite like that, but yes, that's exactly what I mean. It's perfect. There's less chance of one of us becoming attached. I'm not in the right place for something like that. Besides, I'm heading home in a few months so it wouldn't work."

"You could stay."

"I can't!" she said it a little more harshly than she'd intended.

"So, you don't have any feelings for him whatsoever?"

She shook her head. "Look, I like him just fine but no, not in a romantic way." If she hadn't still been so raw after Emmet, maybe it could have gone somewhere. "I'm technically still married."

"No, you're not. You humans and your papers," Locke disagreed. Reece had said something similar. There was merit in the sentiment. Locke seemed to be thinking something through. "You should know that Reece was hurt quite badly. It was a long time ago, but it…" He sighed. "He's had his heart broken before. Ripped out of his chest and shredded into a million pieces."

She frowned.

"I know you're probably thinking that I'm being overly dramatic, but I'm not. It wasn't just that I heard you together. I knew something was up between you before then. I've seen something change in him. I've seen the way he looks at you. Be careful, Hope. I'm worried that Reece might end up falling for you. You might end up hurting him. He might be mostly hardcore, but he also has a heart of gold. Don't stomp on it."

"The last thing I want is for Reece to get hurt. I like him as a friend." That didn't sound right or feel right, but she went with it. "Thanks for telling me all this. I figured as much. I think as long as we keep it to fooling around, we'll be okay. There also needs to be a definite shelf-life on our… whatever it is we have." She almost said relationship, but that didn't feel right either.

"As long as you know what you're doing. You're also a nice person, Hope. It's easy to fall down a rabbit hole. Before you know it, you're in too deep. Even worse, one of you is in too deep while the other doesn't feel the same. It sounds like you have a plan though… that's good."

"We do." She smiled.

"Then I think it's great. Dinner will be ready in about half an hour."

"Sounds wonderful, I'm hungry." She rubbed her hands together. Hope could understand Locke's concern, but it was unfounded. They were being careful. They'd both been clear upfront that neither of them was interested in more. "I'll set the table," she said brightly.

CHAPTER 25

The last couple of days had felt like weeks.

"Good evening, Dr. Bristol," he said, trying hard not to smile at her. He felt happier just seeing her face. Her hair was tied back, and her eyes danced in the sunset. She was beautiful… absolutely radiant. Her dress hugged her soft curves, drawing his gaze down. Forcing his eyes back to her face, he felt warmth flood through him.

"Hi, Reece." She smiled, not being overly friendly, which was good.

"Hello." Locke was grinning broadly as he did up the button on his pants. "Are the Royals here yet?" He looked towards the clinic. The lights were on inside.

"Not yet. Delise and Evander are here already," Reece said. "The Royals should be here any minute. Zaire and Andy are escorting them."

"I'm sure they're excited to find out how the pregnancy is progressing," Hope said. "It's a pity that Leukos was delayed and won't be able to make it."

"I'm sure they are excited," Reece agreed. "Leukos will meet the chicks soon enough. As the king, he has duties that are important to our people."

"I can well imagine," Hope said.

They had delayed the appointment especially so that Leukos could be there, but unfortunately, the conference had gone on longer than expected. He was due back that evening.

"As soon as they get here, Zaire and I will take over. I'll escort Dr. Bristol back home," Reece said to Locke.

"You sure?" Locke asked. "I don't mind waiting. The examination shouldn't take too long, should it, Dr. Bristol?" He turned to Hope.

"Half an hour, perhaps slightly longer." Hope, Delise, and Evander were examining Claire, who was growing heavier by the day. Her laying was imminent. It certainly would not be long before the chicks came. Disappointment hit Reece. They would have to stop seeing each other at that point. The level of risk was low right now; that would change all too soon. Ekon was crazy—that much had become apparent. There was no telling what the fate of the chicks would be should they fall into his talons. The Fallen king could not succeed in his endeavors. Reece was going to tell Hope that they couldn't see each other for much longer. He'd do so that evening. Perhaps they could still have a couple of stolen moments before the big day arrived.

Hope licked her lips. *That mouth.* His balls pulled tight just looking at the little pink tip of her tongue as it swept over her plump lips. It reminded him of how he had felt inside her mouth. As much as he loved her mouth, he couldn't wait to mount Hope again. Excitement surged. There was no way he was allowing anyone but himself to take Hope home. He needed some alone time with her. Craved it. "I can take Dr. Bristol home." His voice was a rough rasp. He cleared his throat, swallowing hard.

"It's been a long day, Locke," Hope said. "You head on home. Reece doesn't mind bringing me." Hope licked her lips again. She sounded far calmer than he did. This was an opportunity for them to be alone. They could take their time a little. They wouldn't have to be quiet either. It might be their last chance. He wasn't giving it up for anything.

"It's your turn to cook and I'm hungry," Hope added, looking at Locke.

Hungry.

Ravenous was a more apt description of what they were. Sexting was a new word he had learned that week. It had been enough to get them by, but not enough to quell their growing need.

"Sure thing." Locke shrugged. "I don't mind either way. I'm making pot roast for dinner."

"Can I have some too?" Andy asked as he walked up, still slightly out of breath from the flight over here.

"You're early." Reece frowned. "We weren't expecting you for another ten or fifteen minutes. I see that Leukos made it after all." He watched as three dragons landed. Leukos had Claire in his firm grip.

"Yes. He told Claire he wasn't going to be here just to surprise her." Andy grinned. "Now, about dinner… I'll even help you cook. You don't mind if I join the two of you, Dr. Bristol?" The male lifted his brows.

Reece felt his feathers rub with irritation. The old Reece would have strongly objected. Instead of shouting, he took a couple of deep breaths. "I'm not sure you should be intruding on Dr. Bristol's personal time." He was happy to note that his voice was even. He wasn't sure why he was quite so possessive of the female. Perhaps ending things between them would not be the worst idea.

"I don't mind if you join us for dinner," Hope said.

Zaire approached them, still pulling on his pants. "What's this about dinner?" the male asked, brows raised.

Andy's grin widened. "I'm having dinner with Dr. Bristol and Locke."

"Sounds awesome! Pity I have to work," Zaire grumbled, looking put out.

"We have an important assignment," Reece ground out, irritation growing. "Let's get back to work, shall we? The Royals are here. We have a job to do." Leukos and Magnar were getting dressed while Claire waited. The three of them were talking and laughing.

"Of course, Reece." Zaire nodded.

Locke and Andy inclined their heads.

"Is there anything to report?" Reece asked Locke.

The male shook his head. "All was quiet today. Nothing out of the ordinary." He shook his head, pushing his hands into his pockets.

"Do not lose focus," Reece warned, looking at each of them in turn. "Do not think for one second that the queen is safe. The laying is almost upon us. We will find out more about the exact timelines after the queen's examination today. Any information regarding the laying is strictly confidential. If this information should get into the wrong hands," he shook his head, "Ekon could end up with the upper hand. We can't have that." There were spies littered within their ranks.

"We won't say anything," Locke said, his whole stance tense, his eyes filled with sincerity.

"You can count on us," Zaire said, nodding.

"I won't say a word." Andy pretended to lock his now closed mouth and to throw away the key. It was stupid. Must be a human gesture. Stupid, but somehow apt. He had to bite back a laugh. Reece didn't laugh while working. Not ever. So he stopped himself.

"I hand-picked each of you, and I trust each of you." He glanced at the Royals, who were now entering the building. "Locke and Andy, the two of you are dismissed. Zaire, you take up watch at the north side. You know the alert signal?"

Zaire nodded. "I do." He jogged away.

"I'll see you all later," Hope said, looking over at them. She turned and walked towards the clinic.

"Later," Locke said, watching her walk away. "Make sure you get Dr. Bristol home safely." Again, Reece was sure there was a strange look in his eyes. It was mischievous. Did he know something? Reece pushed out a breath. *No!* He was being paranoid. This was Locke and he was just being himself.

"I will. You'd better get home and start cooking. You heard Dr. Bristol… she's hungry."

"Yes, sir." Locke gave a mock salute, removing his jeans so that he could shift.

Reece turned to man his post at the entrance of the clinic just as the last of the sun slipped below the horizon. A chill crept into the air.

Delise smiled warmly at Claire. "You are in good health, my Queen. I estimate that you will lay within the next few days."

"How can you be so sure?" Hope asked. "I'm interested to learn all I can from you."

"Of course, child," Delise responded; her warm smile stayed firmly in place. "I go on the size and shape of the belly. You can see that the eggs have moved down… ready to be expelled."

Hope nodded. "Yes, I noticed that." These things weren't an exact science with humans. A fetus could drop in week thirty-four and then sit tight until forty-two weeks. Perhaps things were different when it came to the Feral. She didn't want to dismiss anything.

"And then there's the queen's mammary glands," Delise said. "They are plumper. I would need to examine her nubs. I am sure that she has milk."

"Does this happen close to the laying with Feral women?" Hope asked. "Because it can happen early on in the pregnancy with human women. Milk production isn't necessarily a sign of impending labor."

"You should answer this question, Evander," Delise said, turning to the other healer. "What are you doing on that contraption?"

Evander had just taken his phone out of his pocket. "My apologies, Delise." He bowed his head, putting the device away. "There is a male with feather rot who—"

"It can wait. The queen is more important. I don't want to see you on that thing again." She looked at him with narrowed eyes.

"My apologies to all of you." Evander inclined his head.

"Did you hear the question?" Delise snapped at him.

"I did indeed." Evander's cheeks were a bright red.

"Good." Delise cocked her head, eyes still firmly on him. "I want to see if you have been paying attention, since you love that little block of yours so much."

Hope bit back a smile at the exchange. Delise was as old school as they came, and Evander was a young man. She felt a little sorry for him. The young healer stepped forward. He cleared his throat. "Certainly." His hands were clasped in front of him. "Yes, Feral females produce milk close to the expelling of the eggs, usually a day or two before a female is due to lay. Before that, no milk will appear if the nubs are squeezed."

"That is correct." Delise nodded, taking a step towards Claire. "My queen, I would like to—"

"Um... thanks..." Claire put up her hand. "I'll perform this particular test myself, if you don't mind."

"We'll help you," Leukos said, looking and sounding playful, which wasn't like him at all.

"In that case, I am done with my examination," Delise said. "I am comfortable that all is well with the queen and her clutch. I look forward to the laying."

"That is good news." Magnar grinned. "We cannot wait to meet our chicks."

"Where do you need me, Doc?" Claire asked. "I'm sure there are a couple of tests you need to perform."

"I'd like to check your blood pressure. It's standard—not because I'm concerned with anything."

"Of course." Claire pulled her shirt down, covering her large abdomen.

Hope wheeled the machine over, placing the cuff around Claire's arm, and waited for it to fill with air.

Then she waited for the beep, followed by the reading. "Good." Hope made a note in Claire's file. "That looks just fine."

Hope tore the Velcro apart and removed the cuff from Claire's arm. "Your blood pressure is normal. I'm happy with all the readings thus far as well. You are progressing normally."

"That is a relief." Claire smiled. She was holding Leukos' hand.

Hope opened a drawer and took out some latex gloves. "I want to check your cervix to see if there has been any change. It's normally the best way to predict impending labor. We can see if you are effaced. Perhaps your cervix has started to dilate."

"How exciting!" Claire's eyes widened, then her face quickly fell. "Wait a minute, will it hurt?"

"What does all of this mean?" Leukos asked. His eyes were narrowed.

Magnar was frowning, his arms were folded across his chest.

"Essentially the doctor will put her hand into my vagina to feel if I have started to open to let the eggs out."

"Is that dangerous for the eggs?" Leukos asked, a thunderous expression on his face.

"If performed correctly, it's not dangerous, Sire," Delise said. "I have performed this procedure myself. We normally do it when it's taking a long time for the pains to start."

"Exactly what Delise just said." Hope nodded. "It is a little uncomfortable, but it won't hurt. I will use lubricant. It's also not always a reliable indicator. I've had women who were two or three centimeters dilated, who only gave birth weeks later."

"Why do it, then?" Magnar asked.

"Because it is *normally* a good indicator." Hope shrugged. "It's up to you Claire." She looked at the pregnant woman.

"I would like you to do it, please. We're looking at anything from a day or two, to two or more weeks. It would be nice to get some sort of idea."

"Just wait and let nature take its course," Leukos murmured. He whispered something in Claire's ear, and she giggled.

Magnar took Claire's free hand. He also murmured something, and all three of them laughed.

"The Royals have missed each other," Delise said, smiling. "They are eager to get home."

"Please check my cervix, Doctor," Claire said.

Hope nodded. "Certainly." She placed a large towel over Claire's middle. "Can you remove your tights and underwear, please? Keep this over you to protect your modesty. I will be the one to perform the examination. Can I ask Delise and Evander to please move to that side of the room?"

"Of course, child." Delise and Evander did as she asked, and Claire removed her clothing, which Magnar folded, placing them on a chair. He took back her hand.

Hope used liberal amounts of lubricant before inserting her fingers into Claire's vagina. Claire made a noise of discomfort. "I'm nearly done." Moments later, Hope said, "You're already around a centimeter dilated." She smiled at Claire who shrieked, and clasped her hands together.

“That means it won’t be too long now?” The queen’s eyes were bright.

“It shouldn’t be too long. I agree with Delise, a couple of days. But these things aren’t an exact science. It might take longer. Don’t be disappointed. Try to enjoy the last of your pregnancy. Sleep in and read books. Do all of the things you might not have time for when your hands are full.”

“I will, but I still can’t wait,” Claire said, her voice animated. “I’m not sure if I should be afraid. I have to push out three eggs… three!” She held up three fingers. “I’m not afraid… I’m so excited to meet our boys.”

“It’s interesting that no females have been born in a species and human mating. It is across the board with all the shifters, the vampires…” Hope almost said to herself, pulling the latex gloves off and disposing of them in the correct bin. Then she washed her hands in the nearby sink.

“It is a concern,” Leukos said. “One we will have to address soon. It was one of the items on the agenda at my conference,” he added as he helped Claire to dress. Magnar held the towel in place.

“How interesting.” Hope nodded.

“We would love to stay and chat,” Leukos said, “but I am eager to get home. I have missed my mates.”

“Of course, Sire.” She inclined her head.

“You should come to dinner again soon,” Claire said. “Maybe tomorrow night? If I haven’t popped before then.”

“Popped?” Delise looked concerned.

“If I haven’t laid yet. It’s a human saying.” Claire grinned.

"Not a good one." Delise chuckled softly. "Evander and I need to go. We have a case of feather rot to attend to." She looked at Evander, who looked shell-shocked.

They all said their goodbyes.

"I'll see you tomorrow night," Claire said as they left.

"Fingers crossed," Hope called after her.

"We should invite Reece," she heard Claire say.

Hope's smile widened. Taking her white lab coat off, she found her phone and sent a quick text to Locke.

> *I'm running late. I have some paperwork I need to take care of.*

Three dots appeared. Then a vibration to alert her of an incoming text.

> *By paperwork, you mean Reece. You need to take care of Reece.* He added an eggplant emoji, followed by two laughing emojis. Hope laughed.
>
> *That's exactly what I mean,* she texted back. Followed by. *I will have worked up an appetite.*

Three dots follow by: *Spare me!!!!*

The front door clicked shut. Reece stood there in all his glory. He unclasped his jeans as he strode towards her. "Did you text Locke?" He looked pointedly at the phone in her hand.

"Yes." She sounded breathless. Just looking at him made her insides feel like mush. He was larger than life. So strong and handsome… so intense.

"Did Zaire leave with the Royals?"

Reece nodded; his eyes were golden and beautiful. "I'm going to make you come with my tongue deep inside you." His voice was a rumble.

Holy shit! Just hearing him say it made her throat go dry in an instant.

CHAPTER 26

Reece looked around the room. "Get on the bed," he instructed her in his deeply masculine voice. That alone was enough to send a thrill through her.

Her heart pounded. There was a part of her that had been expecting some small talk. She was glad it wasn't the case. Especially after her conversation with Locke, when he had warned her about Reece potentially falling for her. This was sex. That was all. She couldn't freaking wait. "The desk," she pushed out.

Reece watched as she perched herself on the edge of the desk, pulling her lacey underwear down her legs and dropping them on the floor. She kept her dress on. She'd let Reece peel that off her later.

"Open your legs," Reece instructed her.

"You're being bossy today." She loved bossy.

"We don't have much time and I want to fuck you as well." He licked his lips.

Holy shit! His words caused heat to pool in her lower belly. She felt her nipples tighten. Her clit gave a zing of need.

"You make a good point." Hope slowly shimmied the dress up her thighs. Then she opened up… wide.

His eyes flared with lust as they roamed between her legs. "Fucking gorgeous," he murmured.

Reece moved between her legs. His pants were slightly open. Not enough to see what was going on, but enough to tease. His shoulders were wide. His abs popping. He went down onto his haunches, slowly leaned forward, moving closer and closer to where she needed him the most. "I've been dying to get my tongue inside you," he whispered.

Hope let her head fall back, staring up at the ceiling. Her dress and bra suddenly felt tight around her breasts. Everything felt tight with need and anticipation. When his tongue finally laved her clit, her back arched and a loud groan was pulled from her. That felt amazing.

Reece chuckled for half a second. "No holding back this time. There is no one in the vicinity of the clinic. I made sure of it. We're alone. I want to hear you come. I want to hear all of it. We clear?"

She nodded, not sure she could talk.

He was so damned sexy. Her mouth opened as he laved her again. She pushed out a breath, her eyes fluttering closed.

His mouth closed over that very sensitive, swollen bundle of nerves, and she yelled from the sheer pleasure that moved through her in a rush. She already felt like she was near, and he had only just started.

There was more laving and sucking. Hope clenched her teeth and then moaned. Her hands grabbed onto the edge of the desk. Her eyes were wide, her body felt tense. Poised for release. Already. *What?* Then again, Reece was that good. Plus, it had been a few days since they'd been together.

"Mmmmmm..." He had his mouth over her clit, and he started to hum. The noise caused vibrations that moved right up her spine. Her nipples tightened right up. Then he stuck his tongue inside her while thrumming on her clit softly with the tip of a finger.

That was it.

Done.

Her back bowed again, and she groaned deep, feeling his tongue inside her, his finger on her clit. She groaned so deeply that her throat hurt. He had to know she was coming because he changed places. His mouth closed over her clit, where he suckled her. Using two fingers, he pumped into her. Firm and quick, slowly easing off as she came. Hope was panting hard. The guy was good with his mouth. No, he was better than good; he was fantastic.

Her body felt boneless. She could actually feel the endorphins coursing through her. His tongue still felt amazing on her clit.

His fingers, too.

Oh.

Reece pumped his finger a couple of times. His tongue remained soft, his strokes easy.

It didn't take long for that to change. Before long, there were two fingers inside her again. Deep inside. She could hardly breathe. His tongue stroked her clit. Not too hard, not too soft. Just right. Just so. Just... *Yes... oh god...* Again? No... surely not! She'd never come twice before. Her hips rocked. Hope was humping his face, but couldn't stop. "Oh god!" she moaned. "Oh... oh..." She humped him faster. Her hand in his hair, gripping.

Hope felt that familiar fluttering. That familiar tightening. Everything coiling. "Again?" She yelled as the tightening intensified. "Yes! Yes!" she shouted. Her eyes rolled back, and she was plunging. She could feel her channel squeeze his fingers. She yelled out, shouting his name. Her second orgasm was quick and powerful and left her in a quivering heap.

Holy crap.

Shit.

Holy freaking crappity, crap... Shit!

She couldn't catch her breath. She was sitting there on her desk, next to her open laptop, still moaning. Hope finally forced her gaze on him. His eyes were dark gold and wild. His lips were wet. Reece licked them slowly, making her own mouth feel dry. He gave her the sexiest half-smile she had ever seen in her whole life. He pulled at his pants, and her eyes were drawn to his erection as it sprang free. "I'll give you a minute."

She nodded, trying to catch her breath. Half a minute later, she felt a need unfurl inside all over again when she took in his impressive erection. Hope couldn't help herself; she palmed his cock, watching his eyes flare with desire and his jaw tighten with need. He made a grunting noise. "Can't wait to mount you," he said, his voice thick with arousal.

"Can I mount *you* this time?" she asked, taking her bottom lip between her teeth.

He frowned. "Females don't mount males."

"Sit your ass on that chair." She pointed at the one at her desk. "I guarantee you that you'll love it."

"It's not natural." He shook his head, doing as she said anyway.

"It *is* natural. We're trying it." She straddled him, whispering into his ear. "I'm going to sit on your dick." She giggled softly, feeling so naughty. "I'm going to bounce all over it until you—" His eyes flashed upwards.

He put a finger to his lips.

"What?" she whispered.

"Shhhhh," he said, eyes darting from left to right. He was listening for something. "I thought I heard a noise outside," he whispered. His head cocked to the side. "There it is again. Shouldn't be anyone—"

"I didn't hear anything," she whispered, feeling nervous.

Reece stood up, taking her with him. He placed her on her feet in front of him, noting that his erection was almost gone. He leaned down, picking up her underwear. "Go into the changing room. Hide. Now!" he added when she didn't move. "Stay there, no matter what you hear." This couldn't be happening. It was a false alarm. It had to be.

Mouth dry, panties in hand, she did as he said and went into the room to the side. It wasn't the changing room, though; it was the closet. She turned the light on and look around. There was a whole lot more in there, including mops and brooms; things she could use as weapons. It was more than likely a false alarm. She was reminded of when Reece went to perform checks several times during dinner the other night. That was also based on Reece hearing goings-on outside… same as today.

After pulling on her panties and straightening her clothing, she grabbed the broom, holding it in a defensive stance. It was going to be hilarious when Reece opened up the closet in a few minutes. They could laugh and have sex. Everything was going to be just fine.

"Don't!" someone yelled.

She heard the start of a screech, followed by a loud crash.

"Don't move!" a booming voice shouted.

Shit! Shit! Shit! That didn't sound like Reece. It wasn't him.

She heard a moan. It was loud and laced with pain. That sounded like Reece, but she couldn't be sure this time. She prayed it wasn't him.

"Stay down if you know what's good for you," another voice.

Oh god! This was bad. Was this the Fallen? Were they here? Why? They were early. Far too damned early. *Shit!*

"I said stay down, you bastard. You are outnumbered by a mile. We have more warriors outside, so running would be futile." That answered that particular question. There were a number of them.

"What do you want?" *Reece!* He sounded strong and pissed off. *Oh, thank god.*

"Where is she?" This voice sounded different.

"I'm alone," Reece said.

"Do not lie to me!" someone shouted. "We know that the queen is here. She is being examined."

"Your spies lied. There is no one here but me."

"Could that be?" There was a question in the other voice.

"No! Kwan was clear. He trusts this particular spy. The queen was supposed to be here for at least another five or ten minutes. The king is delayed at the conference of kings. This is the perfect opportunity. Where is the queen? Tell me right now, or you will regret it."

"She's not here! Torture me. I don't care."

There was a loud, thudding noise. Reece grunted, sounding like he was in pain. She covered her mouth with her hand to stop from making any noise. Her heart raced. Her hands felt clammy.

"Where is she?" the voice snarled.

"Stop!" another voice said. "I don't think she's here. We need to go to the royal nest. It's not far from here and I didn't see many guards posted in this area. There are enough of us to overpower them and to take the queen. They were only expecting us once the chicks come."

No!

This was bad! So, so bad.

The other Feral laughed. "Don't you love it when we're underestimated?"

"I do," the first Feral responded with equal humor. "All right, Ambrose and Yuri, tie this bastard up."

"No… wait!" Reece started.

There was a loud thud. "Cradock, you gag him. Put that sack over his head," the Feral said. "I'm sick of hearing his voice and seeing his ugly face."

"Tybalt and Arie…" Hope wasn't listening anymore. She had a few seconds to come up with a plan to save the queen. It sounded like there were a lot of guys out there. They might just get it right. They might just kidnap the queen and her unborn chicks. Hope couldn't allow that to happen. Looking frantically around the small room, her eyes landed on a pile of pillows, sheets, and blankets. There was also a box of medical supplies and some stationery, among other things. Could it work? Probably not in the long run, but she had to try. Her ploy would hopefully buy the queen some time. She scribbled a note on the wall and reached for a pillow.

CHAPTER 27

Blast these bastards to hell!

If they thought he was going quietly, they had another thing coming. Before they could cover his head, Reece elbowed the closest male. If he could escape, then he could alert the Royals and raise the alarm. The male went down, blood gushing from his nose. The second male flanking him, now alerted, saw the blow coming. Ducking, he managed to avoid the worst of it, kicking out as Reece began to make a break for it. He stumbled and the other two were on him in an instant. The ringleader punched him in the face. Reece felt his lip pulverize. He felt hot blood gush. The other male kicked him in the chest. Reece heard a rib crack. He landed a solid punch, before being taken down by the original male he'd elbowed in the face. They got a few violent kicks in while Reece was on the ground. He curled into a fetal position to protect his vital organs, working hard at staying relaxed. There was less chance of bones breaking if he kept calm and loose through his body. He had learned that the hard way.

This was all his fault. He had sent the patrols away so that he could mount Hope in peace. There was only one guard at the nest because he was here instead of there, where he belonged. The Royals wouldn't be paying much attention to anything other than each other. Leukos had ordered an elaborate candlelit dinner and champagne. They weren't going to see it coming. No one had expected this attack or this many males. They had underestimated the Fallen. *He* had underestimated them. Shame flooded him. He'd been so busy sniffing around Hope's snatch that he'd neglected his duties.

It didn't matter that he constantly warned his team to be on their guard. The fact of the matter was that he had let his own guard down, too. He hadn't expected this attack. Not yet. Not while the queen was still with clutch. There were plans afoot to ramp up security after the chicks came. Only after.

He was a fool.

An idiot.

Reece didn't deserve the head guard position.

He deserved to be put to death.

The kicks stopped. "What was that?" one of the males said.

"I didn't hear anything."

"I heard it too," the leader said, eyes narrowed on the closet.

No!

Blast it all to hell!

"You'd better hurry before—" he tried to divert their attention.

"Open that door!" the leader said, pointing at the room Hope was in.

"Wait, I—" They ignored him, opening the door.

There was a squeal. "What have we here?" One of the pricks walked out with Hope. He was grinning from ear to ear.

"Unhand me!" Hope yelled. "Don't you know who I am? How dare you!" She put a hand to her belly.

"It's the queen." Since the queen was the only female this far along with clutch, they bought it immediately. That was the thing—Hope looked like she was with clutch. Why did she look that way? This wasn't right. There was a large, rounded bulge under her tight dress. Her eyes widened as she saw him. She sucked in a breath. With all the blood on his face, he must look frightful. Reece wanted to tell her that it was superficial, but he held back. What the hell was she doing pretending to be the queen? Her act was going to get her killed. When Ekon found out, he was going to have a fit. Hope was in grave danger.

"Our intel was mostly accurate," one of the males said. "The queen *is* here. I'm not sure where Magnar or the healers are." He looked around them like they would suddenly appear.

"It doesn't matter," the leader said. "We've got her." He looked pointedly at her belly. "Ekon will be pleased. Take her."

By feather and tar, he couldn't allow them to take Hope. He couldn't. They would end up hurting her when they found out she was lying. Hope narrowed her eyes at him. She was telling him to keep quiet. He could see it written all over her face.

"Please don't hurt me," she begged. "Don't hurt my chicks." She cradled her belly.

"We won't hurt you, my queen." The ringleader bowed. "Ekon wants you alive and well. Let's go," he told the males. "Cradock, you stay. I want you to bind and gag the male."

They were leaving one. *Just the one?* The male was a big, burly warrior. Reece knew his face looked bad. He had a couple of broken ribs… his collarbone felt like it might be broken too, but he wasn't bad enough to only be left with one male. It would be easy to overpower the male. *Then what?* If he raised the alarm, Hope could be injured and killed when the guards attacked the fleeing Fallen. There was no way he could follow them all the way to Ekon's castle without raising the alarm.

Reece needed to be with Hope to save her. He needed to travel with them. Then bide his time and rescue her. Meanwhile, they would redouble their efforts to keep the queen safe. He needed to talk this male into taking him with them. "I'm a healer," he blurted as Cradock tied his arms together.

The male ignored him.

"Surely Ekon will want the chicks laid and hatched without problems. Humans are soft and weak," he continued.

Cradock began tying his legs. He should kick out and break his jaw… his skull. Reece refrained.

"If the queen were to die during the laying, Ekon would be angry."

Cradock balled up a piece of cloth to use as a gag. "Wait! If you brought me with you and I ended up saving the human if she ran into trouble, you would be the hero. Think about it." He moved his head left and right so that Cradock couldn't get the gag in place. "Ekon wants the queen alive and well. That's what your leader said." He was shouting now, trying hard to get the point across.

Cradock leaned back and smashed his forehead against Reece's skull. It hurt so badly he saw stars for a few moments. His vision cleared just in time to see Cradock standing over him with a table. The table came down hard on him. Not once, but twice… possibly even three times. Everything went black.

CHAPTER 28

They seemed to fly for hours and hours. On and on and on…

In reality, it was probably an hour, possibly less. Hope prayed that the Feral who held her in his talons wouldn't feel that her belly was fake. That he wouldn't feel it was actually a pillow stuffed under her tight dress. The whole thing was held on by surgical tape that Hope prayed would hold. They finally reached a much-reduced version of the Feral lands. Towers dotted the countryside. The creatures flew her straight to the entrance of a tall building that looked to be made up of several towers, all pushed up against one another.

They slowly descended until the beast holding her touched down on a wide stone ledge. His claws scraped on the rocky base as he landed. The creature put her down and started shifting. Hope took the opportunity to ensure that her belly was still in the right place. She needed to try to get away with this ruse long enough for

Reece to sound the alarm. For someone to find him tied up.

Reece's face.

The color drained from Hope's just thinking about all the blood. His gorgeous lips had been an ugly, puffed-up, bleeding mess. His one eye was swollen shut. He looked just awful lying on the tiles in her clinic. Blood spattered all over the white floors. For a second, she'd faltered. She'd been ready to give it all away to help him. She couldn't, though. She knew deep down he would want her to see this through. She needed to keep this together for a little while longer. She needed to give him as much of a chance as possible to keep Claire safe. The queen and her unborn babies were most important.

"Come with me." The Feral took her arm and led her into the room.

It was vast. A fire crackled in the large hearth. Everything was huge, from the long wooden table—it had to be a twenty-seater—to the candelabra hanging overhead. There had to be hundreds of lit candles twinkling above her like stars. The artwork was elaborate as well. Large paintings of men on horseback in the midst of battle. The curtains were a thick red velvet with golden tassels.

A man walked into the room. He was tall and attractive. She could see the resemblance to Leukos immediately. This was when her ploy would be uncovered. Ekon had met Claire. It had been over a year ago, but still. Hope decided to try her luck, anyway.

"Ekon." She tried to sound bored. "Long time no see. I didn't know you were in the business of kidnapping pregnant women. That's an all-time low even for you." She pretended to know him. Praying that they hadn't spent much time together. It didn't sound like it from the stories Claire and Magnar had told.

"Needs must..." He shrugged. "Leukos has backed me into a corner." He turned to the Feral next to her. "You may leave."

"It's my pleasure, Sire." The guy bowed, looking as if he was expecting more. Poor asshole. All he wanted was a little acknowledgment for bringing her in. She almost felt sorry for him... not! This loser had hurt Reece.

Ekon moved closer as soon as they were alone. His eyes narrowed as he took her in. This was the part where he realized that she wasn't Claire and sent his goons back to get the real queen. "You look different," he finally muttered. Just like a man to be bamboozled in this way. If Ekon had been a woman, this would not have been possible. Also, it sounded like the guy was so far up his own ass. Perhaps she'd get away with it after all.

"It's my hair. I dyed it darker. Do you like it?" She touched her ponytail. "My mates love it." Pregnant women didn't dye their hair, but he more than likely wouldn't know that.

"That's the last I want to hear of those traitors." His voice hardened. "You are mine now."

Say what?

She frowned. "What do you mean, yours? I'm mated already."

He got an evil smile she didn't like at all. "I am the true king of the Ferals. If I say you are mine, then you are mine. It's as simple as that." His eyes dipped to her belly. "At least," he got a look of revulsion, "once those things are out of you."

"Things?" She clutched her belly. Even though she wasn't really pregnant, she felt protective of Claire's babies. This guy was completely off his rocker. "My children are not things."

"It does not matter," Ekon blew it off. "We will talk again once you have had this clutch."

It *did* matter, though. It mattered very much. What did he plan on doing with the babies? Thank god she hadn't let them take Claire.

"How close are you to the laying? It can't be long now."

Hope didn't say anything. The less he knew, the better.

"It doesn't matter." He shrugged. "They will come when it is time."

And there it was again. *It doesn't matter.* That line worried her to no end.

"Milos," he called. "Milos!" he shouted, walking over to the wall and ringing a bell. "Good help is so hard to find," he told her.

"What are you going to do with me?"

"You'll go to one of the nests." He flapped a hand. "It has everything you need. My staff will check in on you from time to time."

"Sire," Milos asked from the entrance to the tower. "You rang?"

"From time to time? What if I go into labor?" Her eyes widened.

Ekon gave a shiver of revulsion. It was the only way she could describe it. He did this thing with his mouth and his eyes rolled. His whole body gave a little shake. "You are a female, are you not?"

"What does that have to do with anything?" Her voice was shrill.

"You were made to lay eggs. You will figure it out. I will see you again when you are back to normal." His eyes slid over her body, making her feel some of that same revulsion… although hers was justified. "I'm glad that you have mostly kept your figure. That is something, at least."

Back to normal. Kept your figure. This guy was something else. "I'm a human, pregnant with Feral young." She gripped her belly as if it were true. "Anything could go wrong. Clutch sickness is real. I could die."

"Stop being so dramatic." He flapped a hand again. "Humans can birth our eggs just fine."

"We've had one birth to go on. Just one. Just because that went well, doesn't mean we can rule out clutch sickness or any other labor complications." *Shit!* She was speaking like a doctor. "We were just discussing it at my examination this evening. This delivery will be high risk."

"Who do you recommend? There are a few human females on our soil. One of them? Milos perhaps?" Ekon gestured to the Fallen who looked afraid at the prospect.

A doctor would be nice. This asshole didn't seem to get that. Hope didn't say any of that. She wasn't really pregnant. She didn't want him kidnapping anyone else. It was a case of biding her time and praying that someone rescued her before that madman caught wind of her lies.

"Nothing to say, Claire?" He paused for a few seconds. "You will be just fine. Take her, Milos."

The Feral gripped her arm tightly. At least if she was locked away in some tower all alone, she could hold on to this lie. Every second, minute, hour would help Claire.

There was a scraping of talons on the balcony outside.

"Who is that?" Ekon said, frowning heavily. "I didn't call for—"

Hope gasped when she saw a huge Feral walk into the room. He was half carrying Reece, who was slumped and moaning.

Hope shrieked when she got a better look at him. His hair was matted with blood. He looked half-dead. "What did you do to him?" she shouted.

Milos gripped her arm to prevent her from running to Reece.

"What is the meaning of this, Cradock?" Ekon narrowed his eyes. "Who is this male?"

"He was with the queen. He is claiming to be a healer."

"A healer?" Ekon didn't look convinced. "They only have one male healer, and this isn't him. This keythong looks familiar."

"He *is* a healer," Hope improvised quickly. "Not many Feral know about him. His name is Var, and he's been helping me in secret. Your spies truly aren't everywhere." She shook her head, looking

contemptuous. "I'm surprised they don't know about him too."

"There." Ekon waved to Reece. "You have the healer you wanted. Put them in one of the cage towers together."

Thank god!

Hope breathed a sigh of relief. It was short-lived. What would happen to Reece when they figured out that they were lying? Thank god she left the note back at the clinic. It was just a matter of time. Her throat clogged with fear. She was a woman… Hope was sure they wouldn't hurt or kill her. All bets were off where Reece was concerned. Why had he lied? Why had he put himself in danger?

For her.

He'd done it for her.

CHAPTER 29

The big, mean-looking Feral threw Reece on the bed. The two Fallen left, clanking the steel door shut and locking it with a key. She noted that Milos wore gloves when he touched the metal. She wondered why that was. "This cage is silver-infused. It's no use trying to escape." Milos told her from through the bars. That answered her question about the gloves. "You will find everything you need in the cupboards and the cold box." He pointed at a refrigerator. She looked around them. They were in a regular Feral house, only it was enclosed in a silver cage. It looked like the entire house had been built into the cage. There were tables and chairs, a bedroom area, a kitchen. She suspected that the bathroom would be through the door.

"I need a first aid kit," Hope said. "Var is badly injured."

Milos snorted. "He is a Feral. He will be just fine, my queen. Do not try to escape. I, or one of the others, will check in regularly."

"We need medical supplies!" she shouted. "I'm going to deliver soon. What then?"

"Females for hundreds of years have birthed just fine without the need of such items." He started shifting.

"How did that work out for your Feral women, you asshole?" she shouted after him.

"Don't antagonize them," Reece pushed out. It sounded like he was gritting his teeth.

"Reece!" she cried out, running over to him.

"It's Var." He gave a half-smile and blood leaked from the corner of his mouth. "You are a resourceful female, I'll give you that, but you should not have pulled that stunt. You've put yourself in harm's way."

"What choice did I have? If I hadn't acted when I did, it would have been Claire sitting here instead of me. She would've been alone and afraid."

"Still—" He groaned, more blood trickled from his mouth. Reece clutched his side with his good arm. She didn't need an X-ray to know that the other one was broken.

"Shit!" she said. "Where does it hurt? I think you might have a punctured lung."

"It hurts everywhere, and I definitely have a punctured lung." He winced, his nostrils flaring with every breath. "For the record, I allowed that prick to beat me. I had to get him to take me with."

"That was stupid. What good are you to anyone if you die?" She was panicking and trying not to show it. "You need surgery. Your arm is also broken." It was bent at an odd angle just above the wrist on his right arm.

"I won't die. I need a few hours to heal. I'd appreciate it if you could help me with the arm." He lifted it, wincing.

"Help how? I don't have the necessary equipment. I would need an OR and—"

"What is an OR?" More blood bubbled from the corner of his mouth.

No! No! This was bad. "An operating room. I need medication, an IV to administer fluids—"

"None of those things are necessary. Pull it straight so that it sets correctly."

"What? I can't just pull it. There are—"

"Please, Hope." He grabbed her hand and squeezed softly. "Pull it straight. It's all I need. I have accelerated healing. I'm going to be just fine, I swear. If it sets like this…" He started to shake his head but stopped, his face morphing into a mask of pain.

"Okay… okay, but it's going to hurt."

"I can take the pain."

"Yes, but—"

"Please, Hope!"

"It's Claire, or your highness."

Reece started to laugh, but groaned instead, scrubbing a hand over his face. They were in a real bind.

"I'm sure they'll find out soon that I'm not the queen." Hope felt along his broken arm, trying to determine what was going on inside. Trying to decide how to tackle this.

"Just pull it straight," Reece said again. "You'll need to use quite a lot of strength." He squeezed his eyes shut for a second. "It's a pity that no one saw you. No one knows that you are pretending to be Claire. They might figure it out, though. I hope they do. Otherwise, we will be found out sooner rather than later and Claire will be in danger."

"Actually, I left a note on the wall in the storeroom to say that I was pretending to be Claire. I hope they'll find it since it's small and low down on the wall. I didn't want any of those guys spotting it."

"You're a genius! When you told me that you could be of service in protecting Claire, when I first met you, I thought you were full of nonsense. It turns out I was wrong. I underestimated you, Hope." He gave her a glimmer of a smile. It was tense with pain.

"They have to find that note first and then put two and two together. I don't see how it will make any difference either way."

"My team will look for clues. That closet was left open. They will check that too. I am certain they will find the note. I think that Ekon will find out that I'm not a healer but I'm hoping they'll keep on believing that you're the queen."

"How, though?" Her eyes widened. "Word will get out soon enough that Claire is still at home and that I'm missing. That I lied. I'm sure their spies will hear of it."

"Nope." He pushed out a breath. His eyes were clouded with pain. "They'll see your note and they'll know what to do. It's protocol in situations like this to make that kind of information 'need to know' only. If everyone believes you are Claire, then she will be safe. They will hide the queen to prevent the Fallen from finding out that they have the wrong person. There are very few who will know what really happened; that you were taken instead of the queen. That you are pretending. Our team, the Royals, and—" He cussed.

"What?"

"Do my arm while I'm angry," he growled. His eyes were narrowed in rage.

Why is he so angr—?

"Do it!" Reece growled.

Hope gripped just above his wrist and just below the elbow and pulled… hard. There was a crunching sound as the radius and ulna straightened. She expected the whole thing to collapse as she let go, but it didn't. "We need a splint."

Reece was breathing heavily. His eyes were closed. Sweat had beaded on his brow. "You're in pain. I wish I had something to give you." She touched his hair, smoothing it.

Reece groaned. "That helps." He grunted. "Give me a second."

She jumped off the bed and fetched some water for them both out of the refrigerator.

A few moments later, he opened his eyes. "Thank you. That already feels much better. No splint… necessary."

"Here." She let him drink, which he did, before helping herself. "You should have passed out. You should probably be dead," she told him.

"I'm not a human. I'm fine." His voice was strong and sure. He didn't look quite as pale as he had before. "I'm sure I've stopped bleeding internally. I'm already healing."

"I'm glad." She licked her lips. "What were you saying about the Fallen finding out about me not being the queen?"

"They'll keep it a secret that Claire hasn't been taken. Only a few of us will be told. I trust my team, of course I trust the Royals. I don't trust Shard, and as head guard, he will be told."

"Shard… the guy who came to introduce himself to me?"

"The one who asked you out." Reece looked pissed. His jaw was tight. His eyes blazed, and it wasn't from pain this time.

"You're not still upset about that, are you?"

"I am!" he growled. "That male is a bastard."

"I figured you didn't like him. You said that you were once best friends." She and Reece were having sex. They were also friends. At least, she liked to think they were. She wanted to know more about him. "What happened there? Why don't you trust him? Why do you hate him so much?"

"He lied to me about something very important. He is a selfish bastard."

She kept her eyes on his, hoping he would elaborate.

He didn't. Instead, Reece closed his eyes. "I'm tired, Hope," he murmured. "I need rest."

"Of course. I should probably clean some of those wounds, though, we don't want them becoming infected."

"No." He shook his head, cracking his eyes open for a second. "They won't become infected. I'll wash tomorrow. Right now, I must sleep… it will help me heal. I'm going to need my strength."

"Okay." She reached for a fur, pulling it over him. "How's that?"

"Fine." His teeth were chattering.

"Do you need anything else?"

Reece's chest rose and fell. His breathing was heavy. Was he asleep? Already? Was he pretending because he didn't want to talk to her anymore? Hope didn't like the idea at all. There was only one bed in the room. Hope grabbed a fur of her own and lay down next to Reece, keeping a space between them. It took her a long time to fall asleep.

THE NEXT MORNING...

"Get to your feet!" Reece was yanked out of bed. It was that big fucker, Cradock. The male grabbed him by his healing arm. It hurt like hell's fire, but he didn't make a sound. It felt like the newly knitted bones held. That was something, at least. Hope clutched the covers tightly to her chest, even though she was still fully dressed. Her eyes were wide with fear. He hated how helpless he was.

The sun had only just started to rise. Stars still twinkled in the dawn sky. How did they find him out that quickly? Perhaps this was something else. Why was Cradock there, then? What was going on? What was this all about? Reece didn't like it one bit.

Ekon elbowed the cage door open, walking inside. Two of his guards flanked him. Reece knew that there would be more males on the landing and shifters circling the nest. He was outnumbered by a mile.

Ekon sauntered into the nest, a smirk on his face. The male wore a loincloth made from soft leather. Not many of their males wore this traditional garb anymore. Not since they had started to seriously look at taking human females and studying the human ways. "So," he said as he came to a stop, "you're a healer, is that right?" he asked Reece.

What did Ekon know? It was clear he knew something.

"Yes." Reece nodded. "That is correct."

"Var." He lifted his head in thought. "I don't remember a Var."

"I'm sure you don't recall every male."

"Only the important ones." Ekon scrutinized him. "I see that some of the swelling is down. Still bloody, though. There is only one male healer. My spies were very clear about that. Who are you really?"

"I told you. Not many people know about my existence, I—"

"You can stop with the lies, Reece," Ekon spat.

Reece closed his eyes and let out a breath. His blood ran cold. *Blast it all to hell!*

The Fallen king knew his name. He had to keep his cool. Both he and Hope, as well. Especially Hope. Perhaps her identity was still a secret. It was possible that word had spread about him being missing.

"I thought I recognized you," Ekon said. "It was all that blood and gore." He wrinkled his nose. "Nice disguise. Clever. I actually bought it."

Disguise? Right. His males had beaten him to a pulp, and he'd had to take it.

"Bow to the king," Cradock said in a hoarse voice. "I said to bow!" The male kicked Reece in the knee. He heard it pop as he went down. Pain flared, but he refused to bow his head.

Down on one knee, he kept his eyes on Ekon. "You are not my king," he growled. "Leukos is everything you are not. He's just and kind. He—"

"Enough about my brother!" Ekon threw out. "Leukos will soon be nothing. His heirs buried along with his hopes and dreams."

Buried.

What?

Ekon turned to Hope. She put a hand over her mouth and whimpered.

"I know that you are not the queen," Ekon told Hope.

Blast!

By all that was feathered. Reece grit his teeth, grinding his molars until he was sure they would crack. It could only be someone from the inner fold who was feeding Ekon this information. That bastard was dead. If he got out of this alive, he was killing Shard. He'd kill him slowly, make him bleed.

"Of course I'm the queen." Hope tried to keep up the ruse.

"You are Dr. Hope Bristol. The queen is hiding in one of the abandoned towers on the eastern side of Feral territory. Her mates believe that she is safe there... for now. They are wrong." He laughed, sounding every bit the madman.

"How do you know all of this?" Reece snarled. He knew how this bastard got his information. He wanted to hear it for himself.

Shard! It had to be him.

"It doesn't concern you," Ekon said.

"It does. I'm going to kill the fucker who—"

Cradock elbowed him in the face. His lip split again. Hot blood ran down his chin.

"Shut up!" Cradock growled.

Reece had to work hard not to retaliate. He could snap the male's neck without breaking a sweat. He needed to bide his time, though. Reece had no hope of escaping right then. There was no point in retaliating, but Cradock needed to watch his back when the tides turned. Bastard was going to bleed when that day came.

"You can stay." Ekon pointed at Hope. "Help the queen to lay her eggs. You made some good points last night, Doctor. I don't want my soon-to-be-mate dying. I want her alive and well. You will look after her in the days following the laying. Make sure that she heals quickly. I want to mate her sooner rather than later. I want my seed growing inside her. The future of our people is in your hands, Doctor."

"Claire is already mated," Hope said. "What are—"

"I can do anything I want. I'm the king. Me!" He hit his fist against his chest, his eyes blazing.

"Yes, but—" Hope tried. Reece knew it was futile. Hope may as well be talking to a wall.

"I'm going to put Leukos to death along with that traitor, Magnar." Ekon ignored Hope. "I'm taking my kingdom back. As Leukos' right-hand male, I'm putting you to death as well, Reece."

"No!" Hope shouted.

"Yes, little human. That's how it's done. If I want to take my throne back, I need to make some hard choices. There are those who must pay."

"I need Reece," Hope stammered. "You can't kill him."

Ekon snorted. "What could you possibly need Reece for?"

"He's my lover," she said, picking at a piece of fur in her lap. "I love him." She wiped at her eyes, which were shimmering with tears. "If you kill him, I'll refuse to help you with the queen."

"Of course you will help her," Ekon scoffed. "It is your sworn duty. You will not let the queen suffer. You would not watch her die."

"If you harm the man I love," she shook her head, "I swear to god I won't help you. Not with anything. Not with this. You need me! Humans are weak. The queen might not survive the laying if I don't help her. It's why I was called in. She's got a condition where her pelvis is very narrow. There is a chance she will require a cesarean section."

"What is this ces-ar-ean sec-tion?" Ekon asked.

"It's an operation where the eggs would be surgically removed if they can't pass through the pelvis. We're hoping not to have to go that route because it could harm the chicks."

"The chicks are not important." Ekon curled his hands into fists. "You must save Claire. She is mine. Do you hear me?"

"You need to let Reece stay. I will need an assistant. Reece can help me with the surgery. I won't agree to help Claire otherwise."

"You will help her!" Ekon snarled.

"If you harm Reece… you can go straight to hell!"

Reece knew that Hope didn't mean it about not helping Claire. There was no way she would allow the queen to come to harm. Ekon didn't know that. She sounded convincing.

Ekon turned hard eyes to him. Reece didn't move. He didn't say anything. He prayed that Hope would stay silent as well. If she spoke, she would give herself away. She would come across as desperate.

Ekon finally nodded. "Very well. Let him go," he said to Cradock, who obeyed instantly. "You will help the doctor. I would urge you to swear fealty to me or it will not end well for you. Your female has bought you time. I suggest you use it wisely."

Your female.

Hope… his.

The thought warmed him, so he shoved it away. There was no 'them.' Hope wasn't his, she never would be.

"Let me know what you need, Doctor. The queen will be here soon enough. You need to prepare for the laying," Ekon said.

"I will need a pen and paper to make a list."

"Very well."

Reece watched as they left. The cage door shut with a clang. There was the sound of the door being locked and then cracking sounds as the males shifted before taking to the sky.

"Thank you for saving me," he told Hope.

"He's crazy." She got up off the bed, lifting her dress and tearing away the fake stomach. "I think he's going to harm the babies. He said he's going to bury them." She put a hand to her chest, looking like she was panicking. "He said he doesn't care what happens to them. I don't like the way he's talking." She shook her head.

"I'm sure that Claire will be well guarded. They won't get to her." Ekon seemed to know exactly where she was. If she was in hiding, they might not have a large number of guards drawing attention to her hiding place. He didn't say any of this. He didn't want to scare Hope any more than she already was.

"What if they do?" she whispered.

Reece groaned as he clambered to his feet. His knee was swollen. It was hot and throbbing, but he could stand just fine. It was already healing. His lip, too. It had stopped bleeding and was already scabbed over. "We can deal with one thing at a time."

"This is a nightmare." She wiped at her eyes. "A total nightmare."

He walked over to her, putting his arms around her. "It'll be okay."

"You don't know that."

"If Ekon is stupid enough to take Claire, there'll be a war. Mark my words. Leukos will send every last warrior to free us and to take down Ekon and his generals. I will keep you safe."

She nodded.

Reece let her go. "You shouldn't have told Ekon that you love me." He shook his head.

"It just came out. I didn't know what to do. I panicked. He was going to kill you, and I could see that he meant to do it. It was the first thing that came to mind. I needed him to believe me when I threatened to refuse Claire the care she needed."

"He might find a way to use it against you. Ekon is good at turning people's emotions against themselves."

She shrugged. "We're friends. I didn't mean it. I mean, I don't… love you, that is, so…" She shrugged again. "He won't be able to use anything against me."

"We're not friends, Dr. Bristol. We *were* fucking and now it's over." He hated that his actions had caused this. If only he could turn back the clock. If only. He wanted to punch the wall, to break things, but it would be a useless outlet for what little energy he had. "What happened between us was a mistake," he muttered.

CHAPTER 30

A mistake.

Hearing him say it hurt her. Hope wasn't sure why, since she didn't have anything invested in them. They weren't a couple. They weren't together. They were only ever meant to be short-term. Yet, it still hurt.

"A mistake," she repeated.

"The biggest of my life," he growled.

Her chest felt like a vise was compressing it. *What is wrong with me?* She should feel nothing. Less than nothing. Her eyes stung and her throat felt clogged. Hope struggled to catch her breath.

"I'm sorry you feel that way." She wanted to walk over to him and beat him with her bare hands. It didn't matter that he was all bloodied up already. "You're a real piece of work, you know that? You do realize that I'm a person… that I have feelings? That you just stomped all over those feelings." Hope burst into tears. It was an accumulation of everything that had happened. "I'm crying because I'm here. Because Claire and her babies are in danger. I'm not crying because of you. I made a pact with myself not to cry over loser assholes ever again."

"I'm sorry." His eyes clouded and his shoulders dipped. He took a step towards her, then stopped himself.

"I don't want your apologies. You can go to hell! In fact, don't talk to me."

"Don't say that." He shook his head. "We need to work together if we have any hope of getting out of this alive. We have to be partners—"

"You just finished telling me that I'm less than shit to you. Now you're telling me that we have to be partners? Make up your mind!"

"I didn't say that you were less than shit."

"You treated me like I'm less than shit. You said that what we did was a mistake. You're clearly angry with me for what happened. You blame me, don't you? Just admit it. I can see it written all over your face."

"I don't blame you, Hope." He took another step toward her.

"You're a liar. You blame me. You hate me now. That's what last night was all about. It's why you acted so cold towards me. Like I was the plague or something."

"I don't think that you're the plague or shit, or any of those things. I rate you highly. I happen to like you a lot and *not* as a friend. Not even close. I *don't* blame you." His eyes were blazing. "I blame myself. I'm the trained warrior. I was in charge of keeping the queen safe, of keeping *you* safe, and *I* failed. I was too busy trying to get between your legs to do my damned job. It's me, not you. Never you!"

"I'm sorry," she whispered. Hope closed the distance between them. "I'm so damned sorry. I came onto you. I was the one who initiated sex, even after you explained to me why it would be a bad idea. If it weren't for me—"

"It doesn't matter who propositioned whom. It happened. The attraction between us is… it's strong. It's like this constant hum between us." He drew in a breath. "There I go, making excuses again. Fact of the matter is, I should have made better choices. I should have had more willpower. When it comes to you… I… I don't. I want you. I want you more than I want my next breath. I shake with the need for you… even now."

Hope dropped her gaze and gasped when she saw the tip of his very erect cock peeking out above his jeans. Reece was hard and thick and ready. Her mouth fell open. "You're half dead, and you have an erection." She had to stifle a laugh. Mostly born from the start of hysteria.

"I'm nowhere near half dead and yes, I have an erection." He palmed his cock through his jeans. She loved it when he did that. It turned her on every time. She felt her nipples tighten… her channel, too, as heat swirled low in her belly.

Hope swallowed thickly when she saw a drop of pre-come appear on his tip.

"Ignore it." His voice was a rough rasp. "Sex helps my body to heal. It's a natural response to the trauma I suffered. It will go away… eventually."

"Oh." She felt disappointment rise. "I see." She looked down at her feet.

"Don't look so dejected. I just finished telling you how attracted I am to you and how I can't keep away, even though I should. I broke every rule in my book for you, Hope. As much as I know it was a mistake, I would do it again." He shrugged.

"You broke every rule in your book for *sex* with me," she corrected him. Not for *her*—there was a difference.

"That bastard did a real number on you. You second-guess yourself constantly. You have no fucking idea how beautiful you are. How receptive. How intelligent. How amazing. What happened between us *was* a mistake, but I don't regret it. I don't regret you. This," he touched his cock, "is all you. It's what you do to me. It's my undoing."

It was probably one of the sweetest things anyone had ever said to her, in a bizarre kind of way. It was sincere and kind and sexy. "I know you said that we can't have sex again, but I… I really want you right now," Hope whispered.

"Where sex was a mistake before, it would be beneficial now. It would help me to heal. I would suggest you let me wash up first. I'm disgusting." He looked down at himself.

Always so serious. "I'll help you get clean. I might need to dress one or two of those wounds."

Reece took her hand. "No need. You can bounce on my dick until I come. I believe you promised me something along those lines just before we were interrupted." He smiled at her. It was feral. His smile faltered. "It would need to be the last time for us, Hope."

"I figured as much." She nodded. Hope didn't like the idea. The sex had been off the charts. She doubted she would find someone like him again. Someone who could make her body sing so easily. Someone so compatible in bed. Someone as handsome and cute... funny, too. She forced herself to stop. Her mind was drifting into dangerous territory.

Even now, while she followed him into the bathroom, she could feel her heart beat faster. She was breathing faster too, and Reece hadn't even touched her yet. Her bra felt tight, her dress constricting. She already felt wet, definitely needy.

Reece turned on the faucets, and the shower spluttered to life. He removed his jeans and climbed under the spray. The water ran red as he washed all the dried blood from his body and his hair. There was still bruising on his ribs. They had turned light purple and green. A sure sign that he was healing. His arm looked normal. Aside from an already closing crack on his lip, his face was fine, too. His healing capabilities were remarkable.

Reece took some shower gel and began to wash. She watched as soap dripped down his body. His cock was thick and very erect. He was beautiful.

She pulled off her dress and quickly removed her bra and panties. Then she joined him under the spray. "Did you need someone to wash your back?"

"You can wash me here..." He took her hand and moved it to his straining erection. His eyes were bright. His jaw tense. The hunger in his eyes was almost her undoing.

Reece gently positioned her against the cold tiles. He put one of his legs between hers. His finger slipped between her folds, zoning in on her clit. His eyes stayed on hers. They flared with excitement when she moaned.

When her mouth fell open and her breath came in gasping pants. His finger slid inside her, and his eyes flared with shock. "So wet."

"I'm desperate for you."

She felt his hands shake as he picked her up. "Put your legs around me."

She did as he said.

Hope still had his shaft in her hand. She hadn't even realized that she was doing it, but she had been stroking him softly. Reece anchored her back against the wall. She positioned his dick at her opening, and he slid in easily. Her mouth gaped, and a breath was pulled from her as he bottomed out inside her. *So full! So gloriously full!*

The rest of the world could go to hell in that moment. It was just the two of them right then. They were both breathing heavily while looking into each other's eyes.

"Fuck, Hope," he growled. "You… it… we…" He closed his mouth. Two lines formed on his forehead. He looked like he was in deep concentration. His jaw was clenched, his eyes focused on her.

"It's not exactly what I had in mind, but it'll work." Her hands clutched his wide shoulders. She gave a tight smile and lifted and then dropped. They groaned in unison.

Reece held onto her hips, guiding her up and down. He also thrust into her from below. She let her head fall back. Slowly but surely, they picked up the pace until her breasts were bouncing hard with every thrust. She could feel her orgasm nearing. Could feel the end rushing to meet them… and already she wanted more. So much more.

Reece looked down at her chest like it was the most fascinating thing he had ever seen. Water cascaded down her skin, flowing between the two of them. He was frowning deeply. Despite the fact that she was halfway to a spectacular orgasm, she felt her cheeks heat and not from the exertion.

Then his gaze locked with hers. "So sexy," he growled.

If she could've spoken, she'd tell him that she felt the same way about him. His cock slammed into her. He was grunting. His muscles bulging. She kept bouncing on him, feeling herself get closer and closer and closer. His eyes widened. He grunted and then moaned her name, jerking into her. Hope felt everything tighten for a few seconds before the freefall. She yelled. Her eyes rolled up and her back bowed. He fucked her harder, his hands digging into her hips. It felt so good that she didn't care. Couldn't care about anything other than what he was doing to her. They writhed against each other for what felt like a long time. Their moans and pants slowly ebbing away.

Reece put his head in the crook of her neck, his breath coming in ragged pants. "I want you on the bed," he whispered. "Just once on a bed."

"Yes."

Reece carried her, gently placing her on the furs. He looked down at her for a few moments. Almost like he was burning her image into his memory.

Hope took him in, standing there in the morning light. He was wet. He was magnificent. If they ever got out of this alive, she would cherish this moment. This memory. She'd never felt more desired or more alive than she did right then. She doubted she ever would.

CHAPTER 31

Reece kissed and caressed every part of her. None of her soft skin was left untouched. He laved her breasts until she was crying out. He suckled on her clit, almost bringing her to completion several times. He worshiped her body in the way that she deserved to be worshiped.

Only when Hope begged him to take her did he settle himself between her lush thighs. Only then did he ease his prick into her snug heat. As much as he wanted to slam into her, to mount her with abandon, take her hard and fast, he knew that this was the very last time for them. It had to be. He needed to savor her. To commit this moment to memory.

Slow.

Easy.

Her eyes were wide and hazy with lust. Her mouth was swollen from his kisses. It hung open as he slowly eased himself in and out of her tight confines. He could feel her breasts soft against the hard plane of his chest.

Her hard nubs abraded him. He pulled her legs higher, lifting her thighs.

Her soft moans turned to cries, and her nails dug into his shoulders. He had her spot. Right there. He eased off a little, moving slower… drawing out their pleasure. He wanted this to last. He kissed her neck. Nipped at her earlobe. Then kissed her lips. Swallowing her hard cries.

Every stroke took them higher. Every thrust caused his nerve endings to flare more vividly to life. His heart slammed in his chest. He could feel hers doing the same against him. In sync and as one. Their bodies were slick, sliding against one another. He could feel her pent-up need for him. He wondered if she could feel the same coming from him. If she could feel it in his touch. See it in his eyes.

Her channel fluttered around him. Slow flutters. Slow. Her mouth fell open, and she moaned. Her breath seemed to catch in her throat. Everything stilled for an instant as her whole body tightened around him. Then she was milking him. Her snatch spasming around him so tight it almost hurt. Almost. Hope screamed his name. And they were falling, falling into bliss, falling into each other. He leaned his face down as his orgasm rushed through him. Crashing, smashing, obliterating.

He felt a sharp sting on his neck.

Reece roared as her blunt teeth sank into him. His orgasm flared back to life like a fire fueled with gasoline.

His feathers rubbed. He wanted to bite her back. Every instinct told him to do it. Instead, Reece grit his teeth for a moment and roared again, feeling his seed leave him in hard spurts. He finally slowed, hearing her whimpering beneath him, hearing her trying to catch her breath. He fell to the side in a boneless heap, not wanting to crush her. Reece lay on his back next to her, his chest heaving.

"I'm sorry," Hope pushed out between breaths. "I don't know what came over me. I… I got this urge to bite you. I wanted you to bite me back. Stupid," she muttered.

"No. It's not stupid." He felt for her hand and clutched it. "It's mating behavior."

"It's what?" She sat up.

"It's mating behavior."

"Don't you mean kinky behavior? I've never done anything like that before, and I have to say I liked it. It sure sounded like you liked it too. I guess I've never been very experimental in bed." She chuckled softly.

"I did like it." Fucking loved it. "I'm half lion. We bite during sex to enhance our partner's pleasure."

"My biting you made you come harder?" He could hear that she was smiling. "You're only telling me this now… that we're done?"

"Yes. It makes us come much harder." How did he break this to her without freaking her out?

"Why didn't you bite me back, then?" She gave his arm a playful slap.

"It's mating behavior, Hope."

"You keep saying that, but I'm not sure what you mean, exactly. Mating, as in sex? Surely you don't… You…" She sat back up. "Mating as in marriage?"

"Mates who are committed to one another bite each other. Biting is frowned upon during casual sex."

"Oh, shit!" She put a hand over her mouth. "I'm so sorry. I didn't know. I just… I just did what felt natural.

Why would biting you feel natural?" Her eyes were wide.

"You are a passionate female. You didn't know what it meant."

She shook her head. "I didn't. We can forget about it, since we won't be having sex again, anyway." She sounded disappointed. There was also relief there. He had freaked her out.

"That's why I didn't bite you back, even though I wanted to. Your orgasm would have been two or three times harder if I had, but..." He shook his head. "I vowed never to bite a female again unless she was my mate for life. Not unless we were committed to one another. Biting is supposed to strengthen a relationship. It is one of the things that ties two people together."

"Again? You've bitten someone before?"

He nodded once. "Yes. And it didn't end well. I... I was crushed. When I commit to something, I don't do it by half measures."

"I know, it's one of the things I admire about you," Hope said. "I'm so glad you didn't bite me, then. This could get messy." She pointed between them.

"I hate Shard because he stole my female," Reece blurted. He hadn't meant to say anything. It just came out.

"Oh." She pulled a fur up over herself. "What happened?"

"There were several of us vying for Nerusha's hand—a female in the flock. After months of fighting for her, Nerusha announced that I was the successful suitor. I was beside myself with joy. I was very much in love with her by then. My love for her grew day by day as the mating ceremony grew closer."

"Okay, so you and Shard, as well as several others, were sleeping with Nerusha at the same time while you were trying to win her?" Hope was frowning hard.

"No. There were many suitors for her hand, but Shard and I vowed never to make a play for the same female. We agreed that it could cause a rift between us. We agreed that our friendship was more important."

"What happened?"

He sucked in a breath. "On the day of our mating, Nerusha broke it off with me. She said that she had made a mistake, and that she was in love with Shard. My best friend and the woman I loved both lied to me. Shard had been seeing Nerusha behind my back all along. He broke our vow. He lied. Nerusha cheated. That is why I understand how you are feeling about Emmet and your sister. I have an idea of the pain and disappointment you felt."

"That's awful. She left you at the altar?"

"I'm not sure what an altar is?"

"She left you hanging. Humiliated and betrayed you."

He nodded once more. "The two most important people in my life. Of the two, it was Shard who hurt me the most. Just like your sister has hurt you."

He watched as her beautiful eyes clouded with sadness. "I didn't respond to her text." Hope pulled a lip between her teeth. "The one where she asked me if I knew what signs to look for. She tried calling me a couple of times, but I never responded. Now I feel like a bad person. A terrible person. She needs me, and I'm not there for her. At the same time, I'm still so mad at her."

"You are not a bad person." He took her hand back into his and squeezed. "You are a wonderful person. It is normal to feel this way. When we get out of this, you can call her and start the healing process."

"It's always the good people who get stomped on." She turned towards him. "You're a good guy, Reece. Shard's a jerk. For the record, I would have chosen you."

"You don't even know Shard." His voice hardened up.

"He's smooth and charming."

Reece choked out a laugh. "I'm none of those things. I'm not sure whether you are complimenting me or insulting me."

Hope smiled; it was radiant. "It's definitely a compliment. You're real. You say it like it is. You're not the kind of guy who would blow smoke up someone's ass…" Hope laughed. "You should see your face! That means to tell someone what they want to hear. To say things you don't mean just to make the other person happy."

"No, I wouldn't do that."

"It makes sense why you hate Shard so much. Why you lost it when he came over."

"He is the reason Nerusha is dead. Even after they mated, I continued to feel something for her. It's hard to switch off your feelings, even after a person betrays you."

"I can relate."

He pulled in a deep breath, not liking that Hope was insinuating that she still had feelings for that bastard, Emmet. He didn't deserve her affections. Instead of saying anything about her ex, he went on, "Shard is a selfish prick." Reece ground his teeth, trying hard to find control. He could feel his beast, just beneath his skin… prowling, tail thrashing in anger. "He planted his seed inside her, even though he knew she would sicken and die. He knew!"

"It's my understanding that you guys are wired to procreate. I'm not trying to take up Shard's side here, but you can't really be angry with him for that."

"He killed her." Reece stood. He went to the refrigerator and pulled out two bottles of water, handing one to Hope.

"You probably would've done the same. All of the Feral males—"

"Never!" he snarled.

"Okay, okay." Hope held up a placating hand. She started opening the water and then clapped a hand over her mouth instead. "Shit!" she muttered as she let her hand fall, her chin on her chest.

"What's wrong?" He sat on the edge of the bed.

"It's probably nothing. I'm sure it's not going to be an issue, but I didn't take my birth control last night. I normally take it every night before bed. I'm pretty sure we'll be okay. We shouldn't have had unprotected sex… that's all."

Reece nodded. "Let's not panic about this. There's nothing we can do about it right now." He wasn't sure how he felt. It wasn't shock and horror like he would have expected. Hope would make a fantastic mother.

"I can see you're a little worried. Don't be. It's one lousy pill. I will take a pill to stop a pregnancy when we get back. I'm sure Leukos and Magnar will send help. We won't be stuck here for too long." She pulled some hair behind her ear. He could see that her mind was racing.

"You get pills that can stop a pregnancy?"

She nodded. "I have up to five days to take it. The sooner the better. As long as we are rescued within five days, I can take the pill and I won't become pregnant. It will be a precaution. I'm worrying about nothing."

"Exactly."

"I'm probably not even ovulating." She chuckled. "Even if I was ovulating right now, the chances of becoming pregnant are not that great. The window period is three to five days in any given cycle. I often tell couples not to seek fertility assistance for at least a year. Why? Because these things take time."

Reece pulled on his jeans. He made a noise of affirmation. The thing was, non-humans had strong seed. It was rare for a female in heat not to become pregnant. Since he could see that she was worried, he decided not to set the record straight.

"What are you doing?" Hope asked.

"I heard your stomach rumble. I'm going to make something to eat. The fridge is fully stocked."

Her stomach rumbled loudly, and she put a hand to her belly. "I'm ravenous. I hadn't realized until right this minute."

"We last ate yesterday at lunchtime." He was hungry, too. Injury and mounting would do that to a male. He needed sustenance.

"No wonder, then." She smiled. It lit up her whole face. "What are we having?" She rubbed her hands together.

"Whatever you want." Reece said. "You should get dressed while I am cooking. The Fallen might come back… even Ekon, perhaps. I don't trust any of them. You are a temptation." He looked down at her full breasts. At the pink tips of her nipples and the glistening fur at the junction of her thighs. He felt his prick stir, even though he had just mounted Hope. *No!* He couldn't touch her again. He turned towards the kitchen. Fear rushed through his veins. Genuine fear that made his heart race and his mouth dry. He wanted to mount Hope again and again. He wanted to plant his seed inside her. He wanted to bite her… to mate her. Reece wanted to take her for himself. The problem was that he knew deep down that Hope didn't want him back. Not like that. Not after being hurt so badly by her ex. She was still raw. Still healing. Perhaps there was more between them, but she had convinced herself that she was only interested in what his cock could give her.

Even more importantly, he was not worthy of a female like her. Not after allowing them to become captured. After putting the queen's life at risk. *No!* Reece pushed out a breath. He needed to focus on her safety, on getting them out of there alive. This train of thought would get them killed.

CHAPTER 32

THAT EVENING...

Hope checked on the potatoes. She was making a roast chicken with all of the trimmings for dinner. It was her turn to prepare a meal. That's not why she had offered; she needed to keep busy. It made the time go quicker. It made her think about other things. Things other than the man she was stuck in there with. Other things besides what might be going on outside. Or what would happen to them. She had to stop herself from putting her hand on her stomach… there was that, too. The chance of her becoming pregnant should pale into insignificance beside the very real possibility of dying. And yet she couldn't stop thinking about it, which made her think about Reece all over again.

He was working out. She was trying not to watch, but he was doing push-ups with one hand. Grunting here and there, which made her feel hot under the collar.

Not looking.

Hope was going to focus on making a delicious meal. She wasn't going to think about her missed birth control pill. There was such a small chance that she might be pregnant. Tiny. It was stupid to give it any thought. Even more stupid was how her heart raced at the prospect. It felt like excitement she was feeling.

No!

She and Reece weren't together. In fact, she was still married to another man. One who was expecting a baby with her sister. Imagine if she were pregnant too. It would be a mess. A whole terrible mess. Not how she saw it happening at all. There was no picket fence. No order in her life. It would be wrong on every level.

Reece jumped to his feet in one graceful move. One she hadn't thought possible. He lifted his head, seeming to listen for something.

Wingbeats.

"Let go of me!" a woman shouted from outside as claws scraped on the rocks. "You brute!" the woman shouted even louder. "Asshole!"

"Ow!" a man said. "She's like a hellcat."

"Let me go!" It was Claire.

No!

They had Claire.

Reece had moved to the cage door.

"Step back!" a male voice shouted. She recognized Milos. He was holding Claire's arm tightly. Her face was a mask of rage.

Claire kicked Milos in the shin.

"Stop that, female!" Milos growled. All Hope could see was the spattered blood on Milos's chest.

"I'm the queen, you piece of shit!" Claire screamed. "Let me go!"

"Move away from the gate," Cradock shouted. "This nest is surrounded. Do not try to escape, or the queen might get hurt," he warned Reece.

Every muscle in Reece's body looked bunched and ready. His eyes glowed. "How did they get to her?" he muttered as he stepped back. "How?" He turned to look at Hope. "This is my fault."

Hope shrugged. "I don't know. It's not your fault."

"I know who caused this!" Reece's eyes narrowed. "I'm going to kill him with my bare hands for this."

They watched as Claire was shoved into the cage and the door locked behind her.

"I'll need that list I told you about earlier," Hope shouted to Milos. They pushed a pen and paper through the bars and waited while she made her list of medical supplies.

"You'll have the items later tonight."

"Not good enough," Hope yelled, but they were already flying away. "How are you?" Hope gripped Claire by the elbow and helped her sit on the bed.

Claire's face was pale. Her eyes wide. She was breathing heavily. "Not good." She made a squeak of pain, touching her lower belly. "I think I'm in labor. The pains started soon after they kidnapped me. They hurt Locke. I think he might be… he might…" She burst into tears. "I think he's dead."

CHAPTER 33

Poor Locke!

"No!" Hope gasped. "It can't be." She shook her head. She'd really come to like him over the last few weeks. He was such a great guy who had so much to give. It was clear that he and Reece were good friends. Reece's whole body was stiff; his nostrils flared with every breath he took.

"Are you sure?" Hope asked.

Claire was breathing rhythmically, still clutching her belly. She nodded. "His eyes were… just staring… at nothing. His neck…" She whimpered, another tear rolling down her cheek.

"Was his head removed from his shoulders?" Reece asked, crouching to Claire's eye level. He spoke softly. There was concern in his eyes.

His question made Claire cry even harder.

"That's a bit graphic." Hope widened her eyes at him.

Claire shook her head. "No… just broken." She sniffed. "I'm pretty sure it… That he was…" She sobbed, clutching her belly with both hands. "They ripped one of Zaire's wings off! He fell… bleeding… screaming… So much screaming…" She shook her head. "I'm not sure what happened to Andy." She shrugged. "Couldn't have been good."

"You poor thing. No wonder you went into labor. You are safe here with us," Hope lied. Sometimes a white lie was necessary. Claire was petrified, and it wasn't doing her or the babies any favors.

"Back to Locke," Reece said.

"Reece!" Hope widened her eyes. "I don't think that now is the time." She wanted Claire calm, not hysterical. That meant changing the subject.

"I need to know if they removed his heart from his chest."

"No," Claire whimpered. "There was no removing of anything. Just maiming and killing and then flying off with me."

"I think Locke will be fine. Zaire too. We have superhuman healing capabilities."

"Claire said he was dead. You don't come back from being dead. Can we change the subject?"

"Non-humans can come back from the dead. It hurts like gouging your eyes out or cutting your cock off, but it's possible."

"Sounds lovely," Hope muttered. "I'm glad he might be okay."

"Locke is young and strong. As is Zaire. I'm sure they'll be just fine."

Claire clutched at her belly again. Hope could see it pull tight under her dress. "Here's another one," she groaned. "This one is worse than the last one." She groaned and breathed and moaned.

"You haven't felt any wetness gushing from between your legs?" Hope checked to make sure that her membranes hadn't broken.

Claire grit her teeth and shook her head, groaning low and deep. It took a minute for the pains to subside.

"Let's help her onto the bed," Hope said to Reece. "First, pile some pillows up at the head of the bed. Claire won't feel comfortable lying flat."

He did as she asked. They helped Claire lie back on the bed; her upper body was propped against the pillows.

"This is bad," Hope whispered to Reece as Claire's next contraction started up.

"What?" Claire asked between pants. "What did you say?"

"I asked Reece to help me fetch some supplies." She pushed some hair behind Claire's ear. "I'm going to get you something to drink and a blanket. There are a couple of other items we need. It looks like these eggs are coming."

"No! No, no, no, no!" Claire shook her head hard. "My mates. Magnar and Leukos aren't here. I need them." She groaned, clutching her stomach again.

"They'll be here soon." Another lie she prayed was the truth. "Also, this is your first pregnancy and even though it seems like you're progressing quickly, it usually takes time to fully dilate." Hope prayed that this was true as well.

"Come with me," she told Reece. "We'll be back in a sec." She glanced at Claire, who nodded while breathing through her contraction.

Hope pulled Reece into the bathroom, handing him some towels. "I need to do a check, but I suspect that Claire's labor is moving quickly."

"The eggs are coming?"

She nodded. "The eggs are most definitely coming. Her contractions look quite severe and they're coming fast and furious." She pulled in a breath. "I'm worried. I was hoping and praying they wouldn't get their hands on Claire, but I think Ekon plans on harming the babies. It sounds like he's changed his crazy-ass mind about keeping them. He wants Claire now, instead… not the chicks."

"It does sound like he wants Claire, but we don't know for sure that he plans on harming the chicks," Reece tried. She could see he wasn't convinced. That he was trying to talk himself into believing it. "Who would harm innocent chicks?"

"A madman. Ekon talked about burying them. Also, I don't know if you noticed, but this place has everything a woman could want. From clothing to toiletries. There's nothing here for babies. No cribs, no diapers, or baby clothing. Isn't that strange to you, considering he planned on kidnapping a heavily pregnant woman? He talks about Claire's pregnancy and babies with revulsion. The asshat said himself that he can't wait to plant his own seed inside her. He's disgusting and vile and evil. I'm very worried about Claire and her little ones."

"Ekon is a madman. I agree with you about all of this, but… I don't think we should tell Claire."

"Hell no!" She chewed on her lip. "If Claire has these eggs..." She shook her head. "If Ekon finds out that they are here." She shook her head again, not wanting to contemplate what would happen.

"Is there any way to stop the laying?"

She shook her head. "No! She's too far along. It is her due date and it would therefore be dangerous to attempt such a thing. I don't have any medical supplies, anyway. Even if I did, I would let things progress normally. I have to help her lay these eggs."

"I'll give my life to protect those chicks." His jaw tightened.

Hope felt everything inside her soften as she looked into his determined stare. She took his hand. "I know you will, but..." She gnawed her lips. "I'm really afraid, and hoping to god it doesn't come down to that. Do you think Leukos will find out about this soon?"

Reece nodded. He squeezed her hand. "He will send an army as soon as he does. Ekon didn't think this through at all."

"I hope that they make it here in time." She squeezed her eyes shut for a moment.

"Like I said before, one thing at a time. We can't control what happens outside of this nest. We will tackle this head-on... together."

Hope nodded. "You're right."

Claire wailed from the other room. They quickly walked back. "What took you so long?" she cried.

"Trying to find supplies," Hope quickly came up with.

"Did you see Ekon, or did they bring you straight here?" Reece asked.

"No." Claire shook her head, clutching her belly. "They brought me straight here."

"Do they know you're in labor?" he asked.

"No!" She shook her head some more. "It started to get worse towards the end of the flight, but I held it in. I didn't want them to know. I know that Ekon wants to take them from me."

"Don't think about that now." Hope rubbed the side of her arm. "You're doing really well."

"What happened after Hope and I were taken?" Reece asked Claire. "Was it Locke who sounded the alarm?"

"Yes, it was Locke." Claire licked her lips, breathing hard after a big contraction. "Water… please."

"Blast me! Of course." Reece ran to the refrigerator, throwing it open. He grabbed what looked like ten bottles of water and jogged back. After dumping a pile of them on the bed, he started to hand one to Claire, then cussed, cracking the bottle open. "Can I help you with that, my lady?"

Claire nodded, her face pinched with pain. He held it to her lips. Claire clutched at the bottle and drank deeply. "Thank you," she finally said.

Reece put the bottle down on the side table. "There are plenty more."

Claire started up with her breathing again. "Not again," she moaned.

"Another one?" Hope asked.

Claire nodded.

Shit! This was going too quickly

Reece stood and began pacing. He paced during her entire contraction. As her breathing normalized, he sat down next to her. “My queen, I need to know what happened after we were taken.”

“Andy found your note…” she huffed out a few breaths. “So we knew that you were pretending to be me.” Claire spoke quickly, her face pinched. “I was sent to a nest on the outskirts of—”

“To the east of our lands?” Reece asked.

“Yes.” She nodded. “I was sent with Delise, Locke, Andy, and Zaire. The theory was that if you were here as me, that I would be safe. That the fewer people who knew where I really was, the better. Magnar and Leukos pretended to be frantic with worry. A fake search for me ensued. It was—.”

“That’s good. I take it that they didn’t harm Delise when they came for you?”

Claire shook her head.

“That’s good. She will let Leukos know that you are gone. This is important, my queen. Who else knew that you were fine after Hope and I were taken? Who knew that the search was fake?”

“Is this necessary?” Hope checked in. “Right now?”

“Only those with me, my mates… Oh, and Shard.”

She watched as Reece’s eyes flared with rage. They brightened. Another contraction started up.

“I will need some items to help with the laying,” Hope said to Reece, trying to divert his attention.

“What else do we need?” Reece asked through clenched teeth.

Hope gave him a list of household items that would work. The eggs were coming sooner than anticipated. Claire’s contractions weren’t letting up.

Hope fetched a washcloth and a bowl, filling the bowl with water. She used the cloth to wipe Claire's brow. "I need to check on how things are progressing," she told Claire as her contraction subsided. "Do you want more to drink?"

Claire shook her head. "I'm sure I'm far more than just a centimeter." She gave a weak smile, looking exhausted. Her hair was plastered to her forehead. "I can't believe this is happening." She grabbed Hope's hand. "I can't do this without Leukos and Magnar. I can't!"

There was a loud screech from outside. Then another and another.

Hope looked over at Reece. He had several feathers sprouting from his chest. He looked taller and far more muscular. His eyes were glowing. "Our army has arrived." His voice was gravelly.

Claire sobbed with both pain and relief. Her eyes widened, and she groaned.

"Another one?" Hope asked.

Claire nodded. "Except this time, I feel the need to push!" she yelled.

CHAPTER 34

Reece paced. His feathers not only rubbed but sprouted, too. He felt the need to shift with every fiber of his being.

The feeling of being locked away while a battle was being fought above him was excruciating. It physically hurt. He could hear screeching. Sounds made in rage and others in agony. He could hear thuds, followed by more screeches… louder and closer this time.

He glanced at the females. Hope was positioned between Claire's legs. She was frowning and saying words of encouragement.

It looked like the eggs were well and truly on their way.

His eyes flashed from left to right, following the noises outside. Trying to escape these silver confines would be futile. Touching the silver would simply burn and weaken him. No, he needed to stay and wait. Every protective instinct raged inside him. He had to work hard not to shift. Not to pace faster. Not to throw his head back and to screech himself. All of which would be a useless waste of time, not to mention that it might draw unwanted attention.

"I need to get up," he heard Claire say. She was panting and moaning.

"Yes, that's fine. Whatever is most comfortable," Hope said as she helped her into a squatting position.

There were scrapes on the ledge. Two faces appeared at the entrance. Milos and that fucker, Cradock. They unlocked the cage, pulling the door open.

"Leave now, and I will let you live," Reece warned. Every muscle in him tightened.

"Step aside!" Cradock bellowed.

"We're here for the queen." Milos's eyes were wide. The male looked frightened, and he glanced back. The Fallen were losing. In fact, it sounded like the cries of battle were dying down. This was Ekon's last-ditch effort to get Claire.

"Go now, and I will let you live!" Reece growled again. "If you take one step into this nest, I will end you."

"Let's get the human," Cradock told Milos. "We have our orders. I'm not leaving without her." He turned his cold eyes on Reece.

"Maybe we should run. If we—"

"Do you see yellow feathers?" Cradock growled at Milos. "We will take the queen and then we will leave. Our king was clear."

Claire was breathing heavily. Hope had put herself in front of the queen. Her eyes were narrowed. "You will have to come through me first." She picked up a nearby candlestick, holding it above her head. Hope's eyes burned with fierce determination.

That's my female!

The thought startled him. There was no time to ponder further since Milos and Cradock were advancing. Even though Milos had seemed to be the most reluctant, he charged in first. Reece wasn't sure what the male hoped to achieve. He certainly hadn't thought this through. Reece waited for the last possible second and then ducked out the way, putting his arm up to catch Milos by the throat. The male went down, choking.

Reece stomped him twice while he was down. Both blows were to the head. Not enough to kill the male, but enough to keep him down for a while.

"Thank god!" Hope shouted. Reece heard something metal clang to the floor. The candlestick perhaps? Why had she dropped it?

"Claire!" he heard Leukos shout.

"Sweets." Magnar was there too.

Cradock's top lip curled in a silent snarl. "Next time." He started to back off.

"No! We're having this out," Reece shouted.

Cradock shook his head as he turned and ran.

"Not a chance," Reece muttered as he chased after the male. This fucker had done a number on him too many times to just let him walk away. He seemed to enjoy hurting people. Reece gave Cradock a shove as they reached the ledge.

The male stumbled forward, shifting as he ran. Reece did the same, feeling his jeans rip. It felt good to let his feathers erupt and his wings extend. His tail thrashed as he took to the sky. Reece screeched as he raced after the bastard. Why was it that the biggest bullies always ran the fastest?

When the asshole realized that he wasn't going to get away, Cradock turned and lunged at Reece with his claws. The long, sharp talons caught him across the chest, slicing through flesh. Reece screeched, slashing back. They went at one another with claws and beaks. Falling and falling and falling in a wild flurry of feathers and shrieks. Cradock was a big, strong bastard. Reece knew as they hit the hard, unforgiving ground that he was in the fight of his life.

"Oh, thank god!" Hope shouted, dropping the candlestick with a hard clang.

"Claire!" Leukos shouted. The king was naked, with streaks of dirt across his chest. His eyes were wide as he ate up the floor with long strides.

"Sweets!" Magnar bellowed, coming in right behind Leukos. His face was bloody, as was his right hand and arm. It looked to Hope like it wasn't his blood, since he didn't look injured in any way.

Claire was laughing and crying. Her breath coming in sharp pants that reminded Hope that Claire had been in the middle of pushing out a baby. Not a baby—eggs—the first of three.

"No! We're having this out," Reece shouted from the other side of the room.

Hope glanced over in time to see Reece chase one of the Fallen out onto the big ledge.

Claire moaned loudly. *Shit!* She couldn't think about Reece right then. She heard cracking. Reece was shifting. Claire moaned again. Reece was a big, badass warrior. He could take care of himself… she hoped… prayed. Right now, she needed to keep her head in the game.

"Claire is having these eggs," she told Leukos and Magnar.

"What?" Shock registered on the king's face. "Now?"

"You've got this, Sweets." Magnar sat next to Claire on the bed, taking her hand.

"You're bloody," Claire said between pants, looking at Magnar.

"I'm fine," Magnar growled. "Not my blood."

Claire groaned, her eyes squeezing shut as she gripped her belly. "I need to push. I really need to push. It's coming. Our egg. Our baby." She looked excited.

"What?" Leukos yelled. "Are you sure?" He also grabbed Claire's hand. "My love, I'm so sorry. We should have stayed at your side. Should never have left you. This is all my fault."

Claire groaned again. "Not… your…" She grit her teeth.

"Here comes another one," Hope said. "Help her back into the squatting position," she told the men. "Unless you want to lie down?" she asked Claire.

"Squatting… is… good," Claire said between pants. Her mates helped her up. They held her on each side.

Hope moved to the front of Claire, where she could see what was happening. She really wished that Delise was there. Hope had delivered countless human babies. Eggs, though? *Holy shit!* She could do it, she assured herself. If Reece was there, he would tell her as much.

Reece.

Crap! She didn't want to have to worry about him, too. Thing was, he was good at his job. Amazing at his job. And so was she. An egg… a baby. Tom-ay-to… tomato. She had this.

"Do you still need to push?" she asked Claire, who nodded almost manically.

"Yes!" Claire grit her teeth again. "There is a heaviness… down there." She looked down between her splayed thighs. Just as she did, a gush of fluid splattered onto the furs.

"That's great!" Hope said. "Your membranes have ruptured. It won't be long now, Claire."

"Oh, good!" Her face was pinched with pain. "I can't take much more. I… can't…"

"You can! Push when you're ready." Hope could see that Claire was having another strong contraction.

Claire nodded once, bearing down. She pushed, and she pushed hard, putting her chin on her chest.

Hope thought she saw something for just a second, but Claire stopped pushing and it disappeared. "Again!" she shouted, but Claire was trying to catch her breath. "It's there," Hope told the other woman. "Right there. When the urge hits again, I want you to push with everything you have."

"You saw my egg?" Claire sounded excited.

"Yes!" Hope grinned. "I think one or two more big pushes and you should have a beautiful… egg." She cleared her throat.

Claire laughed. Her cheeks were flushed, and her hair was plastered to her forehead. She looked at each of her mates in turn, who also beamed with excitement. It didn't take long before the next contraction hit.

"Push!" Hope shouted. "Push!"

"Push!" both men shouted in unison.

"You can do this!" Leukos bellowed.

Claire gave a hard yell, and it was there. An egg. It slid right out, landing with a plop on the soft bed. Hope gave a yell, too. Her mouth hung open. She could feel that her eyes were wide.

Claire was breathing heavily, looking down between her legs. "I did it!" she shouted.

There, in the middle of the furs, lay the egg. It was oblong and perfectly white, with brown speckles. It was bigger than Hope had expected. Her mouth still hung open. Hope couldn't seem to close it. "Oh, my word!" she finally whispered in absolute awe.

"You did it!" Leukos shouted.

Magnar threw his arms around Claire. "You are amazing in every way."

Hope touched the egg, being as careful as possible. It was soft and yet very strong, like leather. She knew from her discussions with Delise that it would harden up and become brittle, just like a regular egg, and then hatch in a couple of hours. This one would hatch first. A smaller version of a human baby would emerge. It was a miracle. "Should we move this egg?" Hope asked, not sure what to do at that point. They'd never actually discussed much about what would happen beyond the laying.

"Um..." Leukos looked at Magnar, who widened his eyes as if to say that he didn't know.

Claire groaned, clutching her stomach. "The next one is coming," she groaned. "I... I... feel it. I need to push again."

"Go ahead, Claire," Hope said. "We need to get the next two out as soon as possible." She knew that once the membranes broke, if labor stalled, clutch sickness would set in. Clutch sickness occurred when the eggs turned hard inside the woman, making it impossible to get them to pass. It would mean breaking the eggs internally, thus losing the babies. The woman then stood a good chance of dying too. Although she had told those Fallen bozos that she would perform a C-section, nobody knew if that would be possible. Or if either the mother or the children would survive the surgery. As it stood, Hope didn't have any of the equipment required to perform a surgery. Claire needed to get those eggs out.

It turned out that her worries were unfounded because Claire pushed hard, and another egg landed neatly next to the first. The queen squealed with sheer delight, as did both her mates.

"Brother," a man said from behind them.

Shit!

Shit!

Shit!

It was Ekon. Not now!

Reece shook himself, and dust flew from his plumes in a cloud that slowly subsided. He rose up on his hind legs and took to the sky, flying as fast as his wings would take him. Leukos and Magnar were thankfully with the females. Although he could breathe easier, it was his duty to protect all of them.

He'd been gone longer than intended. He glanced back at Cradock's broken, bleeding body. Reece shook his head. He was growing weak in his old age. He'd left the male alive... barely. Cradock would hurt, but he would live. Perhaps the male would have a change of heart about how to live his life. Mistakes happened. He'd made a few himself in recent times. Although, his... relationship with Hope could not be called a mistake. He was wrong to have said that. The eggs that might, even now, be forming inside her, could not be called a mistake either. He screeched loudly at the thought.

Reece landed on the ledge and shifted, quickly walking into the nest.

Claire was straining. Magnar at her side. Leukos was with… Ekon. What the hell was that male doing here? Reece growled low in his throat.

Ekon had a pathetic look on his face. "I'm so sorry, brother. I don't know what to say or do." The male dropped to his knees. "I swear fealty to you. I will gladly serve you. It was Kwan who orchestrated all of this against my will."

Like fuck!

Blast this male to hell!

Reece rolled his eyes as he strode towards them. "Don't listen to this scoundrel, my Lord," he said. "He planned everything. Of course, he's swearing fealty. He just lost the war." Reece bowed his head. "I apologize for speaking out of turn. I know that you are well aware of all this. There are some things I need to tell you about what Ekon was planning."

"Don't listen to this male," Ekon spat. "I am your flesh and blood."

"Not now!" Leukos snarled. "Sit over there," the true king instructed Ekon. "Get up!" he yelled when Ekon didn't do or say anything. "Go and sit over there. I want to…" Leukos didn't finish his sentence. He locked eyes with Reece.

"I will take care of it, Sire." Reece could see that Leukos was desperate to get back to his mate.

Leukos went back to Claire, who was pushing—hard, from the sound of things.

Reece looked up. He caught Hope's eyes. She gave him a half-smile and then got back to helping Claire lay. He felt warm inside just seeing her.

Reece felt rage burn bright when he looked down at the Fallen king, who was certainly living up to his name. Reece gripped Ekon by the elbow. "You heard the king. Leukos wants you to sit in this chair." He dragged the male over to the seat in question.

"Unhand me!" Ekon growled. "Do you know who I am?"

"Nothing," Reece said in a low rasp. "You are nothing." He threw Ekon into the chair.

"I am the rightful king," he spat.

Surprise, surprise. The male had absolutely no remorse for anything he had done. "You're nothing, Ekon. Like I said before, Leukos is kind and just and everything you will never be."

"Leukos is a fraud! Look at them." He turned his stare toward the royal family just as Claire laid her third egg.

There was much jubilation. The three of them hugged each other. Hope beamed. "Congratulations," she said, looking absolutely radiant.

"It's an abomination," Ekon snarled. "Those offspring are... they're... They shouldn't be. They don't deserve to live."

Ekon launched himself off the chair. He moved far quicker than Reece ever expected, his gaze firmly on the eggs. The male still meant to harm the chicks.

Ekon screeched.

Reece reacted. He was quicker than the male. Stronger too. Ekon had grown soft on his makeshift throne. Reece pummeled Ekon, hitting him hard on the side of his head. He would have no problem ending Ekon's life. He would do so happily, with no qualms whatsoever. There was no mistaking the male's intentions. This was cruel and evil behavior at its worst.

Ekon landed hard at the foot of the bed with a hard groan.

"He meant to harm your—"

Leukos retaliated faster than Reece ever imagined the king could. Especially considering that Leukos spent more time in meetings nowadays than on the field or in the sky. Leukos roared as he removed Ekon's still-beating heart from his chest.

His talons retracted just as Ekon was taking his last breath. The Fallen king's eyes were wide in shock as blood gushed from the hole in his chest. He looked down and then tipped over… dead.

Leukos hung his head.

"I'm sorry, my lord," Reece said. He couldn't imagine what the male must be feeling. Ekon was his brother, after all.

"It is I who is sorry." He looked up at Magnar and Claire. "I should have done that a long time ago."

CHAPTER 35

Reece shook himself, and dust flew from his plumes in a cloud that slowly subsided. He rose up on his hind legs and took to the sky, flying as fast as his wings would take him. Leukos and Magnar were thankfully with the females. Although he could breathe easier, it was his duty to protect all of them.

He'd been gone longer than intended. He glanced back at Cradock's broken, bleeding body. Reece shook his head. He was growing weak in his old age. He'd left the male alive… barely. Cradock would hurt, but he would live. Perhaps the male would have a change of heart about how to live his life. Mistakes happened. He'd made a few himself in recent times. Although, his… relationship with Hope could not be called a mistake. He was wrong to have said that. The eggs that might, even now, be forming inside her, could not be called a mistake either. He screeched loudly at the thought.

Reece landed on the ledge and shifted, quickly walking into the nest.

Claire was straining. Magnar at her side. Leukos was with… Ekon. What the hell was that male doing here? Reece growled low in his throat.

Ekon had a pathetic look on his face. "I'm so sorry, brother. I don't know what to say or do." The male dropped to his knees. "I swear fealty to you. I will gladly serve you. It was Kwan who orchestrated all of this against my will."

Like fuck!

Blast this male to hell!

Reece rolled his eyes as he strode towards them. "Don't listen to this scoundrel, my Lord," he said. "He planned everything. Of course, he's swearing fealty. He just lost the war." Reece bowed his head. "I apologize for speaking out of turn. I know that you are well aware of all this. There are some things I need to tell you about what Ekon was planning."

"Don't listen to this male," Ekon spat. "I am your flesh and blood."

"Not now!" Leukos snarled. "Sit over there," the true king instructed Ekon. "Get up!" he yelled when Ekon didn't do or say anything. "Go and sit over there. I want to…" Leukos didn't finish his sentence. He locked eyes with Reece.

"I will take care of it, Sire." Reece could see that Leukos was desperate to get back to his mate.

Leukos went back to Claire, who was pushing—hard, from the sound of things.

Reece looked up. He caught Hope's eyes. She gave him a half-smile and then got back to helping Claire lay. He felt warm inside just seeing her.

Reece felt rage burn bright when he looked down at the Fallen king, who was certainly living up to his name. Reece gripped Ekon by the elbow. "You heard the king. Leukos wants you to sit in this chair." He dragged the male over to the seat in question.

"Unhand me!" Ekon growled. "Do you know who I am?"

"Nothing," Reece said in a low rasp. "You are nothing." He threw Ekon into the chair.

"I am the rightful king," he spat.

Surprise, surprise. The male had absolutely no remorse for anything he had done. "You're nothing, Ekon. Like I said before, Leukos is kind and just and everything you will never be."

"Leukos is a fraud! Look at them." He turned his stare toward the royal family just as Claire laid her third egg.

There was much jubilation. The three of them hugged each other. Hope beamed. "Congratulations," she said, looking absolutely radiant.

"It's an abomination," Ekon snarled. "Those offspring are… they're… They shouldn't be. They don't deserve to live."

Ekon launched himself off the chair. He moved far quicker than Reece ever expected, his gaze firmly on the eggs. The male still meant to harm the chicks.

Ekon screeched.

Reece reacted. He was quicker than the male. Stronger too. Ekon had grown soft on his makeshift throne. Reece pummeled Ekon, hitting him hard on the side of his head. He would have no problem ending Ekon's life. He would do so happily, with no qualms whatsoever. There was no mistaking the male's intentions. This was cruel and evil behavior at its worst.

Ekon landed hard at the foot of the bed with a hard groan.

"He meant to harm your—"

Leukos retaliated faster than Reece ever imagined the king could. Especially considering that Leukos spent more time in meetings nowadays than on the field or in the sky. Leukos roared as he removed Ekon's still-beating heart from his chest.

His talons retracted just as Ekon was taking his last breath. The Fallen king's eyes were wide in shock as blood gushed from the hole in his chest. He looked down and then tipped over… dead.

Leukos hung his head.

"I'm sorry, my lord," Reece said. He couldn't imagine what the male must be feeling. Ekon was his brother, after all.

"It is I who is sorry." He looked up at Magnar and Claire. "I should have done that a long time ago."

CHAPTER 36

THE NEXT DAY…

"I knew you were too stubborn to die." Reece was smiling broadly, something he hadn't done in the longest time. He was that happy to see his friend alive and well.

"It's time for your draught," Evander said brightly from the doorway, holding up a goblet.

"Now?" Locke growled.

Evander looked down at the floor.

"Fine," Locke sighed. "I'll take it."

Evander walked over to the bed, handing the goblet filled with green, gloopy liquid to Locke. "It will help with pain and will aid you in healing more quickly." He looked at Reece. "Hello."

"Hi," Reece said.

Locke took a tentative sip. He groaned, grimacing. "I think you might be trying to kill me with this stuff, instead," he muttered.

"I'm glad you made it out alive," Evander said to Reece. "I heard that you were there when Ekon was killed."

Reece nodded. He felt himself frown.

"You helped save the queen… our people," Evander went on, sounding animated.

Reece nodded again. He wasn't sure what to say. Several of his people had thanked him for his service. If anything, it made him uncomfortable. He had everything to do with the queen getting taken and very little to do with her rescue.

"I hear that his right hand Feral, Kwan—was that his name? I heard that Kwan died in battle?"

"I wasn't there." Reece tried not to sound irritated. "It is my understanding that your information is correct." He nodded once.

"Of course." Evander lifted his eyebrows. "You were protecting the queen."

Reece held back a snort. *Hardly!* He nodded again.

"Leave us, Evander." Locke sounded irritated, very unlike his normal self.

"My apologies," Evander said to Locke. "You really should drink more of your draught while it is fresh.

Locke made a noise of irritation and took a big sip. Disgust marred his features for a moment.

"One last question," Evander continued. "What was Ekon like?"

"He was an evil bastard." Reece muttered.

"Did he say anything before he died? Did he—"

"He spouted a whole lot of evil shit!" Reece muttered. "Not even worth repeating."

"Go away, healer!" Locke growled.

"Of course! Forgive me." He gave a little bow of deference to Locke, walking backward. "It was good to see you, Reece. Thank you again for your service." He spoke rapidly, quickly turning and leaving the room.

Locke rolled his eyes.

"I don't think I've ever seen you dislike anyone," Reece said.

"He's like a buzzing fly. It's almost like he knows when someone comes to visit. It's buzz... buzz... buzz. Feeding me this crap." He put the goblet down on the side table with a bang.

"You died yesterday," Reece said. "It will take you a little while to get your strength back." He noticed the dark smudges under his friend's eyes. "I'm glad you're still here."

"Me too." His eyes clouded, which was in contradiction with his words. "I'm sorry they took the queen. I fought with everything—"

"Stop there!" Reece looked down at his lap for a moment. He sighed. "I'm to blame for those bastards taking the queen."

"I know why you're blaming yourself and you're wrong."

"You have no idea why I feel this way," Reece argued.

Locke smirked, looking more like his normal self. "Just because you were mounting the good doctor, does not mean that you were to blame for any of what happened."

Reece felt his mouth drop open and his eyes bug out of his skull. He felt everything in him bristle. "How did you know? Did Hope tell you?"

"I'm not an idiot." Locke chuckled. "You wanted to hang around so that you could apologize to Hope after your fight over Shard."

"What's so far-fetched about that?"

"The way you asked me so nicely to do it. I knew instantly that something was up."

"You were off duty. I couldn't command you to leave." Reece sounded exasperated.

Locke snorted. "It's never stopped you before. You were so damned nice…" He shook his head, laughing. "Please give me two hours. I need to make things right." Locke impersonated Reece's voice. "I need to apologize with my cock." He laughed harder.

"You knew!"

"I suspected it when I got home to a broken lamp and a glowing, smiley Hope. If I had any doubt left, it was obliterated the following night. You guys weren't quiet at all. I'm not deaf."

"Why didn't you say anything, you prick?"

Locke leveled him with a stare. "You would've stopped mounting her?"

"Damn straight, I would have stopped. And the queen would never have been taken."

Locke laughed so hard that he ended up gripping his neck. "That hurts."

"What's so funny?" Reece snarled.

"You." Locke took a sip of the draught and screwed up his face for a moment. "That's vile. You've been really hard on yourself. Too hard. You're so busy blaming yourself for everything that you don't see the wood for the trees."

"What does wood and blasted trees have to do with anything? I know it's probably one of those stupid human sayings, but right now I want answers."

Locke sighed. "You're so busy blaming yourself that you're not thinking logically. Let's just imagine that you had been with Zaire at the castle. Hope would've come back with me. Those Fallen fucks would have overthrown you and Zaire. They might've injured or killed Magnar and the king. They would've taken Claire."

"You don't know that—"

"I do! We weren't expecting them. We were unprepared. Ekon was clever to feed our spies misinformation. It left us vulnerable—"

"I left us vulnerable!" Reece hit his fist against his chest.

"You are strong, but you are one male. You would have been overthrown. If you had not been there yesterday, it could have ended badly for Hope and the queen."

"I didn't do anything," Reece muttered.

"You are too modest. You stopped those two Fallen males from taking the queen."

"Magnar and Leukos were there moments later… I didn't stop them." He shook his head. "I need to tell Leukos—"

"You *did* save the queen!" Locke took his wrist in a feeble grip. The male was far weaker than he let on. "You saved her… and Hope, too. You bought them valuable time. None of us are perfect. We all make mistakes. Don't throw everything away. You could not have stopped those Fallen from taking the queen, even if you were in the right place. You fought hard. You did save her in the end, and you should be proud."

"I don't feel proud. I feel like I need to tell—"

"No! It won't solve anything. You'll try to appease your guilt and you'll fail. You may end up losing the head guard position over nothing. Over a moment's weakness. A mistake."

"Hope isn't a mistake!" Reece blurted.

Locke grinned, his eyes brightening up even though he was ghostly pale. "You're in love. Holy shit!" He choked out a laugh.

"Love is a strong word." He shook his head. "No, it's not love. It's too soon—"

"You're in love. Just admit it already."

"I have strong feelings."

"Okay, fine… strong feelings. What are you going to do about it?"

Reece shrugged, feeling miserable. "I don't know."

He looked at the cardboard box he had left by the door.

"What is that?" Locke asked.

"I need to deliver those to Hope. It's medical supplies she ordered… recently." She'd ordered them the previous day as soon as she got back home. They included that pill she had talked about. The one that stopped pregnancy.

"Oh," Locke said. "You're going to take them to her so that you can tell her your feelings."

Reece shook his head.

"You must!" Locke insisted.

"I will scare her. Hope isn't ready for a relationship." Reece shook his head.

"You don't know that. Play it cool. Don't dive straight in and tell her you love her. Take it slow. Maybe ask her on a date."

A date?

No!

It was a terrible idea. "I'll figure it out."

"You're going to talk to her, though?" Locke lifted his brows. Then he yawned, not bothering to cover his mouth.

"Yes," Reece stood. "I'm going to talk to her. Then I'm going to see Leukos."

"I told you not to tell him about—"

"I'm not planning to tell him about mounting Hope during my shift. Although I might still change my mind about that."

"Don't you dare change your mind."

Reece sat back down. "I need to talk to him about Shard."

"What about the male?" Locke yawned again.

"You need your rest." He started to stand.

"What about Shard?" Locke insisted.

"I think that Shard is… was a spy for Ekon. In fact, I'm sure of it. There were a handful of Feral who knew about Claire being in that abandoned tower. I trust you, Andy, and Zaire with my life. Magnar and Leukos would never have divulged that kind of information to anyone… that leaves Shard. I've thought it through. It has to be him."

"I don't think so." Leukos shook his head.

"I know it!"

"You should speak with the males. Delise too. Someone might have said something. It may have been an oversight. I don't think it was Shard."

"You don't even know that asshole. You don't know him as I do," Reece snarled.

"Your opinion of the male is biased. You see the young, stupid Shard who stole your female out from under you. That's all you see. You've let the anger and the hurt cloud your judgment where he is concerned."

"Where the fuck is this coming from?" Reece stood up.

"It's not coming from anywhere," Locke said, sounding frustrated. "Perhaps you are right about him."

"I am!" Reece snarled.

"Think carefully before you approach Leukos with this. Gather evidence."

"Where the hell do I get evidence from?" Reece knew he was overreacting, but he couldn't help it. Shard still had the ability to make him rage inside.

"Keep the possibility in the back of your mind that you might be wrong about Shard. The real spy could end up getting away with it."

"I trust every person who knew. Everyone but him. It had to have been him."

"You need evidence."

By feather! Something that Hope had told him about her ex came back to him. "You're right, Locke. You're absolutely right. Why didn't any of us think about it sooner? We could've weeded out the spies long ago." He started towards the door.

"What are you going to do?"

"You rest up," he said over his shoulder as he walked away.

"Tell me!" Locke shouted after him.

Reece smiled. He was finally going to prove to his flock just what kind of male Shard was.

CHAPTER 37

Hope sighed, trying to adjust the pillow under her head, unable to get comfortable even though the sofa was large. She closed her book, placing it on the coffee table. She'd read the same page over and over. If anyone had asked her what she had read, she still wouldn't be able to tell them. With another sigh, she pinched the bridge of her nose, feeling a headache coming on.

They'd made it back late the evening before, the Royals with their three bundles of joy in tow. Those baby boys were just about the cutest little things she had ever seen in her life. They were about half the size of a human baby, but perfectly formed. Perfectly healthy and gorgeous.

She felt a pang, putting her hand on her stomach. Berating herself, she snatched her hand away. Even if she was ovulating, nothing much would have happened yet. There would be a bundle of cells traveling down her fallopian tubes. It would take days for them to reach her uterus. Then again, Reece wasn't human. Still, there wouldn't be much. Nothing worth getting all teary-eyed over.

The fact of the matter was that she was married to another man. She and Reece weren't together. The Morning After Pill would be there soon, and she needed to just take the thing. No thinking… just doing. It was on the off chance that something was happening inside her. The very, very off chance. She needed to stop with all the drama.

Reece hadn't even bothered to come and check on her, anyway. She squeezed her eyes shut. That wasn't fair. He was a good guy… a great guy. He would make a fantastic father one day. She really needed to stop! Her brain had immediately pictured them together, like a total idiot. *Rewind!* Reece would make a fantastic father with some other woman. Just thinking about it made her feel jealous, which was stupid. He was her rebound guy. It was over… he'd said as much. Their… thing had run its course.

There was a knock at the door.

That was her delivery. She checked her watch. A little later than she expected, but still on time. She opened the door. "Hi, you can put that— Reece!" Her eyes widened.

He was so cute, standing there, a big cardboard box in his hands. "Hi." He smiled. "I thought I would bring you this." He looked down at the box of supplies.

"Oh… um… yeah, thanks." She stepped to the side. "You can put that down on the chest of drawers." Her cheeks flamed when she remembered the amazing sex they had on that particular piece of furniture.

Reece walked all the way into the house, putting the box down on the dining room table. "I thought I would deliver this myself. It has those pills you need to stop the pregnancy."

Reece took a step back and looked pointedly at her packed bags stacked by the wall. "Are you leaving?" He sounded like he was accusing her of something. His eyes were narrowed.

"I'm going home tomorrow. I'm—"

"Running away?" His voice was a deep growl. There was definitely accusation in his stare.

"No!" she half-yelled. "I'm going to sign those divorce papers since I'm not needed here right now. I'm going for one night. I'm not running anywhere." *What was his problem?*

He seemed to relax. "You're coming back, then? The queen needs you."

The queen. Right. She nodded.

"Your pill is in that box," Reece said.

"I know why you came." He was probably there to make sure she took the Morning After Pill. Hope wasn't sure why, but that pissed her off. "You didn't need to bring them, you know."

"I know, but I wanted to." He pushed his hands into his pockets.

"You really are a control freak. I told you I would take the pill, and I meant it. I will do it. Levonorgestrel is highly effective in stopping a pregnancy from happening. We are well within the five-day window. You can go, Reece. I will do what I need to do to—"

"That's just it, Hope. I don't want you to take the pill," he blurted.

For a second, what he had just said didn't register. "I said that… um… What?"

"I don't want you to take the pill. If you are with clutch, I want you to have the eggs. To have our young."

That didn't make any sense. "We're not together."

"We could be. For the sake of our young," he added.

Holy shit! He hadn't just said that, had he? Hope made a noise of irritation as she walked away from Reece, trying hard to focus on the view. Trying to regain her composure. "That's very nice of you to… um… offer, Reece." He thought he was doing the right thing. Giving her an option. He wasn't. Not even close! "But it's not necessary. I don't like the idea of trying to make it work between us for the sake of children. I'm probably not even going to become pregnant."

"We have very powerful seed. A female very rarely doesn't become with clutch if she is on heat."

"That's just it. I probably didn't go on heat… um, ovulate."

"Our seed can live for a long time in a female's body. Much longer than a human male," he pointed out. "You will more than likely become with clutch." His eyes glinted.

"That's a great point. I should probably take another pill in a couple of days just to be sure."

"No! Don't do that. Our species needs young. It would be a shame—"

"Do I look like a breeding machine to you?" She knew she was being harsh, and that this was another one of their cultural differences coming to the fore. But these were babies he was talking about, not commodities.

Babies she longed for, babies she wanted so badly she could hardly breathe. For a second, she wanted to throw caution to the wind and just jump. That second was over quickly, and reason took over.

"No, Hope." Reece shook his head. "You definitely don't look like a machine. You are too soft... too beautiful."

Holy shit! Now he was saying all the right things. Things she had secretly hoped he would say. Unfortunately, he was saying them for the wrong reasons. "Thank you, but we can't do this. We hardly know each other. We aren't in a relationship."

"We could be." His beautiful golden eyes shone with sincerity.

"No!" she said, too harshly. "I just got out of a bad marriage... an awful marriage. Sex is one thing. A relationship?" She shook her head. "Children?" She shook her head harder.

"It could work." He took her hands. "I know you are afraid. I'm afraid too. Think about it, please. Don't take that pill. We could be together; we could be a family."

Family.

It was all Hope had ever wanted.

She shook her head. "No. We haven't even dated. We're not even together, let alone married. I'm still married to Emmet. There is a way that things should happen, and this is not the way."

Reece smiled.

"Why is that funny?"

"You tried to follow a pattern before, with that Emmet prick. You did everything right, am I correct?"

She nodded.

"How did that work for you?"

"I know where you're going with this," she groaned.

"Humor me." Reece raised his brows. "How did that work for you?"

"It was terrible. My marriage sucked. It was a farce… all of it."

Reece was frowning heavily. "Sucked? I'm going to assume that you aren't being literal."

She choked out a laugh. "My marriage sucked, which means that it was revolting on all levels. You're going to tell me that we should do everything the wrong way around."

"I'm saying that I have strong feelings for you."

"Strong feelings?" Why was he so darned cute?

"Yes. I suspect you have strong feelings for me too, and not just for my cock."

"It's not just your cock," she admitted. "You also have great biceps, and a chest that—"

"It has nothing to do with my body. Okay, maybe a little to do with my body."

She giggled. "I'll admit that there is something between us, but I don't think it's enough to bring a child—children—into this world. There would be three." She felt panic well. "I worry, because you guys are programmed to procreate. Maybe this is some of that programming in action."

"All I know is that I like you very much. Don't get nervous when I tell you this…" He licked his lips. "I'm falling for you, Hope. Really, really falling. The thought of you taking that pill…" He pointed at the box. "It makes me feel sick to my stomach. It makes me feel sad to my core. I find myself hoping that you're with clutch. I want this… I want you."

"You do?"

Reece nodded. He put his arms around her, looking into her eyes.

Okay, so this didn't sound like he was doing this because it was the right thing. It sounded like he truly wanted it.

Hope put her hand to her stomach. This time, she didn't snatch it away again.

"Please say yes. Let's be together. Let's—"

"Yes." Hope smiled.

Reece picked her up, holding her tight. "Yes!" he yelled at the top of his lungs.

Hope laughed. They both did.

This was probably the craziest thing she had agreed to since coming here. Coming to Feral lands had been good for her. Perhaps this would be too.

CHAPTER 38

TWO DAYS LATER...

Hope watched as Reece huffed out a pent-up breath, still staring at his phone screen. He'd been looking at the thing for five minutes now.

"I know your shoes are tight, and that it's very noisy here in the city, but we're nearly there. Put your phone away before you fall on your face." Hope elbowed him softly.

"I'm a Feral. I won't fall on my face. My shoes... That's not it." He looked around them, his nose scrunching up. "Although you are right about those things. And then there's the stench. You forgot to mention the stench. This place smells disgusting. It smells of garbage and body odor and... of excrement. Thankfully, mostly urine and not—"

"I get it." Hope laughed. "You're cute. You know that, right?"

"Cute?" He frowned. "I looked up that term, and I don't know if that's a compliment." He slid his phone into his pocket.

"I think it's a compliment." Hope smiled at Reece, who put his arm around her.

"I have to admit," he said, pulling her close, "whatever *you* have to say counts for a lot. A whole lot, since you are carrying my—" His hand slid to her stomach.

She grabbed his fingers. "We don't know that I'm pregnant." She pulled them away.

"I have this feeling." He beamed at her.

"Don't say that. I don't think I am." She smiled while she said it, trying hard not to get excited. "You need to stop saying things like that. I'll take a test in two weeks."

"Twelve days."

"Twelve days. We need to try not to think about it till then."

"An impossibility." He pulled her in closer, his hand rubbing the side of her arm.

"I know, but still." She gave him a pointed look.

He leaned down and kissed her softly on the temple. "You're beautiful, I'd wear a thousand human coverings for you." He pulled on the back of his jeans. "My dick might never work properly again."

She giggled. "Shoes and clothing, Reece." She laughed. So darned freaking cute. "And your dick will work just fine. We'll check a little later, to be sure." She winked at him, then felt a little queasy as she appeared to remember why they were there. "Thanks for coming with me."

"I'm glad you let me come with you. I would've hated the thought of you all alone here in the big city." They had arrived the night before and stayed in a hotel since Hope had given up her apartment.

"I can take care of myself," she reminded Reece.

"I know." He smiled. "You are small but fierce. I've seen you wield a candlestick. I've seen you growl at a Fallen warrior."

She laughed. "Yes, you have. Facing my ex will be a whole other ball game."

"Ball game? I know what each of those words means. I can guess what you are trying to say." He narrowed his eyes in thought.

"So, why were you upset earlier when you were looking at your phone?"

Reece rubbed a hand over his face. "I received the cellphone records I requested yesterday for all of the Feral. I specifically checked one. Shard wasn't in contact with anyone on Fallen territory. There was nothing untoward. At least not in recent weeks. Perhaps he communicated in some other way. When we are done, I'm going to request all his email history as well. There must be something there." He rubbed his chin, the light stubble catching.

"You should look through all the other records first. Maybe you will find the culprit or culprits," she tried, knowing this was a touchy subject.

"I really thought it was him. That Shard was the spy." He sighed. "I still am. It's him, I know it is." Reece didn't sound as sure anymore.

"It might be him, but you should cover all your bases."

"You're right. I will have all of those records checked and delve deeper into Shard too." His eyes hardened.

"Here we are." They'd arrived at the lawyer's offices. Hope pulled in a deep breath. She looked up at Reece. Thank god she didn't have to face Emmet and her sister alone. "Don't be rude to Emmet. I know you don't like him. I mean, he's my ex, so it would be understandable, but—"

"I dislike the male because of everything he did to you. Everything he put you through." Reece's jaw tightened, and his eyes narrowed.

"Please try not to growl at him."

"It will be hard, but," Reece nodded once, "I promise to do my best."

"No... not just your best." Hope was trying to bite back a smile. "You can't growl or threaten him. Please don't hit him, either." Hope stopped walking. "He can be an arrogant asshole, but you can't—" She shook her head hard.

"I won't hit him." Reece got this feral smile that made her stomach flip-flop. "I would kill him if I hit him. Just one blow with this meat sandwich..." He hit his fist against his hand.

"I think that's a knuckle sandwich, but I much prefer your version." They walked into the elevator and she pushed the button for the fifth floor.

Hope's stomach churned. She hadn't seen Emmet in months. The last time she'd seen Lizzie was at the practice a few weeks ago. She'd contacted her sister after getting home from the whole Fallen debacle. It sounded like she and Emmet were back on track. That her sister's fears were a false alarm. They hadn't talked for long; the conversation was stilted. She and Lizzie had a long road to walk. Hope feared their relationship would never be the same. That was life. Some doors closed, while others opened. Reece glanced at her. His eyes softened. It was still weird looking into vivid green eyes instead of his gorgeous golden ones. Since a Feral's eye color was so unique, they had to wear contact lenses when on human soil.

The elevator dinged, and they walked out. Reece took her hand and squeezed. "You've got this."

"I know." She smiled.

"You let me know if you change your mind about that meat sandwich."

Hope laughed just as they arrived at the reception.

Lizzie and Emmet were already there. They both stood up. "Hi," Hope said, still smiling. It was weird; as soon as she saw them her nervousness evaporated. She could tackle this. She could tackle anything she put her mind to.

"Hi," her sister said. Lizzie's belly was rounded. There was no doubt anymore that she was pregnant. Lizzie stepped forward and hugged Hope. It was awkward and thankfully lasted all of three seconds. She took a step back when Emmet looked like he was considering doing the same. Reece put his arm around her.

"Who is this?" Emmet's eyes narrowed. Her ex wasn't as big as she remembered him to be. He was six feet tall. Hope had always considered him to be buff. She was wrong. At least, he wasn't tall or buff next to Reece. His hair looked like it was thinning on top. It was more noticeable since she'd last seen him.

"This is Reece," she said to Emmet before looking at Lizzie. "Reece, this is Emmet and Elizabeth."

"Lizzie," her sister corrected. "It's nice to meet you, Reece." She held out her hand, and Reece shook it.

"Reece who?" Emmet was frowning.

"Just Reece," Reece said, his voice low and gravelly.

"Why is this guy here?" Emmet asked Hope, pointing at Reece with his thumb.

"This guy is Hope's boyfriend." Reece took a step towards Emmet. "I'm here to support Hope. That's all you need to know."

"You have a boyfriend?" Emmet's voice was whiny.

"What difference does it make if Hope has a boyfriend?" Lizzie asked.

"I don't think it's appropriate that she—" Emmet started to say.

"Appropriate? You want to start lecturing me on what's appropriate and what's not appropriate?" Hope laughed. *This man!* He was too much. What had she ever seen in him?

"You can't just bring some guy to—" Emmet started up again.

"Reece isn't some guy, Emmet. He's my boyfriend. I invited him here," Hope said.

"You may go in now," the receptionist chimed in from behind them.

"I don't want him here." Emmet folded his arms.

"Why are you acting like this?" Lizzie said. "It shouldn't matter that Hope has a boyfriend, or that he's here." She shrugged.

"Are you going to start up on me again, Liz?" Emmet kept his arms folded.

"I'm not starting up on you," Lizzie half-whispered. Her cheeks were pink. "Can we just go in and do this?"

"Not if he's here." Emmet looked at Reece.

"Oh, my god!" Lizzie licked her lips, looking down at the carpet under her low heels. "Emmet, this is what we've been waiting for." She took his arm and gave it a tug, but Emmet didn't budge. "Let's get these papers signed so that we can get married." Another tug. "Emmet! Now!"

"I don't think I want a divorce." He looked at Hope with pleading eyes. "I think I made a mistake."

Out of the corner of her eye, she saw Reece bristle. She saw his shoulders tense. He seemed to grow taller.

"What?" Lizzie shouted. "What are you talking about? I'm pregnant with your child. We already had the ceremony. I'm wearing your grandmother's ring."

"I still love you, Hope," Emmet blurted, keeping his eyes on her and ignoring her sister.

There was a loud slapping sound as Lizzie hit Emmet square across the jaw.

Emmet took a step or two back. He looked at Lizzie. "I can't do this anymore!" His eyes had this look of panic.

"*We* are doing this. I'm pregnant, you asshole!" Lizzie shouted.

"You're crazy," he yelled at Lizzie before looking back at Hope. "Your sister is crazy. She follows me around. She checks my phone. She drops in at work at all times of the day. I've lost two clients because of you." Emmet's eyes blazed as he looked back at Lizzie.

"I apologized," Lizzie sobbed, tears running down her face. "It's the hormones."

"No, it's not the hormones. You blame everything on the hormones. I can't take it anymore. You don't trust me," Emmet whined.

"Can you blame me?" Lizzie yelled.

"Yes!" Emmet yelled back.

"I want a divorce," Hope said, starting to turn towards the open office.

"No!" Emmet shouted. "I'll contest. I want you back, Hope." His eyes were glistening.

"Emmet!" Lizzie was still tugging on his arm.

Hope stepped forward, letting go of Reece's hand. You have to do certain things on your own in life, and this was one of them. "I don't love you."

"Don't say that," Emmet tried.

"I *don't* love you. I don't think either of us has loved each other for a long time."

"I do love you, Hope," Emmet whispered. "I made a mistake."

Lizzie sobbed louder.

"You don't love me! All I feel is sorry for you. For both of you." She looked at her sister for a second. "I've said it before, and I'll say it again, the two of you deserve each other."

She glanced at Reece, and they walked towards the office.

"I won't do it!" Emmet shouted. "I won't sign!"

"Can I hit him yet?" Reece whispered.

Hope rolled her eyes and pulled in a deep breath as she turned back. "I ultimately don't need you to sign. I have plenty of grounds for a divorce."

"I'll fight this." He looked pointedly at Reece for a few seconds.

"I'll still win in the end," Hope pointed out.

"Your soon-to-be ex-wife is correct." It was their lawyer. He'd stepped out of his office. Hope was sure that even people down the hall could hear the shouting. "If you don't sign, it'll end up costing you a lot of money in lawyer's fees and you will still lose. I suggest you sign today, Mr. Robertson. It will save you time and money in the long run."

"I don't want to." Emmet sounded like a child.

"I can't believe this." Lizzie stamped her foot, looking like a child, too. The two of them really did deserve each other. Hope watched as Lizzie walked off in a huff. Her sister paused halfway down the hall, probably expecting Emmet to run after her. She started sobbing loudly when he didn't and kept on walking.

Hope couldn't find too much sympathy for her. She felt numb.

"Mr. Robertson," their lawyer said, brows raised.

Emmet's shoulders sagged. He sighed. Then he nodded once and walked towards them.

Reece put his hand to the small of her back. "I'm proud of you," he whispered. Hope was proud of him, too. It would have been difficult for Reece not to react that whole time. To let her stand on her own two feet. But he had done it.

Her heart pounded as she signed. It pounded even harder as Emmet signed as well. This was the start of her future, and she was excited. She couldn't help but put her hand on her stomach for a second. Just a second.

CHAPTER 39

FOUR DAYS LATER...

Reece opened the door abruptly, causing it to bang against the wall. He and his team entered the building.

"What is the meaning of this?" Delise yelled. "What are you doing here?"

Her eyes widened. "Evander! Evander... where are you going?" she shouted after the fleeing healer. He tried to shift, but one of the males tackled him, quickly bringing him down. A healer was no match for a warrior.

Shard held on to the male, grinning. "Not very intelligent, is he?" He swatted Evander on the side of the head. The male cried out. "He's wet himself." Shard made a face. "You're a coward."

One of the others pretended he was going to hit Evander. The male flinched away, and everyone laughed.

"Stop!" Reece shouted.

"You heard our new head guard," Shard shouted. Everyone cheered.

Reece doubted that he and Shard would ever be friends again, but they could get along as colleagues. Particularly since Shard was his second-in-command now. Reece had to bite back a smile. Leukos had called him in the previous day to promote him. "Actually, I'd say that Evander is highly intelligent."

"Can someone tell me what is going on?" Delise put her hands on her hips. Her eyes were bright. "Why are you chasing and beating my healer? Unhand him immediately," she shouted at Shard, who looked sheepish. He even bowed his head. "I can't, Delise. I have orders."

"Please," Evander moaned. "This is a mistake. Please, Delise, help me!"

"What orders?" Delise asked.

"Orders from the king himself," Reece said. "Evander is a spy. It was he who told Ekon of the queen's movements. He was feeding all the inside information to Ekon."

"What?" Delise narrowed her eyes. "Is this true, Evander? It can't be." She looked back at Reece.

"It's true, Delise. We pulled his cellphone records. He was in constant contact with the Fallen. Mainly with a male called Kwan. He was the one who told them that the queen was having a checkup at the clinic that day the Fallen raided. He tried to tell them that the appointment was running early but you wouldn't let him use his cellphone," he told Delise. "He couldn't get the message through in time. That's why they ended up taking Hope and me instead."

"The feather rot?" Delise whispered. "You said that it was a patient with a case of feather rot," she muttered to Evander. "There was no feather rot. You made excuses afterward. We never ended up seeing anyone with feather rot. You lied. How did I not see it?" she muttered to herself.

"Do not blame yourself. Evander was devious," Reece said. "It was because of Evander that Ekon knew so quickly that he had the wrong people. He knew who Hope was, who I was. All of it."

"You were privy to all the information because you were my shadow," Delise was still talking softly.

"Very clever, Evander. Quiet, unsure Evander. You were there, but we didn't even see you," Reece said to the male. "Leukos moved the queen to an abandoned tower nest on the eastern border. The royal guards and Delise went with the queen to keep her safe. You were there. You sent the Fallen a pin location. You are the spy… the traitor. It was you all along." His anger towards Shard had blinded Reece. He'd been so angry for so many years that he had stopped living his life. He didn't want to invite the male to be his friend again, but he also wouldn't throw away more time on hate. He had Hope now. They all did. Hope for a better future.

"Take him away," he told Shard.

"You are right, I am a shadow." Evander spat before Shard could act. "I'm nothing here. I'm not seen or recognized. I'm worth less than dirt. I could've been a general for Ekon. He promised me—"

Delise closed the distance between herself and Evander and slapped him… hard. "You insolent child. Why would you believe a male such as him? I agree with Shard; you're not very intelligent."

"See," Evander snarled. "This is what I have to put up with."

"I am hardest on my brightest students. On my shining stars." She shook her head in disappointment. "You could've had a bright future. Such a waste."

"Wait!" Evander called as Shard was yanking him along. "What? What did you say? What do you—"

"What will become of him?" Delise asked once they were out of earshot.

"It is for the king to decide." Reece looked up at the ceiling for a moment. "I don't think he'll be put to death."

Delise sighed, nodding. "That is something, at least."

"I imagine that he'll be flogged and banished. Forced to live a life of solitude."

"Leukos is a good king. A just king," Delise commented. "Whatever he decides will be the right thing."

"Indeed." Reece nodded.

CHAPTER 40

A WEEK LATER...

Reece knocked on the door.

"I need a little longer," Hope shouted.

"We should be doing this together," he shouted back.

"What? Pee on a stick?" Her stomach was in knots.

"I'd be happy to pee on a stick," Reece said. "But I doubt it would do much good."

Hope laughed, even though she was feeling sick to her stomach. She opened the door. Reece took her hand. "Have you done it yet?"

She nodded, pointing at the neatly folded toilet paper. "It's under there." She gestured at the vanity. "It takes a few minutes. I didn't want to look too soon." She was chewing on her bottom lip so hard she was sure it might bleed.

Reece took both her hands and led them to the side of the tub, sitting on the edge. With a tug, he pulled her onto his lap, closing his arms around her. "Are you okay?"

Hope shook her head. "I'm feeling sad."

"Why would you be sad?" He tucked some hair behind her ear.

"I'm sad because I don't think I'm pregnant." On the same day she'd ended her marriage to Emmet—finally—she'd had some spotting, which had carried on for a few days. It was a little more than just spotting if she was honest with herself. Her menstruation had been almost nonexistent on birth control and it was probably as a direct result of coming off said birth control. Sometimes women bled when they were pregnant; it was possible. "I know deep down inside that it didn't happen. This test is just to confirm that, and I'm a little sad." She wiped away a tear that slipped out the corner of her eye. "My whole life, that's all I've wanted… to be a mom. To hold a baby in my arms. To have a family. I love kids. I love babies. You've noticed how often I go to visit Claire so that I can cuddle." She smiled just thinking about the triplets. Cute as buttons.

"I've noticed."

"It's why I became an Ob-Gyn." She had to blink hard to stop herself from crying more.

"You do know that if there is only one line on that test we can start trying again immediately?"

"You mean that?" She lifted her brow.

"I do." He nodded.

"That would be hilarious, considering we've been using condoms since I stopped my birth control." They'd done that on the off chance she was pregnant and used condoms on the greater chance that she wasn't.

"We can start trying whenever you are ready."

She huffed out a breath. "We should probably tie the knot first."

"I know that particular human saying very well. Are you asking me to marry you, Hope? I thought it was a human tradition for the male to ask the female."

Her eyes widened up, and her mouth fell open for a second. "No! I wasn't… I was just saying. I… um…"

He chuckled. "I know you weren't asking me. I know it's too soon for that."

"Yet we're sitting here waiting on a pregnancy test. I'm praying like hell that it's positive and yet I'm about to break out in hives at the prospect of marriage again. I'm a crazy person."

"Not at all. I think that we've both learned that just because we can't control something, doesn't mean that it's bad. Just because things happen the wrong way around sometimes, doesn't mean that's a bad thing either. I know that you probably don't want to hear this. You haven't been out of your relationship for very long, and you were badly hurt…" He pushed out a breath through his nose. "I'm not just falling for you anymore. I'm in love with you. Totally and deeply. You are the female for me… for always. I know you probably can't say any of that back to me—"

"No. I can't." She felt her stomach churn. "I'm sorry… I'm nervous." She swallowed thickly. "We were supposed to be a rebound thing when we're so much more. I'm going to need time. Even if I do have some eggs growing in here, I need time."

"Take as much time as you need."

"You're amazing. Thank you." She smiled at him. "We can probably check that test." Hope got up off of his lap. "You really don't mind either way?"

"If you are with clutch, it would make me the happiest male on the planet. But if you are not, then it doesn't matter because I know deep down in here," he touched his chest, "that we are meant to be together. That there will be children in our future. That we will be a family. It will happen. Whether it happens now or in a few months… um… if you make me wait years, I might start to get cranky."

She swallowed hard. "That's sweet. I know you mean it, because you don't say things you don't mean. Okay." She licked her lips. "I feel better about this." She walked over to the vanity and lifted the toilet paper, looking at the test.

"And?" Reece asked, sounding animated.

She turned and shook her head. "One line. I'm not pregnant. I'm so sorry." She slowly looked up, locking eyes with him.

"That's okay." Reece gave her a half-smile. "We weren't even trying, and the trying part is half the fun." He stood, walking over to her. Reece wore a pair of sweatpants. He was so sexy. So sweet. So caring.

He was so hers. It was strange because at that moment, knowing she wasn't pregnant—having that pressure, that uncertainty lifted—she realized just how strong her feelings for him really were. "I know I'm only just out of a shitty marriage. I know that I shouldn't have fallen so hard for another guy quite so soon, particularly when I was supposed to be having a rebound relationship, but I have."

"You love me?" Reece grinned.

"That might be taking it a bit far. I— Yes, dammit! Yes, I love you."

Reece put his arms around her. "Does that mean you'll mate me?" He nuzzled her neck.

"Now you're pushing it. The thought of marriage makes me break out in hives, remember?"

He laughed. "I'll just have to work on you… get you to agree. Can we start trying for a clutch right now?" He nipped her ear.

Hope moaned. "No, no, no!" She put a hand on his chest. "Not yet. Let's just have fun. Enjoy us… *this* for a while. I don't want to rush into anything."

"Deal." Reece picked her up. "We're going to start practicing right now. I'm not taking no for an answer." He hoisted her over his shoulder.

Hope squealed.

Reece tossed her onto the bed. Hope bounced twice on the mattress. "Take your clothes off." His sweats were tented.

Reece reached for the side table and pulled out a string of condoms.

"Okey dokey." She tugged her shirt over her head and pulled off her shorts, making quick work of her underwear. When she looked up, he was rolling a condom onto his erection.

Reece growled. "You're so beautiful." His eyes blazed as they took her in. "I don't know where to even start."

"Here." She palmed her breasts.

Reece groaned.

"Or here." She touched herself between her legs.

His groan was louder and deeper this time. "All of the above. As much as I want to taste you, I need to mount you even more."

His eyes were glowing. His features were more angular. She recognized that he was barely in control. It made her heart beat faster.

"Don't be alarmed. It's mating behavior. I can't help it. My beast recognizes you as my mate. I can control it, though. I just might be a bit edgier during sex until you agree to mate me."

Reece looked terrifying and absolutely gorgeous. Her heart hammered in her chest. "In that case, I might never agree."

He threw her a feral smile. "Oh, you will. I can be persuasive."

"Oh, really now?"

"Yes, really. I need you on all fours." He gripped her around the waist and turned her onto her knees. Reece crouched over her, completely caging her in with his big body. His cock was hard and thick between her legs. "These mating instincts are riding me hard. You probably shouldn't have told me that you loved me." His voice was husky.

She giggled. "On the contrary, I should have told you sooner."

Reece kissed her neck. "I love the way you smell." He made a growling noise that was more animal than man. His whole body quivered. "I need you to brace yourself on your elbows. I might make loud noises."

"I'm used to those by now."

"Louder than normal, Hope. I… want to mate you. I'm going to mount you hard. Make you scream. I might pin you down. You can't fight me. You need to go with it." He spoke so softly she had to strain to hear him. Hope was already panting with need.

"Are you going to bite me?" She could hear the excitement in her voice. She wanted him to… so badly.

"Biting is reserved for mates. It will take serious willpower, but no, I can't bite you."

Hope wanted to argue, but Reece nudged inside her, and she whimpered. A couple of nudges later, and he was fully seated inside her.

Oh, god but he was big. Even after having sex quite a few times now with Reece, she thought it was funny that she still felt shock at his size. Her eyes still widened, and her breath sucked back in whenever he entered her for the first time. It was funny. But she couldn't laugh, she could only moan.

He circled his hips, his cock barely moving but hitting all the right spots, anyway. "I will never tire of this… of you." His voice was thick with need. Reece pushed her down on the bed using his body. "We fit perfectly together." He pushed his hand between them, his finger solidly on her clit. Hope moaned.

His thrusts became more insistent, and she gasped.

"So fucking good," he growled, leaving her clit so that he could pull her hands above her head, holding them in place with one of his.

She couldn't move.

Not an inch.

His thick cock punched in and out of her. Reece grunted hard with every thrust.

She was crying out. "Yes," she groaned. Hope was convinced she must be the biggest pervert, because not being able to move, being caged and held down like this, was one of the most erotic moments of her life. She could feel her orgasm building inside her.

She could hear the slapping of his balls. The thudding of his hips against her ass. The wet suction noises. Her pussy fluttered with the start of her orgasm.

She was still well and truly pinned down, unable to budge. She was panting and moaning. Her channel fluttered again. The coiling sensation taking hold.

Using his free hand, Reece gripped her hair and pulled her head back ever so slightly. It didn't hurt her at all. What it did was tip her over the edge. Hope grabbed at the sheets as her pussy spasmed around him. She made this garbled noise.

Reece moaned her name and clamped his teeth on the sensitive skin at the base of her throat. Nowhere near hard enough to break her skin. Hope screamed as her orgasm tore back through her. Her whole body convulsed with the sheer enormity of it. Her eyes rolled back. Thankfully, he held her in place. Her sex was spasming so hard that her eyes actually watered. Swift strokes turned to hard jerks. Reece buried his face in her neck and roared.

Hope must have passed out, because she woke up later in the crook of Reece's arm. "Um… what happened?" Her voice was croaky.

"Oh… hi, Sleeping Beauty." He kissed her on the top of her head.

"How long was I out for?" She swiped the hair out of her face.

"A few minutes."

"Oh, my god! What the hell was that, and when can we do it again?" Her body was still buzzing.

"That was a taste."

"A taste of what, exactly?" She pulled herself up so that she could look him in the eyes.

"A taste of what the mated life would be like."

"Just a taste?" She lifted her brows. "Because if that was a taste, I might not survive mated life."

He chuckled, his chest vibrated. "Oh, you'll survive just fine. I'm afraid I can't bite you again until we're actually mated."

She gasped. "You're terrible. How can you give me an orgasm like that and then take… Oh, I see, this is what you meant by convincing me?" She laughed. "You suck so bad. You do know that a relationship based on sex isn't much of a relationship? And if I agree to mate with you so that I can have mind-blowing orgasms, it would be wrong on all levels? You do realize that?"

"I do, and that's why I plan on giving you plenty of reason to agree to mate me. This was the first of many." He repositioned her on the bed and got up.

"Where are you going?" Hope frowned.

"I'm going to make you flat food. I'm a good cook. I will make sure your stomach is happy. That every part of you is happy. You will agree in no time."

Hope watched as he strode away. She mainly looked at his meaty ass as he walked. Off to go make her pancakes for breakfast after giving her mind-blowing sex. Agreeing to wait as long as she needed before they took the next step. He was perfect. How long would she hold out? She suspected that it wouldn't be long before she crumbled.

CHAPTER 41

FIVE MONTHS LATER...

"Here you go." Hope put three glasses of orange juice down on the coffee table.

"Thank you," Claire said; she had a baby on each breast. "Are you still okay, Trace?"

Tracey nodded. "Yep, I'm doing great." She looked down at the little one sitting on her lap. "How cute are you, Murry?" she cooed.

"Careful," Hope said. "It's contagious." She rubbed a hand over her lightly distended belly.

"No." Tracey smiled, shaking her head. "Locke and I only mated last week. We want to enjoy our life as a couple for a while first. Probably in a few years' time."

Hope and Claire exchanged a look. They both laughed.

"What?" Tracey asked.

"You do know that you're married to a Feral?" Hope said. "I said pretty much the same thing and look at me. I'm laying these precious ones next month. That will be less than six months after I said I wasn't ready to get married again."

Tracey smiled. "Our relationship has moved quickly since coming here a few months ago. Especially since I only planned on visiting. I never planned on staying."

"Exactly. Before you know it, you'll be buying maternity wear," Claire said.

"You're probably right. Locke and I want a big family." Tracey smiled. She was a sweetie. Hope could see why Locke was head over heels in love with her.

"That's good, since the Feral kids come in batches of three." Hope laughed.

"Talking about being with clutch," Claire said. "When is your replacement coming?"

"Next week. I recommended that we hire someone who can stay on once I get back from maternity leave. The clinic is getting very busy. There must be something in the water." She winked at Tracey, who grinned.

"There were four matings this month." Claire lifted one of the babies, using just one arm. "There are seven planned for next month."

"Wow, that's incredible," Hope said. "I'm so glad that things are working out."

"Me too." Claire nodded. Her eyes widened in thought. "By the way, has your sister had her baby yet?"

Hope nodded. "Yes, a couple of days ago. She named him Seth." Hope got out her phone and pulled up a picture of her nephew. "This is him." She showed Tracey and Claire.

"He's lovely," Tracey said.

"I take it that she and Emmet still aren't together?" Claire asked.

Hope had to work not to roll her eyes. "No. He's tried hard to get her to change her mind, but Lizzie won't budge. Thank god. He's a real piece of work."

"You're telling me," Claire said. "I still can't believe he tried to get you back like that."

"He hasn't wasted any time and is apparently dating his personal assistant. Lizzie is convinced that he was cheating on her with the PA."

"He probably was," Claire said.

"Guys like that just can't stop themselves."

"Emmet has only been to see the baby once. I think Lizzie is going to be raising Seth on her own. She's back to living with my folks."

"Serves her right," Tracey muttered. "Sorry, I just can't believe that your own sister had an affair with your husband. It still boggles my mind."

"I'm over it. I'm glad it all happened the way it did, or I wouldn't be here mated to a wonderful man and expecting our children." She smoothed a hand over her belly again. "It's funny how something wonderful can come from something so terrible. Reece is everything to me." She couldn't take the smile off her face.

The End

AUTHOR'S NOTE

Charlene Hartnady is a USA Today Bestselling author. She loves to write about all things paranormal including vampires, elves and shifters of all kinds. Charlene lives on a couple of acres in the country with her husband and three sons. They have an array of pets including a couple of horses.

She is lucky enough to be able to write full time, so most days you can find her at her computer writing up a storm. Charlene believes that it is the small things in life that truly matter, like that feeling you get when you start a new book, or a particularly beautiful sunset.

BOOKS BY THIS AUTHOR

The Chosen Series:

Book 1 ~ Chosen by the Vampire Kings
Book 2 ~ Stolen by the Alpha Wolf
Book 3 ~ Unlikely Mates
Book 4 ~ Awakened by the Vampire Prince
Book 5 ~ Mated to the Vampire Kings (Short Novel)
Book 6 ~ Wolf Whisperer (Novella)
Book 7 ~ Wanted by the Elven King

***Demon Chaser Series** (No cliffhangers):*

Book 1 ~ Omega
Book 2 ~ Alpha
Book 3 ~ Hybrid
Book 4 ~ Skin
Demon Chaser Boxed Set Book 1-3

Shifter Night Series:

Book 1: Untethered
Book 2: Unbound
Book 3: Unchained
Shifter Night Box Set Books 1 - 3

BOOKS BY THIS AUTHOR

The Program Series (Vampire Novels):

Book 1 ~ A Mate for York
Book 2 ~ A Mate for Gideon
Book 3 ~ A Mate for Lazarus
Book 4 ~ A Mate for Griffin
Book 5 ~ A Mate for Lance
Book 6 ~ A Mate for Kai
Book 7 ~ A Mate for Titan

The Bride Hunt Series (Dragon Shifter Novels):

Book 1 ~ Royal Dragon
Book 2 ~ Water Dragon
Book 3 ~ Dragon King
Book 4 ~ Lightning Dragon
Book 5 ~ Forbidden Dragon
Book 6 ~ Dragon Prince

The Feral Series

Book 1 ~ Hunger Awakened
Book 2 ~ Power Awakened
Book 3 ~ Hate Awakened
Book 4 ~ Hope Awakened

BOOKS BY THIS AUTHOR

Water Dragon Series:

Book 1 ~ Dragon Hunt
Book 2 ~ Captured Dragon
Book 3 ~ Blood Dragon
Book 4 ~ Dragon Betrayal

Earth Dragon Series:

Book 1 ~ Dragon Guard
Book 2 ~ Savage Dragon
Book 3 ~ Dragon Whelps
Book 4 ~ Slave Dragon
Book 5 ~ Feral Dragon
Book 6 ~ Doctor Dragon

CHARLENE HARTNADY

CHAPTER 1

She should be happy.

What was she thinking? She *was* happy.

Happy, excited and nervous all rolled into one. Nervous? Hah! She was quaking in her heels. This was a huge risk. Especially now. Her stomach clenched and for a second she wanted to turn around and head back into her boss's office. Tell him she'd changed her mind.

No.

She would regret it if she didn't take this opportunity. Why now though? Why had this fallen into her lap now?

What if it didn't work out? She squeezed her eyes closed as her stomach lurched again.

"You okay?" Rob's PA asked, eyebrows raised.

Jolene realized she was standing outside her boss's office, practically mid-step. Hovering.

"Fine." She pushed out the word together with a pent-up breath. She *was* fine, she realized. More than fine, and she had this. The decision was already made. Her leave approved. She was doing this, dammit. Jolene smiled. "I'm great."

"Good." Amy smiled back. "Just so you know," she said under her breath, looking around them to check that no-one was in hearing distance, "I'm rooting for you." She winked.

"Thank you. I appreciate that," Jolene said as she headed back to her office, trying not to think about it. Not right now. It would make her doubt her decision all over again. She'd made the right one. The only thing holding her back was fear of failure. It was justifiable and yet stupid. She wasn't going to live with regrets because fear held her back. She was going to embrace this. Give it her all and then some. Her step suddenly felt lighter as she walked into her office. *Do not look left.* Whoever designed this building had been a fruitcake. This floor was large and open-plan. Fifty-three cubicles. There were only two offices. One was hers, and one was—*Not looking or thinking about her right now.* Both offices had glass instead of walls. Why bother? Why even give her an office in the first place if everyone could see into it?

It had something to do with bringing management closer to their staff, or the other way round – she couldn't remember. The Execs were on the next floor. *Not going there and definitely not looking left.* She could feel a prickling sensation on that side of her body. Like she was being watched. Jolene sat down at her desk and opened her laptop. Her accepted leave form was already in her inbox. She had to work hard not to smile. It was better to stay impassive. Especially when anyone could look in on her. This was going to work out. It would. All of it.

No more blind dates.

No more Tinder.

No more friends setting her up.

She was done! Not only was she done with trying to find a partner, she was done with human men in general. Jolene bit down on her bottom lip, thinking of the letter inside her purse. She'd been accepted.

Yes!

Whooo hooo!

It was all sinking in. She couldn't quite comprehend that this was actually happening.

The sound of her door opening snapped her attention back to the present. She lifted her head from her computer screen in time to see Carla saunter in. No knock. No apologies for interrupting. Not that Jolene had been doing anything much right then, but still. She could have been.

A smug smile greeted her. "I believe I'm filling in for you starting Friday for three weeks." Her colleague and biggest adversary sat down without waiting for an invitation. "Rob just called to fill me in."

"Yes," she cleared her throat, "that's right." Jolene nodded. *Don't let her get to you.* "I have too many leave days outstanding and decided to take them."

Carla folded her arms and leaned back. She seemed to be scrutinizing Jolene. It made her uncomfortable. "Yeah, but right now? You're either really sure of yourself or ..." She let the sentence drop. "I believe you're going on a singles' cruise?" The smirk was back. Carla's beady eyes—not really, they were wide and blue and beautiful—were glinting with humor and very much at Jolene's expense.

It was her own fault. She should never have told Rob about why she was taking this trip. Why the hell had he told Carla? It was none of her damned business. *Stay cool!* She smiled, folding her arms. "I thought it would be fun."

"You do know that I'm about to close the Steiner deal, right? Work on the Worth's Candy campaign is coming along nicely as well."

"Why are you telling me this?" Her voice had a definite edge which couldn't be helped. Carla irritated the crap out of her.

The other woman shrugged. "It might not be the best time for you to go on vacation. Not that I'm complaining. It works for me." Another shrug, one-shouldered this time.

Jolene pulled in a breath. "I need a break. That's the long and short of it."

"Yeah, but right now and on a singles' cruise...do you really think you'll meet someone?" She scrunched up her nose.

"Why not? It's perfectly plausible that I would meet someone. Someone really great!" she blurted, wanting to kick herself for the emotional outburst.

"It's not like you have the greatest track record." Carla widened her eyes. Unfortunately, working in such close proximity for years meant that Carla knew a lot about her. In the early days, they had even been friends.

"But you should definitely go," Carla went on. "You shouldn't let that stop you," she quickly added. Her comments biting.

"I'm not going to let anything stop me. Not in any aspect of my life," Jolene replied, thrilled to hear her voice remained steady.

Carla stood up, smoothing her pencil skirt. "I'll take care of things back here. The reason I popped in was to request a handover meeting, although I'm very much up to speed with everything that goes on around here." She gestured behind her. "I'll email a formal request anyway." She winked at Jolene.

Jolene had to stop herself from rolling her eyes. "Perfect." She refolded her arms, looking up at Carla who was still smiling angelically.

"I need you to know that I plan on taking full advantage of your absence."

"I know." Jolene smiled back. "I'm not worried."

The smile faltered for a half a second before coming back in full force. "You enjoy your trip. Good luck meeting someone." She laughed as she left. It was soft and sweet and yet grating all at once. Like the idea of Jolene actually meeting someone was absurd.

That woman.

That bitch!

Stay impassive. Do not show weakness. Do not show any kind of emotion. She forced herself to look down at her screen, to scroll through her emails.

Two minutes later, there was a knock at her door. Jolene looked up, releasing a breath when she saw who it was. Ruth smiled holding up two cups of steaming coffee.

Jolene smiled back and gestured for her to come in.

"I was in here Xeroxing—our printer is down yet again – and thought you could use a cup of joe." Ruth ran the admin department on the lower level. Her friend moved her eyeballs to the office next door to hers. The one where Carla sat, separated by just a glass panel.

"You were right," Jolene exclaimed.

Ruth sat down. "Are you okay? That whole exchange looked a little rough."

"I thought I kept my cool. Are you saying you could see how badly she got to me?" Carla was all about pushing buttons. She only won if Jolene retaliated and she'd learned a long time ago it wasn't worth doing so.

"You looked fine. What gave it away and – only because I know you so well – was the way you tapped your fingers against the side of your arm every so often. I take it when 'you know who' said something mean." Ruth handed her the coffee and took a seat.

"Mean doesn't begin to cut it. Thanks for this." She held up the mug before taking a sip.

"What's going on?"

"Things have happened so quickly, I didn't get a chance to tell you. I'm going on vacation." Jolene briefly told her friend all about her real upcoming plans, as well as about what had transpired between Carla and her.

Ruth smiled. "I can't believe you're this excited." She looked at her like she had lost all her faculties. "It's not that big of a deal. Quite frankly, I'm inclined to partly agree with Carla, for once." She made a face. "Maybe you shouldn't be going on a trip right now."

"It's a huge deal, and you're right, I'm excited," Jolene gushed. "One in five hundred applicants are accepted, and I'm one of them. The shifter program is just the place for a woman like me. I'm ready to settle down, to get married and to have kids. Lots of kids. Four or five ... okay, maybe five's too many, but four has a ring to it. Two boys and two girls."

"Two of each." Ruth chuckled under her breath.

She smiled as well and shook her head. "Actually, I'm not too phased about that. I just can't believe they actually selected me."

"You're nuts!" Ruth laughed some more. "Why's it so hard to believe? Just because you've had a bad run doesn't mean you're not...worthy."

"I'm thirty-four. I turn thirty-five in two months' time."

"And that's a big deal why?"

"Because thirty-five is the cut-off for taking part in the program." She had to undergo a whole lot of testing – including ones of the medical variety – and she'd been selected anyway. "I'm so done with guys running away as soon as they realize I'm serious."

"How is being a part of this program going to change anything? I love you long freaking time, but you do tend to scare men away. You're a little ... pushy."

"I'm not pushy! I know what I want and I go after it. After everything I've been through, I'm not interested in anything less, and shifters actually want to settle down. They want kids. They want what I want. For once, I'm going to meet someone who doesn't run scared at the prospect of commitment and family." She sucked in a deep breath.

"Human guys also want commitment." Ruth raised her brows, taking another sip of her coffee. "They want kids."

"Just not with me they don't. None of them wanted anything other than sex or casual dating. Sure, they're more than willing to take the plunge as soon as they move on to the next one, but not with me."

"Have you ever stopped to consider that you're maybe coming on just a little too strong? You can't start out a relationship talking about marriage. Guys can't handle that."

"I'm not coming on too strong. I'm done wasting my time... that's all." Jolene took a sip of her own coffee, feeling the warm liquid slide down her throat. "I know what I want. Casual sex, endless dating..." She shook her head. "That's not it. Even living together. Have you ever heard the saying, 'why buy the cow if you can get the milk for free'? No...not for me. Never again!"

"You seem to think it's going to be different with a shifter. Can't say I know too much about shifters." Ruth shrugged. "Except that they're ultimately guys too."

"For starters they're hot. Muscular, tall and really, really good-looking."

"Okay, that's a good start." Ruth leaned forward, eyes on Jolene.

"They have a shortage of their own women, just like with the vampires. It's actually the vampires who are helping them set up this whole dating program."

"Oh!" Ruth looked really interested at this point. "No women of their own you say, now that's interesting."

"I didn't say no women, just not many women. Their kind stopped having female children, so there's a shortage. They have a natural drive to mate and procreate, which is exactly what I'm looking for." Jolene put her coffee down and rubbed her hands together. "I can't wait to get my hands on one."

"You might just be onto something here. Where do I sign up?" her friend whisper-yelled while smiling broadly. "I can't believe you told Rob you're going on a cruise. Where did you come up with that?"

"I shouldn't have said anything at all." She shook her head. "I don't know why I disclosed as much as I did."

"Yeah!" Ruth raised her brows. "I can't believe he told," she looked to the side while keeping her head facing forwards, "her."

"I know. Thing is, I've made up my mind. I'm going."

"That cow is going to move in while you're gone. She might just get the edge in your absence and take the promotion out from under you."

"I realize that, and yet I can't miss out on this opportunity. I'm willing to risk my career over this. It's a no-brainer for me." She sighed. "Don't get me wrong, I'm freaking out about it, but as much as I love my job, having a family would trump everything. I have a good feeling about this."

"Those shifters sound so amazing." Ruth bobbed her brows.

"I'll show you the website online. They only take three groups a year and then only six women are chosen each time. Just a handful from thousands of applications." Jolene's heartbeat all the faster for getting accepted. She was so lucky! Things had to work out for her. They just had to.

"You say these shifters are hot and pretty desperate?" Ruth smiled, her eyes glinting. "Why didn't you tell me about this sooner? We should have entered together."

"Not exactly desperate, but certainly looking for love. Ninety-six percent of the women who sign up end up mated…that's what the shifters call it, mated. It's not actually the same as marriage, it's more binding. Ninety-six percent," she shook her head, "I rate those odds big time."

"I can't believe you didn't tell me sooner." Even though she was still smiling, Ruth narrowed her eyes. "I thought we were friends."

Jolene made a face. "I didn't tell you anything because I didn't want to jinx it."

Ruth rolled her eyes. "I wouldn't get too excited until you get there. Until you actually meet them." Ruth snickered. "With your luck, you'll get one of the bad apples."

"You shut your mouth. Don't be putting such things out in the universe."

Ruth looked at her with concern. "I don't want you getting your hopes up, that's all."

"Well too late, my hopes are already up." Jolene was going to win herself a shifter. Someone sweet and kind and loving. A man she could spend forever with. "I just wish it wasn't right now. This isn't a good time to be leaving."

"Not with that big promotion on the horizon." Ruth shook her head. "Not when *she* could take it."

"We're both on the same level. We both started at the same time. I hate how evenly matched we are."

"You're the better candidate though. I've never known anyone to work as hard as you."

"Carla works hard too. She's also brought in several big clients in the last couple of months, and she's not going on vacation. She'll be here day in and day out, whispering sweet nothings into Rob's ear."

Ruth made a face. "It's not like that, is it?"

"No, no." She waved a hand. "Sweet nothings of the business kind. It's still a threat just the same to me, and honestly, that's the only downside to this. I stand a good chance of losing to Carla if I go."

"But you are still going anyway." Ruth took a sip of her coffee, frown lines appearing on her forehead.

"I have to." She pushed out a breath. Hopefully, Ruth was wrong about the whole 'bad apple' thing.

Out Now!